F   Jones, Kaylie 20389
JON
        Quite the other way

$18.95

DATE			
NOV 1 6 1989			
DEC 2 1989			
DEC 2 9 1989			
JAN 2 2 1990			
FEB 1 4 1990			
APR 2 1990			
MAY 2 2 1990			

ALSO BY
KAYLIE JONES

As Soon as It Rains

QUITE
THE
OTHER
WAY

QUITE
THE
OTHER
WAY

by

Kaylie Jones

DOUBLEDAY

New York · London · Toronto · Sydney · Auckland

Published by Doubleday, a division of
Bantam Doubleday Dell Publishing Group, Inc.
666 Fifth Avenue, New York, New York 10103

DOUBLEDAY and the portrayal of an anchor with a dolphin
are trademarks of Doubleday, a division of
Bantam Doubleday Dell Publishing Group, Inc.

Library of Congress Cataloging-in-Publication Data

Jones, Kaylie, 1960–
Quite the other way.

I. Title.
PS3560.0497Q5   1989   813'.54   88-30876

ISBN: 0-385-24119-4

BOOK DESIGN BY STEPHANIE BART-HORVATH

Thank you, Carolyn Blakemore,
Julianne Hausler,
and Gloria Jones.

To Robert Decker, Soon-to-be-Ph.D.

Without Bob (he doubtless will beg to differ) this novel would not exist.

and

To W. Marko Antich

For his friendship, guidance, and trust.

One day one of their number would
write a book about all this, but
none of them would believe it,
because none of them would remember
it that way.

—James Jones, *The Thin Red Line*

PART ONE

REMINISCENCE

My father was forty-seven when I was born. As far back as I can remember he always looked old to me, but acted like a young man. One of his knees was somewhat crippled from a fall he had taken stepping off a Moscow tram in the winter of 1943. The story was that he had slipped on the ice and had twisted the knee badly, but rather than take a leave of absence, had allowed the Soviet doctors to operate; at that time journalists were sometimes denied reentry visas for no reason and my father was afraid he would not be able to get back in.

He said the doctors had done a very good job, although they had not been too concerned about aesthetics. A fat, purplish, S-shaped centipede crawled permanently around my father's knee. He said the one good thing about the knee was that he could always tell when a storm was coming. "It always hurts a little," he told me, "but when a storm is coming, it hurts a lot."

I could not imagine being in pain forever and found him extremely heroic.

I discovered rollerskating at the age of eight. I moved quickly from the flat, metal, tie-on skates to the more advanced racing skates with boots attached. The day of the big switch, my father came down into the street to observe me. We lived on a little one-way side street in Paris which was perfect for skating because there was never any traffic.

"I used to be quite the skater in my day," he said. "I even won a championship in Chicago when I was a boy."

"That was a hundred years ago, Daddy," I pointed out.

"I'll bet you fifty francs I can race you to the end of the street and beat you. Where are your old skates?"

"I don't have fifty francs to bet with."

"All right. If I win, you give me ten francs; if you win, I'll give you fifty."

We went upstairs to find the old skates. He adjusted them, making them as long as possible with the little wrench designed specifically for that purpose, and we went back downstairs to the street. My mother followed us.

"Alex," she said, "you're going to do that knee in again, just like you did in Switzerland skiing. If you do this, Alex, I won't speak to you for a week."

"We have a bet going here, Francesca," he said.

All the kids in the neighborhood skated on our street. It was an afternoon pastime. They already thought my father was quite the nut because he liked to play Cowboys and Indians with us. I was the only girl who owned a toy pistol that looked very much like a real gun and fired little caps which you had to place into the cylinder individually. The noise the gun made was fantastic. My father owned one too, and when we played, he was always the sergeant of our team. He taught us how to cover each other—one person attacked while the others fired from behind cars.

On the day of the race, the French kids cheered for my father. He took off down the street like an energetic young boy with his sprig of gray hair flying in the wind. Of course, he beat me by a meter, though I could tell he was holding back and could have beaten me by much more than that. However, he had forgotten how to slide into a break-stop and flew into a parked car at the finish line with a loud bang.

My mother was furious with him, but relieved that he had not "done his leg in" once again. In her relief she forgot that she had threatened not to talk to him for a week, and called him a crazy old man instead. My mother was quite a bit younger than he. She had been a graduate student on an NYU exchange program at the Université de Paris and had ended up in my father's class, The History of the Soviet Union. She married him and never returned to the States.

About their encounter, my mother said, "The only thing I wanted in life was to get married and have children. But most boys my age were frightened of me because I also wanted my master's degree. I argued with them a lot—I let them know I was as smart as they were. At that time women didn't do that sort of thing very much. Your father understood me perfectly well and I fell madly in love with him."

My father said, "All I wanted in life was a yacht. Just a little yacht of my very own to sail around the world in. I took one look at your mother who was the most beautiful woman I'd ever seen in my life and I said 'there goes the yacht.' I've come to the conclusion in my old age that a family is more expensive, but more fun than a yacht."

"One day I'll be rich and I'll buy you a yacht," I promised, "and you can take us around the world." My father liked this idea very much and spent many hours explaining to me exactly what kind of yacht I should buy him.

Besides wanting a yacht, my father wanted to return to the States some day. He wanted me to be American and not French, so I was sent to a special bilingual school which prided itself on its internationality. The student body was comprised mostly of foreigners whose parents worked in Paris embassies or international companies. I went to school with Indians, Iranians, Africans, Americans, Englishmen, Australians, Japanese, Germans, Poles, Czechs, Rumanians, and even some Frenchmen, whose parents also wanted them to grow up bilingual in French and English.

One fall, when I was ten and starting sixth grade, an American boy arrived fresh from Texas. His name was Frederick Thomas and he was tall and tow-headed and had bulging blue eyes that made him look a bit like an insect. He told everyone that his father was "in oil." On the first day he refused to sit next to a black boy whose father worked in the Ghanaian Embassy. No one said anything, including the teacher, because no one knew what to say. This had never happened before. A few weeks later, Frederick Thomas called the Indian Ambassador's daughter who wasn't even black a nigger and was suspended for three days.

I went home and told my father about this, and asked him to explain. I knew about racism because my parents had told me, but what I couldn't understand was Frederick's outspokenness; I thought racists were embarrassed about being racist and kept their mouths shut in public.

"It's his parents' fault. He's probably repeating what he hears at home," my father said. "God." He passed his hand over his long wrinkled forehead and rubbed his whispy eyebrows with the tips of his fingers. "I've been here so long I'd almost forgotten why I left the States."

Frederick Thomas came back to school after his three-day suspension wearing a red arm-band with a swastika in the center of it. He sat next to me in English class and told me how wonderful Hitler's army was. I thought he probably identified with the Nazi youth because all the Nazis I had seen in picture books looked exactly like him. I repeated what I'd heard at home: the Nazis might have had a strong army, but the Russian Army was much more powerful and kicked the hell out of the Nazis before the Americans even arrived. Frederick stared at me in complete horror.

Nothing was said to Frederick about the arm-band, but the school must have called his parents because he stopped wearing it.

Another few weeks passed without incident, and then one day during our after-lunch recreation—it was still warm and we were playing in the park next to the school in our identical navy blue uniform shirts —Frederick walked up to me in the middle of a game of hopscotch and said without warning, "Your father is a Commie bastard."

It was not the words—they really meant nothing to me—it was Frederick's expression that enraged me: the judgmental, haughty disdain in his eyes. Who was he to look down on my father who was not only a hero, but the nicest person I'd ever known? I knew my father had been in some kind of trouble with the American government long before I was born. He always talked about it freely in front of me. He believed he had "done the right thing by refusing to cooperate." I translated words such as these into moving pictures; in my imagination my father was a Robin Hood-type hero who had been tortured by bad people but had not told them what they wanted to know.

I said, "And you're an animal and a racist."

"So what?" Frederick said. "Your father had to leave America because he was a Commie spy."

I don't know what came over me. I stood paralyzed for a moment, and then my knee jammed up into Frederick Thomas's groin. I was amazed at the effect of this maneuver my father had taught me in case anyone ever tried to kidnap me; Frederick fell backward into the pebbles and the dust, rolled into a ball, and started to vomit. I stood above him in a state of complete terror, waiting for him to get up and murder me. But he did not get up. I turned crisply toward the school, and without waiting another instant, went straight to the headmistress's office and turned myself in.

The headmistress, Madame de la Marquette, was French but prided herself on her excellent English, and used it every chance she could get. Before she could say a word I announced that I had fought with Frederick Thomas, and that I thought he might be hurt.

"Sit down, Miss Gray," she said, waving a hand at a chair. I sat down.

"What exactly did you do to Mr. Thomas?"

I said, *"Je lui ai donné un coup de genou dans le zizi."*

"Ah," she said, and then asked what it was that Frederick had said to me. I refused to tell her.

"How can we decide who should be punished if you will not tell us what he said?"

Madame de la Marquette called my father, who worked at home in a study above our apartment, and told him that I had "injured" a fellow student, a boy, who had apparently insulted me. She was confused and annoyed that I would not tell her what the boy had said.

I could hear my father roar with laughter through the phone. "This is not remotely amusing, Mr. Gray," the headmistress said. After a moment, her face turned quite pale and she put the receiver back into its cradle.

"Your father is en route to discuss this matter with us. You will sit here until he arrives," she said quietly.

Although I was quite frightened I found it interesting to sit in her office and watch her conduct business. Madame de la Marquette had extraordinarily long red nails. She used a pencil to dial the phone and to slide papers to the edge of the desk so that she could pick them up. She dialed the infirmary and asked if Frederick Thomas had been brought in. Apparently he had not, and she asked that he be located and sent to her office immediately.

My father arrived within fifteen minutes, although we lived on the other side of town. The end-of-recreation bell had just sounded and students were thundering up the stairs to class.

My father peered down at me as soon as he walked in and winked with the eye that the headmistress could not see. "Hi there, Madame dela Market," he said jovially, as though he'd been invited to tea.

"I'm not telling," I said again. I was near tears and my stomach hurt. My father knelt gingerly on his good knee and whispered in my ear, "What did he say to you, Clinton?"

I was watching my legs swing back and forth under the chair. Finally I whispered back, "He said, 'Your father is a Commie bastard and he had to leave America because he was a Commie spy.' " The tiny hairs sprouting from his ear tickled my nose.

He got up slowly, using the seat of one of the chairs for support, and said to Madame de la Marquette, "This boy is the same one who called the daughter of the Indian Ambassador a bad name?"

"Yes, he's having some trouble adjusting, I'm afraid."

"It sounds to me like he's bringing to school the things he hears at home," my father said. "Poor kid, with parents like that."

"Clinton will have to be suspended for two days," she said flatly. "I'm afraid those are the rules."

"Frankly, Madame dela Market, neither of them should be suspended, in my opinion."

"I want to be suspended Daddy because otherwise he's going to beat me up."

"Do not worry, Mr. Gray, the boy will be suspended as well. We do not tolerate any kind of fighting here, no matter what the cause."

"I think you should bring the boy in here and let's discuss it."

"This is very irregular, Monsieur."

"I don't give a shit what it is, Madame," my father said, raising his voice. His face was turning red and I knew that he was going to start yelling at Madame de la Marquette in about two seconds. I'd been attending her school since kindergarten and knew from experience that the headmistress was the kind of person who never raised her voice and couldn't stand any display of emotion. She wanted to avoid scandal at all costs. She went to the door, pulling down on her short red jacket that matched her skirt and nails and lipstick.

In came Frederick Thomas with a chalk-white face, hunched shoulders, and arms dangling at his sides.

"I'm Mr. Gray," my father said with dignity, extending his hand. I couldn't believe it.

Frederick was caught off-guard and didn't know what else to do so he shook hands with him. Madame de la Marquette went back to her chair behind the big desk.

"Now I think you two owe each other an apology," my father said. "And Madame dela Market is owed an apology and so am I, for disturbing our day's work."

"She kicked me," Frederick said, staring at the floor.

"I'll bet your father's going to kick you a hell of a lot harder than she did for getting thrown out of here twice in a month," my father said. "And I bet he'll be mad as hell to hear you've been repeating the things he tells you privately at home. Should I call him right now at work and tell him what you told my daughter?"

"No," Frederick said.

"What are you so pissed off about?" my father asked.

Frederick gazed up at my father with wistful eyes. "They don't have football here," he said gloomily.

"Well, you could bring your football to school and start a touch game in the park out there. I bet you could get quite a few kids to play."

"They're pansies," Frederick said.

This made my father chuckle because he himself often referred to European men as pansies. "You seem like a smart enough kid, why make trouble for yourself here? There're better ways to get attention."

"I know," Frederick said.

"It's rude to insult people," my father said. "Even if you *are* unhappy."

"I know," Frederick said again, wincing so much his shoulders crumpled inward.

"Madame dela Market, will you let these kids go back to class so you and I can get back to work, and we can all forget the whole thing? Come on you two, shake hands."

Neither of us wanted to shake hands but we did because it was better than getting suspended.

"Monsieur Gray, I believe you could teach your daughter less radical methods of self-defense. And you, Frederick: this is your last chance," Mme. de la Marquette said, pointing a pencil at him. "Next time it's for good."

"Thank you for being so understanding, Madame dela Market," my father said.

Out in the hall, my father asked Frederick if he knew what the words he had said to me meant.

"Yeah," Frederick said, without much conviction, as though he were a bit worried that my father might ask him to explain them.

"That's what I thought. Listen, Frederick, you tell your father that *I* said that I am not a Communist and never was. And you can also tell him that if he has an axe to grind, he can call me. I'm in the book. And, Frederick, if you ever touch my daughter your ass will not be a pretty sight, you hear me?"

"I hear you," Frederick said.

Suddenly, at four o'clock, hundreds of children in navy blue uniforms flew through the big double doors and swarmed the sidewalk in front of the school. A half-circle of parents had formed not far from the doors—they were waiting for the littler children; but all of us, little and big, were yelling because we had at last been liberated. The noise was deafening.

I walked off toward the Metro station, along the park's green gate. I had a habit of running my fingers across the diamond-shaped wire fencing. It made a pleasant metallic sound, like a fingernail across a comb, but louder, and stung the fingertips. I looked over my shoulder several times to see if Frederick Thomas had decided to follow me, but he was nowhere in sight. Then, looking ahead I saw my father leaning against the gate. His hands were hidden in the pockets of his gray trousers, his old tweed jacket pulled back at the waist. He had crossed his legs comfortably at the ankles, and he was observing me. I was embarrassed for some reason, as though I had been caught at something. I must have looked at him strangely, maybe even angrily, because he said in a soft, apologetic voice, "Hell, it was only two hours. I decided to take a walk in the park and wait for you. I don't trust that kid either."

He slung my bookbag over his shoulder (it looked like a purse on him) and took my hand. We walked on in silence for a while, along the gate. I watched the mothers walking with baby carriages and small screeching children running in circles around them. I liked holding my father's hand because he left me room to move around inside the warm and dry cocoon of his grasp.

"You know I try to be a good guy," he said. "I try to see things from other people's perspective. But that kid—you know what it is, baby?"

"What, Daddy?"

"It terrifies me. It makes me feel that no matter how hard I try I just can't protect you the way I'd like to. The idea of some nasty, stupid person hurting you—I just can't stand it. It makes my heart go like this." He held up his other hand and squeezed it into a fist so tight his knuckles lost their color. The gentle, vulnerable timbre of his voice caused my heart to constrict in the same way. I suddenly felt the need to be courageous for both of us.

"Nobody's going to hurt me, Daddy. I promise." I squeezed his hand.

"The best thing to do with mean and stupid people—especially *big,* mean, stupid people, is to be perfectly nice to them. Just smile and act like you don't understand why they're being mean. Most big, mean, stupid people are just as insecure and scared as everybody else and only want to be loved. Mostly. See, no rule works all the time. When you get a little older, I'll teach you other ways of defending yourself." After a long pause he exhaled and said, "I'm not always going to be around."

"You are so too always going to be around!" I said in outrage, and tugged on his arm.

"Whatever you say," he said.

That October, my mother organized a Halloween costume party for my entire class. We wrote out a personal invitation to each student and drew pumpkins and skeletons and witches on the cards with wax crayons.

"Are you inviting Frederick?" my father asked, peering over my shoulder as I admired my artwork.

"No," I said flatly.

"Invite him," my father said.

"Why?"

"Because I said so."

I gave out the invitations at recreation, and because I felt like being mean I kept Frederick's for last. He hadn't expected to get one, and when I handed him his card with his name on it, his face instantly turned red.

He came as Zorro, in a black tuxedo with a cape and a mask and a plastic sword dangling from his belt. He arrived by himself. When I opened the door in my fluffy white ballerina's tutu, he pulled a bouquet of funny-looking yellow and orange flowers out from under his cape and holding them at arms' length, solemnly presented them to me.

"Thank you very much," I said without smiling, and took the flowers from his outstretched hand.

SNOW

To reach my first contact by telephone I went out for a walk in a
blizzard at daybreak, stomach empty and head full of jet-lagged
sleep. The cold white deluge opened my eyes; though I couldn't see a
thing twenty paces ahead, I felt the immensity of the place. All around
the air and the earth were completely white, and silent. The only thing
I could hear was my labored breathing behind my scarf and my heavy
boots sinking in, packing the fresh snow with a muffled, crushing
sound. Once in a while a truck passed up on the road (they managed
always to keep the roads clear) and sometimes the wind howled and
gave me a push or momentarily stopped my progress.

I was trying to get to the phone booth that stood on the corner, half
a mile up the street. There was a closer booth, just at the top of the
incline which was the vast and barren lawn of our Institute, but our
American counselors had told us not to use that phone, precisely because it was too close and probably tapped. This did not make sense to
me. Twelve hundred students lived in the Institute, most of them from
Friendly socialist nations; why would someone bother to tap a street
phone, which the local Russians also used, just to gather information
on one hundred-odd students from Capitalist, Enemy nations? I
strongly considered using that nearby phone, the glass booth looked so
comforting though the wind blew the door back and forth on its

hinges, making a whining sound. I remembered the advice my father had given me as I prepared to leave the house on my first day of American high school. He was always the first one up, before my mother, so he was the one who saw me off that morning. I looked up at him with what must have been, at best, an uncertain face. He patted my head and said in his even voice, "You are entering a completely new environment; don't take liberties until you are personally familiar with the rules."

I moved on past the first booth, huffing and swearing and sweating inside my big black down coat which had been a "going-away present" from my Tante Claire, who believed Moscow was in the North Pole.

I had two *dvushki* and two dimes in my pocket, enough for four tries. Using the phone system was a dreaded, horrible experience; on top of that I hated talking to strangers in a strange language which, up until three days ago, I had only used in a classroom.

In three days I had accomplished nothing. Oh yes, I had gotten ahold of the dvushki, the two-kopek pieces necessary to make phone calls, which it seemed everyone conspired to keep from us wherever we tried to make change. Dvushki were the same size as dimes, but copper, and lighter, and though dimes could do in an emergency, it was certainly better not to use them. *Aha!* might think the Russian who collected the dvushki from the phone at the end of the day, an American has been making calls here, I shall report this to the police and get a little red star by my name for being a watchful and caring citizen. And then maybe a big, stone-faced agent in a trenchcoat would be assigned the duty of watching the booth until an unwitting American showed up. Would he then follow the American? Better not to think about such things, better to use the dvushki.

This is how I got the dvushki. I had met a tall, blond American student from the ten-month program the day before, as I was leaving my room. I saw him running down the hall in sweatpants and a torn sweatshirt. He had a red bandanna tied around his head. He was panting and sweating and his face was almost as red as the bandanna. He stopped in front of the door directly across the hall from mine.

"You are running in this weather?" I said in my messy baby-Russian.

"Yeah," he said in English. "Why not?"

"Because it's minus-five or something out there."

"You guys just get here?"

"Yes," I said.

"Listen, do you have any peanut butter? I'm dying for just a bite of peanut butter, you know? We've been here five months, got five to go, and we ate all ours a while back." He said this apologetically, smiling with very blue eyes that curved sensuously at the corners and made me feel much safer than any other eyes I'd seen since my mother had left me crying at Penn Station six days ago.

"Do you have any dvushki? I'll trade you peanut butter for dvushki." I made a little joke out of it.

He nodded understandingly. "I know what that's like," he said. "Dvushki are gold, man. Specially in the beginning."

"Just wait one second," I said, opening the door to my room. I grabbed the jar of peanut butter I had just unpacked and placed on the book shelf above the desk and was back in the hall in moments.

He unlocked his door with a key he pulled out of his sock and we went into his room. He immediately began to take off his clothes. First the sweatshirt, leaving him in a guinea-T, and then the bandanna. He shook his hair around. It was long and straight and a golden Scandinavian color that never loses its sunny nature, even in winter.

He ate the peanut butter right out of the jar, with an aluminum soup spoon he'd stolen from the cafeteria. "Don't let the aluminum touch your fillings," he said. "*Zap!* Electric shock. Be a good way to get kids to stop eating candy back home. After their first filling, give them an aluminum spoon."

I stood in the middle of his room and looked at the snapshots he had glued to the wall all around his bed. A family barbecue in the backyard of a two-story, two-car-garage house. It could have been Anywhere in America. There was a picture of him sitting on a bench under an oak, kissing a girl with the same blond hair. Their faces were pressed so close together it was hard to tell if she was pretty. I imagined she was very pretty. There were beach shots and ski shots (the girl did not appear in these). Observing his pictures made me feel like I was looking at his underwear drying on a line.

There were two single beds in the room, as in mine, but it seemed the other one here was unoccupied. It was too neatly made up, like a couch. All the rooms I had seen were the same; two beds, one desk with a chair, one shallow closet of varnished wood, two bedside tables of the same varnished wood, a linoleum floor, a plastic radio attached to the beige wall. Only the inhabitants' personalities made the rooms different.

Meanwhile he sat at the edge of his bed, engulfed in the peanut butter, which was extra crunchy—his favorite kind, he said; I felt he would have said that no matter what kind it had been. After four spoonfuls he closed the jar and gave it back to me, along with four dvushki, which he scooped off the edge of his desk. I noticed that he'd left himself two.

"Hey," he said, "don't use the pay phones downstairs, right?" He spoke fast and low, as though someone were listening over his shoulder.

"Of course not," I said.

"You can get dvushki in the change machines at the Central Telegraph Office on Gorky Street. You should go down to the center tomorrow."

"Tomorrow's our first day of classes," I said, bewildered by the idea of heading out on my own, in the snow, after dvushki.

Since our arrival I had been following the other students around to the "tourist attractions," Red Square, the Kremlin. It was embarrassing to be so dependent at my age. At twenty-five I still needed my mother to take me to the train station because I was afraid of getting lost, or getting on the wrong train.

We shook hands. He told me his name was Philip Chase, "with one l," I told him mine was Clinton Gray and that I was very grateful to him. I also told him to stop by if he ever was bored and wanted to talk.

"Bored?" he said. "There's never time to be bored here. You have a boy's name," he observed, as an afterthought.

"Maybe my parents wanted a boy," I said, smiling. My parents had not wanted a boy at all; Clinton had been my paternal grandmother's maiden name. My father had been the black sheep in a family of reactionary WASPs who had lived for generations in a fancy suburb of Chicago. His parents had died long before my birth, and I suppose that by naming me Clinton he had wanted to make up with them in some way, post facto. This was one of those family stories one did not tell strangers.

After I left Phil Chase I took his suggestion, which was to catch the bus to the metro and phone from there. Phil said the phones in the metro never froze, as they often did on the street, and that he was almost ninety-nine percent sure that the phones there were not tapped. In the well-lit, echoing hall was a line of open booths. With trembling hand I placed my first dvushka in the slot and waited for it to drop. It did not drop. I tried another phone, the same thing happened. I decided to watch someone else. A man with a big square fur hat and a briefcase went into the booth next to mine, placed his dvushka, and dialed. When he said *"Allo!"* nice and loud the dvushka descended into the phone. I tried again. Someone picked up on the other end and a woman's voice said *"Allo"* exactly as the man had; the dvushka dropped into the phone. I said *"Allo!"* but the woman on the other end could not hear me. "Allo? Allo! *Allo!'* she repeated. I hung up. By now I was sweating again inside my Arctic coat. I waited for the man to finish, and tried his phone.

"Allo?" the woman said, frustrated now.

"Allo—Rita?" Though our counselors had spent a good half hour of precious orientation time explaining how to ask for someone on the phone, my mind was blank. I suddenly had a terrible urge to pee. Between the gaps of unintelligible words this is what I understood:

"Rita . . . not. She . . . work."

And then I responded in my baby-Russian; "I from New York, from Sarah. I Clinton Gray."

"Ah! . . . again . . . tomorrow . . . nine."

"Excuse me? When?" Now I was yelling, as if that would help.

"Morning, *Morning! Nine.* Good?"

"Good," I said.

She hung up.

I turned around and saw a woman waiting for the phone. She looked at me with tired, interested eyes. Her pale, wrinkled face was framed by a halo of black and gray racoon fur. Her coat had a matted fur collar of a completely different, brownish color. I gave her a friendly smile but received no reaction. Exhaustion once again descended on me; I had the sensation of standing at the bottom of a pool as it is being filled with water. I lost heart and courage and went back to the Institute with two dvushki left.

Now, the next morning, I made it to my booth at the end of the road with fifteen minutes to get to my first class. I took off my fur-lined mitten and placed the dvushka in the slot. My breath steamed up the windows. The receiver was so cold it instantly numbed my ear and arm up to the elbow.

"Allo?" Once again. The dvushka dropped into the phone.

"Allo, Rita?"

"Da!"

The following conversation was a long and painful one, interrupted by "What?" and "Repeat please," but I soon got the most important words through to her:

"My name is Clinton, I from Sarah in New York."

After a short, piercing scream, she said: "Oh my God!" And started shouting into the background. There were three or four voices—including one calm, male voice—shouting at each other at the same time. Rita's high-pitched remarks dominated the others. After a moment she came back to me:

"Where are you? How long . . . here? . . . Come here today?"

"We have classes until three," I said.

"Very well. Five o'clock, metro Medvedkovo . . . last stop . . . orange line . . . first wagon. I will meet you. . . . Do you understand me?"

"I understand. How will you know me?"

"Ha ha ha! Do not worry. I will know you."

2 ▰

RITA

Sitting on the bus, whose windows were completely iced over from the inside, I looked at my little paper map of the Moscow subway system. It was difficult to focus on anything for long. The first day of classes had completely wiped me out. No matter how much sleep I got, the next day seemed worse. I kept finding myself at the bottom of that pool, fighting to keep above the waterline, with the water getting deeper and harder to negotiate.

I felt slightly drunk, unclear; sounds echoed unfamiliarly inside my head. The subway map reminded me of a science book illustration of the anatomy of a big spider. The brown metro line which made a complete circle of the inner city was the outline of the spider's body, and all the colorful lines connected to it—which crisscrossed at the very center and continued on in the opposite direction to the outer suburbs—were its long, spindly legs. Its heart, of course, was in the middle of the middle of the city, at the Kremlin metro stops. And its head? This spider had no head, no eyes. I brought the map closer to my face and stared at it. Once I'd put things back into perspective, I saw that Rita lived at the north end of the orange line, I was at the south, which was strategically wonderful because after my bus ride, all I had to do was sit patiently for about forty-five minutes on one train without having to change lines.

My stop was the first one on the line, so it was easy to get a seat. I leaned back against the window and closed my eyes. After a few seconds I felt exposed and opened them, a reaction to living in New York City for so long; there you always had to be on your guard. But on this metro the feeling was different. People were staring at me, but out of curiosity. Even with closed eyes I could feel their scrutiny; long looks going over my face, scarf, hair, Arctic coat, my bare hands gripping my mittens and the heavy snow boots which were so hot I felt like my feet were being held over glowing coals. Their eyes seemed to come to rest on the plastic shopping bag between my ankles which held the gifts Rita's relative had given me in New York. There were clothes, panty hose, and photographs, carefully wrapped in different-colored tissue paper so that I could tell them apart; which gift for whom, without names attached, to avoid questions from the customs officials on the way in.

I stared back, and this was like playing pingpong. Looks shot back and forth like so many little white balls, skitting here and there, bouncing off the walls until someone would give up. What could be going on in their private thoughts, from which we foreigners were completely excluded? Would no one in the streets address us but the *fartsovchiki* who tried to buy our clothes and shoes and watches and bags as we aimlessly wandered around, trying to "get a feel" for the place? I was dying to talk to Phil Chase about this, about what he did in his free time that gave him no room to be bored. I was dying to know.

And maybe I was imagining the whole thing, maybe they were not looking at me at all.

At every stop an attractive female voice announced: "Warning, the doors are closing. Next stop . . ." And once in a while a polite male voice pointed out that one should yield seats to senior citizens, veterans of war, and women pregnant or with children.

This was my first time alone on the metro; I was noticing things. How quiet it was, how subdued, how beautifully lit up the stations were. Alone, however, I felt exposed. There is definitely strength in numbers. Somewhere in the now-crowded car some men were speaking Spanish, boisterously cracking jokes and laughing. Even though they were probably just having fun together, it seemed that their fun was at the expense of the people around them, which included me. And I too was annoyed and embarrassed, because yesterday and the day before *we* had been oblivious to our surroundings, loudly speaking American and calling attention to ourselves in a way that guests should not in such a serene environment, particularly enemy guests.

I was fifteen minutes late getting to Medvedkovo. When I stood up to leave the train, blood rushed to my head; in my temples and throat I felt and heard it pulsating. *Boom boom.* Is this fear, I wondered, or simply exhaustion? I had not eaten a meal of any kind since our arrival. Bread and cheese, bread and cheese—easy to find, easy to ask for in the barren stores—and more bread and cheese. I had tried the Institute cafeteria at lunch, once. I could not recognize any of the dishes. I saw only brown mush and ran out of there, confused, embarrassed. I was sorry for them, our hosts, whoever they were; they surely were trying their best to feed us properly. Everyone else was eating the stuff, why couldn't I?

In five months, I told myself, you'll have time to get used to it.

I stood on the platform at the front of the train, trying to look inconspicuous. My pulse was still pounding inside my head. I leaned up against a pillar of some kind and for a second, pressed my forehead against its cold, smooth surface. Then a tiny woman in a tattered brown sheepskin coat came running down the stairs toward me. Her feet beneath the long coat were so small they looked like a child's.

"Clinton?" she said, pronouncing it *Kellint'n*. She grabbed my elbow and tugged on it. It was the high-pitched, energetic voice from the telephone.

"*Da!*" I said.

"*Slava Bogu,*" she said, pressing her hand to her heart.

I had not considered what would follow, what kind of questions she would put to me. Getting there had been my primary concern. Now that she was a solid reality, a tiny woman with heavy-lidded, deep-set eyes and an ancient face, I worried that she would not like me, would not understand me, that I might commit some irreparable faux pas. I had thought and thought about what to wear to this meeting; whether to get dressed up, whether to dress down. Which would be most appropriate, which would say more about me and my background? I had finally decided to wear my second-best sweater, a turquoise and gold wool one which my other tante had made me for Christmas, especially for this trip.

Rita glanced fleetingly at the plastic bag dangling from my arm and her cheeks flushed slightly.

"Come come come come come quickly with me. Tea we shall drink, and then food we shall eat with my relatives and all will be much much better for you poor dear little kitten coming all the way so far by yourself from America!"

She said this so loud my heart practically stopped. My *God,* here we were standing in the most public place of all!

"You must not to speak so loud," I muttered.

"Poo!" she said, lifting her hand and pushing air to the side. "Nonsense. I am an old lady."

She gripped my arm above the elbow and pulled me along, just slightly behind her. She was almost running and in the boots I had a hard time keeping up. She carefully explained the directions as we went along, "for the next time." We took yet another bus (she made me repeat its number several times) for three stops and then got off in front of a row of tall, gray buildings which looked exactly like my Institute and the developments surrounding it. It was hard to imagine that I had gone all this way, from one end of the city to the other, to find myself in seemingly the same place.

3

RELATIVES

Everyone wore slippers at Rita's. The two other people for whom I had brought gifts were standing in slippers just inside the door as we came in. They were Rita's cousin Anna and Anna's husband Igor; I recognized them from a photo their relative had shown me in New York. Rita introduced them as her sister and brother.

"Just look at this coat, Anya," Rita said. "It looks like the *vatniki* the *zeki* wear in Siberia, ha ha ha!" She pulled at my collar from the back, trying to get the coat off me. "Tell me," she asked, "is this stylish nowadays, in America?" She used the word *modny,* which I had been hearing constantly in the past few days.

"Yes," I said, "I think it is stylish, especially with young people."

"Funny thing!" Rita said, shaking her head, her eyes distant and dreamy.

"What is a zeki?" I asked.

Rita and her cousin glanced at each other quickly. Anna had large brown eyes which smiled constantly, but in that fraction of a second I saw an angry flash in them as she looked at Rita.

"It's a joke, do not be offended," Anna said in a soft, tremulous voice. "It means political prisoner. *Politzaklyuchëniy,*" she said. That was a word I knew from "Soviet Literature and Society," the best graduate course I had ever taken, because the professor, Vika Erikson, had loved the Soviet Union with a nostalgic, passionate sadness I had never seen in any professor before.

"Take off your boots," Rita said, hovering about me like a noisy hummingbird. There was a pile of slippers on the floor beneath the coatrack from which she extracted a pair with little pointed heels and blue pom-poms at the toes.

Igor stood a little to the side, observing the scene. He was a swarthy man with a sly look in his eye. He watched me suspiciously, but not without amusement, as though he considered himself a knowledgable man who could not be easily fooled. It was hard to tell exactly how old he was, though he was well over fifty, and at least ten years younger than Rita.

Rita shouted "Teatime!" and clapped her hands. She prodded me into the rectangular, wallpapered kitchen. The formica-topped table set against the wall was covered with chocolates and cakes and hard candies, and, of all things, halvah.

Anna stayed at the stove, her solid, square back stooped over some dish she was preparing. Her silver bracelets tinkled and glinted as she worked. She was in a black wool skirt and white angora sweater, and wore a set of round onyx earrings that had a tiny diamond at the center and matched her necklace and one ring.

"Is that halvah?" I asked.

"Oh yes," Rita said. "Here we have everything." She made that circular gesture, pushing the air away from herself. At the center of the table stood a bowl of small, yellow apples. Some were bruised, some were shriveled, but by God, they were apples. There were little, greenish oranges in the bowl as well. My tongue and throat remembered the mouth-puckering taste of fruit and my stomach growled in outrage at the punishment it had been enduring the past few days. Across from me, at the head of the table and under the window, sat Igor, who seemed entirely consumed with his tea and chocolate-covered waffles, which he delicately dipped into the cup before each bite. Holding the cup with his hand curled around the rim, he sipped with a loud sucking sound. The window was a mirror reflecting us, the warm light, and the lavish table. The night beyond the plants on the windowsill was completely black.

"So you and Sarah are friends," Igor said, smiling in his foxlike way. His teeth were a pattern of ivory and gold.

"*Nyet,*" I said, reminding myself to keep it simple because I spoke so poorly. "We are in the same yoga class for people with bad backs."

"Bad *chair*-backs, you said!" Rita laughed merrily. "Bad backs is not the same thing as bad *chair*-backs."

"Yes," I said. "Sorry." *Spina*—back; *spinka*—chair-back, I reminded myself.

"Leave her alone," Igor said. "She speaks well for an American."

"That is right," said Anna from the stove. "Sarah has always had a bad back. Is her back better?"

"Much better," I said. "The yoga has helped much."

"And Arthur, how is his health?" Anna asked.

"Not good," I said. This had all been rehearsed over cups of coffee in a small café near the yoga center.

Remember to tell them, Sarah had said, *that Arthur's health is terrible and that I'm afraid we're going to have to move to Florida.*

"They might have to go to Florida," I said.

"What is wrong with Arthur's health?" Igor asked. "That man is strong as a *byk.*"

What the hell's a byk? I wondered.

"He has a bad heart," I said.

"So do I have a bad heart." Igor slapped his chest. "I had two *infarcta* last year."

Anna went over to him and placed a hand on his shoulder.

"*Nu, kushaite! Kushaite!*" Rita pushed the waffles, the fruit bowl, the chocolates, over to me.

"Leave the girl in peace, Rita," Igor said dismissively. "We have dinner coming and you want to fill her full of sweets."

Sometimes there were words I heard but did not understand—these I tried to remember so that I could look them up later—and sometimes I simply didn't understand the sounds at all. Most often if I understood the rest of the sentence, I could fill in the blanks.

"My dear, I am certain she hasn't eaten in days, just look how pale her face is, and her eyes have big circles. Poor little girl coming all the way from America in the middle of winter! And what a winter it has been. Now it is February and better, but in January poor Igor, with his heart. When it was thirty degrees of frost, he could not leave the house for three weeks." Rita moved frantically around the little kitchen as she said this, going to Igor, coming back to me, leaning close to my face, waving her arms around.

Igor liked this attention; he blushed slightly, comfortably. He looked at me with a half-smile, almost proudly, as though he had performed some kind of feat.

"How terrible," I said. "Simply terrible." This was remembered from a dialogue my class had memorized a few years back. I meant it, however. It was inconceivable to me, minus-thirty centigrade. The poor man could not even leave his house.

"Truly," Anna said.

"Could you not go away somewhere?" I asked.

Igor shook his head solemnly. "Too sick," he said.

Sarah had given me a quick rundown of her Moscow relatives in the coffee shop. I had not quite caught the connection until now. Sarah was a real New Yorker. These were her husband Arthur's relatives. *Watch out for that Igor, he's a sly devil,* Sarah had told me. *He's into some fishy business. A gangster of some kind.*

You probably mean he trades on the black market, I said, big expert that I was.

Yeah, like I said, he's a gangster. Knows everybody, has lots of pull with higher-ups over there.

Rita had taken my plastic bag when she'd helped me off with my coat. The color-keyed tissue paper seemed ridiculous to me suddenly; as if they wouldn't know what was for whom without my help once the gifts were opened. But because I had promised Sarah in New York, I said, "In the bag I brought are presents from Sarah. The blue paper is for Igor, the purple for Anna, and the red for you, Rita."

"Ha ha ha!" Rita pealed in her high voice.

"Next time you will come to our apartment. It is two floors above in this building." Anna was once again speaking from the stove.

"Thank you," I said. "And there are photographs in an . . . an . . ."

"Envelope," Rita said, finishing for me.

"Yes."

Out of nowhere, she asked, "Are you Jewish?" which Sarah had also asked in New York. Sarah had been suspicious as to my reasons for wanting to be in Moscow in February.

"No," I said, almost apologetically. I wanted to tell them that all my tantes were Jewish, that I had no family except for my mother, and all her girlfriends, for some reason, were Jewish. The tantes worried about me, bought me things; they felt personally responsible for my education and well-being, for my successes and failures. This sounded so absurd that I said nothing at all.

Lifting his chin slightly, Igor asked, "So what interests you about the Soviet Union that you'd come here in February? You're at that Language Institute, right? You want to teach Russian in America?"

"*Nyet.*" This was to be expected, it invariably came up in any conversation I had with anybody about Russia. Often I lied, especially to strangers and at New York cocktail parties, where truth isn't highly valued anyway.

My mother understood my interest in Russia in the way that she understood everything about me—without a word being said. What she didn't like, however, was the fact that my trip was to be five months long and that three of those would be in winter.

But you could go in summer!

I told her it would not be enough.

Enough what?

Time, I had said, simply.

I chewed and swallowed the sweet and mealy bite of apple slowly, considering my choices.

"My papa," I said, trying to be careful to use the correct words, "was here during the war. He was a journalist and got to know Russia very well. He wrote books about your war that Americans didn't like very much in the fifties." At this I smiled sheepishly, because it was a habit.

"What is his name?" Igor asked, leaning forward.

"He's dead. He died almost ten years ago," I said quietly, feeling my voice strangling inside my throat. "Alexander Clinton Gray."

"Bozhe moy!" Rita shouted, "I know his books! I know his books! I was in Murmansk working with Lend-Lease during the war! I know everything about him! Comrades, we have the daughter of a famous person in our house!"

After that they started calling me *Clintonotchka* and offered to get me tickets to the Bolshoi Ballet that very week.

4

CUCARACHAS

My roommate Isabel was four years younger than I, a senior at Yale. She was reserved, materialistic, and territorial. She had out-lined her space in our room on the first day; she knew which shelves in the shallow closet would be hers, which desk drawer, which bookshelf. She placed a carefully selected number of her belongings in each of these storage areas, without saying a word. She had chosen the bed closer to the window and had unfolded her pile of Institute sheets and blankets with a deft snap of her wrists. She kept her peanut butter, dried apricots, and soup mixes in a locked suitcase under her bed. Property didn't mean much to me. Beside the ankh ring and the silver bracelet that had belonged to my father—which I never took off—and my camera and flash—gifts from my ex-fiancé—I didn't care if I went home without a thing. Most of the clothes and consumer goods I'd brought were meant to be given away before the end of my stay. I was going home to an empty apartment anyway, a new future.

But, I hadn't brought a hotpot. Isabel kept hers hidden away in the cabinet under her bedside table. In the morning I needed coffee before I could function, and had to ask to borrow the hotpot. She invariably made a face. Why hadn't I brought my own? Good question. Why hadn't I? I had brought other things I was sure would be appreciated, I figured people would be willing to share. I was wrong.

It seemed almost inconceivable that I would be living in this space with Isabel for five months. She was a person to whom I would have had absolutely nothing to say under other circumstances.

The night I came home from my first meeting with Rita and her relatives, I was drunk. My new Russian friends had uncorked a bottle of sweet champagne and a bottle of vodka to celebrate my arrival. We drank the vodka in shots, intermittently, all through the dinner of duck roasted with apples and prunes. They had gone all-out, and I was so happy to be treated so kindly that I enthusiastically drank to every one of their many toasts—to friendship, to their relatives back in America, to understanding between the people of our powerful nations, to peace on earth, to health, to success, and so on.

I came in five minutes after the midnight curfew and hung my coat on one of the hooks in the tiny hall next to the bathroom. When both Isabel's and my coat were hanging, it was hard to get into the room. It was particularly difficult drunk, and I kept getting entangled in the heavy folds, unable to find the light switch.

Isabel was already in bed, but not asleep. She was lying on her stomach reading a textbook; the green plastic desk lamp shed a rectangle of light on her pale hair and delicate, almost translucent face.

"Some guy came by and left you a stack of dvushki." She did not look up but pointed to them with the tip of one neatly manicured finger. There was an edge of displeasure in her tone which announced that in her opinion, this was somehow wrong. I could see her telling people: *Clinton Gray is such a flirt. She got some guy who's not even on our program to give her oodles of dvushki.*

Under the pile of dvushki was a note from Phil Chase (I had to close one eye to read it) explaining that he had made it to the center that day and that I owed him fifty kopeks for the twenty-five two-kopek coins he had left me.

"When did he come by?" I asked, trying with great difficulty not to slur. I wondered if I was speaking just a little too slowly. I couldn't tell anything from looking at Isabel.

"About ten minutes ago. I'm turning out the light, all right?"

"Fine," I said on my way out the door. "I'll be back in a couple of minutes."

Phil was in a good mood and pulled a bottle of hunter's vodka out from its hiding place, between his bed and the wall. There was a new dry law in the Institute: absolutely no alcohol was allowed anywhere in the building.

"Before the new rule everybody used to get crocked. The Bulgarians upstairs told me there were parties in the rooms that went on all night. It's all politics; no one really gives a shit, as long as you're not obvious about it. No one wants to get in trouble. If *we* get into trouble, the bureaucrats take a beating from the top."

We did not once mention the vodka, because Phil had told me he believed the room was tapped.

I didn't need to drink any more, but when Phil passed me the bottle I matched the length of his swig. It practically killed me. The honey-colored vodka tasted of sweet, powerful spices, almost like licorice, but not quite. I had always been alarmed at new, unfamiliar tastes. But whenever I made friends with a person of the opposite sex, I felt the dangerous urge to play macho.

At one point Phil stood on his hands and walked across the room to the closet, and back. He was giving himself his "drunk test," he whispered. I showed him my yoga head-stand, which involved positioning your interlocked fists and elbows so that they formed a tripod. I had not accounted for the weight of my boots and fell over like an old tree.

What did we talk about? I asked myself the next morning as I lay in bed trying to remember. I had to get up and get ready for class. The entire room was spinning around me; I felt like a sneaker in a washing machine.

Nothing important, I hoped; certainly nothing came to mind.

Isabel was preparing to take a shower. She walked away from the closet with matching powder-blue towels wrapped around her head and body.

"Next time please turn on the light, so you won't go banging into things. You could hurt yourself."

"I'm sorry," I said, pulling the covers over my head.

Five seconds later a bloodcurdling scream came from the bathroom. I threw the covers back and ran. Isabel's escape was blocked by my arrival, and she pushed to get me out of the way.

"Cockroaches! Thousands of them! All over the place!" The girl was ashen, you'd have thought she'd found a corpse in the tub. Why the bugs had picked that moment to make their appearance, I couldn't imagine. There hadn't been a single one up until then.

Our bathroom was shared by two women in the room next door and they, too, had come running. Maria-Manuella Concepcion, aka Ceppie, looked in with a mildly concerned expression on her small, delicate face. She was wearing a long T-shirt that said WACKO AND CO. in blue lettering across the chest. Isabel and I watched from the hallway while dozens of cockroaches scurried for the cracks in the walls. Ceppie stamped her feet. "Okay, you bastads!" she said through her teeth. "You not goin' to fuck with me. I'm used to yous bullshit."

She had never spoken with a Spanish accent before that morning. Her English was flawless, eloquent. We had sat together on the flight from New York to Frankfurt. She had talked about Dostoevsky, but without the slightest trace of pedantry. She simply talked, her enormous, almond-shaped eyes seeming to lose their focus, as though she were remembering a respected uncle.

"America appears in practically every one of his books, did you ever notice that? America represents many people's hopes, dreams, and fears too. Svidrigailov—you know, the dirty old man in *Crime and Punishment?* He tells everyone he's going to America, and then blows his head off. And in *Brothers K,* Dimitri's last hope is to escape to America because they're going to send him into exile in Siberia; *his last hope* is to escape to America. This *means* something. Dostoevsky saw the contrast way before his time." She told me she had written her senior thesis at Harvard on the subject.

So who was this street kid in our bathroom?

Isabel ran off and returned shortly with a can of Raid, which she handed to Ceppie without crossing the bathroom's threshhold. Ceppie gave the can a good, vigorous shake and sprayed the evil-smelling mist into every crack and corner.

"Watch out, they might attack you!" Isabel yelled.

"Don't be stupid, Isabel, they don't attack, only the water bugs attack," Ceppie said. "You can tell this chick never lived in a big city."

I could sense that Isabel was about to protest: she took in a short breath and opened her mouth. She must have thought better of it, because not a word came out.

Ceppie was shaking her head and laughing. "The water bugs do attack sometimes. They look just like these fuckers but they're seven times as big. We had 'em in our apartment because of the restaurant next door. The Board of Health finally came and closed that shithole down."

Ceppie had a deep and slightly raucous voice, but its singsong quality gave it an attractive gentleness. She was not very tall, maybe five-three, but svelte and muscular. Her nails were short and her hands looked hard, even bruised, as though she'd spent a good deal of time punching walls. She was not the kind of person with whom one would want to pick a fight.

"I hate to say this about my own people, mang, but did you ever see a clean Puerto Rican bodega?" she asked no one in particular.

Ceppie's roommate, a tall, heavyset, quiet woman, returned to their bathroom door with four Roach Motels in her hands. She spaced them evenly at the foot of her door, facing into the bathroom.

Her barricade reminded me for some reason of the Maginot Line. Ceppie stood with her arms crossed, leaning against the bathtub, taking in this operation.

"These are Communist roaches, man, they're never going to go for that bourgeois shit."

I laughed, but the tall girl ignored her.

When it was my turn to use the bathroom, I was hardly thrilled. I had lived in New York City long enough to have ceased screaming every time I saw a roach, but my hatred of them had not diminished. Making sure to turn on the light a good thirty seconds before entering, I stamped my feet to announce my arrival, and went in. The spray seemed to have had an effect. With my mind still far from clear, I gazed around this bizarre little room. The floor and wallpaper were a brownish yellow. The toilet faced the tub and had a wall to itself, between the two doors. It was a strange contraption. The wooden seat was removable, so every time you sat down it slipped and one side shot up in the air. You had to aim carefully, a skill which I was in no state to master at the moment. The "receiving" area was not a water-filled hole, but a flat, slightly concave porcelain plane which stared up at you like a glass eye and presented to you all the things you really would rather not see, before you flushed and had it all carried away by a short and unreliable jet stream.

The sink was an inch or two away from the tub and the two shared a long, swan-necked faucet which swiveled from side to side so that you could fill one basin or the other but not both at the same time. The pressure was surprisingly strong, and there was hot water. I took this as a good sign.

Ceppie knocked as I was taking my shower.

"Is that you, Gray?"

I told her to come in.

"This bathroom isn't so bad," she said. "In my grandparents' place the bathtub is in the kitchen."

"I have a writer friend who lives in the East Village in one of those old five-story walk-ups. Her bathtub is in the kitchen. She has a fourteen-year-old son, I don't know how they do it," I shouted over the water.

"People get used to anything, believe me."

Back in the room, Isabel sat perched at the edge of her bed, doing her eyes. She was holding a little blue purse mirror, up close to her nose. As she glanced up at me she spotted a big fat cockroach running toward her across the floor. She screamed and lifted both legs in the air as though they'd been hanging over the edge of a canoe on the Amazon and she'd just noticed the crocodiles. She grabbed her Raid from the bedside table and hit the bug with a good stream, forming a puddle on the linoleum floor. The noxious smell made my head spin and my stomach rise.

I needed coffee. I wanted to eat. There was some bread and cheese in a plastic bag on the windowsill, but it had been bought by Isabel. Mine had been finished the day before. On the desk lay the apples and oranges Rita had given me to take home to my friends, but I could not stomach fruit now—too much acid.

"These are for you, too," I told Isabel. "My friend gave them to me and told me to share them."

I was sick of separating our things; I was sick of asking her for her hotpot to boil water for my instant coffee, which I had brought from home in a plastic bag (of course, I had forgotten to bring dairy creamer, and hated coffee without milk.) That afternoon, after class, I decided I would go on a serious food hunt.

With twenty minutes left before first period, I went down to the cafeteria. Phil had mentioned that the kasha at breakfast was the Institute's best meal. I had never tried kasha, but as Ceppie had said, people get used to anything.

5

CEPPIE

Confused as to how to proceed on my food hunt, I phoned Rita's cousin Anna from the phone booth on the corner. I knew that Anna did not have a job, that she stayed home and took care of her ailing husband. I called for moral support, more than anything, but I never made it shopping that afternoon.

Anna told me to come over immediately. They had somehow gotten two tickets to a performance of *Swan Lake* at the Bolshoi for the next evening, and Anna wanted me to come pick them up. She also said she would feed me, so I forgot about my shopping and took the long metro ride out to their side of the city.

Anna's apartment was bigger than Rita's. The dining room and living room shared one large space. A heavy crystal chandelier hung from the low ceiling, and below it was a large antique mahogany table surrounded by six upholstered chairs. The pattern on the upholstery—red velvet roses on a beige background—was in direct conflict with the gold paisley couch and the furry red, green, and gold acrylic pillows which adorned it. The wallpaper was purple, blue, and white stripes and the rug was an orange and blue oriental with a complicated pattern. On the large oak cabinet which took up one wall were hundreds of porcelain statuettes and silver- and gold-plated figurines.

Anna was very proud of her apartment, especially of this room. She took me down the hall and showed me the guest room, but not the master bedroom. Igor was sleeping. Along a wall in the hallway was a glassed-in cupboard where the family photographs were exhibited. "It is a nice apartment," Anna said in her gentle, tremulous voice.

I agreed enthusiastically that it was beautifully arranged.

Rita showed up at five o'clock with the Bolshoi tickets and Igor appeared from the back of the house. Anna prepared the most delicious dinner, easier on my stomach than the rich, gamy duck of my first visit. We had *pelmieny,* the Russian answer to meat ravioli, in chicken broth; then Anna fried up little round patties of ground chicken with onions and breadcrumbs, called *kotliety,* which we ate with barley, and pickled cabbage cut into thick round slices. "I am so sorry this is such a simple meal," Anna said. "We did not plan ahead this time."

"Oh, no!" I said. "This is wonderful. Simply wonderful. I am so happy."

I was completely starved. I'd had nothing to eat but the Institute kasha which, as it turned out, was quite delicious. Hot and sweet, and filling. The little chewy granules of wheat gave you the impression you were eating something substantial, and the comfortable feeling of being full lasted well into the last of three one hour-and-a-half classes.

Ceppie came to my room later that night to ask if I would go hunt for food with her in the morning. She told me that earlier in the evening, a most extraordinary thing had happened to her.

She described the episode with such clarity and detail that even now my recollection of it is similar to the images I have of my parents' first meeting, of their honeymoon, of their first fight—oddly, I remember being there. Ceppie's Russia, like my parents' early life together, became a substantial and intrinsic part of my own life.

At around five, coming back from a four-mile run, Ceppie had heard Latin singing and guitar playing coming from the municipal kitchen on our floor. She was passing that way, so she stuck her head in. Around one of the two large formica tables some Cubans were listening and singing along with a guitarist. Ceppie greeted them in

Spanish and the guitarist waved her in, pulling up a chair for her from the second table.

"Where are you from?" he asked, without waiting for a reply. "We're from Cuba." He explained that most of them had been in Moscow studying at the Institute for over a year, and that sometimes they got homesick and gathered like this, in the kitchen, for a taste of home.

"So *where* are you from?" he asked again. Ceppie found him very attractive. "He has humorous eyes," she told me, "absolutely pitch-black, like coal." She said his hair was so black it seemed to have a blue tint.

"I'm from New York City," Ceppie answered flatly, being careful to employ a neutral tone. The Cubans stirred in their seats.

"From New York City?" the guitarist repeated.

"Yes. The West Side of Manhattan; you know, like in *West Side Story?*"

"But where are your parents from?"

"Puerto Rico," Ceppie said. "We came to New York when I was six."

The guitarist seemed to like that.

"So how's New York City?" someone else asked. All five of them, including the heavyset black woman cooking at one of the stoves, looked at Ceppie with good-humored curiosity, waiting for her response.

"New York City's good if you're rich, shitty if you're poor," Ceppie said, shrugging and extending her hands, palms up.

In response to her comment, they started arguing among themselves.

"See! That's what I've been telling you for years."

"Bullshit, man. It's propaganda."

"Ask her if she can walk in her Central Park at night. No one can walk there at night, that's what they say on the news."

"It's true," Ceppie said calmly, "most people don't walk in the Park at night. *I* walk in the Park at night."

"You're not scared?"

"No, but I guess it depends on what section of the Park we're talking about. In some places, I know people. I grew up with some of those guys who are out looking for trouble. They don't mess with me, they like me. They know I went to a good university and everything. You know Harvard?" The guitarist said he had heard of it. "Also, I have brothers."

The Cubans laughed and nodded understandingly.

Ceppie did not tell them, as she told me later, that one reason she dared to walk in the Park at night was because she was a second degree black belt in karate. She had never been attacked, but one day she hoped she could test herself, find out if all that karate training had been worth the trouble.

The black woman was frying up a large skilletful of onions and peppers, and some kind of stringy meat. Behind that a pot of rice was boiling, and its gentle odor mingled with the pungent sweetness of the frying onions and meat. The smell made Ceppie's mouth water and her knees tremble. Her last meal had also been the kasha of that morning, but she didn't usually eat much, and was surprised at her own reaction to the smell of the home-cooked Cuban food.

"So you just got here with the Americans?" the guitarist asked. "You shouldn't worry then. After a week, everything here will seem normal to you."

"Yes." She ran the back of her hand over her sweat-covered forehead and closed her eyes. Suddenly she didn't feel well at all. The four-mile run had wiped her out.

Without a word, the black woman came over with the skillet. The guitarist slid his dessert-sized plate in front of Ceppie, and someone else presented her with a spoon. The woman heaped food onto the plate, then set the skillet down in the middle of the table and went back for the rice. "No, no. Really, I can't take your food from you. There's not enough for everybody." Ceppie was served rice first; two large spoonfuls on top of the fried meat.

"Armando already ate," the black woman said, gazing at the guitarist out of the corner of her eye. Ceppie thought the woman was slightly insulted by her refusal.

"It's true," Armando said. "I already ate earlier, at my friends'."

So Ceppie ate. She chewed and swallowed slowly, with a relish she remembered from early childhood. At first, in New York, things had been difficult. The food they ate wasn't always good. Her mother had to make things last. "When it was something good, something I liked," she assured me, "then I was happy like last night."

She sang with the Cubans for a long time, neglecting her homework. They drank red Georgian wine out of opaque mugs, in case the *dezhurnaya*, the floor mother of sorts, looked in unexpectedly. Armando said there was one dezhurnaya who liked to drink with them and never gave them a hard time, but she was off duty tonight.

The next morning, when we set out after food, Ceppie was a tad hung over. We had a hard time climbing the incline that led from the Institute to the street. The snow was not deep, it hadn't snowed during the night. But the air was so cold it froze the hairs in your nostrils as you breathed. It hurt the eyes. Ceppie had an empty khaki backpack slung over her shoulder and looked like some kind of guerilla in her drab olive army jacket that had a fur-lined hood and came to her knees. We were huffing up that hill with our heads tilted downward against the wind, determined to get to the store and back before our first class.

The Cubans had let her in on a couple of their secrets: where they shopped in the neighborhood, and that she should go to the stores in the morning, because after classes it was already too late. The stores were emptied of anything worthwhile by noon.

"I swear, when they gave me that plate of food I almost cried. I'm going to buy them a bottle of something, something from one of those hard-currency stores. What do you think I should get?"

"I don't know. French cognac?"

"French *cognac?*"

"Why not?"

"Isn't that terribly bourgeois?"

A blueish hue preceded the sun. More windows began to light up, bringing mysterious character to the completely neutral, bland, unattractive housing complexes we passed. We lived in one of Moscow's newer developments; less than fifteen years earlier the area had been completely wooded. Even now the boxy, five-to-ten-story buildings seemed unfinished, lacking either paint, a sidewalk out in front, or something not essential but important enough by American standards to give them a neglected, ramshackle appearance.

"Looks just like the Bronx to me," Ceppie stated reassuringly. "Better than some parts, for sure."

"I've never been to the Bronx; I've only driven through on my way to New England." I felt very middle class suddenly. But I didn't see any sense in pretending to be something I was not, especially with Ceppie, who seemed to see right through all of that.

She laughed quietly. "My Auntie Clarissa lives in a section of the Bronx you wouldn't want to visit with your complexion."

An enormous silence surrounded us. It was lovely and peaceful walking in the growing light.

A moment later, Ceppie added, "It's funny how people can come from such different worlds, but over here they get thrown together and everybody acts like they're equal. Back home you probably wouldn't talk to me. My brothers would scare you to death. After this we'll never see each other again."

"I hope that's not true. Maybe you'll take me up to your aunt's when we get back."

"Maybe you'll freak out." She placed her small hand on my shoulder. "But I don't think so."

There were few streets connecting to the narrow main one on which we lived and were now walking. To our left, people were beginning to emerge from the footpaths that led into the courtyards of the housing complexes. On our right was Institute land: an expanse of snow resembling a choppy sea stretched downhill for more than a mile to the edge of a forest of silver birches. From the middle of the forest, a skyscraper reached up into the clouds. Here and there, in the expanse of snow, a tall building identical to the Institute stood alone.

"Easy to get lost around here. No numbers, and all the buildings look exactly the same," Ceppie said.

The sun appeared, a red-hot silver dollar rising above the trees. We passed a new building site dug deep into the snow-covered earth. In the middle of the cleared area stood a gigantic yellow crane. There was construction litter everywhere: piping, barrels, cement slabs, crates, broken bottles.

A young man jogged past us in a purple sweatsuit that looked like it had been purchased in the sports department of Bloomingdale's. Suddenly, at the next intersection, civilization seemed to stop. There was nothing but a wasteland of construction pits that stretched as far as the eye could see.

The birch trees beyond the snow stood like a silent army of silver-limbed ghosts. In my mind, Old Russia and its romantic literature had always been synonymous with birches. Prince Andrew had met Natasha in a birch forest, and found that she represented what was honest, simple, and profoundly Russian; he fell madly in love.

"I feel like falling in love," I said, and immediately regretted it.

"Jou ang eberybody else," she said in her Spanish accent, which she seemed to put on and take off like a costume. She punched me in the arm, and winked. "You were looking at the birches, right?"

"Yes."

"You know, birches like these must be seen to be believed." The beauty and simplicity of what she'd said made me laugh.

AT THE
BOLSHOI
WITH
PHIL CHASE

Phil Chase had not been in his room the night I came home to the Institute with the two tickets for *Swan Lake*. I did not mention the tickets to anyone, not even Ceppie, because I very much wanted Phil to go. He could think whatever he liked: that I was being nice by repaying his kind welcome; that I was a lonely newcomer; or, that I was asking him on a date. The ambiguity gave me an odd sense of security. Either way, it was an extravagant invitation; I knew tickets to the Bolshoi were an expensive rarity.

The next morning, with ten minutes left before first period, I crossed the hall and knocked on his door. Under my arm was the one notebook I had brought with me from the States and was using for all my classes; I had not been able to find Soviet notebooks anywhere yet.

Phil opened the door. He was wearing thin gold-rimmed glasses, and a light blue shirt under a royal blue sweater. Just a half-inch of shirt collar was visible above the neckline of the sweater. He looked like the serious older brother of the man who two nights ago, had worn a guinea-T and walked across his room on his hands. I was taken aback, and stood in the hall staring at him as though I had knocked on a stranger's door.

"Is something wrong?" he said.

"No! You look so different, that's all."

"It's good to look serious for class, so I dress up a little."

He was holding a pile of notebooks and textbooks, ready to head downstairs. I felt betrayed somehow, as though he had purposely fooled me. I thought I'd gotten to know him a little. He had not seemed complicated to me, just a very nice, easy person, someone I had felt comfortable with, had drunk seriously with. And here was someone I actually felt threatened by because he looked too handsome. The sweater brought out the peppermint blueness of his eyes. The slight bump on the bridge of his nose was hidden by his glasses. He looked noble, with full lips and a square jaw that gave him a strong, determined look.

"I have tickets to the Bolshoi. Would you like to go?" I must have sounded a little sharp, unpleasant.

"When?" he asked, not seeming all that thrilled by my disclosure and invitation.

"Tonight. I came by last night to ask you but you weren't in."

"I got back pretty late," he smiled. "My friends never let me leave on time to make curfew."

"I only got the tickets last night."

"I can't go tonight," he said simply. "I'm supposed to go see some people I haven't seen in weeks. They're pretty mad at me."

Now I was hurt, but I didn't want him to know so I shrugged indifferently.

"All right," I said. "No big deal, I'll ask my friend Ceppie." I walked out the door and down the hall. I heard him lock his door, and I felt his eyes on my back. I noticed for the first time that the hall floor, under the strip of green carpeting that ran down the center was of blond parquet. What a pretty floor, I thought as my eyes suddenly and incomprehensibly filled with tears. I walked faster.

"Clinton," he called after me. "Hey!"

I stopped, but I didn't turn around. I tried to make my voice sound as though I were truly concerned. "We're going to be late."

I must be tired, I thought. It really was not a big deal; Ceppie and I would have just as good a time at the Bolshoi together. Without men. Now I was pissed off at myself for not having asked her first.

I felt him approaching me. His presence overwhelmed me, like an undertow pulling me down.

"I'm sorry," he said, more gentle now. "I really would like to go."

I could have said a number of things.

"No big deal," I said instead. It shocked me that I could not control my disappointment or hide the fact that I was insulted.

I pounded quickly down the six flights of stairs, but Phil easily stayed within two feet of me. When we got to the long wooden hallway which connected the dormitory to the academic building, he put his hand on my shoulder, passed me like a car on a highway, and took off at a run down the hall. When he was gone, I felt worse, though up till then all I had wanted was for him to disappear.

Ceppie was not in my first period group, which was Grammatika. Today we were to discuss our backgrounds; where we were from in America, and why we had become interested in Russian. I didn't want to be singled out; it was nobody's business but mine that my American father had spent most of World War Two as a journalist in the Soviet Union. I also realized I didn't really want to share my memory of him with these strangers. I was going to have to make something up fast. While I was going over this in my mind I didn't have time to think of Phil, nor did I hear a word the other students were saying.

There was a ten-minute break between Grammatika and our next class, which was a Soviet History lecture that was referred to as "The World According to Lenin." It was held in the main auditorium. I stood outside the door of that vast room and waited for Ceppie, who was, of course, late. She always went to the *bufyet* for a quick cup of black coffee between classes. She said she could not stay awake otherwise.

I watched a group of Africans walk by. They were dressed in green and brown tunics with intricate black circular patterns painted on the material. I strained to understand the language they spoke, finally realizing it was bastardized French. Then three young men in red floor-length gowns and round red hats passed. Monks? Couldn't be. They looked Indian, but I was not sure.

The bell sounded and people began to disappear into the classrooms.

I was about to go in and find a seat when I saw Phil running toward me with his long-legged gait. He was slightly out of breath.

"I just ran out to the street and put a call through to my friends," he said, pushing his hair away from his eyes with the flat of his hand. "I told them I have the flu."

"Did you run out there without your coat? You're going to *get* the flu," I said, and knocked on the paneling behind me. Everything in the academic section of the Institute was made of wood.

I was feeling very confused. I was completely charmed and flattered, but I was still angry. My vanity said, *Tell him you already asked someone else!*

"It was only a couple of minutes," he assured me. "It's not cold out today. So. What time do we leave?"

Our seats were in the last row of the orchestra section. The row was raised a foot above the others, and ran in a half-circle around the theater. From there we had a perfect view of the stage and the loges at its sides, but we could not see the main loge that was right above us, where the Important sat. The only thing in the theater that reminded you that this was indeed Russia in the 1980s was the enormous banner above the proscenium arch, which glorified the Communist Party of the Soviet Union. It was a red chariot of some kind, in complete conflict with the surrounding decor. Phil and I were very quiet. No one in the audience spoke above a murmur.

"Have you been here before?" I whispered to Phil.

"Once," he mumbled back. "But I was sitting way the hell up there somewhere, I couldn't see or hear a thing. Your friends must be some important people to get these seats at a day's notice."

"I have no idea who they really are," I said.

Phil looked like a successful artist in his tweed coat and paisley tie. He was still wearing the blue shirt of the morning, and his glasses. I had done my best to get dressed up. This was no easy feat considering the cold outside, the heat inside; did you wear your snowboots with a skirt, and replace the boots for shoes once you got inside? Or did you wear layers of socks with a good pair of leather boots and leave it at that? I wore my best sweater, a cream-colored cashmere my mother had bought on sale at Bergdorf's for forty-nine dollars, a straight black skirt with giant snowflakes in the print, silk long underwear, both top and bottom (a gift from a third tante), and my black leather boots with three pairs of socks. By the time we sat down in the theater I was about to die of the heat.

I leaned over, took off the boots and two of the pairs of socks, stuck the socks in my bag, and put the boots back on. I was considering doing the same with the long underwear, but the Russian sitting next to me was already upset about the socks.

Once the ballet started I had the sensation that I had stopped breathing. The dancers leapt so high in the air I feared for their limbs, the way I feared for the young gymnasts while watching the Olympics on television. Phil sat motionless beside me. As I'd look over at him, I could see the ballerinas flitting back and forth, white butterflies in the lenses of his glasses. His lips were shut tightly, there was no expression on his face. He was completely absorbed.

I was suddenly assailed by the strangest recollection, which I realized may have been nothing more than a vision instilled in me from my mother's endless tellings of the stories of my youth. I saw myself as a tiny girl sitting between my mother and father at the ballet in Paris. The Russians had come to town. My mother had been worried that I would not be able to sit still through the entire ballet, and told me the story of *Swan Lake* before and during the show. After every dance I clapped and shouted, "Bravo, Madame! Bravo, Monsieur!" at the top of my lungs. After the last curtain, I refused to leave. I believed, in my three-year-old's mind, that a ballet was like a movie; if you sat long enough, the show would start again. I grabbed hold of the seat and screamed and cried when my parents tried to take me away by force.

"Encore! Encore!" I screamed. People were staring and my parents were embarrassed.

Not knowing how to quiet me, my father suggested we go backstage and meet the dancers. "They're real people," he explained calmly. "After all that work they have to take a rest."

"Can we touch the little people?" I asked, probably under the impression that they were three inches tall, because of where we sat.

"We can certainly ask," my father said.

So the three of us went backstage, and stood in a furious crowd of autograph-seekers and ballet aficionados. With me on his hip, my father worked his way up to the dancers, who stood inside a protective circle of Soviet guards. He explained in Russian that his terribly stubborn child would not go home until she had personally been introduced to the dancers. The prima ballerina lifted me up over her head, spun me around in her powerful little arms, and kissed me. She held me for a while, perched on the waist of her fluffy tutu, while she smiled and signed autographs for the people. For years I told anyone who would listen that I had met a real Russian fairy princess.

After that, I loved all the Russians.

That night at the Bolshoi, the audience shouted and clapped with complete abandon after every dance. They were not afraid to be expressive here. It was a release of some kind. The audience loved the dancers and the music; I could feel their indescribable pride. I loved the dancers, too; I loved everyone in the crowded theater. I wanted to tell my father: *Now I understand what you must have felt for these people. I am starting to understand everything.* But there would be no such conversation. Ever. He had been dead for almost ten years now. How could something hurt so much after ten years?

In the middle of *Swan Lake* I began to cry. My eyes and nose ran so badly that I had to reach into my bag for some toilet paper, which I always carried with me because there was never toilet paper in public places. After I'd wiped my face and quietly blown my nose I put my hands in my lap and gripped the crumpled ball of tissue. I felt comfortable and safe in the darkness surrounding me. Phil's warm, solid hand suddenly appeared on the armrest. He squeezed my left wrist, then laced his fingers through mine, while his face remained glued to the stage, completely absorbed. I was afraid to stare at him and only glanced sideways without turning my head. Neither of us moved for the rest of the first act. During intermission we went to the bufyet and had a fruit juice with whipped cream and chocolate shavings on top.

With this we had little sandwiches of butter and red caviar. Phil waited in line and paid for them while I went to the lady's room to wash my face.

During the beginning of the second act I waited in vain for him to reach for my hand again. After twenty minutes I put my left hand on his knee, and he took it between his palms, resting his hands in his lap.

What did I know about Phil? I had learned on the night of the hunter's vodka that he was from Long Island, that his father was a professor of mathematics at SUNY Stony Brook, that his mother was of Norwegian descent, that he had a brother and a sister and a blond ex-girlfriend with whom he'd been desperately in love, but something had gone wrong. He liked to surf, and was a lifeguard at the ocean in the summertime. He was getting a Ph.D. in Russian Studies at a university in California. So what did I really know about him?

I had been crazy in love only once, in college. Because it had happened to me, I believed in the *coup de foudre,* that you *could* meet someone and immediately fall in love. You could die from it, like a fever, and no amount of logic ever helped anyone in that situation. I was relatively certain that I had nothing to worry about now. That fever had passed, and I had become incapable of such feelings.

I was not an angry person, I did not blame Adam, my lover in college, for what had happened to me. I still felt affection for him. But I never saw him; he scared me too much.

It is the newness of the place, I told myself. You're alone and scared and Phil's a nice guy.

Nevertheless, my emotions were causing me to worry. My hand in Phil's lap began to sweat but he did not let go.

7

THE
U.S. PASSPORT
AS AN
APHRODISIAC

Phil Chase and I sat pressed arm to arm on the long and crowded metro ride home from the Bolshoi. I waited for him to ask me why I had burst into tears in the middle of the first act of the ballet—I was in a careless mood and wanted to tell him secrets—but he paid no attention to me. He was busy watching Muscovites get on and off the train. Two old drunkards were arguing over which of them was unhappiest. With each big jolt of the train they fell into the crowd, which stumbled backward in a collective wave. No one said a word to the drunks but everyone watched with solemn, disapproving glances.

Phil's even temperament exuded a complacency toward life which I envied. It was impossible to know what went on behind his stolid face, and I watched him alertly, looking for clues.

He was a methodical and organized person. I could tell from the cleanliness of his room and from the way he pulled things out of his backpack without looking for them, as though he knew exactly where each item was placed. He also waited a long time between cigarettes, but when he lit one it was with determination. He would light and then smoke the cigarette quickly, inhaling with such relish that the ember glowed bright red, and the look of sober control would momentarily fade from his face. When his hair fell into his eyes he would push it back with a swift raking movement that had become involuntary, like blinking his eyes. Most importantly, I felt that he was capable of strong emotions, but for some reason avoided them. This bothered and fascinated me.

As I sat watching him on the metro, I wanted to ask him what had possessed him to take my hand during the ballet, and hold it so tightly that sweat drenched our palms. I had a sudden desire to kiss him. I wanted to look through his wallet and his backpack, put my face against the clothes in his closet. The slightest look from him sent a flush through my body; his preoccupation with his surroundings and not with me sent my heart to my knees. He battered my emotions, and, though outwardly I seemed as calm as he, inwardly I felt at the mercy of a sudden ocean storm.

"Why don't you have a roommate?" I asked, breaking our silence with a pointed question—or a neutral one—depending on how he chose to interpret it.

"I do. But he's having an affair with the Director of the Bulgarian Program. She has her own room 'cause she's the Director. When they have a fight he comes down. He gets antsy once in a while, tells her he doesn't want to be so serious, and she throws him out. I think she wants an American husband in the worst way. He took most of his clothes and his shaving gear up to her room. So basically, I have my own room. Except when they fight."

"I hope he gives you a warning when they fight."

"Why?" He looked at me blankly.

"Well, in case you want to have a girl in yourself."

"That hasn't happened yet," he said. "It would be complicated to get involved with someone in the Institute. Paul—that's my roommate —couldn't get away from his Bulgarian even if he wanted to. There are a couple of Russian girls I like, but they can't come into the Institute. Plus, I can't tell if they like me or if they like my American passport. You'll come to notice pretty quickly that a U.S. passport is a hell of an aphrodisiac around here."

The walk from the metro was a treacherous one. The paths were frozen, uneven, and dark. We waited ten minutes for a local bus that did not arrive. Phil took me by the arm and started for the Institute.

Though they were flat, my New York City boots slipped out from under me at every step. I was forced to hold onto his arm as tightly as I could. Just before the Institute was the Path from Hell, a three-foot snowbank that ran along the edge of a fence which cordoned off a construction pit. The other side of the snowbank was the dark, icy street. One slip and you were dead, if a car happened along at the wrong moment. Phil gripped my arm and led the way, holding the wooden fence with his other, gloved hand.

Before we reached the lighted area in front of the doors, Phil spun around and kissed me. It was completely unexpected and I fell into the thickness of his sheepskin coat. I could not feel his body through our layers of clothes, which was disturbing, but his mouth was like a steamy pool, an oasis in the biting cold. A warm mist floated around our heads. When he moved away from me I found myself staring up at him with a dreamy expression. Then I was revealing my hand in this card game and it made me angry because not only did he have the Royal Flush, he also had all my money stacked on his side of the felt.

"Thank you for asking me along," he said. His voice sounded deeper, hoarse and quiet.

"You're welcome," I said. "Thank you for being so helpful these first few days."

My tone was perfectly agreeable, but devoid of sentiment. Anger was, and had always been, my emergency switch. It was a cold and calculated anger that slammed shut my emotions like a huge iron door, when I felt I was losing control. I turned away and headed for the Institute doors.

We showed our student passes together, climbed the stairs together, but when we reached our hall, he went to his room and I to mine. Not another word was said. I felt like a sleepwalker.

That night, when I had calmed down, I wrote him a note before going to bed:

> Dear Philip—Are you shy or vain? Are you afraid or indifferent? I can't seem to tell, and I need to know. —Clinton.

But I did not slip it under his door.

The atmosphere in my room had become much less tense since my successful expedition to the grocery store. I had come back with enough food to last Isabel and me a week. I had found *kolbasa* (which looked and tasted exactly like bologna), milk, yogurt, fresh bread (the loaves had been hot from the oven when we'd bought them), butter, mixed preserves of unidentifiable fruit, cheese, and—miracle of miracles—sprats! Sprats, like the eggplant caviar that came in glass jars, were a deficit item, which made them a delicacy. I dutifully waited in line for ten minutes for the sprats, and came home with four tins which were much appreciated by my roommate.

There was a sill on the inside of our window, which served as our refrigerator. Overnight, the milk had frozen solid and our fruit was frostbitten. Isabel complained in muted tones as she prepared for her shower, but did not deny me her hotpot, which was crucial to me. After two cups of coffee (I held the carton of milk over the boiling water to thaw it) and a few slices of bread and preserves, I decided to set out once again to make phone calls from the booth at the end of the street.

This took immeasurable will. I couldn't imagine why I was so terrified of using the phone, of asking for a person and explaining who I was. It did not occur to me at the time that I might have possessed an unnatural fear of rejection in general. I was only aware of my fear of being rejected by Phil Chase, and this took precedence over my fear of the telephone.

As I opened my eyes that morning my first thoughts had been of him: how did he sleep and what were his dreams? I was relieved that I had not slipped the note under his door.

I looked through my coded phone book and picked out a number to call. This was a little like picking a card out of a deck.

I chose the number of a young playwright my wonderful professor of Russian Literature had given me before my departure. Vika Erikson was secretive about her connections in the Soviet Union, and did not hand out numbers indiscriminately. I knew nothing about her relationship with the playwright, except that they had been friends a long time. Also, "young," in Vika Erikson's seventy-five-year-old eyes, could mean anything. I had no idea whom I was calling.

"Allo?" An old woman's voice answered.

"Allo, may you call Andrej to the phone, please?"

"Who is phoning?"

"A student of Professor Vika Erikson from New York." I remembered too late that it was always better not to mention the United States on the telephone.

"Wait a moment, please." The woman did not sound the least bit thrilled. The receiver was put down with a bang. Quite a while passed before a man's voice came on the line.

"Allo?"

"Allo, my name is Clinton. Professor Vika Erikson gave me your number. I am one of her graduate students. She . . . ah . . . asked me to send her regards." There was a long pause.

"I was expecting you. Vika phoned me last week. How is she? I haven't seen her in many years."

"All right. As you know, she is unhappy. Her husband died a few months ago."

"Yes, it's terrible."

"Yes."

Another long pause.

"Listen, I am very busy right now. One of my plays is in . . . and I have no time. I practically sleep at the theater. Are you interested in seeing a rehearsal?"

"Yes, of course. With great pleasure."

"Can you come tonight?"

"Yes."

He gave me directions.

I wore the same outfit I had worn to the Bolshoi the night before.

Andrej was waiting for me in front of the theater. He was around thirty-five, of medium height, thin, with small shoulders and thick black hair. His eyes were hazel; the left one wandered, which gave me the impression he was preoccupied with something going on behind me while he talked. Andrej dressed Western-style, in Wrangler corduroys and a blue-and-white-striped sweater. The only thing that gave him away as a Soviet was that the shirt beneath the sweater was of a completely different pattern and color. We shook hands quickly, and he led me into the theater by the elbow. We sat together in the third row.

Andrej explained in a whisper just before the curtain went up that the play was about to open. It had been ready months ago, but he had had some trouble with the censors, and had been obliged to rephrase some of the dialogue. But he felt he had done it without harming the theme.

"There is a good amount of slang in here. I am afraid you will not understand completely. If you need to ask me, you will. All right?"

I did not understand everything, but the gist of it was clear to me. The play is about a Moscow underground rock 'n' roll group in the late 1980s. The band's lead vocalist, a girl of around seventeen, is having an awful time trying to decide whether to give up singing and go to college, or to continue with it, and take a labor job somewhere to support herself. She has problems with her family (the parents and two sisters and she all live together in a two-room apartment—the right half of the stage). Her father, a veteran of World War Two, reminds her constantly that she has nothing in the world to complain about, and talks (almost nostalgically, it seemed to me) about the miseries he experienced during the war. Both parents do not see anything good ever coming of her singing with the rock group. And most importantly, the parents know that she is obsessively in love with the organizer, and lead guitarist, of the band.

Completely shocking to me was the freedom with which the characters discussed their problems. Their average salary is around one hundred and fifty rubles a month, and a guitar costs close to a thousand. They starve themselves and cut all sorts of corners to pool their money for instruments. They cannot even afford guitar strings, much less guitars, or amplifiers, or microphones. They all work labor jobs in the daytime, and none of them can make ends meet. At one point in Act I, in the crowded garage where the group meets (the left half of the stage), the drummer writes a fan letter to a drum company in Hungary. In Act II an entire drum set arrives all wrapped up, with a letter from the president of the drum company saying he'd never received such an extraordinary fan letter in his life. "Use them well," he writes. The young drummer cries.

The musicians wear jean jackets and sport rather conservative punk haircuts (meaning they aren't mohawks, or streaked red and orange) but they definitely make a statement about their need to express individuality. In America, they would have seemed mild.

In the garage is a tape player. The musicians listen to old scratchy, faded Beatle songs, over and over again. "Girl," in particular.

Andrej leaned over and asked me in a whisper if I thought having the tune sound scratchy worked. "It's supposed to be a little sad," he explained.

"It's terribly sad," I said. I felt he didn't want me to think they couldn't get ahold of a clear recording of the song if they had wanted to.

"I can't believe this play is being allowed," I said.

"It was very difficult, I must tell you."

"What did you change?"

"The ending," he said. The play ends well. The band is discovered by a relatively liberal young Communist who organizes youth concerts. He believes that Soviet youth is floundering, and must be allowed to express itself. He sees no harm in allowing kids to play publicly, as long as the songs are not anti-Communist. For every sad, depressing song, there must be a happy, optimistic one. The band leader is not certain that complying with these demands is ethical. Nevertheless they give it a shot, and agree to audition before the judging committee.

"What is that?" I whispered to Andrej.

"Oh yes. Every artistic creation must pass before a committee, just as this play did, before it can be released publicly."

At the end of the play one of the less important band members goes off to Afghanistan. I was flabbergasted.

"You see, the way I had it end before was that nothing happens with the organizer. The kids can't make up their minds. A little like Beckett, you know, waiting for Godot and Godot never comes? But it was categorically refused that way. It's okay now, it moves with the times."

"It's a miracle," I said.

"Yes. Well, Afghanistan without a happy ending just wouldn't work."

"It's wonderful," I said.

He asked me if I had time to get a snack before going home. I said yes. We climbed into Andrej's little Lada car whose heater was broken and went to the Union of Theater Employees. Andrej flashed a card at the linebacker *babushka* who blocked the door to the restaurant. Outside the building an enormous line of people waited to get into the café next door.

The inside of the restaurant was palatial. Large chandeliers hung from the ornate ceiling, the windows were covered by thick velvet curtains, the tables were crowded with laughing people who all seemed to have had a good deal to drink.

Andrej ordered a bottle of champagne and a bottle of Georgian cognac. "I am sorry but they no longer serve vodka here," he explained, "It's part of the new War Against Alcoholism."

"But cognac is as strong as vodka," I said.

"But cognac is cognac and vodka is vodka," Andrej pointed out. He turned to the waitress, who looked ready to fall asleep on her feet. "Do you have any caviar tonight?"

"*Nyet,*" she said.

"Come on, now!" he said, piqued and incredulous. "We have a very important guest here," he gestured toward me with an open hand. "We can't send her home to her country without trying our caviar."

"All right, I'll see," she said.

The appetizers were extraordinary. Besides the little crystal bowl of red caviar, there were slices of salmon, slices of beef, egg salad, potato salad with green peas and mayonnaise, little cheese and meat pies. There was a fresh cucumber salad as well. I was ecstatic, and drunk by the time the entrée of mushrooms baked in sour cream arrived.

Phil Chase should see me now! I thought.

"Your restaurant reminds me of the writers' union in *The Master and Margarita,*" I told my host.

Andrej laughed. "Exactly right! We artists have certain privileges, but there are serious restrictions as well. But all the same, you are seeing a part of Moscow's 'khaigh laife.' "

"Your play is extraordinary. I never thought I would see a play so —what?" I wanted to say daring, risqué, something to that effect. In Russian, it was impossible.

"Two years ago I was in serious trouble for writing something much less controversial. It is surprising even to me. They want plays like this now."

"What was the theme?" I asked.

"I will tell you another time."

His wandering eye looked over my shoulder at the table behind us. It made me want to turn my head.

"You are the daughter of Alexander Clinton Gray."

"Yes."

"Vika told me. What are you looking for here? People? Information?"

"Yes. I have nothing to start with. He threw everything away before I was born. He never talked about being here during the war—sometimes he would say he had great friends in Moscow. But of course, they are not in his books."

"Ah yes, his books. They were published here in the early sixties. They were so in demand it was impossible to find them. Of course, I was a child then. But later, I read several. I remember the one about Stalingrad particularly."

"That is certainly the best one."

"I'll help you, if you want." He patted my hand, as he might pat a child's. "Here, drink." He poured me a tumblerful of cognac. I noticed suddenly that he had not had anything at all to drink; he had filled his champagne glass, but had barely touched it.

"I will be completely drunk," I said.

"I will drive you home," he said.

"I can sit in a taxi."

"Absolutely not." As if he'd noticed my watching his glass, he added, "I cannot drink because I am . . ."

"Excuse me?"

"Zarulëm." He pantomimed driving.

He insisted on pulling into the Institute parking lot, though I'd asked him to stop at the top of the snow-covered lawn.

"Why?" he asked. "It's cold."

"It's dangerous for you."

"Yerunda," he said. Nonsense.

I noticed that he looked around rather carefully before pulling in, and he did not go all the way to the Institute doors but stayed in the shadows.

"Tomorrow I have the last rehearsal," he said. "But the next day, I will come for you. What time?"

"Four o'clock," I said. "Do not come in here. Stay up on the road."

He laughed lightly. "All right." Then he tried to kiss me. I shook his hand enthusiastically and jumped out of the car.

Of all the coincidences in the world—just ahead of us was Phil coming up the path through the snow. He stopped when he recognized me, but only for a second.

"Who was that in the car?" he asked as we went in and flashed our student passes at the old lady sitting in the glass booth, half asleep. "Good evening, Vera Borisovna!" Phil said to her with great enthusiasm. "How do you feel this evening?" His Russian seemed flawless. The old lady smiled at him. That was a first. It was 12:15 A.M., fifteen minutes after curfew.

"That one likes me," he muttered as we moved on down the well-lit hall.

"I was out with a famous playwright who tried to kiss me."

"What did I tell you?" Phil muttered. "That U.S. passport is a goddamn aphrodisiac."

"Thanks a lot, Phil."

"Oh Christ, I didn't mean it like *that*. I just don't want you to get into trouble."

My blood was suddenly pounding in my head. He cares! I thought. He cares! Which caused my knees to weaken and my mouth to go dry.

"You do something to me. It scares me. I'm not used to it." My voice trailed off; I needed to cough but refused to. It seemed inappropriate somehow.

"Isn't that strange? You do the same to me."

"Well, one would never know," I said with mild exasperation.

"Come home with me and I'll show you."

I asked if he was drunk.

"Not particularly," he said.

The matter-of-factness that descended upon him after we entered his room surprised me at first. While I sat paralyzed on his roommate's unoccupied bed, Phil put things away, hung our coats in the hall, and unfolded the bedspread and the top sheet. He took his red bandanna out of his backpack and placed it over his bedside lamp, muting the harsh light and giving the room a reddish glow that reminded me of the bordellos I'd seen in movies. He was casually battening down the hatches, as though he were experienced in these matters, and felt completely at ease.

I was reminded of my father, who had behaved similarly preparing for a hurricane, twelve years before. We had just moved to Florida from France. When he'd heard the news over the radio he had calmly gone about the house closing the shutters and bringing in the patio furniture. "How unexpected, Clinton," he had said good-humoredly as I followed him around, wide-eyed. "Your first year in America and we're going to have a hurricane. It sounds like the worst of it will hit the Carolinas. I don't think it will be a bad one. It should be fun." He may have been more concerned than he seemed, but he obviously did not want me to worry. On the other hand, my father often warned me that I would be extremely lucky if I managed to get through life without having to really suffer. But his presence always reassured me, and at that time I was relatively certain that nothing terrible would ever happen to me.

Phil showed no signs of apprehension and I was thankful to him for that. It made me stop imagining all the little things that could go wrong. Gradually his stolid composure left him. Later, the bedside lamp went crashing to the floor, along with his dictionaries and the water glass. The sheets were twisted into a humid pile. I was not aware of anything until it was all over, when I realized I was cold and the wind was howling outside his window. He got up and untangled the bedclothes, tucking them in at the foot and covering me with top sheet and blanket. I started telling him things I was certain I would regret having shared with him by morning.

"I almost got married once. In fact, until a few months ago I was engaged, but I backed out. You want to know why?"

The room was dark now, except for the meager light wafting in from other Institute windows. His face was distorted by shadows and I didn't recognize it. I felt safer not looking at him. His heart beat reassuringly against the side of my head.

"Why?"

"I don't know why. Because I thought love would get easier and easier to understand as I got older. No way, it only gets more complicated. There wasn't any heat in our relationship. But heat is something I'm scared of, so it seemed okay to me to live a very calm life together. I thought it would be good not to worry about being in pain. But then my mother took me out to lunch one day, a couple of months ago, and said 'You and Dave already act like an old married couple. What's the rest of your life going to be like?' I cried right there at the damn sushi bar, went home and called it off."

What I did not tell Phil was that the weekend before that lunch, I had gone by train to visit Dave in Philadelphia. He had a small part in a production in Philly and we had not seen each other in two weeks. On the train I realized that I had not really thought about him much during the week, but I *was* beginning to miss him as the train approached the station. I decided to be romantic when I stepped off the train; so I threw my arms around him and planted an open-mouthed kiss on his lips. He turned his head to the side, pointing to his sealed lips.

"Bubblegum," he said. "Brand-new piece."

My heart dropped but I did what I always did with my disappointments. I locked it in a case and threw it into the closet, on top of all the other cases I had managed to accumulate over the years. I could barely open the closet door, but it was not until I had that sushi lunch with my mother that the entire pile came tumbling down on my head.

"Do you always listen to everything your mother says?" Phil asked me.

"No. I'm as rebellious as most daughters, but she was right. I loved him but there was no passion."

"And we have passion," he said, almost with dismay. Then, as though this next thought were completely connected, he added, "My mother is schizophrenic. She's been whacked-out for fifteen years. Sometimes she's okay, sometimes she's not. The weirdest thing is I can't tell the difference. But she gets stuck on things sometimes, and won't let up. Then I know she's off the deep end, and I go wild." He breathed out a sour laugh.

I wanted to tell him I had fallen in love with him three days ago— it had been almost immediate—but I was afraid of shocking him. I tried to show him instead, without saying a word. Our brief conversation was the eye of our hurricane. The rest of the storm lasted most of the night.

His Soviet-made alarm clock rang at six, tearing me out of a dreamless sleep. The sound was so loud and shrill it could have been an Institute fire drill.

It took me a long time to find my clothes, my shoes, and my bag. I leaned over to kiss the back of his neck on my way out.

"Listen," he said soberly. My heart sank before he'd finished his sentence. "Don't get too worked up about this. I've got a lot of things to resolve in my life. This is a bad time for me to be getting involved." I felt he wanted to erase the whole night.

"Do me a favor," I said in a completely flat tone, "don't hurt my feelings. And don't insult my intelligence."

He called me back, as I opened his door and went out into the silent hall. My eyes were brimming with tears. The dezhurnaya was not at her desk at the end of the hall; she was probably sleeping, like everyone else.

8

THE DOG
FROM HELL

M y roommate Isabel and I became friends at around the same time
my mung beans and alfalfa seeds sprouted into mounds of
healthy, crunchy legumes.

On our third day in Moscow, realizing that our peanut butter jars
would not be empty for quite some time, I had appropriated two large
glass jars from the cook who ran the Institute bufyet. I bribed her with
a lipstick and an eyeliner. Back in my room, I poured a centimeter of
beans into one jar, a centimeter of sprouts into the other, and filled
both halfway up with water. I placed the jars on the floor of our closet.
Isabel observed this process and complained that she would forget
about the jars, accidentally knock them over, and ruin her shoes. She
said our room (in which, in the early morning, we could often see our
breath) was too cold to grow anything in anyway. The next morning,
after covering the tops of the jars with cheese cloth which I secured
with rubber bands, I emptied the water, rinsed the beans and seeds,
wrapped the jars in long underwear and put them back in the closet
exactly where they had been before, but this time lying on their sides. I
scrupulously rinsed out both jars every morning for four days, watching in awe as the beans and seeds grew and grew (the anemic-looking
health food store salesman had assured me they would but I hadn't
believed him) until both jars were stuffed with sprouts. I moved my

sprouts to plastic bags, and announced to Isabel that we were now the proprietors of the only fresh, live legumes in the American group. Isabel was delighted and retracted any and all complaints. I started the process all over again, while Isabel and I ate the sprouts that day for breakfast and dinner, in cheese and kolbasa sandwiches. After the second day of the sprouts' fruition, she told me that she was feeling much better, "less cranky," she said, due to the rise in her intake of natural vitamins.

She was indeed less cranky, for on the morning that I came home from Phil's room in my wrinkled outfit of the night before, with mascara smeared around my eyes, she did not chastise me. She was one for organization and following the rules, which included sleeping in your own room every night. I had been expecting her wrath, but all she said was, "Ah! Thank God you're all right. I was worried. You look knocked out."

How perceptive of her. I felt like my insides had been dynamited out of me. The night had seemed like an extraordinary dream until Phil's morning warning that I should not take it all so seriously. Now I didn't know what to think; I had lost all perspective.

Isabel fixed me with her pale, sharp eyes.

"Maybe you should sleep," she said. "I'll tell your *starosta* that you're sick."

The Americans were split into four groups of ten. Each group had an elder, appointed by our American counselors, who was asked to report absences and general displays of bad behavior. Although my starosta was more liberal than the others, we had only just begun our marathon of classes, which would continue for five months, and I did not feel right about skipping so soon.

"I'd better go," I said.

"Listen," Isabel said, sitting down beside me on my bed. "You need some sleep." Her shoulders were slightly hunched, and her pink Lanz of Salzburg nightie hung like a curtain over her body. Only her toes stuck out at the bottom.

I felt guilty and wondered if I smelled like sex.

"Also," she said, "I have to take some things to a woman later today, and I would really appreciate it if you would come with me. It's a complicated situation, a terrible one, in fact, and I need some moral support. I know it's a lot to ask. But will you come?"

Her eyes had lost their haughty, displeased look and she seemed like a vulnerable little girl. I was suddenly no longer afraid of her. Considering that I had thought she despised me, I was touched.

"Sure I'll go. But why me?"

She shrugged lightly and smiled. Isabel had angular features, a pointed nose and chin. Her smile rounded her chin and eyes and softened her face completely.

"Well, you're my roommate," she said. "You're older. And you've been out almost every night since we've been here; I figure you must know something about the way these people think that I don't."

"Are you kidding? I don't understand anything around here."

"I think you should stay in and sleep." She patted my shoulder with a flutter of her hand. "I'll tell your starosta you have cramps. That always gets men." She said this in a whisper, looking at the contraption hanging from the center of the ceiling, which was our code for the Bug, aka Igor. If Igor was good at his job he already knew that I'd been up all night. But the good news was that the Institute bureaucrats generally left us alone. It was our own counselors we had to worry about.

I got undressed and crawled between my cold sheets. I slept without dreams, without a further thought for Phil, until Isabel came back from classes at three o'clock.

We left the Institute at four. Once we were out of the building and trudging up the icy path to the bus stop, Isabel began to tell me the story behind this meeting. Above us, thin cables resembling telephone wires were strung between the Institute and the building across the street. Large, slate-gray crows with the markings of pigeons planed, swooped, and landed on the wires. Their lonely cries tore through the stillness. They dive-bombed the netted bags filled with perishables that hung outside the Institute's windows.

I wondered if the wires were listening devices. What other purpose might they serve? I did not want to worry Isabel, and listened to her story without saying a word.

"I'm being thrown in the middle of this, you see." She exhaled a cloud of steam which floated off above her granny hat of black felt. It had a scarf sewn to it at the ears which tied together under her chin. The cold had turned her nose and cheeks pink immediately, as though it had slapped her hard on each side of the face.

"As long as we pretend we don't know anything about it, we'll be fine. Do you understand?"

"Not really," I said, out of breath. Just a short walk through the snow was an exhausting ordeal, especially since the Institute lawn was an uphill slant, until you reached the street. To cross to the bus stop you had to climb over the snowbanks left by the ploughs. Many people were waiting for the bus, which meant one would be coming soon. Isabel and I picked up our pace.

"I have this professor of Russian Lit at Yale, Albert. He's young for a professor, and we became friends. I babysit for his five-year-old daughter. Lena is about the most beautiful child I've ever seen. She has these blond corkscrew curls and big blue eyes. Anyway, she is half-Russian. She was born here in Moscow."

The bus was coming. We ran toward the stop, our feet dragging in our heavy snow boots. Isabel went right on with her story.

"Albert was here on a ten-month IREX"—International Research Exchange—"scholarship at Moscow University a little more than six years ago. His field is Nineteenth-Century Theater. He was working on his Ph.D. dissertation, and he met this girl at a party at the University. Albert says she looked like a goddess. You see, Albert is not that good-looking, he's thin and tall—not someone you'd notice. But they fell in love. Well, *he* fell in love. Maybe she fell in love too, I don't know. This girl, Vika, was only sixteen, still in high school, but she told him she was eighteen."

We barely squeezed onto the bus and stood pressed against the doors, so Isabel spoke in a mumble, close to my ear.

"Albert said they had a pretty wild time together. They smoked a lot of pot—I didn't know they had pot here, did you?—and they drank a lot and then guess what happened?"

"I can't imagine," I said wryly. "The girl got pregnant?"

"The girl got pregnant. Doesn't sound *too* familiar, does it?" Isabel twisted her rather full lips into a sly grimace.

"Byvaet," I said. It happens. Everyone said this in Moscow.

"Albert asked her to marry him and that's when he found out she was underage. They had to get her mother's consent. Vika was six-months pregnant when Albert's student visa expired and he was forced to go to Germany. He reapplied in Germany and came back on a special visa, as a guest or a relative or something, and lived with Vika and her mother. They stayed four or five months after the baby was born, then he got them out."

"Are they Jewish?"

"No. And I know that's strange. They don't let Russians out very often. But this was a special case, because he came back and lived here with them, and there was a baby. So I suppose the authorities didn't put their marriage into the 'ficticious marriage' category. They let them go.

"So he took Vika and Lena back to Yale. He was still working on his dissertation and didn't have a red cent to his name. They lived in an attic in New Haven. Vika got thoroughly depressed. Albert wanted her to go to a Yale shrink and he wanted her to talk to some recent immigrants too, but she wouldn't do either. He said she'd just mope around the apartment all day in her nightgown. He was teaching a class and working on his thesis, and making pizza at one of the college hangouts. The apartment became a total wreck: dishes in the sink, rotten food in the fridge, dirty clothes all over the place. She started to neglect the baby. Albert would come home and the baby would be screaming her head off. Vika hadn't changed the diapers all day."

We got off the bus and entered the metro, flashing our monthly transport passes at the woman in a blue uniform and a pillbox hat who guarded the turnstiles. It was rush hour again. I always seemed to be on the metro at rush hour. There were many old women with netted shopping bags and cardboard boxes getting on the train. We let them have the seats and stood facing each other, against the far door.

"Albert got the flu at work one day and came home early—" Isabel was watching me carefully. "You look like you know what's coming and you don't believe it. He found Vika in bed with a very dubious-looking character. They were both on heroin. He found a needle and paraphenalia lying on a tray on the floor by the bed. The baby was in her crib screaming. She was hungry."

"Jesus Christ."

"I'm telling you exactly what Albert told me," she said apologetically, as though it hurt her to be repeating it, and the whole thing was simply too awful for words.

"Albert told Vika that if it ever happened again he was going to take Lena and leave. It happened again and he left."

"How long could she have been on smack, for God's sake?" I practically yelled in her ear. Big, tired, moonlike faces turned and stared at us from all directions. The Russians, who never seemed bothered by either the heat or the cold, kept their hats on and their coats buttoned up to the collar. I, on the other hand, had taken off my scarf and opened my coat and was sweating profusely.

"I suppose they weren't on the best of terms before he caught her," Isabel said, "because tracks are visible. They couldn't have been sleeping together."

It was not hard to envision the young Russian beauty in a flimsy, torn negligee, slinking about the apartment, getting paler and paler, more and more unhappy. What had "Amerika" meant to her before she arrived? What kind of America had she expected from Albert? Wealth? Excitement? Parties? Had Albert been too exhausted to help her when it was still possible? It didn't make sense to me, but I could imagine Albert, weary and covered in flour from making pizzas, opening the door of his attic apartment and finding his ordered life in ruins.

"After he threw Vika out," Isabel continued, "she called a few times, looking for money. She never asked about the child, never wanted to see the child. Then Vika disappeared. Albert filed for divorce—desertion and drug addiction—and got custody of Lena.

"Here's the hard part: Vika's mother still lives here in Moscow. Albert keeps in touch with her. She knows Albert and Vika split up, but she doesn't know anything about the drugs."

"If it were my kid, I'd want to know."

"Well. That's none of our business. Natalia Ivanovna—that's the mother—has astronomically high blood pressure and Albert thinks it might kill her if she finds out. Plus—can you imagine?—she's a widow, and Vika is her only child. All we have to do is deliver these presents from Albert, and get out of there. We don't know anything. All right?" Isabel stared at me suspiciously, as though she thought I might betray her. "We don't know *anything* at all."

Night had completely enveloped the streets. The four-lane avenue was crowded with trolleys, buses, and cars. The wide sidewalk was frozen and glimmered like a dark pond in the yellow glow of the street lamps. Isabel grabbed hold of my arm as we slid downhill toward the curb. Two workers in blue padded jackets were standing there smoking, waiting for the light.

Isabel approached them. "Excuse me, please, would you be so kind as to tell me please where is So-and-So Street?" I saw distrust in their beady, slightly drunken eyes. They ignored us and crossed the avenue as soon as the light had changed.

"Maybe you should try a shorter version of that," I suggested. An old lady was pulling a shopping cart down the sidewalk behind us. Her shuffling feet moved so slowly she seemed to be going backward. Isabel went to help her with her cart.

Once we got her to the corner, Isabel asked, "Excuse me, please, So-and-So Street?"

"Tam, na perekrёstke." She pointed ahead with a crooked finger in a crocheted glove.

"What's a *perekrёstok?*" I asked Isabel. She took her pocket dictionary out of a large black bag and searched through it by the light of a shop window that displayed a pyramid of generic blue tin cans with pictures of fish on them. FISH it said on each can.

"It means intersection," Isabel said, putting the dictionary away quickly and looking about to see if anyone had noticed.

"We look like foreigners anyway, Isabel. Don't worry."

The courtyard of the apartment complex was surrounded by a metal gate that also served as a snow fence. We followed a path that had been cut into the snow up to the door. The dezhurnaya sat heavily behind her desk. Her menacing expression suggested that it was *her* job to know who came and went, and to report, if necessary.

"Kuda vam?" she barked. She had a wart between her eyebrows and a black mole on her chin that was sprouting long black hairs.

"Number Twenty-eight," Isabel said haughtily, as though we had every right in the world to be there. "Natalia Ivanovna is waiting for us."

"Take the lift, there," she said, pointing with her chin. "Fifth floor."

A layer of thick red vinyl covered the door, nailed at the edges with large round tacks. A little space had been left for the peephole. It looked like soundproofing to me. Isabel pushed the buzzer. A dog began to bark furiously from behind the door.

Natalia Ivanovna was of medium height, and phenomenally fat. Her heavy wheezing indicated that just getting to the door was a trial for her. She wore a white housedress speckled with purple flowers, and a brown turtleneck that was the same color as her hair. She had no ankles; her legs ended and her feet began without demarcation. Next to her big, square, slippered feet stood the dog, a black-and-white mongrel with a body shaped like a blood sausage and legs like four birthday candles. His teeth were long and brown and he liked to bare them a good deal.

"Grrrrrrrgrrrrrrr."

"That's enough, Sharik," Natalia Ivanovna said, as though she were praising him for having made a nice poop.

"What a sweet little dog!" Isabel said, not entirely convincingly.

"Come in, girlies, don't be shy. Take your coats off." She moved away from the door and opened another door immediately to the right. The dog would not let us by. His furious growls wracked his fat little body with such force that his back legs slipped out from under him on the linoleum floor.

"*Scat, dog!*" Isabel hissed. His tail disappeared between his legs, and he turned away, offended.

We followed our hostess into the living room. Two antique lamps shed a golden light over the old wallpaper, the large oak cabinets, and the round coffee table. Above the threadbare couch on which she sat hung a black-and-white photograph of a truly beautiful girl playing the violin. Her eyes were half shut, as though she were too enraptured by the music to notice the photographer. Her torrent of blond curls was tied back with two large bows of white gauze, one on each side of her face. They resembled a fairy's wings and gave her an enchanted look.

I thought: this cannot be the junkie Albert divorced.

"That is my baby," Natalia Ivanovna said, following my gaze. "She was in a special school for gifted children. She played in concerts, that one. She was the best violinist in her class, even better than the boys."

Natalia Ivanovna's eyes were partially shielded by a pair of thick glasses. Her expression was blunt, unyielding, yet questioning at the same time. Grief was not visible in her eyes, but in the lines surrounding her mouth, which seemed to pull her lips down, giving the impression she had spent too much time gritting her teeth.

"I am Isabel and this is my friend, Clinton."

"You live in Yale, Isabel?"

"Yes."

"And you, where do you live in America?"

"In New York City."

"Do you know it well?"

"What?"

"The City."

"Yes. I have lived there for over four years now."

"I will show you an address, you will tell me if it is a good address, or a bad address, all right?"

"I will try."

She was not looking at us now, but into space.

"The last letter I received from my Vika was from New York City. It was one year ago. I wrote back immediately, but my letter came back here. I don't understand?"

"Maybe she moved and did not tell the post office." I felt helpless, and my artificially comforting tone made me feel like a liar and a hypocrite.

"You think? She asked me for money, the poor child. Yet she *knows* I cannot send her rubles! They have no value in America, and in any case, it is against the law!"

Isabel and I shook our heads slowly, helplessly, at the same time.

"Tell me," she went on, speaking loudly now, "in America do you not have laws that prevent a man from marrying a girl and taking her far away from her own ones and then leaving her—not taking care of her? Why does Albert refuse to see her? Why does he not give her money?"

"I think . . ." Isabel thought for a second. "I am certain that something must have happened between them. There are things between people that others do not know."

I was proud of her; she was trying to put forth a careful suggestion without lying or entangling herself.

Natalia Ivanovna clenched her teeth. "My darling could never hurt a soul. She is the fragile one who is so easily wounded."

As if to change the subject, Isabel reached into her bag and brought out a carton of Marlboro Lights, an enormous pair of black, fur-lined nylon boots, and an envelope. She placed the cigarettes and the envelope on the coffee table, and handed the boots to Natalia Ivanovna. She took off her slippers, and pointing her square toes, shoved her feet into the boots. The couch sighed with relief as she stood up and walked across the room.

"Good Lord, these are ugly! And heavy, too," she said. "Tell me, is this the style now in America?"

"Well," Isabel said, slightly offended since she had dragged the boots all the way from New Haven to Moscow in her already overcrowded suitcase, "they are the newest . . . thing . . . in winter boots. They are warm."

"I told Albert I wanted boots to match my coat. It's brown, you know. Albert knows my coat," she laughed. "I have had the same winter coat for ten years. I don't understand how he can be a professor and have such a windy head."

She sat down again, put on her slippers and left the boots on the floor. Sharik pounced on them immediately and began to chew on the fur lining.

"Stop that, Sharik," Isabel said, leaning forward, but not too close.

"Grrrrrr," growled Sharik, and stared at her with his mean little eyes. *You just try to take them from me,* he seemed to say.

Isabel handed Natalia Ivanovna the envelope.

"Albert gave me these photographs of himself and Lena at Christmas."

Natalia Ivanovna tore open the envelope and stared down at a snapshot of Albert decorating the tree. It was a skinny little tree but it was covered with large, colorful baubles. She put her thick thumbs on Albert's face and moved the picture to the back of the pile. The next three were of Albert and she riffled through them as though shuffling an old deck of cards. Then she came to a picture of Lena opening her presents, a little blond cherub with large, intelligent eyes.

"*Oy,* my little Lenotchka! How she's grown. Let your babushka have a good look at you." Her eyes brimmed with tears. She brought the picture to her lips and kissed it with a loud smack.

"She looks just like Vika, don't you think so?"

"Yes, she does," Isabel and I agreed.

"And like me when I was younger," she added.

From the hallway came the comforting odor of dough frying. I was relieved at the thought that she would soon feed us, and we would not have to talk so much.

"Olya—Olga Vladimirovna—who lives with me, is preparing *cheburishky.* She is a better cook than I, God knows," she chuckled, still staring at the picture. Her cheeks jiggled wildly.

And then, as though the next thought had just come to her out of the blue, she asked, "Why does Albert refuse to let my Vika see the child? In her letter from a year ago she tells me that she called and called but he would not allow it. Then Albert moved and now she cannot find him."

"I believe," Isabel said slowly, "that is not true. On the . . . on the . . ." She glanced at me quickly. "How do you say 'on the contrary'?"

"Naobarot."

"Eto naobarot," she said. "Albert told me that Vika disappeared completely. She did not ask to see the child."

"Albert is lying," Natalia Ivanovna said, and her jaw clamped shut.

"Lena is very well," Isabel said gently. "I take care of her when Albert must go out. She is a happy, intelligent child, very sweet."

Natalia Ivanovna shook her finger at us. "I told Vika the first time she brought Albert to my house, 'this is not the man for you.' She did not love him, I could see that immediately. She felt no—how to say this—no physical love for him. You understand, many nights he slept here, on this very couch, she left him here while she went out with her girlfriends. He was too old for her. She was just a child. 'Vika,' I told her, 'Do not do something stupid with this man just because he comes from over there.' "

A tall, well-shaped blond woman opened the adjoining door. She was wearing a white housedress with several buttons missing at the thigh. She held it pinned together in her hand.

"Please come have something to eat," she said, smiling coquettishly. Her features were large, and separately they might have seemed coarse, but all together they made a truly handsome face. We followed the two women into the dining room, which was also a bedroom. Olga Vladimirovna took the chair at the head of the table closest to the kitchen, Natalia Ivanovna sat at the other end, by the bed, and Isabel and I sat across from each other.

While we ate, the conversation remained limited to our impressions of Moscow, which was quite a relief. The meat pies were delicious. We ate them with a cold pepper salad that came in a store-bought jar.

Olga Vladimirovna, tucking a strand of hair behind her ear, said suddenly, "I have been to America. I was an Aeroflot stewardess in my day."

"I am not surprised," I said. "You are very pretty."

"Oh, Aeroflot pays no attention to such things. My husband, God rest his soul, was an engineer for Aeroflot, which is how I got the job.

"We stayed in New York City many times. On the avenue next to the park. It was so hot I thought I would die. Horrible place, New York City."

I didn't know what to say, so I said nothing.

"And that park—full of black people and brown people who do not like to work. And at night they steal your pocketbook if you are not careful."

I thought of our suite-mate, Ceppie, and felt the urge to defend New York City's underprivileged the way she might have, had Isabel asked her along instead of me. Maybe Olga Vladimirovna might appreciate something along Marxist lines, such as: *but as you know, Capitalism leaves those black people and brown people very little choice.* I didn't have time to respond, Olga Vladimirovna was on a tear.

"Here, everybody works. There are no homeless and no unemployed in the Soviet Union. Jews only want to leave because they are lazy. Here they make their money the easy way, speculating on the black market. But it's not good enough for them, so they want to go to America. But in America they have to work like normal people, and they don't like that. Then they want to come home. Ha ha ha!"

I stared across the table at Isabel, whose face had suddenly been invaded by red blotches, giving her a consumptive look. A blue vein had appeared on her neck.

"That is a . . . a . . . general generalization," she blurted out.

"Don't misunderstand me," Olga Vladimirovna said, "I know some very nice Jews. We have a neighbor for example. A dentist. He's just like a Russian."

"But," Isabel said, turning pale now, "just because someone is Jewish does not mean they are not Russian!"

"On your passport, it says you are Jewish if you are Jewish, and Russian if you are Russian," Olga Vladimirovna responded flatly. "And Ukrainian if you are Ukrainian, and so on."

A completely helpless anger flooded over me, just as it did back home, when American acquaintances called me an apologist for the Soviet system. I did not consider myself an apologist, I just felt that before passing judgment people should have all the facts. These arguments were exhausting and could not be won one way or the other. There was no use arguing with Olga Vladimirovna, but out of principle, I felt I had to say something.

"But Russian Jews do not have their own republic," I said. "Ukrainians have a republic, and Russians have the biggest republic. But Jewish people do not have one."

"They certainly do," Olga Vladimirovna pointed out. "Well, not a republic, but an autonomous Jewish region. We gave it to them. It is in the Far East, near the Chinese border." She seemed quite proud of this fact.

"But what if they are born in Moscow, and live in Moscow their whole lives? Why would they want to go to Siberia?"

She shrugged. "Why not? They want to go to Israel and America."

"Now, now, Olya. No need to politick with the girlies. Get the tea, please." Olga Vladimirovna gathered our plates and disappeared into the kitchen.

Just then my feet began to boil inside my boots. It seemed odd to me suddenly that we had not been offered slippers. I took one boot off by tugging at its heel with my toe. Sharik, who had obviously been patiently waiting for such a moment, attacked my socked foot. I kicked him with the other boot as hard as I could.

"Aiiaaiii!" he yelped.

"Here, Sharik." Natalia Ivanovna lifted him to her lap and fed him a piece of cheburishka. While he chewed his eyes peered angrily at me over her plate. She reached into a drawer by the bed and pulled out a stack of letters and photographs. She handed me Vika's last letter. The return address was in the heart of Alphabet City—on Manhattan's Lower East Side. I would not have walked down there, even in the daytime, for a thousand dollars.

"Is it a good neighborhood?"

"It is a young neighborhood. Many young artists live there because it is not expensive."

"Ah. That is good, then?"

Alphabet City was hell—shooting galleries, junkies, and burned-out buildings—but what was I supposed to tell her?

"I have a friend who lives not too far away. I can write her and ask her to go see your daughter. We can write through the American Embassy."

"Really? You will write your friend?"

"I will." My friend Beatrice was a writer I had met at a Columbia University party. She lived on Avenue A and Tenth Street. She was the toughest, most courageous woman I knew. If anyone would go looking for Vika, she would. It might even give her a good story. Beatrice was always looking for good stories.

A thought hit me and all at once I could barely breathe: Vika could be dead. AIDS was devastating the junkie community of New York. My head began to spin. What would I tell Natalia Ivanovna if her daughter were dead? *I'm so sorry, Natalia Ivanovna, your daughter is dead.?*

If her daughter were dead, wouldn't someone have notified her?

If her daughter was alive, her chances of surviving were not good. All the newspapers said intravenous drug users and homosexuals were falling like flies in New York City. For some reason I kept wanting to believe that the whole thing was a big misunderstanding, and Vika was absolutely fine.

What could Natalia Ivanovna have done to her daughter to receive no news for a year? It was possible that Vika was like the dog Sharik, sour from too much love and permissiveness.

My mother had given me that much love, but she had not been that permissive. She had a sharp tongue, and her advice was always good. She never lied, and never wanted anyone to feel sorry for her, even at her lowest moments, when she was most in need of compassion. I thought of her frightened eyes as she had put me on the train to go to my U.S.S.R. orientation. Maybe she was thinking that she might never see me again, that I might stay in Russia and never write to her, never think about her again. She might have been worried about sickness, that I might fall ill and no one would be there to help me. "Don't worry, Mommy," was all I could find to mumble as I tried desperately not to cry in front of her.

Maybe Vika had missed her mother terribly, and maybe she had never missed her at all. In any event, it would not hurt for Beatrice to try to find the girl and ask her to please write her mother.

"You are crazy, my dear," Isabel said in the elevator. "You are going to get involved in this thing."

She was holding Sharik in her outstretched arms, his back to her and his face inches from my chest. Natalia Ivanovna had handed him to Isabel as we were leaving. She said that little Sharik needed his walk and we should drop him in the courtyard on our way out. He was so smart he would find his way back all by himself.

"Careful, now, Isabel. No brusque movements," I said.

"Don't you worry," she said. Sharik was growling, but in a more subdued tone. Apparently he did not like the idea of being dropped from such a height. She held him at arm's length until she'd deposited him in the snow in the courtyard. He chased us all the way to the gate.

Isabel's composure collapsed as soon as we were out in the street. Tears began streaming down her face. They froze before they reached her chin.

"That Olga is a Nazi," she said.

"You can't argue with people like that. It only makes you feel sick. Let's take a cab home. I'll pay."

There were few cars on the avenue at this late hour. We waited at the corner a long time.

"Maybe Natalia and Olga get it on?" I said.

"Lesbians?" After she got over her shock, Isabel began to laugh.

We both howled with laughter, tears streaming from our eyes as we stood hunched and gripping our stomachs. The occasional passerby stared at us in amazement. We tried pinching our noses, and looking away from each other, but we could not stop. Finally, in the distance a car appeared. As it approached I spotted the little green light on the passenger's side of the windshield, which indicated that it was an empty cab.

The car pulled up and stopped at the curb. I opened the back door.

"Where to?" asked the driver in an angry voice, turning his head.

"Ulitsa Golkina. The Institute there." We were at the opposite end of the city.

He shook his head. *"Nyet."*

"I can't take any more of this shit today," I said to Isabel; then to the driver in Russian, "Nonsense. Ten rubles and a pack of American cigarettes."

"Get in," he said.

We climbed in quickly. It was a small victory, but I felt disproportionately ecstatic, like a child who has just convinced a parent to fork over money for a new toy.

9

A LOOK
AT THE
KHAIGH
LAIFE

We had one completely free day a week, and that was Sunday. Wednesday was excursion day, but Saturday was a school day, just like Friday. So if we intended to be bad and not come home to the Institute by the midnight curfew (1 A.M. on Saturday nights,) we were better off sleeping over at our Soviet friends' on either Tuesday or Saturday nights. On Wednesdays we could show up at the excursion site on time and pretend we were coming from the Institute; or we could come wandering in on Sunday afternoons as though we'd just been out for a walk. Some of the American students seemed to think they were in winter camp, and came traipsing in at nine-fifteen on school mornings, just in time to make their first class. The Institute Director's office windows looked out on the front doors; he was perfectly aware of who came and went and probably made a little note in his black booklet. He would almost never accuse, however, because blatant infractions of the rules did not make anyone look good.

My second date with Andrej the playwright fell on a Saturday night, but this was by no means intentional. I waited for him at the top of the Institute driveway, as arranged. Snow was falling heavily, silently, and I felt conspicuous standing there. I pretended to be engrossed in my pocket dictionary. Fifteen minutes late, Andrej pulled up in his little, muddy white car and honked the horn, waving wildly though he was only four feet from where I stood. The loud blasts ripped through the silence, terrifying me. In a panic, I jumped in and told him to drive away quickly.

"Ha ha ha!" he laughed, slapping my knee, which was sticking out of the split in my big down coat. "You think you are in a spy movie!"

Andrej was wearing a gigantic red fox hat that covered his entire head down to his earlobes. Only his hazel eyes peeked out from under its brim.

"What a nice hat," I said.

"You want a hat like this? I will get you such a hat tomorrow."

"No, no. That is not what I meant."

"A young foreigner like you should not be going around Moscow in this cold without such a hat. Let me get you a hat. A hat just like this one, but for ladies."

"Andrej, you really must be careful. They watch us."

"My dear girl, I am going to take you to meet a man who writes films and plays and holds the Order of Lenin. Let them follow us. He is friends with the Minister of Culture and has met with the General Secretary. With me, you have nothing to worry about."

Boris Mikhailovich Toropov lived in one of the oldest neighborhoods of Moscow—most of Moscow, Andrej explained, had burned down at one time or another—in a building dating back to the early nineteenth century whose windows looked out on a park crowded with tall, snow-covered trees. At the center of it was a pond turned skating rink where bundled-up children sailed round and round to classical music.

The ceilings of Boris Mikhailovich's apartment were at least fourteen feet high. A long, well-lit corridor led from the front door to the living and dining rooms. There were so many doors connecting to this hallway that I supposed Boris Mikhailovich housed and supported a good number of people.

When Andrej and I came in to the dining room, we found the family gathered at a large antique table. An old woman in a black shawl, her hair tied in a little gray knot on top of her head, sat knitting beside an elderly man who had a laurel-shaped crown of white hair.

There was a very pretty young woman of about twenty-five, another woman who was closer to thirty-five, and a man of indeterminate age who leaned over the table with hunched shoulders and pretended he was alone. All were drinking Earl Grey tea out of matching porcelain cups and intermittently munching meringue tarts.

Andrej first introduced me to Boris Mikhailovich, the balding, elderly man, then introduced the old lady as Auntie, the young woman as Masha, the youngest woman as Sonya, and the other man as Ivan.

"What an extraordinary apartment," I said, and immediately was shown around by Sonya. She was a beautiful, dark-eyed girl with perfect Slavic features—large, almond-shaped eyes, high cheekbones, a thin, straight nose, and full lips. She wore a long purple sweater and blue jeans.

The apartment had all the trappings of a middle class Western home. It had a modern bathroom with a European toilet and a bathtub adorned with fancy chrome spiggots; there was a dishwasher, a refrigerator with a large freezer compartment, and a food-processor in the kitchen. In Boris Mikhailovich's study was an IBM Selectric III typewriter and a Sony TV and VCR. Sonya showed me all these things with apparent nonchalance, as though such opulence were commonplace in Moscow. But there was still a twinkle of pride in her dark eyes.

I committed a blunder. I said, "Your father truly has the most beautiful apartment I have ever seen." She exploded into laughter. "He is my husband," she said, rolling her eyes and smiling, pulling back her pink lips and exposing even pinker gums and a row of perfect white teeth.

I was still blushing when we got back to the dining room. Andrej was putting down his cup and commenting on how much he adored English tea, especially Earl Grey. The lamp above the table looked like a Tiffany and shed a peaceful, amber light on the circle of faces below it.

For a long time Boris Mikhailovich sat without saying a word. He was listening to a little Aiwa radio which lay on the table next to his cup, through a listening device in his ear. He had an aged, professorial face. His eyes were gray, small, and piercing, but friendly and less intimidating than they might have been without the heavy, dark half-moons beneath them. He was not fat and not thin.

"Papa is listening to 'Voice of America,'" the other woman pointed out.

It was then that I realized that Boris Mikhailovich's daughter—whom I had thought was his wife—was not half as pretty as his wife, whom I had thought was his daughter.

"Tell me about SPID," his wife asked me.

"Speed?" I asked. I had no idea what she was talking about.

"AIDS," Andrej put in in English. "Here it is called S-P-I-D."

In Russian, this was barely possible for me. I knew no medical terms, nor the names for most organs of the body. I tried my best to explain what I knew, which was not much.

"Our papers have said that it was invented by your Pentagon. They were testing a new . . . and something went wrong. Is that true?" she asked.

"What? Why would the American government invent something to kill Americans? What a crazy idea. No. They don't know where it is from. Maybe Africa. They don't know."

"*Nyet, nyet,* to kill Russians, not Americans. Someone broke the tube by accident." She pantomimed the germ flying away by wriggling her fingers in an upward motion.

"No, no, I don't think so." Why did I not think so? The idea was so farfetched to me it seemed hilarious. On the other hand, I became concerned because I could not explain why this idea seemed so absurd to me. I had always believed there was fundamental truth in what I read in the American papers and heard on TV. I was surprised that such privileged and cultured citizens were not more suspicious of the Soviet propaganda machine and did not see it our way: we in America were a democracy and therefore our media informed us more honestly. But then, of course, we in America had not heard much about the Shah of Iran's torture chambers, d'Aubuisson's death squads in El Salvador, or about Madame Marcos's three thousand pairs of shoes, until way after the damage had been done and America was forced to admit to having supported leaders who were a tad maniacal. But this also was a matter of perspective; in America, it was viewed as a simple fact that *anything* was better than Communism, and concessions had to be made. I began to wonder for the first time in my life if I might not also be programmed to a certain degree.

By the time Boris Mikhailovich was finished listening to "Voice of America," I was exhausted.

When he gave the gathering his attention, everyone listened and no one spoke unless asked a question directly.

Could a well-educated man believe that the Soviet papers told the whole truth? I wondered. He probably believed that in the name of Communism concessions also had to be made, and the truth was relative to the cause. Maybe he listened to "Voice of America" to get a more rounded picture. And maybe he believed, as Lenin did, that to oppose your enemies, you had to know their philosophies as well as you knew your own.

"They have stopped . . . 'Voice of America,'" Boris Mikhailovich said to no one in particular, and shook his head dreamily.

"What does that mean?" I asked Andrej quietly. He was sitting next to me.

"You know, mixing up the signals. Now we can get it without problem."

"Really?"

"Yes," he insisted.

"Well, what shall we have to drink?" Boris Mikhailovich asked, rubbing his palms together.

"*Oy*, Borya, let's have Amaretto!" his wife said.

"I'm not drinking," his daughter said.

"Ha ha ha, my little alcoholics," he said good-humoredly. "At least you, little daughter, have sense. What about our guests? What would you like? Sonya, open the . . ."

His wife went to an oak armoire that had an ornate mirror in the center of it, and opened a cabinet door. Inside was a stash of liquor bottles ranging from gin to cognac.

"Sonya will have Amaretto, I will have Scotch—" began Boris Mikhailovich.

"Clinton likes cognac best," Andrej put in.

"Bring the cognac out, Sonya."

It was Rémy Martin. Sonya laid out little matching crystal shot glasses, and filled each one to the brim. Then the toasts started. To the new Leader, to peace, to nuclear disarmament. After two shots, my Russian improved tremendously.

"Mmmmmm, I simply *adore* Amaretto," Sonya said, sipping. Her face lit up entirely.

After a little while, without asking me any questions, and as though I had been brought here for this very purpose, Boris Mikhailovich started talking about my father and the war. He did not speak in the rapid slur he had employed earlier, so I could understand almost everything. Later, I asked Andrej to fill in the gaps.

Boris Mikhailovich took in a deep, wheezing breath and exhaled while he spoke.

"Here, the general feeling was much better toward the Americans than the British during the Great Fatherland War, because we thought that Roosevelt wanted to open a second front much earlier, and was being hindered by Churchill. I think this is not true at all. I think it was quite complicated. Our papers nevertheless were kinder to Roosevelt than they were to Churchill. In the summer and fall of 1942 we thought everything was lost. And the Americans and British believed this as well. They waited to see what would happen at Stalingrad. Now the U.S. and Britain say they helped us greatly by sending arms and provisions, but it was barely anything. Lend-Lease was absolutely minimal until 1943."

Boris Mikhailovich took a little notebook and a pen out of his chest pocket and drew two parallel, slightly diagonal, slightly curving lines. The area between the lines he colored in; left of the left line he drew a long, amoeba-like shape; to the right of the right line, he drew several rows of X's.

"Stalingrad was built on the west bank of the Volga," he said, hammering the pen into the amoeba-like shape, "so that as the fascists attacked the city, they still had not reached the river. After fantastic fighting and unimaginable losses, the Red Army eventually retreated to the bank of the Volga. 'There is no land beyond the Volga' became an Army slogan. This meant they would stay put or die. So they held the west bank—a strip of literally a few hundred meters, you understand —and therefore they held the river." Now he drew arrows which started at the X's and went toward the amoebic form. "And beyond the river on the east bank was the Soviet artillery with its Katyusha rockets." He hammered the pen into the X's. "All provisions and troops were ferried across the river by night, under fire.

"September until mid-December were the worst months. It is impossible to explain the street fighting that went on, fighting not only for buildings, but for rooms and floors. Some days there were over two thousand casualties on the fascist side and probably as many on ours, though exact figures have never been clear.

"No foreign correspondents were allowed access to the front while there was any chance of Soviet defeat. In the first week of February, after the fascists had surrendered, many correspondents and even political missions were allowed to visit the ruins of Stalingrad. Yet in mid-December, with victory within our grasp, Hitler's 6th Army under General Paulus remained trapped within the cauldron and the situation was not completely secure. Your father was given permission to visit a region a hundred kilometers or so northwest of Stalingrad, where it was relatively safe.

"They allowed your father because his articles stressed the heroism of the Soviet Army, and he pushed for American involvement and aid. His Russian was exceptional—most journalists arrived without knowing a word—and he was well liked in Moscow. Correspondents have never been trusted, but he was trusted more than most. The government kept close track of the journalists, of course. Yet in December, when your father was permitted to travel to that region, there was enormous optimism and joy in the army and in the leadership because the fascists had been encircled after months and months of the most brutal fighting with the most astronomic losses on both sides. I don't know what happened, but in the general sweep of things, your father, while on this expedition, temporarily disappeared.

"You see, your papa and I shared a mutual friend, a Colonel Gavrilov. He was an army cameraman who had received many, many medals for courage. You understand, he held a camera while the men next to him were holding guns, and being fired upon. He is responsible for some of the best footage of the war, and not only at Stalingrad. Gavrilov had enormous connections, and somehow during this expedition, he got your father close, very close to the fighting. Almost to the east bank of the Volga. This is absolutely an exception, an incredible thing for a Western journalist!

"Hitler forbade Paulus to surrender Stalingrad, you see. At that time, during the period between the encirclement and the failure of von Manstein's attempt to break through to Paulus, the fighting went on in the city. And they fought quite bravely, those starving, frozen German soldiers. Apparently your father spoke to wounded Soviets, *and* to German prisoners, without official permission. In short, he saw and heard too much. I don't know exactly how Gavrilov smuggled your father in so close. Maybe he passed him off as a Soviet." Boris Mikhailovich brushed the air away from his face, as though this were an irrelevant point. "It is unknown exactly. Of course they were found out, and it caused quite a stir. Your father was sent back to Moscow, but they did not throw him out of the country. He had already written those extraordinary articles. He was too precious to us to throw out. You see, we *wanted* pro-Soviet feeling in America. We wanted the second front desperately. While from 1941 to 1944 the United States sat and waited to see what would happen to Russia, twenty million people died here. Your father saw it with his own eyes. He was on our side, so to speak. So, temporarily, all was forgiven.

"After the war, Gavrilov was exiled along with many other soldiers who had been captured by the fascists or had simply associated with Westerners. It is unbelievable, simply barbaric." He shivered and shook his head in disgust. "Most of those who had worked with Lend-Lease were shot or exiled. Gavrilov died in Siberia in 1952, of pneumonia.

He was quite a good poet. Have you read his poems? . . . Never mind. He is unknown in the West."

I had never heard of Gavrilov. My father had rarely mentioned his time in the Soviet Union during the war. He claimed it was a "thing of the past" which was better left alone. I thought suddenly of my Soviet-Jewish friend Rita, who had welcomed me to her house not even a week before, and had given me the Bolshoi Ballet tickets. She had mentioned working with Lend-Lease in Murmansk during the war—had she been exiled as well? She had spoken of it with such enthusiasm that it hardly seemed possible.

"Gavrilov was rehabilitated along with many others after the death of Stalin. A book of his poems was published during the thaw in the early sixties. Mostly they are war poems, sensitive war poems. Isn't that a contradiction? But it is true. He believed courage was impossible without fear. This was not a philosophy of which Stalin approved. Gavrilov was a bit crazy, he followed no one but himself. I do not believe the episode with your father was what got him exiled to Siberia; however it was certainly used against him. He was accused of giving away secret information to the enemy. That was a horrible time, after the war. Almost like the purges of '36–'38. Everyone was afraid."

There was a long silence while everyone watched Boris Mikhailovich pull his thoughts together.

"Is there anyone still alive of his family?" I asked.

"There is a daughter somewhere. Shall I find out? I will call my friend who is in the Ministry of Culture."

And after a moment, he added, "Gavrilov liked your father quite a bit. He thought he had a Russian soul."

"My father's governess was Russian. She came to America when the Red Army won the Civil War." I said this wondering if it was a mistake. Boris Mikhailovich had spoken quite openly of his country, and I felt it was only correct to respond accordingly. It seemed to me that Russians were Russian no matter where they were, or what their beliefs might be.

The old aunt, who had sat knitting in silence since our arrival, looked at me suddenly with her slightly murky eyes, and smiled.

"How old do you think I am?"

She had been introduced as "Auntie," but I did not know whose auntie. Boris Mikhailovich himself was close to seventy. I did not want to commit another blunder.

"Seventy," I said.

She laughed in a tiny voice. "No, no, my dear. I am ninety-five. I have lived through seven wars, but I have never considered leaving my country."

Auntie's dark skin looked like the leather of an expensive, well-worn glove. The fine creases only added to her attractiveness. She had little sagging jowls on each side of her round chin. The blue of her eyes was clear and deep.

"To stay young and healthy one must always turn the other cheek, and accept what God has given one with joy. I have never fought with anyone, and do not plan to start now."

She laughed, and everyone joined in.

"I was also from a good family," she said dreamily. "But my father believed in Lenin. We have always believed in his philosophies."

"Lenin was a brilliant man," I conceded, which did not say much, but made her very happy.

"Borya believes that also," she said, going back to her knitting. "A few wrong turns have been taken, but we are back on the path again, praise God."

"Sonya," Boris Mikhailovich said, "get some food out here, will you?"

Sonya got up and left the table. We drank more toasts, while I thought about my father and felt the old familiar ache building up in the center of my chest.

"Do you know, Boris Mikhailovich, that I miss my father terribly much. I never knew these things you've told me. I never knew them at all. It makes me feel far, far away from him. And how fortunate you all are to be together."

"Thank the Lord," said Auntie, crossing herself.

Sonya came back with a platter of cold cuts and cheese and a basket of bread. We drank more toasts.

Hours passed. Andrej had not talked much during the evening, but when he spoke it was always to make a thoughtful, intelligent comment. He helped me with the words I did not understand, and found the words I was looking for when I got stuck. Yet he never interrupted me or put words in my mouth.

Finally Andrej leaned over and, tapping on the face of his watch, informed me that it was time to go if I was to make my curfew. I told him I couldn't care less about my curfew. The cognac was making me feel quite bold. By the time Andrej convinced me to leave I was drunk, but so was everyone else, except Andrej and the daughter who had given up drinking. It turned out that the hunched fellow with the misanthropic attitude was her husband. He did not seem to get along with either his wife or his father-in-law. He drank a good deal, and more than made up for his wife's abstinence.

"That is the real khaigh laife," Andrej whispered to me in the elevator. "I am so pleased they liked you. You see, Boris Mikhailovich was my *nastavnik*."

"What's that?"

"A teacher of sorts, but not in school. He helped me with my work as a playwright."

"A mentor?"

"Yes. Mentor. We have that word as well."

"Thank you. Thank you so much." I said.

"For what?"

"For bringing me here."

"You say thank you but now your Institute doors will be locked and you will be in trouble. Look, it is already quarter to one." He showed me his watch again, as though I would not believe him otherwise. The watch swam in and out of focus before my eyes.

"You little drunk," he said, laughing. "Listen, I'll take you home to my mother's. Don't worry, she is like a tiger about me and women. She will not let me near you."

"Good," I said, and laughed. At first he seemed slightly shocked, but then he laughed also.

"Why do you live with your mother when you are so successful?"

"I am just recently divorced. I have a twelve-year-old son. I am waiting for permission to buy a cooperative apartment. It is such a long process. Completely ridiculous."

In his car with the broken heater, I suddenly wanted to cry, and did. I was drunk enough not to feel odd about releasing the painful buildup in my chest.

"Do you know that in your country I have cried more times in one week than I have in a whole year at home?" I reached into my bag for my eternal wad of toilet paper.

"What is it?" Andrej said softly. "Your father?"

"It is the world. You know, it can be a terrible place. Terrible. He left America, my father. You know that man, McCarthy? My father left because he thought America had gone completely crazy. He thought the Cold War was completely crazy. He believed it was invented on purpose. When they asked him to come and . . . and— what is that word?—to stand in front of the committee against Communism, he told them he would not cooperate because the whole thing was a fake! For a while he was protected by the university where he taught. It was a private university very much to the left. Then he went to France."

"Protected by the university?" Andrej laughed. "Good Lord, here they would have all been shot—him, and the whole university."

"You cannot compare our countries, Andrej. Yes, they did not shoot them, but people's lives were completely ruined. And my father was not even a Communist!"

"Communist, not Communist, what does it matter? People are people."

"Are you in the Party?"

"Yes. I joined at twenty-one. That is unusual because until twenty-six, there is the Komsomol—the Young Communist League. You understand, in university I was the best student in my department; I was asked to join." He explained this as though he were apologizing. "I believed. But now I believe with moderation."

"I think you are a truly good man," I said. "You are not obliged to be so kind to me."

"It is good that you are coming to my mother's house. I want her to meet you because before you leave here, I would like for us to get married."

"But you don't even know me!" I said in a high-pitched voice I did not recognize.

"I know you well enough," he said calmly.

10

THE
NIGHT
OF THE
MATRIARCH

We drove on in silence. Andrej's eyes remained glued to the dark road. I watched the sky. Moscow's at night was royal blue—the deep, rich, elegant color of fairytale skies.

I remembered something I had not thought of in years: at six, I had gone to a girlfriend's house to sleep over for the first time. When night fell I cried so much that my friend's mother called my parents and asked them to come fetch me. When I saw my mother at the door, all fear and embarrassment abandoned me. I flew to her and wrapped my arms around her thighs. After that my parents had jokingly nicknamed me Sleepover Clinton.

I wanted my mother. *Dear Mommy, your Sleepover Clinton is at it again.* . . . Only this time she's twenty-five and she's halfway around the world. No one would save me tonight.

I blamed only myself for missing the curfew.

In a completely serious tone I said, "Listen, Andrej, I like you very much but I could never marry you. I have to go home after this. My mother is there."

"Your mother can come live here with us."

"My mother is afraid even to come *visit*. No. Listen, do not talk about such a thing anymore. Never. All right?"

"*Nu, ladno.* I will try. But if I can't help myself, you will forgive me."

"No, I will not forgive you."

"Ha ha ha! How funny you are."

It was absurd. They were so unlike us! I suddenly recalled Phil Chase's darkened Institute room—his earnest blue eyes fixing me almost submissively from peculiar angles, and myself glaring back, feeling temporarily strong and in control of him. I had not spoken to him since. Was that normal?

Andrej was telling me that he wanted me to get pregnant; he wanted a beautiful, intelligent son with dual citizenship. Was *that* normal? A man who had never kissed me?

"But what if it's a girl?" I laughed nervously.

"All right, so a girl," he conceded.

Although I was flattered by his advances, and my vanity was touched, I was not stupid enough to believe the man had fallen in love with me after knowing me two days. If he wanted a *mariage de convenance*, why not be straightforward and businesslike? *Clinton, I would appreciate it very much if you'd do me a favor and marry me.*

No, I would say, equally unmoved by this new approach. *But if you like, I can try to find you someone.*

I was completely lost and had no idea what to say. I wanted my little, clean, Institute bed. I wanted Phil Chase. All the cognac I had imbibed at Andrej's friends' luxurious apartment began to churn in my stomach.

The wipers squeaked back and forth and left white arching streaks on the windshield. The road was so black the sky hung over it like a velvet curtain. Andrej had not turned on his headlights.

"Turn on your . . . your . . . lights, there. For the car."

"There's no need. Only on school holidays," he said. "Look. All the other cars do the same."

It was true; the cars kept their parking lights on until they approached another car.

"This is very dangerous," I said hopelessly.

"Energy must be conserved." Andrej squeezed my knee.

"Stop it, Andrej. Please. I have to tell you this. I . . . I have someone already. I love someone else."

"What kind of man would allow you to go all the way to Moscow for five months? An idiot, that's what."

"*I* am the idiot! We should have left the party when you said it was time."

It was immediately apparent that his mother was of the same opinion. She opened the door as soon as Andrej started fiddling with the lock. In front of us stood an elderly woman with two long gray braids and a parchment-like face. She glared at me with undisguised contempt.

"*Oy!* Andrusha," her voice trembled. She pulled the lapels of her ragged green dressing gown together tightly around her throat.

"Mama, this is my friend Clinton. She is an American student. She is a student of Vika Erikson in New York. Remember her?" He spoke to her in a smooth, even voice.

"It's two o'clock in the morning, Andrusha," she said. "Is this a way to bring a guest home?"

Andrej gently took his mother by the shoulders and moved her out of the way. He led me into the living room. A solitary lamp with a red shade glowed in a corner. Enormous, somber oil canvases covered every inch of wall space. It was too dark to see what they represented.

"Mama, she must stay here tonight. She will sleep with Klara here, in the living room, and I shall sleep in Klara's bed, understand? They have a law at their Institute; she cannot get in now, the doors are locked."

"Such laws are made to be respected," she said. "Girls should not be out so late at night."

"That's enough, Mama," Andrej said evenly. "Go back to bed. Wake up Klara and tell her she must sleep in the living room. Go on."

She went off grumbling to herself. Andrej attempted to explain.

"My mother still thinks I am twenty. You see, ever since my divorce —more than a year and a half ago—I have been staying here. I sleep in the living room. But I am looking for a new apartment. What do you think"—his voice dropped to a whisper—"would you like to live in a big apartment like the one you saw tonight? If you marry me I will get an apartment like that one."

"Don't be silly, Andrej. You don't listen to me, do you?" I was annoyed now, and embarrassed.

His sister came out of the bedroom. Klara was between twenty-five and thirty—it was hard to tell because she was half-asleep and the light was dim.

"I'm so sorry to . . . bother you," I said, searching foggily for words.

"Oh, it's nothing," she assured me in a warm, kind voice. She began to arrange the two perpendicular couches in the living room, taking bedclothes out of a cupboard drawer. The mother stood behind Klara, directing operations.

"Not like that, Klara! What are you doing to that bed? Here, let me."

"It's all right, Mama," Klara said, "go back to bed."

Andrej approached me and wrapped an arm around my waist. I tried to wrench myself free but he would not let go. The mother winced. I wanted to hit him.

Very fast, in a half-whisper, she said, "It isn't enough for you to have the entire Soviet Union, you have to go after Capitalists." She said the word *Capitalist* like a swear word, the way some Americans said *Communist*.

"Be quiet," Andrej mumbled menacingly. "I am speaking to you seriously."

"Well, I'm going to bed," she said, but she did not move. She stood in a corner with her arms crossed over her chest, staring at me with a puckered-up face.

"I am coming too," Andrej said, and tried to kiss me. I gave him a push and ran for the couch-bed his sister had just made.

"When are you going to become serious?" the mother said as he led her off down the hall.

Klara and I lay down to sleep in the darkened room. Our heads were inches apart, our bodies at ninety-degree angles on the two couches that fit against the walls and met in the corner. I had taken off my jeans and sweater, and left on my cotton turtleneck and underwear.

Once the light was turned off down the hall and the apartment had become entirely silent, Klara rolled over and said, "Mama adores him so much she makes life impossible for the women he courts."

"We are not . . . There is nothing between us," I said. "We just met a few days ago. We are friends." A few weeks later, in Grammatika class, I learned that there were three expressions for "friend" in Russian. *Drug* or *podruga*—meaning boyfriend or girlfriend, or very special friend; *priyatel'* or *priyatel'nitsa*—meaning friend; and *znakommiy/znakommaya*—meaning acquaintance. Of course, speaking to Klara I used the plural of *drug,* which confirmed what she already thought.

"Yes, friends. Well. In any case, I will give you my number at work. You must call me if you have any problems with Mama."

"In what sense, problems? What do you mean?"

"I don't know. We'll see."

Though it was close to noon, it seemed like the crack of dawn when the mother woke me up; she was fussing loudly, setting the living room table. She complained that it was improper to bring guests home without warning because she could not prepare a decent meal without advance notice.

She brought an absurd amount of food to the table; no one needed that much food first thing in the morning, especially on a hangover. Klara was delicately setting down the forks and knives and telling her mother to speak more quietly. When she glanced at me I saw her features for the first time. Her nose was slightly hooked, her eyes large and a deep brown color. She had a tiny round chin while her cheeks were high and flat. Her short, thick hair was parted in the middle, and curled under slightly just below her ears, giving her face the shape of a heart. When she saw me observing her, she smiled conspiratorially and made little charming exasperated faces which seemed to indicate that I should be patient and humor her silly old mother, just as she did.

I also noticed that the oil canvases were still dark and gloomy. A barely discernible face here, a fruit bowl of gargantuan proportions there. During breakfast they had laid out all kinds of cold cuts, a meat jelly the color of liver that jiggled like cellulite on a fat person's legs, cheese, black bread and white bread, jams, fried eggs, pickled tomatoes, and tea as strong as coffee. The mother addressed her comments to Andrej and Klara.

"How does your little friend like Moscow?"

"She is having a grand time because *I* am showing her the khaigh laife. Isn't that so?" Andrej said.

"It must seem awfully difficult to her, compared to the easy life in Capitalist America," she said. On *easy*, she snorted. "But what do you expect? Life would be just as fine here except *we* had the Great Patriotic War to fight. We are just getting over the damage the fascists caused. But you people don't know anything at all about that."

I opened my mouth to protest, but Klara closed both eyes for a long second, and shook her head. Her cheeks were flushed. Was this her position in the family unit: to sit in silence and maintain peace between Andrej's girlfriends and her mother? I wanted tell the old lady to go to hell American-style; in the worst, most atrocious language I could muster in Russian.

"But your friend is not eating," she said to Andrej. "Look how skinny she is. She must eat. Tell her to eat!"

"She is eating, Mama, look. There, a piece of cheese."

"All the girls adore Andrej," she said, staring at one of the paintings behind me. After a deep sigh, she added, "Of course, Andrej must do what he likes with his life. It is not my affair. With one ex-wife already and a son, and a—"

"That's enough, Mama," Andrej snapped, angry for the first time. His mother's face registered shock, then horror, then grief, then collapsed, shrinking in upon her puckered-up mouth. Her eyes brimmed with tears and she said nothing else.

"I'm sorry," he said quietly. No one spoke for an eternity. Klara flicked on the television set. We watched an old movie. The KGB man was an honest, trustworthy, handsome, blond hero, and the CIA man was a dark and slimy murderer who slit peoples' throats in the middle of the night.

About an hour into the movie, Andrej pushed his chair back from the table and said, "Clinton must get back to her Institute."

The mother cleared the dishes, setting them loudly on top of each other, and disappeared into the kitchen. Klara took me aside and handed me a little piece of paper with her work number scribbled on it.

"When you call please attempt to sound Russian," she smiled. "If not Russian, then at least Polish. Say your name is Katya. I will know it is you."

"All right," I said, smiling back. "Thank you." Then I made a serious face. "What is the problem with your mother?" I asked. "What did I do?"

"You are a nice girl," she said, and kissed me. "It is not your fault. It is Andrej she is angry at. Don't listen to Mama."

Back in the car, Andrej seemed in a terrific mood. I was out of my mind with joy at the prospect of going home. He didn't seem to notice that I wasn't talking to him. I blamed him for putting me through that ordeal; he could have explained our relationship to his mother.

"You must phone at four tomorrow, after class. I will wait for your call." He reached for my knee again. I caught his wrist in midair and threw it back at him.

"Your classes are an absurd waste of time. You will learn a great deal more with me and my friends than you will in class," he said. "I want you to see only me."

"Don't be stupid. That is impossible," I responded furiously. Half-expecting him to throw me out of his car, I said very slowly, "I think your mother is a bitch."

I knew the word from the movie *Patton*. "*Suka*," I said, which also implied the rest of the expression that General Patton employs to insult his Soviet counterpart who approaches him at a banquet, wanting to toast their mutual victory over Germany.

I had heard that the Russians were like the Italians about their mothers. Recently, for example, I had been told that the worst insult you could throw at someone in Russian was "I fucked your mother." But I did not see how to apply this expression to the present situation.

Andrej sat bolt upright and clenched the wheel. Before he could speak I said, "How could you take me there when you know how she is with your female friends?" Again, I said, *"podrugy."*

"You don't understand," he said quietly.

"She is a tyrant," I said. "Like Ivan the Terrible."

"She is a good woman," he said blandly, almost smiling now. "A very good woman. You do not know her."

"That is certain."

"She will get used to you."

"But I do not want to get used to her," I said. "I do not love you, Andrej. Do you understand? I love someone else."

"Who? I'll kill him."

"That wouldn't help. Listen, will you be my friend?" Again, *drug.*

"Of course," Andrej said. "Call me tomorrow at four. I'll wait for your call."

When I slammed the car door shut at the top of the Institute driveway, he was blowing me a kiss. His wandering eye looked vulnerable and sad. I felt guilty for some reason; maybe because I already knew that I would not be calling him the next day.

11

CEPPIE
ENRAGED

I marched right into the Institute, past the linebacker dezhurnaya who guarded the front doors. I felt I had a cardboard sign attached to my forehead that said CLINTON GRAY MISSED CURFEW & SPENT SATURDAY NIGHT OUT, but the dezhurnaya did not even look at me or at my student pass.

In our room, Isabel was sitting on her bed with a pillow between her back and the wall. Her long legs in dark wool tights extended straight into the room like two broomsticks with fur-lined slippers dangling from their handles. On her lap was a notebook in which she was writing very slowly. It was probably her essay for the next day's Grammatika class: "My Home Town." Dictionaries of all kinds and sizes fanned out on both sides of her. I had the same essay to write for my Grammatika class, which unfortunately was a more advanced group, comprised of graduate students who—unlike me—really did want to become professors of the Russian Language and were hell-bent on learning to speak and write without mistakes. I had already been pegged as the class idiot by our prodigiously narrow-minded teacher. (I used my imagination to cover for not having studied the readings, but she could not cope with any variations on the theme.) I had not even begun to think about this essay and panicked, certain that most of the other students in my group had finished theirs the night it had been assigned.

"I forgot about that damn essay," I said.

"I figured you had," Isabel said in that slightly reproachful tone which always managed to make me feel guilty and defensive even when I didn't deserve to.

"I got stuck somewhere, Isabel," I said. "It was too late—"

"Don't talk about it here," she interrupted, looking up at the ceiling, our code for Igor the Bug.

I took off my clothes, which smelled of cognac and cigarettes, put on sweats and heavy socks, and sat on my bed to begin to write "My Home Town." I was immediately stuck. Where was my home town?

"I was born in Paris, France, but my parents are Americans," I wrote. No; I crossed this out.

"I was born in Paris, France, but my father was and my mother is American."

I started again on a new page: "My family lived in Paris, France, until I was thirteen, when we moved to America. After that we lived in many places, but Paris is where I was born though I am not French."

I tore out both pages and started once again: "My home town is New York City."

I found it easier to write about New York, because I could look at the city with an objective eye. I was not attached to it, nor to my memories of it. Trying to write about Paris was impossibly painful for me. I blocked the city out of my mind as soon as we moved back to America.

"New York City is dirty and horrible but is the cultural center of America," I wrote.

"Your friend the twelve-monther came by looking for you last night at one in the morning," Isabel said without looking up from her essay. I dropped my ballpoint pen and it rolled away on the linoleum floor.

"Well?"

"He came in looking sort of sheepish. I think he really wanted you to be here. When he saw that you weren't, his face dropped." Isabel pulled on her chin, elongating her already long face. "He started to leave you a note and then changed his mind. He walked up and down, up and down. He saw your sprouts on the windowsill and asked me if you had grown them or if it had been my idea. I said you had grown them and he could have some if he wanted. He said he was surprised you would think of such a thing and ate the whole darn bag of mung sprouts in two bites. Good thing he didn't find the alfalfa, that's all I have to say."

"The next batch'll be ready in a couple of days," I reassured her. "What did you tell him?"

"Nothing. I was pretty cold, actually. You know, after what you told me and everything. I think he didn't behave as a gentleman should. I didn't tell him what I thought of him; I just said, 'Clinton can take care of herself.' He brought you flowers but he took them away with him."

"Isabel, sometimes you really piss me off." I couldn't stand the thought of Phil leaving with his flowers, it made me feel sick to my stomach.

"The day before yesterday you said you didn't want to talk to him!" Isabel pointed out in a hurt and righteous tone.

But I hadn't intended to be rude to him. I had avoided him the last few days to protect my feelings rather than to punish him. It was the statement he had made the next morning, warning me away from attachment, the cold ambivalent tone he employed, and the unnerving ring of his Soviet alarm clock: I had awakened to find that the rare intimacy we'd shared had immediately become a parody of itself. Feeling emotionally betrayed was an unpleasant reminder of a period in my life, after the death of my father, when I'd almost lost my mind.

Phil's words had also reminded me of my father's advice when I turned thirteen and started having periods regularly. My father explained to me that men would say just about anything to get a girl in bed. "Even after they've got you there they'll keep on lying; the oddest thing is they usually believe what they're saying at the time." I had not listened to him. I thought my father was being overly protective. Later on, I decided my father had been overly gracious to men.

Phil had not lied to get me in bed; he'd only gotten cold feet in the morning because he too had felt disarmed that night.

But he'd come back with flowers. He'd come at one, just as I was sitting in Andrej's car thinking of him. That was fate for you.

"Isabel," I said, my voice trembling, "If some guy came by here with flowers for you, I wouldn't send him away without at least offering to take the flowers, even if I thought he was the world's greatest jerk." I got up and stormed out of the room, leaving "My Home Town" lying on my bed.

A slim crack of light showed beneath Phil's closed door. I knocked quietly, and waved at the floor dezhurnaya who was sitting behind her desk at the end of the hall. She was talking on the phone, but looked up and nodded to me.

"Vkhoditie!" Phil yelled.

He was also sitting at his desk, bent over a notebook with his back to the door, wearing his guinea T-shirt and sweatpants. One of his enormous dictionaries lay propped up before him at a slight angle. Next to it, four red roses drooped in a bottle. The buds had hardly opened. Roses cost a fortune in Moscow in the winter, and rarely lasted more than a day.

"Hi," I said. He turned around, swinging his legs so that they straddled the back of the chair. There was a little hole in the crotch of his sweatpants. He said nothing at all and gazed at me with his impenetrable blue eyes.

At that moment the slight bump on the bridge of his nose only added to his attractiveness, strengthened his features, while his full and sensuous lips counteracted this completely and gave him a slightly boyish look. There seemed to be no constants at all; Phil's face changed every time I saw it.

He still said nothing.

"I stayed at the movie director's—"

He brought one index finger to his lips, without a sound.

"Come on, Phil. They don't know who the hell I'm talking about. We don't even know if they listen."

"Believe me," he said.

"Well, I slept in the living room with his sister. They have this sort of couch that takes up two walls and connects at one corner, like this." I made a ninety-degree angle, fingertips touching. "He lives with his mother. But listen to this, Phil: he asked me to marry him!" I laughed lightly.

His mouth twisted into a wry grimace.

"Be careful," he said. "That doesn't sound good."

"Yeah, really. I told him he doesn't even know me."

I thought: Andrej's never even *kissed* me. You've kissed me *every-where.*

"Odd thing, isn't it?" I said.

I laughed again in a silly way and turned my eyes from him to the wall above his bed where he kept his photographs. The picture of him kissing the blond girl was gone.

"What happened to the blond girl?" I asked.

"Oh, that was over a long time ago," he said, offhandedly.

"I mean the picture."

"I've been waiting for you to come back since that night," he said.

"Listen, I didn't miss the curfew on purpose. I didn't stay away to be mean, either. My feelings were hurt."

"I guess I didn't need to say what I said. Sounds to me like you've had a lot more experience dealing with men than I have dealing with women. What I meant to say is . . . Well, after the program ends I'm taking the Trans-Siberian to the Far East. Then I'm going to travel around the world till my money runs out."

There was a completely determined tone in his voice, and the muscles around his jaw hardened. It all started to make sense, and I began to feel frightened again.

"I'm not asking you to fill up all the gigantic holes in my life, so don't panic. I'm trying to take care of that myself for once, and I'm on the right track. That's why I came here, Phil. I didn't come here to fall in love."

"I didn't either."

"I'm not looking for a husband, for God's sake. I already told you the other night that I just got *out* of an engagement."

I had no idea where this was coming from; I didn't know if I meant it, or if I was making it up as I went along. It sounded pretty convincing to me, and to Phil, too, I thought. I had a solid base from which to work in Moscow, and I felt much more determined, and directed, than I had when Phil and I had spent the night together just over forty-eight hours ago.

"I have things to do here," I said. "I'm looking for information about the person I loved the most in the world. He's dead, but there are things I need to know. I'll tell you about it some time, if you want to be my friend."

"I am your friend," he said, and got up, lifting his leg over the back of the chair. "Is it possible to be friends with somebody and sleep with them too?" He picked up the bottle with the roses in it and came toward me. I was still standing near the door, ready to leave if that was what he wanted.

"If you don't fall in love with them," I said.

"Here," he said. "Some old babushka was selling these in the metro. They're dead already."

"You know, when I'm not with you you don't affect me this way. If you want to stop this thing you'd better say so right now."

"No," he said. The kisses he planted all over my face seemed to grow long winding roots that paralyzed my good senses and caused my heart to pound so loudly I was afraid he might hear it.

"Listen," this took a good deal of courage on my part. "No matter what happens, when the program's over, the program's over. We'll still be friends."

"Stay here," he said. "Stay here until tomorrow."

It was already getting dark outside.

"I have a damn paper to write on 'My Home Town'," I said. "And I haven't even decided which home town to write about. I don't really have one—a home town."

"I'll help you. I think they file our papers," he whispered in my ear, "they use them as psychological evaluations. So you write something as bland and innocuous as possible, with correct grammar and no opinions."

"All right," I said, kissing him on the chest, on the arms, on the neck. He was much taller than I was and these were the parts of him directly in front of my face.

A loud banging on the outside door interrupted us. Phil moved away from me and yelled out his usual *"Vkhoditie!"*

It was Isabel. Her face was green, as though she were seasick.

"My dear," she said, swallowing with difficulty, "I think you'd better come back right away. Maria-Manuella just came home in a complete rage. Something must have happened to her today, and she . . . she . . ." Isabel looked up at the ceiling, put her finger to her lips, turned toward the bathroom door and pretended to punch it, in slow motion, with a limp wrist. "There's a"—she cupped her hands into two joining half-circles—"this big! What do we do?!"

"People get tossed out of here for less than that," Phil muttered, and was out the door. He had not met Ceppie, but he knew she and her roommate were Isabel's and my suite-mates; if they were sent home for destroying government property, we would be too. We all had been informed that guilt was collective in the Soviet Union.

Although Ceppie was the person I felt closest to and liked the most in the group, I had barely seen her in the past four days; we chatted a few times late at night when we both got home from our various rendezvous.

The three of us piled into the little hallway that led to Ceppie's room, fighting for space like Russians trying to squeeze into the metro train when the doors are closing. The hole in the bathroom door was not as big as Isabel had indicated, but was still a good three inches long and one and a half inches high. Ceppie had punched clear through the flimsy 3/4-inch-thick door of unvarnished wood.

From the hallway we could see her sitting on her bed, hunched over and gripping the wrist of her right hand. Her knuckles were not bleeding, though they seemed more bruised than usual. Ceppie's roommate, Elsa, was not home. She had met a black marketeer in Red Square the first day, and had not spent a night home since. Phil was inspecting the hole, mumbling, "How the hell did she do that?"

"She's a black belt in karate," I said.

"Wonderful," Phil said.

Isabel composed herself and went into the room. She leaned over Ceppie with her fists on her hips like an angry schoolteacher and demanded to know what had possessed Maria-Manuella to behave in such a manner.

Ceppie looked up at Isabel. There were black streaks of mascara from her eyes to her chin. This surprised me; Ceppie didn't seem one for mascara or any other kind of cosmetic.

"Don't call me that," she said, biting her lower lip. "Only the nuns and the family call me Maria-Manuella. It's Ceppie to you."

"This is very unusual," Phil said, his eye against the hole in the door. "She must be very pissed off. I'm going to talk to the dezhurnaya. One of you guys better come with me. We're lucky 'cause it's Lidya Dmitrievna today. She likes me."

"I'll go with you but you do the talking," I said.

Phil stopped in his room for a moment, then we walked down the long hall on the strip of green carpeting. I watched as Lidya Dmitrievna grew bigger and bigger and more menacing, and I broke out in a cold sweat.

"Good afternoon, Lidya Dmitrievna," Phil said. She was knitting at her desk, a blond woman of around forty who wore her hair in an enormous bun at the base of her neck. The knitting needles went click click click.

"*Privyet,* Phil," she said without looking up. "Only it's not afternoon, it's evening now."

She put down the knitting needles and, elaborately lifting the sleeve of her left arm, tapped a nail on the face of her enormous Swatch watch. It was of many colors; patterns that went round and round in hypnotic circles.

"I am so pleased you like the watch, Lidya Dmitrievna," Phil said. "Every time I see you wearing it it makes me very happy. I found two extra batteries I thought I had not brought. They are so little I lost them. Here you are."

He placed a tiny envelope on the desk next to the phone.

"You are too kind to me, Phil," she said, shaking her head and blushing slightly.

"This is Clinton from 622," he said.

"Gray, *da?*"

"*Da,* Lidya Dmitrievna."

"We have a problem," Phil said conspiratorially. "Can you get the master here today?"

"I think we can get the master, what is the problem?"

"I think you should come take a look," Phil said. So the three of us went back down the hall to number 621, which was Ceppie's room.

"*Oy!*" Lidya Dmitrievna brought a flat hand to each side of her face. "What is this?"

No one mentioned the hole. We spoke around it as though the problem were a leak in the sink or some such routine mishap.

Phil brought Lidya Dmitrievna into the room, where Ceppie still sat hunched and motionless at the edge of her bed.

"Concepcion, *da?*" Lidya Dmitrievna said.

How she knew all our names was beyond me. I had never said more than a passing "Good morning" or "Good evening" to her.

"A little tiny person like you?" Lidya Dmitrievna asked.

"She is very very . . ." I couldn't remember the word for upset.

"In love," Phil said. "And her heart is completely broken."

"Only love can do such a thing, it is true." Lidya Dmitrievna uncrossed her arms and patted Ceppie on the head. I was afraid Ceppie might try to bite her. She was full of pride; she did not like compassion; and she certainly would not appreciate being patted on the head.

"But such a little tiny girl!" added Lidya Dmitrievna.

"These are very serious girls, Lidya Dmitrievna," Phil said. "They do all their homework and never miss classes."

"The Americans are much more serious than the others—especially the Africans—it is true," she said, and nodded pensively. Phil led her out into the hall. I followed them.

"Nevertheless this is very bad," she shook her head. "Very irresponsible. Never in all my years—"

"The master will come today, Lidya Dmitrievna?" Phil interjected, looking straight into her eyes and frowning.

"Yes. As a favor he will come today. Later," she added in a whisper, "when there won't be so many people around."

He walked her down the hall. I heard Phil ask her with great concern if her son was doing better in his classes, and then their conversation faded into mumbles. I went back into the room and sat down next to Ceppie on the bed.

"Don't worry," I said loudly, "the master is coming and the leak will be fixed."

"Who's the guy, *mujer?*" she asked me. "Our fairy godfather or what?"

Isabel was standing above us with her arms crossed, tapping her foot.

Shortly afterward Phil came back with a full bottle of Pertsovka vodka and handed it to Ceppie. "For the master," he said.

"I have a bottle of cognac I bought to give the Cubans," Ceppie said, looking up finally.

"That's good," Phil said. "Any cigarettes?"

"I've got a carton of Marlboros," I said.

"Good," Phil said. "Two packs should do. Ceppie's got to do it, though."

"Thanks, mang," Ceppie said to Phil in a flat tone, wrapping herself in her Puerto Rican accent. "Jou saved my ass an' are now considered a friend for life."

I walked through the bathroom to my room, gathered my notebook and dictionary and the cigarettes and brought them back.

"I'll stay here with you till the master comes," I said.

"No, mang. I gotta think."

"Phil lives right across the hall," I said. "That's where I'll be if you want to talk."

I stared through Phil's open closet door at his duffle bag crumpled up on the floor. Above it hung four or five long-sleeved cotton shirts, the tweed sports jacket he had worn to the Bolshoi with me earlier that week, and a couple of pairs of pants. He did not own many clothes.

"Okay, let's write that essay."

"Thank you, Phil. How can I ever thank you?"

"We'd better write the essay first. Otherwise we won't do it, I fear."

"You're unbelievable. Where's the master going to find one of those," I asked pointing at the door.

"He'll take one from somewhere else."

Ceppie knocked on Phil's door at ten o'clock. I had just finished recopying "My Home Town" into my homework notebook. This was my innocuous last paragraph:

> It is nice to get out of New York City in the summer because the weather is very hot and humid. Some weekends I go to the beach to visit my mother. If I stay in the city I go to Central Park and watch the roller skaters and the children doing tricks on bicycles. They dance around big music boxes that are all playing the same radio station. Sometimes there is a hat in which you put money for them. New York is a complicated city and very frightening for people who do not know it well, but I love New York because it is my home town.

Ceppie was wearing her army jacket with the fur-lined hood. Her face was drawn, her eyes swollen from crying.

"The master came," she said. "He reminded me of my father and I told him so. Did I tell you my father's a plumber?"

Phil was at his desk, writing his long essay on Methodology. His topic was how to use the verbs of motion in Pushkin's *Yevgeny Onegin* to teach foreigners how to understand Russian verb tenses.

This was rather amazing to me, as I could read no more than two pages of *Yevgeny Onegin* in an hour.

He reached under the desk and brought out a half-bottle of hunter's vodka, pulled the stopper out with his teeth, took a swig, and handed the bottle to Ceppie.

"Thanks," she said, coming forward. She took a swallow and passed it to me. "You guys want to take a walk with me? Mister Phil's got ESP I think. That was a good one, 'she's in love.'"

Phil left his desk, pulled a wool sweater on over his T-shirt, and grabbed his coat, which had been lying on his never-present roommate's bed.

We walked away from the Institute, down the road toward the endless row of construction pits that marked the end of the inhabited world. The moon was full above the birch forest and cast a ghostly silver light over the expanse of snow and the trees' white branches.

"Clinton and I took our first walk this way," Ceppie said, as though reminiscing about something that had taken place years ago. "Maybe it's the full moon that makes me crazy."

Phil sighed deeply and said nothing.

"I was here before, Clinton," she said. "Last summer. I never told you but it wasn't because I didn't trust you; I just never told you."

"At the Institute?" Phil asked.

"No. We stayed at a hotel for six weeks. It was one of those special student groups organized by Harvard."

We walked far, listening to Ceppie's story. Phil, in the middle, linked an arm through each of ours. The snow squeaked softly, reassuringly, under the soles of our boots.

Ceppie's story broke my heart. Several weeks later, she took me to a party and I met the people she described to Phil and me that night. It was strange to recognize them in the crowded apartment, even before she pointed them out to me.

The previous summer, Ceppie had gone alone to Gorky Park and had sat on a bench in the sun, next to the big basin from which spouted numerous, extravagant fountains. Classical music filled the air, wafting from old-fashioned megaphones that surround the basin. She was reading *The Great Gatsby,* one of the American novels she had brought along to give away. A man approached her and sat beside her on the bench. She continued to read without looking up, thinking that he might be after her Levi's jacket or her Nike sneakers. After a while he leaned toward her and said in Russian, "Are you what is called a Black American without privileges?"

Her skin was the color of milk in coffee, and her hair was dark and curly, but no one had ever mistaken her for Black. She turned to him in surprise, and saw now that he was young, around twenty, tall and dark-eyed with wild black hair that pointed upward like a flame. He had a pale, delicate, intelligent face.

"I am not Black, but I am Hispanic, another race without privileges," she responded. She did not know how to say "minority" in Russian, or if such a word existed.

"What nationality are you?" the young man then asked.

"I am a Puerto Rican American."

"Ah." He nodded pensively. "That is a state, then, in America?"

"No. Puerto Rico is to America what Bulgaria is to the Soviet Union."

"But Russians like Bulgarians," he said. "My name is Misha."

"My name is Ceppie."

"Will you come to a party with me tonight, Ceppie? My friends are very educated about America, but they have not met many Americans. Most Russians know more about America than Americans know about Russia, isn't it so? We all have read Mark Tvain, Irvin Shaw, Djek London, Djon Steinbeck. My favorite is Villiam Folkner because he writes like a Russian. What book are you reading? My friend who is giving this party reads English very well, but I cannot."

"This is F. Scott Fitzgerald," she said. *"Velikiy Gatsby,* it is called."

"I don't know it," he said, shaking his head. "It is probably anti-Soviet, then?"

"Not at all. I don't think so. It is about a poor man who becomes rich so that he can marry a rich girl. It makes the rich look very bad."

"I am certain my friend will know of this book. He loves American movies best of all. You can come to his party and tell him about new American movies."

"Why not? I'll come with you." Ceppie's street sense was very keen, and she was not apprehensive at all.

They took the metro to the Avenue of the Enthusiasts stop in the northeastern section of Moscow. From there they took a bus.

The friend's apartment was big by Russian standards. There was a bedroom and a living room, and a kitchen which held a table that could seat six. On top of the refrigerator and on every imaginable inch of shelf space were empty, Capitalist beer cans. Ceppie saw Budweiser, Heineken, Miller, Miller Lite, Amstel, Kronenbourg, Dos Equis, and dozens more, many she had never seen before. She was shown the bedroom by the proud owner of the apartment, the redheaded Grisha. Above the double bed he had pasted the jackets of all the books he had read in English. They were mostly sci-fi novels: *Space Dogs, Vampires from Mars, Thunderella*—titles Ceppie had never heard of. There were cassette tapes of all sorts of American rock 'n' roll everywhere. Even though the alcohol laws had become stringent in Moscow, everyone arrived with a bottle of something—wine, vodka, Georgian and Armenian cognac. Ceppie had brought nothing but her book, which she gave to Grisha, apologizing for not having brought anything else.

"You are a guest," he said. "Guests bring nothing the first time. But I accept the book with pleasure."

He had no jaw to speak of and when he smiled his mouth completely overtook the lower third of his face. Ceppie noticed with dismay that most of his teeth were rotten, and some were even missing in the back.

Ceppie tried to control her drinking. She was generally not a big drinker, but they filled her glass every chance they got. When no one was watching, she'd pour her shot of vodka or her glass of wine (they mixed everything indiscriminately) into someone else's. There was an endless cacophony of rock music—both the stereo in the living room and the cassette player in the kitchen were going at the same time—blasting through the apartment. People were dancing and singing, and there was much stumbling, and even some tears. Ceppie remembered one girl standing by the bathroom, crying because she was a failure to her devoted mother. Ceppie's head was spinning. She took a corner seat at the kitchen table and tried to collect herself. She had not eaten since morning, and the prospect of food at this party seemed slim. Misha joined her. His eyes were red and completely sad.

"Do you like our party?"

"Very much," Ceppie said.

"It is like this all the time, however, and I would so much like a change."

"What kind of change?"

"I don't know—a change."

Someone across the table from them, a girl, said to her, "You are sitting at the corner of the table, you will not be married for seven years, ha ha ha!"

"Quick," Misha said, "A toast against that."

"I am hungry," Ceppie said. "And drunk."

"Let's go to my apartment. I have food."

Pushing his dusty books, notebooks, and pens aside, Misha spread a tablecloth out on his work table—he was an engineer of some kind. The bed was the only place in the room to sit other than the one chair that came with the work table. There was a bookshelf crammed full of books (they were everywhere, even under the bed), a closet, and a window with a little balcony. On the balcony flowers of all colors bloomed in little clay pots. Ceppie was amazed.

"Do you grow the flowers yourself?"

"Of course. Please speak quietly. This is a communal apartment. My neighbors are curious. If you run into them in the hall, say you are from Latvia."

"Aren't Latvians pale and blond?" Ceppie asked.

"True," he said pensively. "All right then, from Armenia."

They ate kolbasa and cheese on black bread, and drank strong Azerbaijani tea. Ceppie went home to her hotel in a cab at three in the morning. Misha asked her to meet him the next day, which she did, and every day thereafter for the rest of her six-week visit.

Misha had been graduated from Moscow University and held a degree which overqualified him for the job he had sorting silverware in a factory. "They train you and give you hope for a better life and then they tell you there is no place for you in the field for which you are trained," he told her. He was completely disillusioned, but his nature was gentle, and he was not angry. He lived a small and comfortable life, making occasional deals on the black market to make ends meet, and to give him something exciting to do. He dealt in Western blue jeans, was the go-between for some kind of a large underground operation. He never asked Ceppie for anything Western, but he did ask her to sleep with him on several occasions. Each time she declined.

"Why not?" I asked her that night as we walked and walked under the full moon with Phil between us.

"*Ay, mujer.* You don't understand anything." She looked over at me, across Phil, with her swollen eyes. "I have never slept with a man."

Phil breathed out a long jet of steam but still said nothing.

"I believed he loved me," Ceppie said. "But I was scared. It's one of those things; you wait and wait, and then it becomes such a big deal you can't just throw it away without some kind of commitment."

"I've only slept with three women in my life," Phil said, looking straight down the road into the darkness.

My God, I thought. I'm Number Three. Everything became clear to me. I was shocked to learn that their experiences had been so different from mine; they did not have ex-lovers in their pasts who had been and always would be as nameless and faceless as the birch trees.

"They say the first time is supposed to be awful," Phil continued. "Not at all. It was wonderful. I was in love. Blind as a bat in love."

An indescribable knot of pain obstructed my throat. Who were his two others? Which one had penetrated his soul and left no room there for me?

"Why not sleep with him now, Ceppie, if it's still going on?" Phil asked.

Ceppie told us that once, last summer, she had spent an entire day at Misha's apartment. They had planned it ahead of time; one weekday morning Misha called his job and said he was sick. When Ceppie arrived, no one else was home. The hot water had been turned off during the night because pipes in the sector were undergoing "prophylactic work," and Misha was heating a huge pot of water on the stove for his bath.

"Get undressed," he told Ceppie, "I will give you a bath."

She took off all her clothes and sat in the tub. With a large wooden ladle he poured the water over her head and back and soaped her down. "This is what we do at the public baths," he explained, massaging her shoulders with a rough, spiky sponge. Then she did the same to him. For her, this had been enough. It had meant the same thing to her as making love and she had not wanted to spoil it. Still wrapped in a towel after her bath, she offered to marry him. She told him she would return to Russia as soon as she could, and would stay for at least three months, which was the amount of time one needed to file marriage papers. Then they would get married and she would get him out. Misha had agreed, saying that even if he did not hear from her for a year he knew she would come back and he would still be waiting for her, no matter what.

Now, six months later, she had been back a week and had spent most evenings at Grisha the redhead's parties, waiting for Misha to show up. Calling Misha's apartment was complicated, because he shared one phone with his neighbors and had asked her not to call unless it was a total emergency. All regular messages had to be relayed to him through Grisha. Misha had finally appeared at Grisha's on the fifth night, looking pale and depressed and dissipated. He told Ceppie he had new neighbors who were hard-line Communists and would not appreciate his involvement with a foreigner. "I can still be Armenian," Ceppie suggested. "It wouldn't work now," Misha said vaguely.

Finally, that very Sunday morning, he had agreed to have her come to his apartment. Ceppie went armed with condoms. It was time, she decided. She wanted to prove to him that she was dead serious about him.

They had been sitting at his work table sipping tea and not talking because Misha seemed nervous, and Ceppie did not know how to approach the subject of her virginity. The door to his room flew open and a shapely Russian girl with gorgeous long blond hair traipsed in as though the room belonged to her.

"I'm sorry, Misha," she said. "I waited for the bus for twenty minutes, got to the metro and realized I forgot my notebook. I couldn't go to the meeting without it."

She shrugged, picked up her notebook which was lying on the bookshelf, and left without saying a word to Ceppie.

"Is that your new Communist neighbor?" Ceppie asked in a completely neutral tone.

"Yes," Misha said with a straight face.

"You don't have to lie to me," she said.

"I'm not."

She took the condoms out of her bag and dumped them on the bed.

"Here," she said. "You can use them with her."

She left without saying another word; Misha sat slumped over his tea with a look of complete dejection on his face, but did not attempt to stop her. She controlled herself on the bus and metro, clenching her fists and biting her lower lip until she reached home. When she got back to her dorm room, Ceppie punched the hole through the bathroom door.

12

THE
HEROINE–
MOTHER

Andrej the playwright seemed to be under the impression I could not manage in Moscow without him. To prove him wrong (as well as to punish him for having put me through a night with his mother the Matriarch from Hell) I did not phone him on Monday as agreed. I knew I wouldn't when he dropped me off on Sunday. I waited five days before heading out, after classes, to call him from my usual telephone booth down the street. This is the conversation I had with Mrs. Andrej:

"May Andrej be called to the phone, please?"

"Andrej is out of town."

"Out of town? For how long?"

"It is unknown," she said.

"It is Clinton. Please, would you pass on to him that I phoned? What day should I try again?"

"I don't understand," she said bluntly, and hung up.

This was obviously the kind of "problem" Andrej's sister had anticipated, and warned me I would run into with their mother. Outraged and fuming, I dialed Klara's number at work with a trembling hand. "Attempt to sound Russian," she had told me—"Or at least Polish"— but it occurred to me as I asked for her that I did not know their last name or patronymic, which was the only proper way to ask for a person in a public situation. A Pole would certainly know that.

"May Klara be called to the phone please?"

"Klara?"

"Da."

"Who is calling?"

"Katya."

The receiver was put down. A moment later I heard a woman's voice.

"Yes?"

"Klara?"

"Yes."

"It is Katya. I have lost Andrej. Your mother said he is out of town."

"He went to Leningrad for the opening of his last play," Klara said.

Now I felt hurt—abandoned, like a slighted mistress—which infuriated me doubly because firstly, I was not his mistress, and secondly, *I* was supposed to be punishing *him*. And here I was battling a hellish matriarch for a son I did not even want.

"The play I just saw?" I asked Klara, trying to calm down.

"No, no. The last one. It is about the blockade and is just opening in Leningrad."

"Why did he say nothing about it?"

There was a long pause. "I don't know," Klara said. "I am sorry. *Nu,* listen, I have a number for you. Boris Mikhailovich called yesterday and said you must call a woman named Vera. Understand? She is the woman you are looking for. Shall I read you the number?"

"Yes. But Klara, listen—when does Andrej return?"

"It is not certain."

"How do I find him? Your mother does not like me," I said, and laughed uncomfortably.

"No, she is only old-fashioned," Klara reassured me. "You must call me here in a week. I will tell you everything. Katya—this is important —Boris Mikhailovich is not sure this Vera will want to talk to you. If she seems angry, do not tell her from whom you got the number; it is a secret, understand?"

"Of course." I said. She read me the number three times, slowly.

"Thank you so much, Klara. Will you meet with me?"

"In a week, if Andrej is not back."

"Thank you."

"I kiss you."

"I kiss you. Until soon."

Petrified, I stood in the booth with my forehead against the ice-cold metal phone. It was said that this Vera's father had died in exile owing to his friendship with my father. How would *you* feel, I asked myself, if it were the other way around—if your father had died because of her father?

My father's heart had always been weak, and the meager rations and bitter climate he'd endured in wartime Russia had wiped out his resistance permanently. His nature, it seemed to me, had also been especially sensitive, and the struggle and violence he'd witnessed during the war had marked him for life. I could blame the whole country if I wanted to. I could blame that bastard McCarthy, too, for forcing my father to leave America. The point was not to blame anyone and to find out everything there was to find out.

The metallic cold pierced through my skull like a drill and brought tears to my eyes.

I placed a dvushka into the slot and waited for my breathing to stabilize.

I dialed the number.

"I am listening," a woman said in a tone that forewarned that this was in fact the last thing in the world she wanted to be doing. I could hear children screaming in the background.

"Is this Vera?"

"I am listening."

"I am the daughter of Alexander Clinton Gray." My voice cracked on the last syllable. I did not know how to proceed, so I waited for her to respond.

"Now you stop that, Sasha," she yelled into the background. *"Petya, you get that away from him now!"*

I heard loud whining and a few outraged screams, then she said into the phone, "Can you come today?" in a completely matter-of-fact tone.

"Yes," I said without even considering the fact that it was already late and getting dark.

"All right," she said. We made arrangements to meet at a certain metro stop near the center of the city.

"Can I bring you something?" I asked.

"No, nothing," she said. "Thank you."

"Some wine or vodka?" At that time it was practically impossible for Muscovites to get ahold of liquor. The liquor stores were open from 2 to 7 P.M.—and this was a big improvement, because just a few months ago, we'd been told, stores had been open only from two till five, and workers left their jobs to go stand in line in front of the liquor stores. The government had raised the price of a bottle of vodka from two rubles to ten, but that had helped very little. Non-alcoholics who enjoyed a bottle for a celebration were the ones who were punished; alcoholics were now drinking perfume and robbing houses to buy alcohol on the black market. Russians now made their own moonshine, *samogon*, which killed more people than cancer.

After a pause the woman said, *"Oy,* but I wouldn't want you to go to any trouble."

"It's not a problem, really."

We had a hard-currency Beriozka store right on the other side of our birch forest, in the lobby of a newish skyscraper hotel that was on the same bus route as the metro. Only foreigners were permitted to shop there.

"I'll stop on the way," I said. "It is easy."

As I hung the receiver back onto the phone, a cloud of exhaustion descended on me at the prospect of the endless bus and metro rides I was about to undertake.

And it had begun to snow. Enormous flakes danced in the air and tickled my face as I walked toward the bus stop. Across the street students were lumbering down the snow-covered driveway toward the Institute. With the snowfall came the familiar, comforting silence. The sky had dropped completely to the ground. Through the white shroud the Institute's yellow windows twinkled brightly. At the bus stop people stood clustered together under the shelter.

How strange—sleep was becoming another rare and valued bourgeois commodity. There were the obvious other ones besides alcohol, the expected ones: toilet paper, fresh fruit, fresh vegetables, fresh meat, a dvushka for the public phone; but sleep . . . I thought of the old Portuguese nanny who had cared for me as a child. She used to say that sleep was the only pleasure man was given free of charge. For this reason, she took her sleep very seriously and reprimanded me sorely for always trying to get out of my nap. I wondered if her life in Portugal had been as absurdly difficult as most Russians' lives were.

I got off the bus in front of the hotel and walked toward the Beriozka store, which had white curtains hanging over the large windows so that the ordinary Soviet passerby could not see what was for sale inside.

"It's disgusting," Phil had said when I'd asked him about the hard-currency stores. "You know what *Beriozka* means? 'Little Birch Tree'— the soul of Mother Russia, the best of what Russia has to offer her honored guests. Just go take a look in one of them: we can buy for dollars everything the Russians can't get their hands on. At first I refused to use them. But then after about two months I realized I was just making my life miserable. Plus, we can't pretend to be Russian. It's hypocritical. We're like visitors at the zoo."

This Beriozka specialized in Russian furs and amber jewelry. There was a clothes section which I took a quick look at, out of curiosity; on a rack hung absurdly overpriced polyester shirts and jackets from Hungary and Poland. Dime-store quality at best. The store sold both Western and Soviet alcohol and a few dry goods from West Germany and Switzerland such as powdered fruit juices, chocolates, and nuts. There was Chianti Classico Riserva Ducale in the wine section. Two and a half rubles a bottle. In New York City at my corner liquor store the same bottle cost over seven dollars. Once the two and a half rubles were converted at the official dollar exchange rate (around two thirds of a ruble to the dollar) and I was charged the ninety-kopek fee for cashing a traveler's check (it did not matter if the check were for ten or one hundred dollars, the charge was the same), the bottle cost just a little more than it did in New York. I didn't mind. I also bought a bottle of Moskovskaya vodka and four jars of West German powdered tropical fruit mix—the label stated in German that the mix was enhanced with ten important vitamins. I thought these might make a nice gift for Vera's children.

The plastic bag the cashier handed me had a painting of a Russian *matryoshka* doll on it, with the word BERIOZKA printed above it in large letters. This outraged me; not only was I forced to use these stores, but now the whole world had to know about it. The languid young cashier had bright red hair. When she bent over her register I saw that her roots were growing in black. She handed me a piece of paper with the amount in dollars scribbled on it. I thanked her in Russian and she said "You're welcome" in English. She observed with curiosity as I shoved the plastic sack into my big black bag before going out into the street. The bottles clanked loudly against my hip.

As soon as I was out on the street a somber-looking character in a flimsy raincoat accosted me. He was not wearing a scarf or hat; it was snowing heavily and his face had taken on a blueish hue.

"Student?" he said in Russian, smiling as though proud of the big black gaps in his teeth.

"Yes." I kept moving toward the bus stop.

"From where?"

"U.S.A."

"Please, I will pay you." He pushed a handful of ruble notes at my chest. "Will you go back in and buy me cigarettes and vodka?"

"It is not allowed."

"Look, I have many rubles."

"I can't. It is not allowed," I said, a hard edge in my voice. I thought, KGB in disguise; our counselors had warned us about such types. They railroad you into exchanging money on the street, or buying something in the Beriozka, then cart you off in their black car, question and body-search you and then send you home as an example to the others. I had been told the KGB was especially fond of catching Americans in these situations of *khooliganism*.

"Here," I said, reaching into my bag and taking out the full pack of Marlboros I carried around in case I had to bribe a cabdriver, or met a Russian who smoked. "It's a gift." I ran toward the bus stop without looking back.

I waited for Vera on a stone bench at the very front of the subway platform and watched trains for twenty minutes. A computerized digital clock above the arch of the tunnel told you the exact time, and how many minutes had elapsed since the departure of the last train. I observed that the maximum time between trains was 1:06. Fantastic! I considered writing a letter to the New York Metropolitan Transit Authority suggesting they send a delegation to study the Moscow Metropolitan named for Vladimir Ilyich Lenin. In the Moscow metro there was no graffiti. There was no crime. A drunk, once in a while, vomited or fell on you in a crowded train, but that was only very late at night.

Writing to the MTA would probably get my name on some CIA blacklist, if it wasn't on one already.

An icy wind blew in from the tunnel and zipped around the marble pillars of the well-lit station, which had chandeliers hanging from its high, arching ceiling. I wrapped my wool scarf more tightly around my head.

Tomorrow, I decided, I would get a hat.

My nose began to run and I became depressed.

I felt someone approaching and looked up. A woman in a black wool coat and cap stood before me. Little white flowers had been sown into the stitch of the cap. She had a wide, Slavic face and coal-colored half-moons below her eyes.

"*Zdrastvuytie,*" she said.

"*Zdrastvuytie,*" I said.

"I am sorry, I had to wait for my neighbor to get home. The little ones are too wild to be left alone. The oldest has piano class today. I forgot." She shrugged, and smiled for the first time. She had spaces between all her front teeth.

"Shall we go?"

Heading up the escalator she reminded me to pay attention to the way we were going for the next time.

"I am sorry. I have caught a cold. With children it is always like that. And my nose." She pointed to a red spot above her right nostril. "I have . . . all the time."

I had never heard the word she used. "May I look?"

"Pazhaluysta."

I brought my face closer and realised that she had a patch of cold sores the size of a nickle there. They were the typical liquid-filled bumps, tiny as the blunt end of a straight pin, erupting from a rash.

"That is herpes, in English," I said in a low voice. "I have the same thing, but on my lip, here." I pointed to a corner of my lower lip. "It is the worst thing in the world." When I had an outbreak on my lip it was not a fourth as big as the one on her nose, and it still felt like a lightbulb was attached to my face.

"It is," she said.

"I have medicine. I can bring you medicine next time."

"Medicine for this? Is it possible?"

"It is very new. We have an . . . an . . . ." I wanted to say epidemic, but had no idea what the word was. "We have many people who suffer with this. There is medicine for the pain and to make it go away faster, but there is no cure yet."

"Incredible!" she mused, shaking her head. "The luxury of Capitalism. You really have medicine for this?"

"Da."

"In Russia they will never have it," she said dejectedly, her head sagging between her large shoulders. "It is not important enough. We are used to suffering."

Vera's courtyard, a large square at the center of a block of gray buildings, was completely submerged in snow. The ends of several seesaws protruded at odd angles from the choppy expanse, reminding me of sinking battleships. There were scraps of paper and metal and rubber littering the ploughed footpaths. The tree branches sagged with the weight of accumulated snow.

"My children are wild because they are inside most of the day," she said.

"How many do you have?"

"Five," she said.

"*Five?*" I said. "I thought no one had five in Russia."

"No one but a person as stupid as I." She punched me in the arm, hard, and let out a loud, raucous laugh. "I am a *mat'-geroinya.*" A heroine-mother, she said.

"What does that mean?"

"After your third, you become a heroine of the Soviet Union. I have privileges. I don't wait in line when I shop. I don't have to wait in line for anything—except alcohol," she said. "And that is a tragedy, because I love to drink." She winked at me, her dark and thoughtful eyes crinkling at the corners.

"I love to drink, too," I said.

"And our fathers did also, or so said my mama. I never knew my father, do you know?"

"I'm sorry," I said.

"I don't care much," she said.

We got into the elevator and she pushed the button for the third floor. Nothing happened.

"*Blyad!*" she hissed, and jumped up and down. The elevator shuddered wildly. It lurched, gave a big burp, and began its climb.

"What is blyad?"

"Ha ha ha! Look it up in the dictionary. It won't be there, most likely. It's a bad word for *prostitutka,*" she said conspiratorially. "Don't tell your professors where you learned it."

"Now I know three bad words in Russian," I said.

"Which?"

"Son of a bitch; I fucked your mother; and whore," I said.

This really cracked her up. She guffawed and slammed her hand against the elevator door. It began to shake like a child with a fever. My heart sank, I was certain we were going to crash to the bottom and die. What would our fathers think of that?

"Do Russians and Americans go to the same heaven?" I asked Vera jokingly.

"Of course," she said. "There is no Communist heaven. You live a Communist existence so that you can go to Capitalist heaven. No listen, without joking, I should not speak that way. I am a believer— *pravoslavnaya.*" Orthodox, she said.

"Are you a believer?" she whispered as she unlatched the door.

"No," I said. "I am an atheist."

"How long are you here for, five months? Good, I have five months to convert you."

The hallway was quite dark. We removed our heavy coats and Vera added them to a gigantic pile of coats of all sizes which hung from hooks right by the door.

"The children are sleeping, praise God," she smiled. "Take off your boots." I did. On the opposite side of the hall was a set of deep shelves which had been stuffed from bottom to top with pairs of slippers. Vera swiftly dug through them, pulling out tiny ones and enormous ones to find a matching pair for me, which took quite some time.

I counted five doors as we walked the length of the apartment to the kitchen.

The walls of the kitchen were decorated with ancient icons, some carved of wood, some embossed and painted bright colors. The figures' heads were often encircled by gold halos.

At the large, square kitchen table sat an old woman whose skin was so thin and ancient it resembled wrinkled silk. Her eyes were humid, but sharp.

"The children are sleeping," she smiled impishly, as though she'd accomplished a feat.

"Thank you, Anna Yefimovna. Anna Yefimovna is my neighbor. She helps me. A great woman. This is Clinton."

"Very pleased," I said.

"Very pleased," she said.

"Sit, sit," Vera said. "I have fixed us something to eat. What a pity you did not call two days ago. It was Fat Tuesday—I invited all my friends and we ate blini with salmon and sour cream. Now I am fasting until Easter. No meats, no meat products, and no milk products. And of course, no alcohol. But today is special, I will have a little drink."

"Fasting must be very difficult here."

"One adapts."

I took the Beriozka sack out of my bag and stood the bottles of wine and vodka and the jars of fruit mix on the table.

"*Oy,*" Vera said. "Do you think God will forgive me? After all, today *is* a special day. Shall we open one?"

"Of course," I said.

"What is this?" She picked up the Chianti and inspected the label. "French wine?"

"Italian."

"*Oy,*" she said. "What luxury."

"These are for your children. Fruit juice of some kind. It is in German, I can't read everything but I know it has vitamins. Ten vitamins."

"Fantastic. We give them something good for them but they think it is bad for them so they like it even more. What minds you Capitalists have!"

"Some wine, Anna Yefimovna?" Vera asked her neighbor as she uncorked the bottle.

"Oh, I mustn't."

"Just one finger."

"All right. I've never tasted Italian wine. But just one finger."

We drank the wine from tiny stemmed glasses.

"I made a borscht with vegetable stock because of the fast, you see. I am sorry for you that there is no meat in it." She dropped a heaping tablespoon of sour cream into my bowl. Disintegrating, it slowly turned the soup from red to pink. It was the most delicious beet borscht I'd ever tasted. There was a salad of soft cheese and minced garlic, and bread and kolbasa sandwiches. Vera touched none of this.

Anna Yefimovna sat with us and talked in a high, lilting voice about living alone. She was a widow, and had one married daughter who no longer had time to stop by. "But that is all right," she said. "She has her own little ones now and has to live her own life." Her eyes brimmed with tears as she spoke of her dead husband, whom she visited once a week at a cemetery on the other side of town.

"We were so young when we married. Fifty-four years ago," she said dreamily. "We barely knew each other then. But what a kind man. The kindest man in the world. He is gone five years now and I still cannot get used to it."

"It is terrible to be alone," I said. "My mother is alone now."

"Yes," she agreed.

"I'll take my medicine now, Vera, and leave you two in peace."

"Stay, Anna Yefimovna, have some borscht."

"No, no. Just my medicine."

Vera poured a green brew out of a jar into a cup and gave it to the old lady. She made a face as she drank it down.

"You should not be going to the cemetery in this weather, Anna Yefimovna. It is not good for your heart."

"On the contrary, it is the only thing besides you and your children that is good for my heart."

As she stood up to leave she gripped the back of her chair with swollen, arthritic fingers. Standing, she was only a little taller than I was sitting down.

"What a nice, pretty girl you are," she said, patting my shoulder lightly. "I am sure we will meet again."

We sat in silence for a moment, and then I heard a baby crying outside the window.

Vera opened the double-glass doors that led to the balcony and an icy wind blew into the room. She carried in a large bundle of cloth and laid it down on the kitchen table, swiftly pushing the dishes aside.

"This is Seryozha," she said, and deftly began to unravel the bundle. Under five layers of quilt was the baby, wrapped in a white cloth contraption, arms pinned to his sides. Vera freed him and lifted him in the air. He was dressed in a one-piece, padded red suit with hood and feet attached.

"Vera, it's freezing out there!"

"All children must have an hour of frost a day. I don't have time, with all the others, to take him for a walk in the street. So he takes his nap on the balcony."

"He will die from the cold."

"All the others had their hour of frost a day, and they are healthy as byks."

"What is a byk?" I asked.

Vera brought a fist to each temple, index finger extended. "Like a cow," she said. "But of the masculine gender."

She changed the baby's cloth diapers right on the kitchen table. He started to scream.

"I must feed little Seryozha. Yes yes, right away," she cooed.

As Vera was stirring a concoction called *Babymiks* into warmed water, a terrible scream came from down the hall and a child screeched, *"MAMMMMAMMMMMMMAAAA!"*

A stampede followed. Two little boys came tumbling into the kitchen, the dark-haired one arriving first. Tears streamed down his face and his nose dripped blood. His voice was wracked by terrible sobs.

"Mam—mmaaa Saa-sha h-h-hit me with his f-f-fist in the nnn-o-se!"

Sasha had been in pursuit as they arrived. His amber-colored, leonine hair curled frantically around his head and his face blazed with fury.

"Mama, it's not true. Petya hit me with his car right here." He pointed to a purple spot on his forehead where the car had hit him.

Then he saw me sitting at the kitchen table, looking at him. My hair was almost the same color as his, though I'd had mine streaked before leaving the States, while the golden tint in his was completely natural. He came forward with a determined expression and reached up and pinched a strand of my hair between his fingers.

"Look, Sasha," Vera laughed, "a relative of yours all the way from America, ha ha ha!"

Sasha was perplexed and stared at me in silence a long while. His irises were large and just a touch darker than his hair. He resembled nothing so much as a tawny jungle beast.

"Are you my relative?" he asked.

I was tongue-tied.

"Look, you have the same hair. Darker at the top and lighter at the bottom. It's rare here, hair like his. See, Sasha is surprised," Vera said.

"Would you like some good fruit juice from Germany?" I finally managed to ask the child. It was a very strange feeling to be speaking to a child in Russian. His native tongue, so natural to him, was such a trial for me. I could not say a whole sentence without making some kind of grammatical mistake.

"What is she saying, Mama? What is she speaking?"

"She's speaking Russian with an accent," Vera said. "She wants to know if you want to try the German fruit juice she brought you."

"Who is older, Sasha or Petya?" I asked him, enunciating carefully.

"Petya is older. I am four and he is five."

"But Sasha is our wild one," their mother said.

"I WANT SOME JUICE FROM GERMANY. I WANT SOME JUICE FROM GERMANY!" Sasha chanted in a voice too loud for such a little body. Soon they were both yelling in unison *"WE WANT SOME JUICE FROM GERMANY!"* It sounded like a student street riot.

"Silence!" Vera yelled, putting the baby down in his highchair and going to the sink. She brought tea cups to the table and measured two heaping spoonfuls of the pink powder into each one. The children stood in silent anticipation, eyes wide and tongues out, looking up at their mother like kittens waiting for their milk. The baby screamed his head off, legs and arms flailing the air.

She gave Petya and Sasha their cups. The children scuttled out of the kitchen and disappeared down the hall.

"Tell me, do you think it is worth it?" Vera mumbled. "To have five is pure hell. But they are my only joy in life."

"The government must be happy with you."

"Not really. They are happy with three. But after the fifth, it is 'Very nice, Comrade. But you should stop now.'"

"Why?" This contradiction did not make sense to me.

"It is unknown. Maybe because I am Orthodox they do not like me. Maybe because with that many babies it is impossible to work. There is a deficit in all . . . By profession, I am an engineer. I was an . . . in a factory of building materials. I stopped working because of the babies. Personally I do not believe in abortion. But do you know, most Russian women have four, five abortions? It is our national means of birth control. I know one woman who had seventeen. It is horrible."

"But what about other means to stop it *before?*"

"It is a cultural problem. Russians do not like it."

"I don't understand."

"Oh, it is possible to get such things. But Russians prefer abortion. It is free, it is like going to get a tooth taken out. Next day you are back at work, and the whole thing is forgotten."

"What if you became pregnant again?"

"I would have another child. It is a sin to have an abortion. But do not worry, that will never happen. My husband and I are— We have no relationship any longer."

The baby was temporarily appeased by the *Babymiks*. Vera held him sitting on her lap. Soon he began to moan and his tiny hands reached out toward the plates of food on the table. She gave him a piece of bread, then a piece of cheese, then another piece of bread.

"Tell me, do you have a Russian lover?"

"No."

"Good. Forget about Russian men. They are swine. I have five sons, and God forbid they should take after their father. A worse swine than their father does not exist."

"Maybe you can help me," I said, and began to tell her about Andrej. I told her that he had asked me to marry him, that his mother thought I was after him and had hung up on me that afternoon (I had to pantomime this), when I had tried to reach him.

"It sounds bad," she said angrily. "He only wants to marry you because you are American. He wants the privilege of being allowed to travel to the West. That is certain. What is his family name?"

"I don't know. He is a playwright. One of his plays just opened last week in Moscow. Now he has disappeared. And no one will tell me anything." I described the dress rehearsal I had seen the week before.

"*Ha!*" She slapped the table. "Andrej Sokolov. He is a bad playwright."

"I thought his play was very good."

"His themes are five years late! He is a coward. He writes about things *after* they become perfectly acceptable."

"If he wrote unacceptable plays, they would never be seen and he would be in prison."

With the baby on her hip she went to the phone and dialed a number. She spoke to someone for a few minutes, her words coming so fast that I could not understand a thing. She slammed the receiver onto the phone with a bang, and went brusquely back to her chair.

"Your Andrej is married, my dear," she said in a victorious tone, as though she'd won a bet.

"He is divorced," I said, becoming defensive.

"Yes, he is divorced, but—*I fucked your mother*—he is also married! He has a brand-new wife and a brand-new baby in Leningrad. She is a costume designer at Lenfilm. In fact, he is in Leningrad right now."

"How do you know all this?" My chair seemed to be sinking into the floor. My heart began to pound in my head.

"I just asked my friend who is an actress. Moscow is nothing but a big village filled with peasants. Everyone knows everything about everybody. You don't believe me? Ask him next time you see him."

We heard the front door open and close. An uproar followed down the hall. The little shouting voices mingled with an older, deeper voice.

"Shhhh. That is Oleg, my husband."

"He still lives with you?" I said, my lower lip drooping from all her disclosures.

"Of course. Where else should he live? He always goes to bed early. Then we will continue to talk."

13

THE HEROINE-MOTHER II

Expecting a big brute of a man to come blasting into the kitchen, I was taken aback when a tall, lanky fellow with sunken shoulders and a sunken face opened the door. He stopped short as soon as he noticed me, but composed himself quickly and greeted me with a little nod.

"Please be introduced," Vera said. "This is Oleg, my husband. This is the daughter of my father's friend Alexander Clinton Gray."

Oleg gazed at me fleetingly, nodded, and turned toward the stove. He lifted the lid of the enormous soup pot.

"Borscht?" he said.

"Of course," Vera said.

The two older boys came in behind him. The eldest resembled the father; he had the same build, the same dark red hair and victimized expression in his eyes. The younger child resembled Vera the most. He was around twelve, olive-skinned, dark-haired. His shoulders and arms were large and powerful-looking and his body moved sluggishly, as though he were just becoming accustomed to being big.

The eldest came to the table and seized the opened jar of fruit mix. "Mama, can I?"

"Of course," she said.

"I can't read it."

"It's German, not English. Here, Volodya, a person for you to practice with." She turned to me, "Volodya speaks English very well. Say something, Volodya."

Volodya stared at the floor.

"How do you do?" I said.

"I am well, thank you." Volodya had an English accent.

"Is your teacher English?" I asked slowly.

"Noo, she is a Russian lady."

"You speak very very well."

"Why, thank you soo much."

He went to the sink, filled a cup with water and brought it back. He poured at least a half-ounce of powder into it.

"Eto slishkom." That's too much.

He winked at me slyly.

The father came to the table with a bowl of borscht and sat next to me.

"So. Where are you from?"

"The United States."

"Of course, but where?"

"New York City."

He gazed at me sideways, addressing an invisible person sitting beside me. The look in his eyes reminded me of the way dogs at the pound will peer at you from behind their bars, wagging their tails wildly because they know you are their last chance. Oleg made me feel uncomfortable.

Vera was standing by the sink with her back to us, peeling potatoes. There seemed to be hundreds of them in the sink but she worked with the steady swiftness of a machine. The pot designated for the peeled ones filled up at the speed of a Charlie Chaplin movie.

"How did you find Vera?" her husband asked, looking down at the soup.

I was suddenly surprised that Vera had not asked me this herself. Was Vera pleased to see me? It seemed she was. I still did not feel justified in breaking that unwritten Soviet rule: never talk about one set of friends with another. No one trusted anyone outside the unit.

"From a friend of a friend of mine. An old man who was also in the war and knew Vera's father."

"Ah," he said, nodding, and left it at that.

"Do you know that I was born in jail?" Vera said loudly, turning only her head away from her work. Oleg blushed crimson.

"Yes, for some reason they arrested my mother too, in 1947. But she was pregnant so they did not send her to Siberia with my father. My sister, who was only fifteen, bought my life for a bottle of vodka. She sneaked it in under her dress and gave it to the guard. Otherwise they would have taken me away and raised me in a good Communist orphanage." She laughed and slammed the pot of potatoes onto the stove. "And now I would most probably be an outstanding Party member instead of a mat'-geroinya."

The children came and went. The first jar of fruit mix was finished by dinnertime, and Vera hid the other three high up in one of the cabinets. The two eldest picked at the plates of food she'd put out for them, the younger two scrambled in and out from under the table, pinching and punching my legs and howling with laughter. They brought me all their toys to inspect. There were fire engines, little cars, bouncing balls, plastic clowns, plastic puzzles. I ooh'ed and ah'ed in admiration of each new toy. The baby sat, naked from the waist down, on his father's lap. He was a fat, pink baby with cellulite on his legs and an expression of constant apprehension on his face. At first I did not understand this look. Then I noticed that whenever Oleg was not paying attention, Sasha the lion pinched or bit the baby's hands and feet. The baby howled, but Sasha managed to slither away unnoticed.

The children's dinner of boiled potatoes and hot dogs was served while they watched a television program entitled *Good Night, Youth* on the big TV that stood on a shelf across from the table. It was a cartoon, with flowers and blades of grass singing happily while the birds build nests with the help of the bunnies and beavers. Then the birds help to collect important supplies for the bunnies' and beavers' winter living. At the end the flowers and the blades of grass go to sleep, the birds fly south while the bunnies and beavers wave goodbye.

After the program ended there was much screaming and crying;

Sasha took away Petya's toys, the eldest tried to interfere and was punched in the stomach. He left the kitchen, outraged, refusing to eat. Kolya, the one who most resembled their mother, went after him. The baby defecated all over his father's lap. Oleg stood up with a look of calm acceptance on his face, apologized, and placing one hand under the baby's bottom, carried screaming Seryozha away. Both father and baby disappeared into the bathroom for a while.

As bedtime approached, the screaming and running around crescendoed to a feverish pitch, and it took both parents and Volodya, the eldest, an hour to quiet the others enough to get them into their pajamas. The three little ones slept in the first room down the hall. It was a large, square room, with yellowing wallpaper, torn in spots. There was one closet and a Soviet-made stereo, a double bed against one wall, a single against another, and a crib by the door. The large windows in the far wall looked out on—of all things—an Intourist hotel. A blue sign blinked РЕСТОРАН, restaurant, all night long.

Sasha and Petya were corralled into their bedroom and the trouble continued. While one was being tucked in, the other would get up and charge out of the room. When that one was finally cornered by the father and carried in howling, the other would start jumping up and down on the bed. Meanwhile the baby stood in his crib, gripping the railing, and howled. I offered to help but was finally told to go sit in the kitchen: my presence was agitating them.

I sat in complete bewilderment and stared at the TV screen without understanding a word that was said. I thought: a man so gentle and helpful who obviously loves his kids, she calls a swine? To me she seemed fortunate. One thing I felt instinctively about Russians was that they were more like the French than like the Americans in the way they approached relationships: personal questions were never asked when you first met someone, not even "what do you do for a living?" Information of that kind was only offered, and it was not my position to ask questions.

I tried to concentrate on the television. It was a news program of some kind. Kolya came in and sat with me. He was in tattered pajamas,

too tight around his shoulders and waist. His slippers were three sizes
too big for him.

"That is New York," he said, pointing at the screen. It was a shot of
the subway stop at Broadway and Ninety-sixth Street.

"Yes. I live near there."

"Look at the *bezdomniy,*" Kolya said. The homeless person was
digging into an aluminum garbage pail, pulling out soda cans. He took
a sip out of one of the cans, tilting it upside down.

"*Oy!*" I said.

The camera moved into the subway, where two black men in tattered clothes and woolen caps were interviewed.

"Look, their clothes are like my pajama," Kolya said.

The voice-over was in Russian. I couldn't understand a word of
what was said because I kept hearing the English syllables beneath the
Russian.

"They sleep in the metro," Kolya said.

"Yes," I said. What was I supposed to say? "It is one of the biggest
problems of New York."

"Why?"

"I don't know why."

"They say at school that we don't have those people here, but Mama
says that's not true. Here they put them in prison so no one will see
them."

"You must not say to your teacher at school what your mama tells
you at home."

"Of course not. I am not crazy." Kolya looked at me with his
heavy-lidded, slightly bulging eyes, which had the same dark half-
moons below them as his mother's. Their expression seemed to indicate
that in his opinion, I was either completely naive, or completely stupid.

"How many to you are there years?" I asked.

"How many to *you?*"

"To me there are twenty-five years," I said.

"And to me there are only eleven. When to me there will be
twenty-five, to you there will be . . ." He counted under his breath,
looking at me.

"Thirty-nine," I offered.

"To Mama there are thirty-nine now. You will be too old for me to marry," he said dejectedly.

Vera came in and quietly shut the door behind her.

"*Kolya!*" she said in a loud whisper. "To bed immediately!"

"Will we see you again?" he asked.

"I hope so very much," I said.

Kolya got up lazily, his big shoulders drooping, and ambled out of kitchen.

"Oleg is sitting with the little ones," she said. "Every night it's the same. He sits with them, and when they fall asleep, he goes to his room and falls asleep himself."

"Where do you sleep?"

"With the little ones. My mother lived with us for many years. She had a room to herself at the end of the hall. After the birth of Seryozha we gained the right to have the apartment to ourselves. But she never moved to her own place, she died less than six months ago, just as her application to move was approved. Now Oleg sleeps in there. For a while he slept here, on this couch."

The couch against the wall, behind the table, was all of four feet long.

"How could that be? This couch is too small for a man his size," I said.

"He likes pain. He slept in his work clothes and in the morning he changed before going back to work. Every day like that, for more than eight months."

I stared at her, shaking my head.

"Russians are strange, yes? Mine is a particularly miserable . . ."

"He seems so nice. *Sladkiy,*" I said, meaning sweet, as in sugar. I did not know any other word to express this.

"I tell you he is a swine. I would divorce but with five children it is very difficult."

A question which in fact bothered me: why the five children—especially the newest—if everything were indeed so bad?

As though she were reading my mind, she said, "Sometime I will explain everything. But not now." She brought an index finger to her lips.

"I have one photo of our fathers together, would you like to see it?"

"Of course, with great pleasure!"

"And I have one letter—God only knows how it got through. It was sent to my mother in 1956, from France." She left the room for a few minutes and came back carrying a shoebox filled with pictures and yellowing pieces of paper. She rifled through the contents, pulling out a picture now and then and showing it to me. The first was of herself as a child—"I was a real street kid. I had to fight all the time because the other kids called me jailbird. That's why I'm so strong-willed. Look at Kolya, he has my build exactly. And my gentle nature, which has been destroyed by too much anger. I hope that will not happen to him."

She took out a picture and gazed at it with admiration.

"And this is my sister—she had a different father—who bought my life for a bottle of vodka. Of course, this is just a few years ago."

The picture was in color. Her sister had dyed blond hair piled high on her head, and an incredible amount of makeup around her eyes and mouth. She looked hard as a brick.

Vera pulled out a few more pictures, stared at them, and put them in the bottom of the box.

"We will look at those another time," she said sullenly. "Ah, here it is."

She handed me a yellowing black-and-white photo of two men standing close together under a blooming cherry tree. One of them was on crutches.

"That's my papa!" I shouted, jumping from my seat. "He had an . . . an . . ."

"Accident?"

"Yes. He fell off a tram."

My father was a head taller than the other man. His hair was cut very short, which was strange because all my life his hair had been long, down past his collar, and his eyebrows, which I always remembered as thick and gray, were black, like two grubs above his eyes. His expression was the same however: chin jutting defiantly while his mouth curved up just the slightest bit, as though he were smiling at some private joke. Vera's father, Gavrilov, seemed protective. His arm was wrapped proudly around my father's shoulders, as though he were presenting him for an award. His smile was broad, open, and kind.

"My mama, God rest her soul, told me they were completely wild together. Your father took my father to places he was not allowed to go—restaurants and so on. And my father took your father to places Americans were not allowed. They thought they were being smart. You know, before the war there were the purges. It was a time as bad as we ever had here. Then, the war brought new literature, new freedoms. People needed God and love of the homeland and history and poetry to go on fighting. After the war Stalin refused us those same freedoms, and many, many people who had taken advantage of them were sent to jail."

Tears were streaming down my cheeks.

"It is not anyone's fault," she said slowly. "It is the system that is to blame. It is a system based on deceit and lies. For seventy years they have been telling us it will get better, Comrades, it will get better. But nothing ever changes. It is not your father's fault my father died in Siberia. It is the fault of Stalin and the sons-of-bitches who worked for him."

"Yes," was all I could manage to say.

"You see—they were friends, and now we will be friends." She opened the bottle of vodka because we had finished the red wine.

"Here—to them," she said, holding her glass aloft. We drank. She refilled the thin-stemmed glasses.

"My papa—he had trouble back home after the war," I said. "He was a professor of Soviet History and Journalism at a university. It was known that he was not a Communist, though he wrote good things about the Soviet Army during the war. But there was a great fear of Communism in America.

"And there should have been! And there still should be!" Vera interrupted, slamming her fist against the table.

"I don't agree with you," I said.

"You don't agree? What, are you Communist!"

"No, no. I believe in understanding each other. Not fighting. That's all. In 1954 they asked my papa to come before a committee and prove that he was not a supporter of the Communists, but he refused, on principle, because he supported the right of each person to believe what he wants. There is a part of our Constitution that says a man is allowed to say and think and write what he believes. My father knew this committee was trying to take away that right."

"So they sent him to jail?"

"No. He lost his job at the university and went to France before anything more could happen."

"Incredible. Here they shoot you for that."

Vera slid her fingers into an envelope and brought out a sheet of paper. In the center at the top were my father's initials. The handwriting was unknown to me, the letter written in a careful Cyrillic script. The only letters of my father's that I had seen were written either on a typewriter or in block letters. A strange, uncomfortable jealousy pinched my heart.

"He wrote this to my mama," Vera said. "You know, he could have come back, after 1960. He never did."

"He married my mother, and then I was born."

I had trouble deciphering the script. I had to ask Vera to explain certain words, to read other ones aloud to me.

20/X/56

My Dear Natasha,

For the past few days I have been wild with grief and horror. A French newspaper included your husband's name in a list of "recently rehabilitated" artists—I had no idea anything so terrible had happened! I have lived the past ten years with the belief and the hope that great men such as your husband would continue to bring change and honor to your brave, young country. Since the doors of a cold peace were closed on our friendship ten years ago, I have not lived a day without thinking of you.

When I was denied a tourist visa several years ago, I believed that it was simply a question of politics. Now it seems I was completely wrong. I imagine the worst things and have nightmares. I wake up covered in sweat at the thought of your husband's suffering. I fear I am to blame and there is nothing I can do.

I only hope that my other close friend did not suffer because of me as your husband has. I pray she has found a happy life, as I pray you have.

I am constantly reminded of the absurdity of this world when the newspapers speak of the possibility of another World War.

My heart is forever with you,
Sasha

My heart was slamming against my ribs like a bird trying to escape from a cage. I drained my glass and poured myself another drink. A puddle formed at the base of the glass.

"Who is the other close friend?" I asked Vera.

She looked at me, sipping her vodka slowly.

"I do not know," she finally said.

"You do not know? Swear to me."

"Your papa never talked about it?"

"Never. He said everything was better left alone. Please, Vera. Who is she? Is she alive?"

"I think she is dead."

"Can you find out?"

"I can. But your papa himself said such things are better left alone."

"I don't care. I must find out."

PART TWO

PART TWO

14

A VISIT
WITH RITA

"What am I doing here?"

Phil Chase had just shaken me awake and was peering down at me with a concerned expression. As I stared at him from my groggy alcoholic stupor, I remembered that just yesterday I had vowed never to sleep with him again. We had been sharing his single bed every night for the past week and a half. Since I'd met Vera a week ago, I had spent most of my evenings sitting in her warm kitchen surrounded by her noisy children. It was a haven for me, a place in which I could temporarily ignore the thoughts that were bothering me. Phil and I spent the hours of midnight to eight together, but he insisted on keeping his life outside the Institute separate from his love affair with me. I had not met a single one of his Soviet friends and he had not met mine. I never brought this up because I did not want to argue with him. Therefore we had an immensely affectionate, erotic sex life backed by nothing. At night I believed he was in love with me; in the morning I felt like a complete stranger and awakened depressed and lonely.

Why did I do this to myself? I couldn't answer that question, so, finally, I had promised myself to stop. But as I had sat in the safety of Vera's kitchen and the midnight curfew had approached, my resolve had weakened with each shot of vodka, until, by the time my taxi pulled up in front of the Institute, it had completely dissolved.

"You've got class in a half an hour," Phil said. "Got a little trashed last night, I gather. Came in here crying your head off. You said a lot of strange things and then you passed out right on top of me. You're heavy, you know that?"

I sat up, my head spinning wildly, and noticed that I had slept in my clothes. The alcohol I had consumed at Vera's was emanating from my pores like a noxious gas.

"I'm sorry," I said.

"No problem," Phil said. "Were you with your friend again—the one with all the kids?"

"I sure was."

"I gather she's a great booze hound, like us. I'd like to meet her some time."

"That's a change of tune. Okay, the next time I go, you're coming with me, or I'm not sleeping with you anymore. I've had enough of this."

"That's what you said last night."

I had gotten drunk entirely on purpose. I had wanted to build a roadblock in my mind so that no further convoys of frightening emotions could pass through. I had been thinking about Phil and how much better life would be if he were sitting next to me at Vera's table, sharing the vodka with us and playing with her kids. Then suddenly Vera informed me in an offhand manner that my father's "other close friend" was still alive. Vera's sister had told her that the woman was not only alive, but in Moscow. There was a phone number, but Vera did not particularly want to give it to me. I became frightened because this woman's very existence was another of the things I wanted desperately to avoid. The reality of her was a slap in the face.

"I don't know this woman," Vera said guiltily. She began to hand me a little slip of paper, and then pulled back. "I don't know what kind of relationship she had with your father. But don't tell her that you got her telephone number from me."

"Of course not," I said, reaching for the paper with a trembling hand. Vera crossed her arms and hid the paper against her chest. I tried another tack. I put my palm up, like a beggar, the back of my hand pressed against the table so that she would not see that I was shaking. "Please," I said.

She finally gave it to me and I felt completely alone, abandoned and betrayed not only by Phil, but also by my father. I was jealous of Phil's Soviet friends, whom he kept from me like a man would keep his wife from his mistress; I was jealous of this unknown woman, the "other great friend" of my father's letter. She had known him before my mother or I had even been a thought in his head. Jealousy had always affected me like the flu. Now my stomach became upset and I could not eat the dinner Vera had prepared. All my muscles ached from a pain that started somewhere near the heart.

"I couldn't stand to see you cry like that," Phil said. He ran his hand lightly through my hair. "We'll start doing more things together. I promise you. All right?"

"All right."

He kissed me, trying to pry my mouth open with his tongue, but I pushed him away, embarrassed by my breath.

I went back to my room, took a cold shower, and dressed for class. Even after brushing my teeth and dabbing on cologne I smelled like vodka. This was not going to be an easy day.

In first *para,* I sat next to Edmund Byrnes, the only person I trusted in my group because he was as lazy as I and didn't take the classes too seriously. Just a few days before, Edmund had cornered me in the hall, sworn me to secrecy, and asked me the odds of impregnation when a condom broke in the middle of a girl's cycle. His breath had been as bad as mine was today, and his poor eyes had beseeched me to reassure him.

"Pretty good, I would imagine," I had said.

"*Fuck!* She gave me this Soviet-made rubber, you know. Well it's just like everything else they make—unreliable. What am I going to do now?"

"Wait and see. When was her last period, do you know?"

"Like ten days ago." He was a tall fellow with dirty, curly blond hair and a pale and serious Germanic face.

"You'd better get some American condoms," I had suggested.

"How?"

"At the embassy clinic. Or ask someone. I know lots of people brought them."

"What do *you* use, if you don't mind my asking?"

"I'm on the pill. I can't help you there, Edmund. Sorry."

I was drunk through this first para, which was our grammatika class. The teacher was explaining the different forms of the verb "to look." When you added any one of your basic prefixes to *smotret'* you got just about anything you wanted: to glance at, to look carefully, to look over, to look through, to observe, to look around. . . . And of course there was the problem of tense—you could do all these things repeatedly, or just once, or just once while you were in the process of doing something else. I didn't give a damn about any of it, but kept my head buried in my notebook and wrote furiously for an hour and a half.

By second para I was merely tipsy. We looked at slides of the Tretyakov Gallery, which was fortunate because the paintings were fascinating, the room was dark, and I didn't have to talk. By lunchtime I was sober and sick as a dog. Since the only sensible thing to do was eat, I went to the cafeteria and ate three lunches (on a hangover my belly was a bottomless pit). I had kasha with thin strips of meat in a brown sauce, potatoes with thin strips of meat in a brown sauce, and rice with thin strips of meat in a brown sauce.

Fortunately the last para of the day was the lecture course on Soviet History, the one we had nicknamed "The World According to Lenin," so I was able to relax in the back of the auditorium and write a letter to my mother.

When the bell finally rang, I made it up the stairs without too much trouble, gripping the railing and pulling my weight up behind me. Other Institute denizens stampeded past me like a colorful herd of mountain goats.

My mind was set on one thought: bed. I planned to sleep until the next day. I stopped by the dezhurnaya's desk to check for mail—none of us had received anything yet, neither through the embassy pouch nor the Soviet mail. And once again, sadly, there were no letters waiting for me. Meanwhile I was writing three or four letters a day, including to people I hadn't spoken to in months who didn't even know I was away in Russia. It helped me feel connected to home.

The dezhurnaya looked up from her knitting, handed me a little folded piece of paper and said, *"Dievushka,* there was a phone call for you." I unfolded the paper and read "Call Rita Abramovna as soon as possible." Her work number was scribbled below. I stood with my mouth hanging open while the dezhurnaya smiled at me complacently, as though taking phone messages for American students was a normal occurrence.

"Thank you," I said, and went to my room to get my coat.

It had only been three days since my last visit with Rita and her relatives. I had been seeing them about once a week, but phoned every few days to keep them informed of my activities and progress so that they wouldn't feel forgotten. But it seemed obligation had a completely different meaning to Russians than it did to us, and every time I refused an invitation to visit Rita, she shrieked with dismay into the phone. It was becoming more and more difficult to call her.

Rita apparently felt that it was my obligation to spend more of my time with her and her relatives. Andrej had felt the same way until he disappeared—I should have room in my life only for him. And *he* had a lot of nerve, considering what I now knew. And even Vera, whom I had been seeing more than anyone, had insisted just last night that I come back to see her today. She had been offended when I'd said I had to stay home and study. It was inconceivable to any of them that I might have more than one group of friends or other obligations, including my life at the Institute. They were completely unreasonable, like young siblings vying for parental attention. The pressure this put me under was thoroughly exhausting.

Huffing my way up the icy slant of the Institute hill, I decided not to walk all the way to the booth at the end of the street. In defiance of everything our counselors had told us, I called from the one that was just across the street and supposedly tapped. If Rita could phone the Institute *and leave her phone number,* why should I knock myself out hiking a half a mile in the snow to call her back? I was feeling sorry for myself and my head hurt. My obligation to call Rita back was interfering with my privacy, and adding to my misery.

I dialed the number begrudgingly, ramming my middle finger into the little metal holes and following them around to the finger-stop, where it would invariably get pinched and stuck.

"*Clintonotchka!*" Rita shouted into the phone. Her voice was as loud and as high-pitched as Vera's little children's formidable screeches of indignation. "*Where did you disappear to? You promised to call yesterday and you forgot!*"

"I did not forget, Rita. I had a very important day yesterday. I told you, I have met a person whose father knew my father." I spoke slowly, in a soft, quiet voice, hoping to influence her to lower her own.

"*What is her name?*"

"I cannot say here."

"*We were worried about you, little soul!*"

"Rita, you must never phone the Institute. It is very bad for you."

"*Nonsense. I spoke to the director of the dormitory, who took the trouble to look through all the lists of American students to find your room number, then connected me to the floor dezhurnaya, who was very kind as well.*"

"I am speaking seriously, Rita. We were told many, many times at the orientation that they certainly watch us and listen to us."

"*Never mind!*"

"Rita, please don't scream. I cannot understand what you are saying."

She lowered her voice a tad, but not the pitch. "I am an old lady and it is not a problem, I promise you."

"But it could become a problem for *me.*"

She was silent for a moment, and then proceeded in a completely different, lighthearted tone. "Well—it doesn't matter. I have tickets for you for the Moyseev Ballet tonight."

Now a black cloud descended on me. I was going to have to trek out to her place all the way on the other side of the city to get the tickets, kill a few hours somewhere, and then trek on to the theater, which was probably near the center. That meant two bus rides and a forty-five minute metro commute at rush hour just to get to Rita's. I really was not physically up to this. "I think I am getting sick," I lied. "I am very tired and I must rest."

"You cannot be sick today, this is the Moyseev Ballet! *You must come here immediately to get these tickets!"*

"I am feeling very badly, Rita. I cannot go all the way to your house and then to the ballet. Not today."

"I went through much trouble," she said woefully, her voice finally dropping three decibels. I had mortally insulted her once again.

"I am sorry," I said. "I have been very, very busy and am completely—completely—without strength."

"And where have you spent all these nights?" Rita asked in a grief-stricken tone.

"I told you, I have met a person who knows about my father," I said.

"What person?" she asked.

I said nothing.

"What is their family name?"

My heart began to pound in my throat and temples. Something seemed terribly wrong. Phil Chase, who had been to Russia twice before, had been the one to warn me about the unwritten law: never mention one Soviet friend's family name to another. Soviets operated within family units—they called each other sister and brother even when they were not related—and anyone outside the nucleus was considered a potential informer.

I had already told Rita all about Andrej, his mother and his sister, and about Boris Mikhailovich and his strange family. Although I had not mentioned their last names, she had recognized them immediately. They were famous. Their fame eased my dismay: fame was a protective cloak.

But why was she asking me about Vera? Pure curiosity? Some kind of parental concern? Over the phone?

"I don't know any family names," I finally said.

"Ha ha ha! Well you must find out their family name. *It is obligatory.* When you tell me I will find out for you who they are."

I turned my eyes away from the telephone box as though averting them from Rita's gaze. Outside the booth three teenagers, a boy and two girls, were approaching carrying cross-country skis on their shoulders. The boy was telling a joke. He guffawed and slapped the prettier, taller girl between the shoulder blades. She slapped him back without cracking a smile. The other girl was laughing but the boy ignored her. They passed by oblivious to me and my anxiety, and I watched their backs heading down the hill toward the birch forest.

"It is not your business, Rita. It is my business." I attempted to sound distant, displeased. Russians often said Americans spoke atonally, without emotional connotation—well, I tried at least to sound firm.

"Will you come to us tomorrow then?" she said, as though she had not heard me.

"Yes," I said. "I will come tomorrow, after classes."

"*Nu, ladno.* It is a great pity about the Moyseev Ballet."

"I am sorry."

"Until tomorrow, then," Rita said.

I headed back down the hill toward the Institute, remembering something Vera had said to me just a few days before: *Don't be fooled by some nice old lady who tells you she worked on Lend-Lease and doesn't add that she spent five years in jail after the war; she is an informer. I fucked your mother, I know what I'm talking about.*

I knew that the Russians were alarmists and liked to exaggerate, but now I had something else unpleasant to think about.

The next afternoon I was in a much healthier state of mind, and the interminable trek to Rita's side of the city did not seem a bother at all. It gave me time alone to think. Rita and her relatives had shown me such kindness and hospitality the first week, but I was beginning to see their generosity in a different light.

One of the points our orientation leaders had made over and over again was that some Soviets might befriend us in order to get their hands on Western goods. At the time I had believed this warning to be pure anti-Soviet propaganda, but then Phil had warned me of the aphrodisiacal qualities of an American passport and I noticed a strange phenomenon around the Institute. Fantastically unattractive girls like

Ceppie's roommate, Elsa, were having wild, passionate love affairs with tall, handsome (if a tad sleazy) Soviet men. Late at night these couples necked in the shadows, beneath trees or in dark corners away from the Institute's lights. Interestingly, these men were so westernized you could not tell they were Soviet. They wore jeans and down jackets and moon boots and sported Walkman earphones under their ski hats. I had to ask myself: are they really in love with the unattractive girls, or are they in love with the West?

I enjoyed bringing vodka, wine, chocolates, and powdered fruit mix to Vera and her children. It was a token of my appreciation. I had brought Rita and her cousin Anna baubles from America as well, but every time I had been to her apartment Rita had acted dissatisfied, and had asked me for something else, something more. Once I was wearing a pair of antique glass earrings I had bought at a flea market in New York City and Rita, reaching under my hair and fiddling with them, had asked me straight out if I would give them to her. I considered for a moment, and then said that I would give them to her before I left Russia. Until then, I wanted to keep them. She nodded slowly as her eyes glazed over, as though counting the number of weeks until my departure.

Another time she asked me if I had any cassettes of Western music I might want to part with. And then, on my most recent visit, a strange scene had taken place.

Rita's cousin in New York had given me fifty dollars to buy Rita a gift in a Beriozka store. I had not known how to approach the subject up until then because it was not a large sum of money and I was afraid of insulting her. As always, her cousin Anna and Anna's husband Igor ate dinner with us, and I was embarrassed to bring it up in front of them. But during dinner Rita asked me if I had a Walkman. When I responded that I did, she asked if I would sell it to her. I told her it was not mine, I had borrowed it from a friend, which was the truth. In an offhand manner, hoping to appease her, I brought up the money.

"Your cousin Sarah in New York gave me a little money to buy you a gift in the Beriozka store. If there is anything you want—"

"How much?"

"Fifty dollars."

"Fifty dollars!" She stepped away from the table, fork in hand, and spit over her right shoulder. *"What can you buy in the Beriozka for fifty dollars? Nichevo!"* Nothing, she shouted, and stomped out of the room. Anna, Igor, and I sat in silence a moment, and then Igor asked me about my classes. Their faces registered no change whatsoever. We could hear Rita fussing around in the kitchen down the hall, as dishes rattled in the sink and cupboards opened and closed. Two minutes later she came back completely calm and smiling, a bottle of Georgian wine in her hand.

"Never mind," she said in a tiny angelic voice. "We shall discuss that matter another time. Now we will eat and have a wonderful time. Clintonotchka, your Russian has already gotten so much better! Isn't that so, Anya?"

I had not known what to make of this.

I rang the bell. Rita opened the door and said in her incredibly powerful, childlike voice, *"You are a very bad girl."* She shook a finger an inch from my nose. *"It's not every day that a person gets tickets to the Moyseev Ballet."*

"I am sorry," I said glumly. I wanted to say, *I never asked you to get me tickets—why are you trying to control my life?*

My father used to tell me that a person would impose guilt on another as a means of control. It was another form of imprisonment. My parents had tried to keep me guilt-free but the Portuguese nanny who had been responsible for me when they were not around had made up for their lack of pressure tenfold. Consequently, I had terrible attacks of guilt coupled with even worse attacks of anger because I understood that I was being manipulated.

At that very moment I was suffused with guilt for having gotten so stinking drunk with Vera that I could not function well enough to take Rita's tickets and go to the ballet.

"Take off your coat," she said, her hands already on my buttons. "This is a funny-looking coat, ha ha ha! Very warm?"

"Yes. Almost too warm," I said.

"How much costs a coat like this?"

"It was a gift from my aunt. I do not know but probably around two hundred dollars. It is the nicest present my aunt ever gave me."

"Ah," she said. She grabbed a pair of slippers inside a cabinet by the door and slid them in front of my feet.

Five minutes later Anna and Igor arrived, already in their slippers. Anna was as usual very stylishly dressed, in a purple wool dress with matching amethyst earrings and a necklace. Igor was pale and seemed exhausted. His face had taken on a grayish hue, and his eyes and cheeks were sunken.

"How do you feel, Igor?" I asked.

"I have not been sleeping well."

"His blood pressure is very high," Anna said in a worried voice.

"In America the doctors say that for blood pressure it is important to eat a certain way."

"What do you mean?" Igor said.

"You must try to eat more vegetables, and rice, and foods that are not fried. Eggs and meats are not very good."

"Here it is difficult to cook like that," Anna said. "Can you make me a list of foods that are not good for him?"

"Certainly."

Rita's apartment was quite big though not as lavishly decorated as Anna and Igor's. There was a living room/dining room with one couch, a big closet, a cupboard, a large TV set on a little table, and a dining table and chairs. There was a bedroom at the end of the hall, and next to it was the kitchen. There was not a single bookshelf or book in sight, which did not mean she had no books; they simply were not displayed. We sat at the table, which had been set for dinner, and I wrote out a list of foods that had a high cholesterol content. Unfortunately, all these foods were staples of the Russian diet. Russians could not survive without their fried meats, fried potatoes, fried meat and cabbage pies. Pastries and breads were crucial, and they added butter to everything. As I was writing, Rita brought in dinner—halved potatoes baked with a slice of bacon on top, and some kind of meat lying in a pool of thick sauce. Igor's face brightened considerably at the sight of the food. He lifted his knife and fork even before the food had reached the table.

"Try to eat less salt, and more fruits and vegetables," I said, dismayed. "You must try to boil and steam things more. No oil."

"Igor eats one apple or one orange a day," Anna said hopefully. There was deep concern in her large brown eyes. I felt terrible for having brought up the subject at all. I was amazed that they knew nothing about diet, that a doctor had not told them. It was probably useless in any case, because of the erratic supply of certain foods.

I changed the subject. "I brought you a little gift." I went to my bag, which I'd left out in the hall, and came back with two one-ounce vials of Opium perfume that I'd bought at the duty-free shop on the airplane. This was, in a sense, an apology for missing the ballet.

"Oh, how nice!" Anna said. "Thank you." Rita had gone back to the kitchen. When she heard Anna's exclamations her little feet pattered furiously down the hall toward us.

"Thank you," Rita said, lifting the vial and inspecting it. Her eyelids were large and of a brownish hue; they hung low over her eyes giving her a sleepy, longing expression. The look in them now was more forlorn than usual. The perfume had not compensated for the tickets.

We ate in silence, almost as though eating were so important that it should not be interrupted by idle chatter. When she had finished, Rita said, "We must go together to the Mezhdunarodny Tsentr and find something to buy with the fifty dollars."

This was the fanciest hotel in Moscow, built by Armand Hammer and used rather exclusively for conferences and special business missions. It was said that they asked for a hotel pass at the door, and many American students from the Institute had already tried to get in and had been turned away. I had gone there with Phil one afternoon. We got dressed up, acted as though we owned the place, and marched right past the guards. The Art Deco interior was something to behold. I felt as though I had been beamed Star Trek-style from gray Moscow to a Hyatt Regency hotel, crossed with a modern, suburban American mall. Canned muzak wafted in through invisible speakers while the glass

elevators went up and down inside the lobby. There were plants growing everywhere. There was an expensive Japanese restaurant, a German
restaurant, a bar, and a little café in the lobby. There was a food
Beriozka, a jewelry store, a bookstore, and several clothes stores where
you could buy the latest Western fashions. The "drugstore" section of
the clothes store sold Western deodorant, and had the best selection of
French perfumes in the city. All these goodies could only, of course, be
purchased with hard currency.

Most importantly—our orientation leaders had harped on this fact
as well—the ordinary Soviet citizen is categorically forbidden to enter
the hotel. We spotted a few Soviet diplomats and their wives, some
tourists, but no ordinary Russians. The penalty for bringing a Russian
in is severe: the tourist may be expelled from the country; the Russian
may lose his apartment and his job.

"No," I said with finality. "You tell me what you need and I will go
buy it alone."

"How can I know that when I don't know what is in the stores?"

"I will go there and look and then tell you."

She stared at me with her woeful eyes a long time and said nothing.
"The last time Sarah sent somebody to see us we went into the *tsentr*.
She was a diplomat. No one said a word to us."

"A diplomat has diplomatic . . . diplomatic . . . a diplomatic
passport. They can do whatever they like. I am a student. It is different."

"You are an American citizen, *They will do nothing to you,*" she
shouted.

"I don't care, I won't go with you to the *tsentr*," I said. I spoke
slowly and calmly and stared at her angrily to enforce my point.

"I am a poor woman," she said after another long silence. "I have
nothing in life. I need a winter coat."

"But I looked in a Beriozka yesterday—"

"Which one?"

"In the hotel near where I live. A jacket made of . . . made of
. . . not natural material costs more than fifty dollars. I cannot buy

you a coat. But a nice sweater or dress I can buy you. And," I added, "if it is more than fifty dollars I will pay myself."

"How much more can you pay?"

"I am poor as well. I am a student and I have a stipend and a mother who helps me out but I do not have enough money to buy you a coat." I could not believe the anger in my own voice, but none of them seemed to notice. Rita pulled her chair around from the head of the table so that it was right next to mine. She leaned against me, her hand gripping my forearm. Her breath was sour against my face. I tried to put some distance between us but she would not let go of my arm and only moved her mouth closer to my face the more I tried to back away. I felt extremely uncomfortable, and embarrassed by my discomfort. My face, I knew, was flushed—but Rita did not seem to see this at all.

"We will take care of you here. *You need not spend any dollars on anything at all. Do not buy anything in the Beriozky.* Igor will get you everything—vodka or wine or anything and you can save your dollars."

She must be crazy, I thought. Every time I want to visit someone I should let them know in advance so that they can supply me with wine and vodka? It was absurd.

"There are things in the Beriozka I get for my friends which you cannot get," I said.

"Like what?" Rita said, defensive now.

"Fruit powder with vitamins for my friend's children."

She fell silent. Her mouth puckered up and I was afraid she would begin to cry.

"That's enough, Rita," Igor said. "Stop yelling in the child's ear." More gently, he addressed me. "There's no need for you to spend dollars. What for? It is pure robbery."

I decided there was no point in arguing with them and gave up. I did not say another word about it.

In a lighter voice, Rita said, "But tell us again about Boris Mikhailovich's apartment."

"Beautiful," I said. "He has all Western things. A beautiful typing machine, a Sony television, a dishwasher in the kitchen . . ."

"See," Rita said to Anna. "And it is all through the government. Good Communists are rewarded for their good deeds."

"Rita . . ." I finally said, "I can give you the fifty dollars and you yourself can decide what to do with it—"

"*Nyet!*" she said, putting up her hand with her palm facing me. "*Never! I* am a good Communist, a Party member. I hold a medal for being one of the greatest food inspectors in the Soviet Union. It is against the law to take dollars! I don't even want to *see* dollars. Dollars are the poison of the Capitalist West!"

I couldn't believe I had heard her correctly and sat there staring at her heated face while a stupid smile distorted my own.

"However," Igor said, leaning forward—he was dipping a halved potato in the meat gravy and smacking his lips as he spoke—"we are having a terrible shortage of . . . coffee in Moscow."

"What is that?" I asked.

"Coffee in the jar, you know. Not the beans. We can get the beans, no problem. I will give you fifty rubles to buy me as much coffee as you can buy in the Beriozka for that amount." His lips parted into a wide smile, exposing his glinting gold teeth.

"Maybe someone in your group wants to sell their winter coat. You will not sell yours?" Rita put in.

"*Nyet.* I already told you it was a gift and my aunt will be angry."

"*Nu, ladno.* Soon, on a Sunday we will take you to a very nice restaurant and we will dance and have a very nice time. You can bring a friend—another student, if you like. Isn't that right, Igor?"

"Certainly," Igor said.

After dinner we watched a movie about World War Two in which a platoon of foot soldiers held off an armored unit by gripping detonated grenades against their chests and throwing themselves beneath the tanks. Igor walked out of the room on several occasions. Anna told me it was because he was a veteran and such movies reminded him too much of his own experience.

I left them at eleven. Rita insisted on giving me five rubles for a taxi (it cost ten to get home from where she lived). She accompanied me downstairs and we stood beyond the four-foot snow bank out in the street and tried to hail a cab for ten minutes.

"We will be your family in Moscow," she said, kissing me goodnight. Her breath formed a damp cloud around my face. "Do not worry about anything."

I was so completely exhausted I nodded off in the cab. *Do not worry about anything.* These words rang in my ears and I awoke with a start. The streetlights and house lights and red and blue and white neon signs flew past in my peripheral vision. I had lost all sense of direction, felt dizzy, and closed my eyes again. I was reminded of the merry-go-rounds and rollercoaster rides of my childhood: you're flipped upside down and thrown from side to side and you laugh and scream from nerves and fear because you've temporarily allowed strangers to take control of your life.

15

IN
THE
BIRCH
FOREST

I had carefully copied the name and phone number of the woman who had known my father during the war into my little black booklet. This booklet contained all my contacts' numbers, my appointments, and homework assignments. Although I kept all the dangerous information coded, the booklet never left my side. I carried it around in my bag all through the day and slept with my bag next to the bed at night. I saw the booklet a thousand times a day, and was incessantly assailed by pangs of guilt—time was running out. I scolded myself for not calling the woman, but every day I found a new reason not to.

Today's excuse was that Phil Chase had invited me to go to the movies. Just beyond our birch forest was a movie theater which was showing the hottest film in town, *Pokayanye* (I looked this word up in my pocket dictionary; it meant "repentance"), which was a film about the horrors of Stalin's dictatorship.

This was a good excuse, because every Russian I'd met had insisted that seeing this film was "obligatory" and at that time it was extremely difficult to get tickets. Phil had done the only intelligent thing, which was to stand in line and buy tickets for the next day.

A series of iced-over steps led to a terrace about twenty meters back from the frozen sidewalk, on which stood the large, one-storey theater building. It had a flat roof which slanted toward the back. There were no glittering neon signs inviting you to the movies, but there were a few color posters pasted out front on billboards announcing the present and coming attractions. The front was all glass and to the left you could see the long ticket line, which did not seem to be moving at all. There were two booths, one for today's showings, one for tomorrow's, and the queue for tomorrow was indeed shorter.

We went in through the glass doors and gave our tickets to a very small, very fat woman who was so suspicious she inspected each ticket by bringing it up to her nose and squinting at it a long while. The slate floor was muddy, the walls were of plain wood paneling. At the back of the large hall was a balcony, and a flight of stairs which led down to a bufyet—the line there was incredible. The movie would start in five minutes but twenty or thirty people were still standing patiently in the stationary line, bundled up in their heavy coats and hats. From above I could see the coffee machine steaming, the little ham, kolbasa, and cheese sandwiches spread out on the bufyet's counter, and glasses of orange soda lined up in rows.

The film caught me completely by surprise. It takes place in Soviet Georgia (Stalin was Georgian, but then so was the director of the film) and the plot follows the pattern of a dream. The Ionesco-like incongruities make it impossible to pinpoint the time historically, but the symbolism, to anyone who had survived the Stalinist period or knew anything about that period is flagrant. The Dictator wears Mr. NKVD Beria's famous bifocals, has Stalin's forehead, Mussolini's jodphurs and riding boots (and operatic voice), and Hitler's terrifying little mustache. His henchmen wear armor (their visors always closed) and ride horses and carry ancient weapons. I supposed this was so the Dictator could seem international and eternal, but the Soviet symbols prevailed. In one scene, a little girl and her mother search through a massive number of cut-down trees that are stored in a field. The overall effect is of a cemetery. They are hoping to find the name of the little girl's father carved on the base of one of the trees. During the purges of '36–'38, citizens who were taken away in the middle of the night and were never heard of again often ended up in Siberian labor camps; there they carved their names on the bases of the trees they chopped down in the hope that someone would find them and let the world know they were still alive. While the mother searches in vain, the little girl plays in a pile of wood shavings, letting the sawdust run through her hands like sand. (In Russia today there is an aphorism left over from Stalinist times: "When you cut down trees, bark will fly.") When the child begins to play in the sawdust, the old woman to my right, who sat rigid in her coat and hat, suddenly began to sob into her hands.

There is a show trial in a garden of flowering weeds. The garden is surrounded by a white stone wall. A woman dressed as Justice stands with a blindfold over her eyes and scales in her hand, while the accused in a torn white robe confesses to a string of ridiculous acts of espionage and treason. A gasp went up from the audience, swept across the theater, and then subsided. Just in front of us three teenagers shifted in their seats, whispering to one another and giggling. I wanted to pull them by their hair and force them to watch the screen. This is when I began to cry, because it was all so awful and they were too young to understand the terror, the disappearances. The show trials of '36–'38 had been erased from their history textbooks.

Coming out of the theater the people were completely silent, as though to talk about such a film in public would be pure idiocy. Phil and I stood in the street and watched the crowd disperse. It was an odd feeling to come out of a movie and have nowhere to go for a cup of coffee or a drink. People huddled wordlessly at the bus stop. The bus ride home would take only fifteen minutes, but the wait for the bus might be forty-five at this hour of the night.

We didn't mind. These were the little things one got used to—a great deal of time was spent waiting. And I was content: I was here for five months and then I would be home again, but without Phil. For now I was with Phil, and as long as he was happy to be with me, I looked no further than that. Life was stable, difficult, but stable.

Looking up at him out of the corner of my eye I thought about the herculean efforts I made every day to avoid him, to go out on my own, to be independent. But when I knew he would be in front of a certain door, waiting for a class to begin, or in the cafeteria at the end of classes rather than at lunch break because the line was too long then, I found myself drifting toward those places. In my mind I made a thousand excuses for being there that had nothing to do with him. "Hey there," Phil would say as though it were a coincidence. He was never annoyed or displeased to see me although he never seemed overjoyed. Keeping a formal distance, we would chat about this and that until long after everyone else had left.

On some nights, when I got home to the Institute, I would not knock on his door but go straight to my room across the hall. I conducted these experiments because while I wandered alone around the city I would imagine that his interest in me was waning. But if I had not knocked on his door by a quarter to one, he would come by and ask me over for a drink or leave me a note if I wasn't in. Invariably I ended up spending the night with him.

I thought about these things while we waited for our bus, but said something completely different. "It would be nice to have someone to discuss that movie with who had lived through the purges." I would never have asked Rita, because Rita had probably been busy writing letters to the NKVD denouncing her neighbors.

Out of nowhere Phil said, "Why don't you call that old lady?"

"What old lady?" I was apprehensive suddenly.

"The one you keep talking about, the one who knew your father."

I stood paralyzed for a moment, as though he'd slapped me in the face.

Phil looked at me with the sober, complacent expression I had come to expect, but still could not fathom. It was not condescending, it was not distant, it was not derisive, but it always seemed to put him in a position of control, which infuriated me.

"I'm afraid she'll hang up on me," I said quietly. In the street, when we spoke English, we spoke in muted tones so as not to attract attention, not to offend.

"Bullshit," Phil muttered. Close to fifty people were now waiting for the many buses that stopped there on the corner. No bus had passed in quite some time. The cold from the layer of ice that covered the cement beneath our feet was slowly beginning to creep through the soles of my boots.

I stamped my feet and danced around in a circle.

"Why don't you just mind your own business?" I said angrily. "You know what *I* think? I think you want to make me completely insecure."

But what I really thought was that by calling the woman I would somehow be trespassing, I would be breaking some taboo, like a cowboy trampling over an Indian tribe's sacred burial grounds.

But how different a man could my father have been forty-five years ago? I often tried to imagine him as a young and vulnerable man, not an old and wise one, as I had known him all my life. In 1942 he would have been twenty-seven, exactly Phil's age. I could not imagine Phil Chase in a fistfight, much less caught up in the middle of a war. How sheltered and spoiled we were; my generation had even been spared Vietnam!

"Do you want to know what I think, or not? If not, I'll be quiet, because you're right, it's none of my business," Phil said. "But I like you and I can see this thing's driving you nuts."

This was one of the things that drove me nuts about Phil: *I like you.* How dare he say "I like you" to me? Why not spare me and say nothing at all? His choice of words seemed cruel to me at times. And this was a person who took words seriously. He had written two B.A. theses, one on Death in *War and Peace,* and one on the use of etymology in *Ulysses.* Of course, he could have been lying or exaggerating about this; how would I ever know?

"All right, what do you think?" My tone was unpleasant, nasty, and suddenly I didn't like myself.

"Of course there's the possibility that she'll hang up on you and that would be that. But worse, she might invite you over and tell you all kinds of stories about your father that you don't want to hear because he might turn out to have a different past than the one you imagine and admire."

"Go to hell, Phil," I mumbled, on the verge of tears. The Russians had begun to watch us with their usual distant curiosity.

"When you're loaded and you crawl into my bed at night you talk about him—or don't you know that?"

"I know that."

I also knew that by not calling Yelena Davidovna, I was undermining the very object of my trip.

"Come on, there's a booth right outside the theater. Call her. Come on. I won't listen." He tugged at my coat sleeve and then pulled me away from the bus stop. The people at the bus stop watched us go. Russians were always curious when they heard a foreign language— especially English.

"It's past ten!" I argued.

"It's all right," he said. "Do you know a single Russian who goes to bed before midnight? Anyway, even if you wake her up, this is going to be the surprise of her life; she's going to be thrilled, I guarantee."

The booth was an open one, protected on both sides by glass and attached to a metal pole. When I'd finished dialing I turned and watched Phil's back in his sheepskin coat. He was smoking a cigarette, blowing the smoke up above his head and observing the mob at the bus stop. There was something about the way he held his shoulders back and the way his jaw curved to meet his neck that made me long to kiss him even as I wanted to hurt him. A woman's voice came onto the line after the second ring.

"Allo?"

"Mozhno k telefonu Yelenu Davidovnu pazhaluysta?"

"Ya slushayu." The voice was gentle and deep; it had a vulnerable edge.

"Govorit Clinton Gray." I said, this is Clinton Gray speaking.

"Clinton Gray . . . Clinton Gray . . . *Kak eto mozhet byt'?"* And then she repeated in English, "How can it be? Can it be? It can't be. I don't belief it can be. Are you wife or are you daughter?"

"Daughter."

"Daughter. You are alone here in Moskva?"

I thought about her question for a moment and replied, "Yes. But I study with a group of students."

"Won't you come to my house for tea, *dochka?"* She called me "little daughter." "Tomorrow afternoon. I shall prepare a nice tea."

I said, "I would be honored to come to tea."

"Good, good, dochka. Take my address. I will expect you at which time?"

"At four," I said.

"Wonderful! At four there will still be daylight."

Phil was just behind me when I turned away from the booth. His full lips had curved into a slightly self-satisfied smile. "What?" I said.

"When are you going?"

"Tomorrow," I said. "After school."

Our bus still had not come so Phil decided he wanted to walk home through the birch forest. The night was warm in comparison to most; it was not the minus-fifteen-degree weather we had been experiencing, and the wind was still.

"What are you, crazy?" I said. "There's tons of snow in there."

"There are paths. I run in there every day. You can wait here for the bus, but I bet I can get home before you do."

I did not want to wait for the bus by myself, so I followed him into the woods.

Within a minute we were swallowed up by the ghostly trees. Everywhere I looked there were trees glowing silvery-white, and no light but the stars and the half-moon in the sky reflecting off the trees and snow. I held on to the hem of Phil's coat and stumbled along a few feet behind him. I was wearing a long wool skirt over silk long underwear, heavy socks, and my snow boots, and did not feel the cold at all. It did not matter here if you wore snow boots with skirts. If you wanted to wear a skirt or a dress you had to wear your snow boots, because wearing New York City leather boots was absurd, as I'd learned the hard way. All the girls had left fashion and style behind somewhere back in the first week.

The paths were frozen, uneven, slippery, and covered with snow in some areas. It was a good thing that I was wearing the snow boots. Once in a while I looked up and saw the silver branches reaching for the stars. They reminded me of beggars' arms.

"Phil!" I tugged on his coattail. "Phil, would you have left me there to wait for the bus, really?"

"No."

"Are we always going to be competing like this, to see who'll give in first?"

He stopped and turned toward me. I could barely see his face, only his glasses reflecting the long silver trees. His normally full lips were a thin, shadowy slit.

He took two steps in my direction and lifted me up, reaching into the split of my down coat, which was held together by three big, widely spaced buttons.

"You're a jerk, Phil, you're going to tear these buttons off!" I laughed and wriggled out of his grasp. He dropped me and I sank deep into the snow at the edge of the path. I sat up and pressed my back against the slick bark of a tree. This is when an Arctic down coat comes in handy, I thought. I will write to my Tante Claire and tell her about this.

Phil crouched, and as he crawled toward me his knees on the bottom of my coat pulled us further into the snow. Our breaths hung around us, white like the snow and the trees and the stars, but of a vaguer density, a paler hue.

He pulled me away from the tree so that I was suddenly staring at the trees' crooked fingers and the royal blue sky. My scarf kept my hair out of the snow.

"You are going to get us arrested. Get up."

"Please," he said with a heavy voice while his finger undid the buttons of my coat. His hands slid toward the inguinal patch in my silk long underwear. His fingers bent into fists as they gripped the thin material, and he tore the patch apart in opposite directions. I gasped but by then it was too late.

Beneath the long underwear was my bare skin. The cold hit me for only a second, and it was not unpleasant. Lying deep in the snow bank, I felt as though I'd become a fraction of the earth. Phil's face pressed hungrily against mine.

He undid his coat so that it enveloped us like a small blanket, while mine lay below us like a short down quilt.

"Who are you? Who are you?" I asked him, breathing in his hair, his neck. I thought I would have recognized his smell even blindfolded in a crowded room. "Where did you come from?"

"From Long Island," he mumbled.

His glasses were knocked off his face and afterward it took us ten minutes to find them.

When we reached the doors of the Institute Phil was still trying to brush the snow out of my coat. "You look like the Michelin tire man after a blizzard," he said, slapping at my back. No amount of slapping would coax the white powder off. The shining in Phil's eyes reminded me of the stars. We went into the lighted hall. I stared at his profile while he naturally and calmly greeted the old gate-watcher, who shook her head at us in disgust. "You Americans are mad!" she said. "Playing in the frost like children!"

He had been mine for a few seconds but now he was his own again, and I felt completely alone.

16 ▮▮▮

YELENA DAVIDOVNA'S SKIES

We had two means of sending and receiving mail: through the American Embassy pouch, which was carried by a diplomat to Helsinki and mailed from there twice a week, and through the Soviet mail, which arrived in a completely haphazard manner, sometimes once a week, sometimes three times. People said there was no rhyme or reason to the Soviet mail. A letter might take a month to arrive, while another might arrive in five days. It operated within its own, weird twilight zone.

Each day, after classes, everyone stopped by the floor dezhurnaya's desk and searched through the pile of mail. Even the first week, when we all knew that nothing could possibly have arrived yet, we looked. And each day we grew more and more apprehensive.

Three and a half weeks passed before I received my first letters, because I alone had not known that American students were allowed embassy mail privileges. It seemed that every student in the group had appropriated the Helsinki Embassy address before our departure. My roommate, Isabel, for example, received seven letters before I received one. My apprehension increased with each day. I imagined the most horrible scenarios: the Soviets were monitoring my mail, or worse, someone dear to me had died and all my friends and family were trying to decide who should be the one to write me.

Finally—and coincidentally, the night I called Yelena Davidovna—
I came home to find two airmail envelopes on my bed. My anonymous
benefactor had carefully separated the letters so that I would see immediately that there were two. Their blue-and-red-striped trim and colorful stamps jumped out at me from the white pillow as soon as I entered
the room and I ran to them the way a child rushes to the tree on
Christmas morning.

They had come through the Soviet mail and were from my mother
and my Tante Claire. Although each letter was completely characteris-
tic of its sender, both my mother and Tante Claire had a way of
addressing me that made it seem as though time, for them, had stood
still. I suddenly felt that I was not twenty-five and in Russia at all but
eighteen and away at college.

Feb. 3

My Dear Baby,

Nothing much to report. Your Tante Steph's son Dan is in the
dry-out place again. We all thought he'd stopped drinking for
good the last time but I guess not. It turns out he likes cocaine as
well as booze and was selling it in the street and got caught.
Yesterday your Tante Steph called and yelled at me. She said it's
completely unfair that I have such a good child when hers is so
rotten and I yelled back that it's not my fault that I have such a
good child. Now we're not speaking.

My neighbors Fred and Paula are getting divorced. Fred says
it's because she kept buying diamonds and putting them on his
credit cards and not telling him about it. I believe she did do that,
because I always thought she was a bitch and only married him
for his money (who else would marry a man as short as that?) I
also believe if she'd put out a little he would have let her buy all
the diamonds she wanted.

Your Tante Claire is crazy as ever. Last night she took me to a
fancy Italian restaurant because she thought I was depressed about
you leaving (which is true but I don't like her to know that) and

she ordered a pasta putanesca, which is made with anchovies. Now you know Claire has been allergic to fish ever since she was born and when we were roommates in college I wasn't even allowed to cook fish in the dorm kitchen which was about a mile down the hall from our room even though everyone else did. Well I forgot that putanesca had anchovies in it and only realized it when I tasted it because we both ordered the same thing. As soon as I tasted it I knew Claire was going to go into convulsions on the floor and I'd be spending the next eight hours baby-sitting her in the hospital. It was already too late to stop her though because she'd taken several bites and was commenting on how delicious this sauce was. So I decided not to say anything and watch what would happen. She ate the whole plate and said, "My goodness Francesca, this is the best sauce I ever tasted! I wonder what's in it?" She wanted to ask the waiter for the recipe. I told her that was the rudest thing I'd ever heard, only low-class people ask for recipes in restaurants. So guess what? Your Tante Claire is not allergic to fish, after all, which is what I've been telling her since we were seventeen. But don't tell her I told you because she'd be angry at me. She wants to know if you are wearing her coat. Please wear it because in the New York Times it said it is —15 degrees over there. I hope you are warm enough. Please write to your Tante Claire when you have time. It would make her very happy.

I miss you and am very proud of you. *I think the Russians are great people and I hope they take good care of my baby.*

I read a terrifying article in the Daily News this morning. An American girl went to Australia on vacation and was eaten by a crocodile. Please be careful where you swim. I love you,

Mama

Tante Claire wrote:

February 3
My Dearest Godchild,

I am writing you because I had dinner with your mother last night, and have to tell you that she misses you so much it is upsetting. But she keeps her chin up and pretends she doesn't miss you as much as she does. We had a lovely dinner at an Italian restaurant and I tried a new sauce I never had before. I have to tell you your mama is as crazy as ever because she thinks after knowing her for over forty years I can't see that she is lonely and needs a boyfriend. I am trying to fix her up with a French conductor friend of mine. Actually he is a friend of your Uncle Sydney's whom we met in France. He is bald and has seven children from his previous marriage which ended badly (his wife committed suicide) but he is a brilliant man and has a good sense of humor.

Your mama is still in love with your daddy which is understandable. They had such a special relationship. But it is time now for her to stop mourning and to get out in the world. Don't tell her I told you this because she will be angry at me for not minding my own business.

There is news every day about Russia in the papers and on the TV and your Uncle Sydney and I think about you all the time.

Are you getting enough to eat and are you warm enough? Have you met nice Russians? You don't have to write to us if you don't have time but it would be nice to hear from you. Here is a joke I heard yesterday:

President and Mrs. Reagan are in a fancy restaurant and the waiter comes up to take their order. Mrs. Reagan says, "I will have the sole meunière." The waiter says, "Very well, and your vegetable, Madam?" "Oh, he'll have the same."

I thought it was pretty funny. Your Uncle Sydney sends his love and says he will write to you soon. Be a good girl and don't get into any trouble. All my love,

Your Tante Claire

Every few days I had been writing them innocuous letters concerning the weather and the food I was eating. I talked about the Soviet stores and the deficit items. "There is no toilet paper in any public bathrooms, so we carry around our own." I told them vegetables and fruit were scarce but my new friends were feeding me so well that I was never hungry. I did not want to worry them any more than they already, naturally, did. "My coat is so warm I am constantly sweating in the street even though it is zero to −15 centigrade most days." Through the embassy mail, I had already written them about the famous Soviet war hero/playwright who had known a good deal about my father, I had written about Vera, I had written about her children and her strange husband. I had written about Phil—something to this effect: "Guess what? I am having an affair. But don't worry, he's American. He is from Long Island and is tall and blond and a surfer. It doesn't look like it's going to get serious. After this he's going around the world till he runs out of money."

This information concerning Phil would be a little upsetting to them because they were constantly (even when I was engaged to my ex-fiancé, Dave) trying to marry me off to a Successful Man. My mother wanted him Rich, regardless of his profession; Tante Claire, herself a poet, wanted him to be a Respected Artiste, regardless of his financial situation. Dave was a rarely employed actor who worked as a word processor at night and whose family was penniless, which put him on both their shit lists. Their obsessive desire to see me married seemed odd to me, as they had been great feminists in their day and had not married young themselves.

They became jealous if one was privy to information and the other was not. For this reason, they tormented one another by telling each other all their friends' and relatives' secrets; needless to say, I had not mentioned Yelena Davidovna's existence to either of them in my letters.

I tried to imagine how they were reacting to what I wrote them.

"There is no toilet paper anywhere in public places."

Claire: *Clinton can't be serious.*

Francesca: *Why can't they make toilet paper? What's so hard about making toilet paper?*

"They stand in line for things like cucumbers."

Claire: *Isn't that funny! That's always the part we leave in the little tossed salads we get in restaurants.*

Francesca: *I hate cucumbers, they give me indigestion.*

"The metro is beautiful and only costs five kopeks."

Francesca: *So what? I've never been on a subway in my life. What does it cost to take a cab, or does such a thing even exist?*

Claire: *God, Francesca, you are so bourgeois.*

And what would Russians understand of their American letters? A boy is sent to a *sanitarium* for dealing drugs? A couple divorces because the wife spent too much money on diamonds? Joking about a President's senility in the mail? A psychosomatic allergy to fish—a food that is a formidable and necessary staple of the Soviet diet? It wouldn't take an avid Communist to comment, *What a remarkable display of bourgeois decadence!*

My mother's attitude toward my interest in Russia was not one of dismissal, although she admitted that personally, Russia did not interest her in the least. "If I had an extra couple of thousand dollars to blow, I'd go to Italy and rent a villa by the sea with maids and cooks. You can keep Russia, I'd rather travel in comfort and style," she'd said. And my father's life before they had met, as far as I knew, did not exist for her at all. We had never, ever spoken of it.

In the past week, a thought which had taken root in my mind years before had grown disproportionately large and oppressive: it was possible that my father had avoided the subject of his time here during the war because my mother had been unable to cope with the fact that he'd been in love with someone else. Why else had it taken him fifteen years to marry after he'd returned?

I put the letters in my suitcase under my bed, locked it, and went to Phil's room. That night I slept badly. I dreamt that my mother was crying, her face buried in her hands, because of something I had done. Phil had to shake me awake. "You were crying in your sleep," he said.

The next day, after classes, I left for Yelena Davidovna's with an apprehensive heart.

Yelena Davidovna's street was called the Bulvarnoe Koltso, the Boulevard Ring. It was a large street which ran in a circle around the very central part of the city. I came out of the metro in front of the statue of Pushkin on Gorky Street. Gorky Street reminded me of the

Champs Élysées. It led to Red Square and the Kremlin the way the Champs Élysées led to the Place de la Concorde and the Tuileries. There were shops and theaters and hotels and a constantly bustling crowd. The statue of Pushkin faced the Bulvarnoe Koltso, a beautiful boulevard split by a long park lined with enormous trees.

I walked along the alley between the trees. Children ran and shouted in the snow-covered playgrounds, and women sat on newspapers on the park benches. It was a beautiful, bright, crisp day and the sun was blinding, dazzling against the snow.

I watched the children tumble about in their bulky coats, their faces completely obscured by colorful scarves and hats. As the numbers on the buildings approached Yelena Davidovna's, it became harder for me to breathe and walk. I sat down on a vacant bench to gather up my courage and reorganize my thoughts.

In the last week I had come to believe that my trip to Russia was a long wave on which my life was precariously balanced. Some day it would come crashing down, and I along with it.

I had applied to graduate school my senior year of college because I didn't know what else to do. What did one do with a Bachelor of Arts in Russian? I moved to New York and halfheartedly attended Columbia University. I became restless and quit after a year. I found a decent, not very challenging job organizing grants for struggling Soviet immigrant writers. I liked my job and for a while I felt important in a small way, but after several years I realized I was fooling myself. The only thing I wanted to accomplish in life was the thing I feared the most: to live for a time in Russia. I went back to Columbia and took out a loan. After another semester, I applied to the Language Program in Moscow.

This "obsession" with visiting the Soviet Union, as Dave had termed it, had been a severe handicap in our relationship from the start. He could not understand why I had not gone to Russia while in college, or directly out of college. Why had I waited another four years? How do you explain to someone something you barely understand yourself? I told him that up until that point, I had not been psychologically ready. "When are you going to be psychologically ready to get married," he countered, "in another ten years?"

"Maybe," I said. That was the beginning of the end.

My New York apartment was now emptied of Dave's belongings, which meant it was bare. At twenty-five I was still in graduate school and still without my master's degree. I had the increasingly discomfiting feeling that I had accomplished absolutely nothing in my life. And I was going home to nothing.

I sat for a while listening to the children and wishing that I had married Dave and stayed at home and had a child of my own. It was hard to breathe, the air was so cold. I thought about my mother and felt that I was betraying her somehow. I got up resolutely from the park bench and went in search of Yelena Davidovna's house.

There were two unmarked buzzers next to the door, as was customary in communal apartments. I rang both and waited in front of a big double door.

A minute later the left half of the door swung open slowly, and before me in shadow stood a woman close to my height. She stepped back and let me in. She switched on a hall light, and for a long moment we stood in silence, staring at each other.

Her hair was completely white, cut short along her jawline and parted on the side. She had sharp gray eyes and fine features, an aquiline nose that was strangely rounded at the tip, and a long mouth. Her back was small and straight and she kept her chin jutting slightly forward.

"What an extraordinary surprise," she mumbled, speaking in Russian. "I am speechless." She let out a little laugh, and asked me to remove my coat. Slippers were given to me. I followed her down the short hall.

"This is a communal flat," she whispered, pointing to a closed door to the right. "I have been living with these same neighbors since 1951 and I still hate them." She began to laugh but was interrupted by a terrible fit of coughing.

She opened the door at the far end of the hall and we entered her apartment.

Walking behind her I noticed that her little pointed bones were discernible beneath her dark slacks and dark turtleneck sweater. It was hard to determine her age, but she was certainly over seventy, and probably closer to eighty. She walked slowly and assuredly, though her right arm was folded in just below her chest, like a broken wing.

"Today is a glamorous day is it not? The sun shines in through my windows." She opened the door onto a small, well-lit room, which held a bed, a desk, a cupboard, and an entire wall of long, thin drawers. We went into the next room, which was slightly smaller and stacked from ceiling to floor with books. There was a small round table set for tea, and a couch with an old, beautifully embroidered shawl draped over its back. The window had a balcony that looked out onto the narrow park in the middle of the boulevard.

"I watch the children for many hours," she said, looking out the window.

"I just sat in the park watching them as well," I said. "They are wonderful."

"They are wonderful," she said. "Shall we have tea?"

I followed her back out to the hall, past the communal bathroom, w.c., and into the kitchen. She had set a kettle on the stove, and many little cheese and ham sandwiches on a plate. A fancy chocolate torte stood in a box on the counter. Her hands, especially the right one, were gnarled and the joints resembled the knots on the branches of old trees.

"Would you be so kind as to lift the kettle for us?" she asked me. "Pour here," she said, pointing with difficulty to a little teapot. "You know Russian-style tea? Very strong in the teapot, and water is added after. We shall take the food out to the library."

I was overwhelmed by the amount of time she must have spent standing in the cold kitchen slicing bread and cheese and ham to make these little sandwiches.

We sat at the round table. Her china didn't match but all the pieces were beautiful and old and seemed to go perfectly with the white lace tablecloth.

"How do you like Moskva?"

"I like it very much. It is so different than America, or France."

"Yes, you were many years in France."

"Yes."

"Your father, he finally went back to America?"

"Yes. When I was thirteen. We lived in Florida, where he taught at the university, then we lived in Connecticut, then in New York City."

She lifted her cup slowly, put it down slowly, then ate one sandwich, taking tiny bites. She lit a strong-smelling Soviet, nonfilter cigarette, all with her left hand.

"I have been painting the children outside the window," she said. "It is so difficult, because the light is different every day, the children are different every day, and they run run run! Like little rabbits. Before my right hand became so bad I could have done it in one day. Now I remember what was yesterday, and I add to what is there today . . . and so I get a very different kind of painting. Would you like to see?"

"With great pleasure."

She went into the other room and returned a moment later dragging a low easel along the floor. She left it about four feet from where I sat. In the watercolor the snow on the ground and in the trees was blue in spots and yellow and pink in others. The little bundled-up children had been captured in movement, running in their clothes of indeterminate, earthy reds and browns. The tall trees were many shades of gray, meticulously outlined and painted so that they seemed the most permanent, the most stable forms in the painting. The sky was a fantastic burst of blue and purple clouds, which seemed to be carried by a strong wind. There were vague golden strips of light peeping through the clouds.

"It is beautiful."

"You see, it is almost like many days, different weathers."

This aquarelle was a formidable feat. I could not imagine how she had managed with her hands in their condition. Yelena Davidovna stood back from the painting and gazed down at it with tenderness. The matter-of-factness with which she treated her ailment made it impossible for me to mention it or to ask questions. She had somehow managed to accept it, and work regardless of her handicap. It seemed to be a subject she felt was not worth discussing.

"Your papa liked to draw," she said, coming back to her seat and pouring me more tea. It was a slow and careful process and I wanted to take the little teapot from her hands.

"My papa?"

"Yes. He was terrible, but we laughed a good deal. You understand, in October of 1941 I did not leave Moskva when the city was evacuated, because my father was in the hospital and could not be moved. My mother, my sisters, my aunts and uncles all left, but I stayed with my boy. The city was getting cold and there was so little food. During the time of greatest peril, when the Germans were only fifty kilometers from the city, my boy and I hid in the bathroom of our apartment because it had no windows, the walls were thick, and you could not hear the bombs as much there. After we knew that the Germans would not take Moskva, like all mothers who stayed I sent my little boy to camp so that he would be warm and have enough to eat. You know the government took good care of the little ones, as best they could. But on weekends my little boy would come home to me, skinny-skinny, and he cried so often and so much I did not know what to do.

"When the Germans approached Moskva, your father was evacuated east to the Urals along with all the diplomats and correspondents. Entire embassies were moved by train to Kuybyshev. He did not want to go, your poor papa! He had arrived from England in September, sailing through the Arctic Circle with a convoy of arms. The trip took a month; he arrived in Moskva, a month passed, and then he was evacuated.

"We met during that month he was in Moskva. We became friends." She used the plural of *"priyatel'*, meaning close friends but not implying anything more. "He came back from Kuybyshev in the middle of December. He came straight to my flat. You know he was not like most correspondents. Most arrived and did not speak Russian at all. But your papa spoke extraordinary Russian, with a pre-revolutionary turn of phrase, like an aristocrat! He got around Moskva like a mouse inside the walls of an old house. And he wore Soviet-made clothes and was completely fearless. Fearless to the point of recklessness, and I told him so.

"He often brought sugar, apples, little things for the boy from the diplomatic store. Foreign correspondents had the same privileges as diplomats but sometimes even for them there was no sugar, no apples, no meat. He liked to draw funny faces, cartoons. My little boy was so entertained by him with those silly drawings. He was in Moskva two weeks and then they sent him back to Kuybyshev until the middle of January."

"Does your son remember my father?"

She put her cup down slowly and gazed at me with a stricken expression. Her eyes seemed to grow dark, as the sky in her painting, and I felt as though I'd said something irreparable.

"He died of cancer of the stomach ten years ago," she managed to say in a whisper. "I understand what you must have lived through losing your papa. But I promise you that there is nothing worse, no fate on this earth worse than outliving your own children."

"I'm so sorry," I said in English. "I had no idea."

She sat straightbacked and poised, her left hand in her lap and the right one folded up under her chest. The large grandfather clock by the wall ticked loudly. We sat in silence a moment, and then she said in Russian, "Would you like to see more paintings?"

"Certainly."

"The sun comes through the window in the other room better this time of day. Come in there."

She dragged the easel along behind her.

"Please, let me," I said, trying to move in and take it from her.

"No, no, my dear. I am fine. I do this all the time."

The long, thin drawers were filled with paintings and she took them out in piles of five or six at a time.

"I had an exhibition a few years ago," she said with pride. "I am in the Union of Soviet Painters and I was given an exhibition by the government. I have been painting the same way for sixty years; the critics said I have developed greatly—I say they have changed their minds about what is good and what is not."

"And did you sell your paintings, then, at the show?"

"Oh no, my dear! Artists are not permitted to sell. Only the government buys the work. Although, under the table, anything is possible. I could never live on the pension I receive." She laughed lightly at this.

They were mostly water color landscapes of different regions of the Soviet Union; the Russian birch trees, rivers, and peasant huts in the country as well as villages in Turkmenistan's arid land, the mosques, and camels; there were some of Estonia and Latvia, and some of Soviet Georgia. In the midst of a landscape of nervous lines would be a meticulously depicted hut, a boat, the trunk of a tree, or a church. "I am here!" each seemed to say; they were little manifestations of individuality. The depths and immensities of her skies were annihilating. You could almost see the movement of the light, the roll of the clouds. One sky might be bright pink, glowing, while below it the world would be serene, already dark, calm, and at peace. When the clouds were black and purple and seemed to rush forward, the earth below might be bathed in a strange, pale and comforting light. The sky outside her window began to darken and cast shadows across the room.

"What a pity," she said. "They are not as good in false light."

"Night comes so fast here in winter," I said.

"Yes. And the electric light washes the color out of everything. Come, shall we have more tea?"

We went back to the room filled with books. Night fell completely and the boulevard disappeared outside the window. Now the yellow light inside the room shone in the window panes, reflecting the books, the table, and Yelena Davidovna's white hair. I reached for the teapot before she could and filled her cup.

"I should not have told you about my son," she said dejectedly. "It is not nice to tell others of one's sorrows. Would you like a glass of vodka?"

"If you would."

"Certainly."

I wanted her to tell me where the vodka was so that I could get it, but she insisted on getting it herself. It was in a cabinet by the grandfather clock. She brought two tiny crystal glasses back in her left hand, and the bottle tucked up under her arm.

"My young friends take good care of me," she smiled happily.

"They are all friends of my son. They have not abandoned me although I tell them they are wasting their time watching over an old fool like me. But they continue nevertheless to shop for me, cook for me, entertain me. In fact, they will be here soon," she looked at the clock. "You must stay for dinner."

"Let me pour," I offered.

"*Nu, ladno,*" she conceded. We drank a toast to each other, to our meeting.

It was quiet and warm in the room.

"What a courageous girl you are to come all the way here by yourself," she said after a while, appraising me with her clear eyes.

I laughed without heart. "Not at all. I should have come many years ago."

"All things happen when they do." She turned and gazed at the window. "How dark it is!" she said.

"Your country is strange that way. In the morning it is still black when I go to class, and almost right after class, it is already dark."

" 'In winter I get up at night' . . ." she chanted in her throaty English. " 'In winter I get up at night' . . ." She paused as though the words were on the tip of her tongue and it seemed strange to her that she could not remember them.

" 'In winter I get up at night/And dress by yellow candlelight'! Da, that is correct. A *potom,* after that? I don't remember."

" 'In summer, quite the other way/I have to go to bed by day.' " I began to choke as I remembered my bedroom in Paris and my father sitting on the edge of my bed, looking like a mad scientist with his whispy white head bent over a book. It was either bedtime or I was sick; the memory was unclear and I could not remember if there was light coming through my windows. My father was reading me that poem and tears were falling from his eyes. I believed he was crazy.

"It's not even a sad poem, Daddy," I said, patting his hand.

"But it's a *beau*tiful poem," he said. "It's too good for kids."

He'd cried when he read me *Stuart Little* and *Charlotte's Web.* I would not allow him to read to my girlfriends when they came to visit because I was afraid he would cry in front of them and I thought they would laugh.

"A potom?" Yelena Davidovna asked me.

"I also don't remember."

The doorbell rang and I tried to get up but Yelena Davidovna insisted on answering the door herself. Before getting up, she placed her twisted hand on mine and said in Russian, "There are so many stories I can tell you. We must get together often and I will tell you all that I remember. Another thing—I do so hate to ask you this—might it be possible for you to get me American aspirin? It seems to be the only medicine that lessens the pain in my hands. We have aspirin but it is not as good and it hurts my stomach terribly."

"Of course! Of course! I will get you thousands of American aspirins. Enough to last you ten years!"

She laughed lightly at this. "Not that many, my dear dochka. I will not be here that long."

17

A BATTLE OF WILLS

"You're walking crooked like an old peasant—what's in the bag?" Phil asked. It was Sunday afternoon and we were on our way to the bus stop. Rita had invited me to the restaurant and had told me to bring a friend. I had convinced Phil to come along by telling him that he had probably never, in his six months in Moscow, encountered a more rapacious, confusing, and wily wheeler-dealer than Rita. I also told him I needed a buffer against her unrelenting demands.

"Well, the husband of her cousin gave me fifty rubles to buy him freeze-dried coffee at the Beriozka," I explained.

Phil made a disgusted face and said, "Give me some of those jars," extending his hand.

"He gave me a fifty-ruble bill. What do I do with it?" I had been carrying the bill around in my wallet for the past few days, unable to get rid of it. I had offered it to the cashier at the Dieta, the Soviet-style supermarket up the street where I did my weekly shopping, but she had refused to change it. The cabdriver who had brought me home from Rita's a few days before had also refused to take it.

"Are you nuts? It's illegal for students to carry currency higher than ten-ruble notes. Don't you know that? Why do you think they pay us our stipends in ten-ruble notes?"

"I knew, but he gave me fifty rubles, so I took it. I was embarrassed anyway and he said it wouldn't be a problem."

"Give it to me. You know the *militsia* are allowed to search your wallet right in the street? If they find it they'll arrest you for dealing on the black market."

I quickly took the fifty-ruble note out of my wallet and handed it to him crumpled up into a ball.

At the metro station he asked me to wait for him by the row of public telephones. He stood in line in front of the booth where you bought your monthly transportation pass. Behind the ticket window was a yellow drape which hung all the way down to the arch-shaped hole through which you transacted. You had to bend at a ninety degree angle to get a glimpse of or to be able to hear the person with whom you were dealing.

The queue moved rather quickly and in five minutes Phil came back and handed me five ten-ruble notes.

"This is the safest place to change big bills. They do it all the time and don't ask you any questions—but you're screwed if there's a militsia man behind you. Don't ever let anybody give you big bills like that. Just refuse, okay?"

"Okay. Sorry."

We arrived at Rita's apartment at four o'clock. She stood in her little vestibule and openly looked Phil over from head to foot. She led us into the living/dining room, and we sat at the table for an hour and drank tea while the TV blasted away in the corner.

In a jovial tone, Rita began to ask Phil questions about himself. Since I was not the object of her interest, I took the opportunity to study her from this comfortable distance. Her face and hands were pale and dry and specked with large, light-brown freckles. Like heavy drapes, her eyelids hung over her irises right to the top of her pupils, giving her eyes a strange, ambiguous expression of languor and impenetrability. Languid she was not. Her relentless vitality conflicted with the drooping eyelids, making her seem comical, almost puppetlike at times. Her lips, like her skin, were pale and parched, and when she spoke her tongue appeared white and often stuck to the roof of her mouth. She gave a general impression of thirstiness.

She began by asking Phil where he was from. He said Long Island, and she asked in an excited manner what kind of neighborhood his parents lived in and if they were near the sea. He said they were not far from the sea and she asked what his father did for a living. Phil said his father was a professor of mathematics and Rita asked him if professors of mathematics made a lot of money in the United States. Phil said they did not. It was apparent from her sly smile that she did not believe him. Then she asked how long he'd been in Russia. He said six months. Did he have many Russian friends?

She had been giving thoughtful nods to all his responses like an interviewer looking to hire someone for an important position, and Phil had fared quite well until she asked about his Russian friends. Phil told her quite bluntly that he made it a rule never to discuss his Russian friends with strangers. Her face froze in mid-nod and she was temporarily thrown off her tracks.

It took her about four seconds to recover. She picked up speed, so to speak, and pushed right on over the rocky terrain like a little Caterpillar bulldozer.

"But I am not a stranger! I am a friend of your friend!"

Phil said nothing and sat back, completely poised and relaxed. I was proud of him.

Rita then asked Phil if, as a ten-month student, he had a private telephone and if he did, would he please give her the number so that she could reach me without going through all the trouble of phoning the Institute.

I was aghast and at the same time fascinated to observe how Phil would handle this request.

"I do not have a phone and in any case you must never phone the Institute," Phil said flatly.

I could see by the way she was tilting her head that she was becoming impatient.

"I know there are fifty in Clinton's group. How many in your group?" she asked him without skipping a beat.

"Ten," he answered.

"Your director must have a phone. Clinton's director has a phone but she cannot give the number because there are too many students in the group and the phone is used only for emergencies. But you are only ten therefore there is no problem."

"I do not know anything about Clinton's director or his rules," Phil said. "My director has a phone, yes, but I will certainly not give you the number. They listen to all the directors' phones and Russians would be completely stupid and thoughtless to call."

Rita became hurt; her head tilted downward and her lips sagged at the corners. Phil gazed at her with interest.

"I am a Party member," she said pointedly, "I am an old woman. They can do nothing to me. I have nothing to worry about." She leaned forward suddenly and gripped his forearm. Phil did not flinch. Her voice went up a decibel. *"It is hard for me to reach Clinton and I want the number of your director so that I can phone you and leave messages for her. I get tickets to the best programs in the city. I have to speak to her so that she can come get the tickets."*

"Nevertheless I will not give you the number," Phil said slowly. Then he changed the subject.

"You are lucky to have such a big apartment."

Rita said nothing.

We all turned our attention to the blaring television. A high-ranking official was discussing the changes that were taking place in the Soviet Union. He mentioned that there would soon be a new law allowing a certain amount of private enterprise in the commercial sphere. There was something said about restaurants and taxis.

"It is a miracle," Phil said loudly. "It is simply a miracle. Things are getting so much better. Private enterprise will improve the quality of life."

Rita gasped. *"Not at all!"* she screeched. *"How can you say such a thing?* We must achieve a higher quality of life through Socialism, not Capitalism. *The Soviet Union must achieve Communism through Socialist means!* If we employ Capitalist methods, it will only prove that Communism has not been successful in the Soviet Union!"

Phil threw his head back and laughed uproariously. Rita gazed at him with her head tilted comically to the side. He stopped laughing and asked her politely to repeat what she'd said because he might have misunderstood her. She repeated exactly what she'd said in a little, tender voice.

"I would like to believe that such a thing is possible," Phil said, his expressionless eyes on her face, "but there is corruption everywhere in the bureaucracy. Your consumer goods are terrible. Everybody knows that Soviets prefer Western goods. What about those Soviet Capitalists who take advantage of this? I would even say that in certain circles, the taste for luxury exceeds ours. By allowing some free enterprise, the government hopes to get rid of black marketeering and help the consumer economy, doesn't it?"

Rita seemed to listen to Phil but it was apparent that she was not paying attention to what he said. A condescending smile was on her lips, and her eyes seemed to be asleep.

"You know nothing about the Soviet Union," she said vaguely. "Your Western press looks down at us from the ceiling and tells only lies."

"I have been here for six months, Rita Abramovna, and have not read a single Western newspaper. It is *your* papers which say that the corruption is enormous, that enterprise directors and managers have gotten fat at the expense of the people. It's the middle-level bureaucrats who have the most to lose from these reforms."

She shrugged and looked away. "Enough. It is all nonsense. We have been trying to improve our light industry ever since the war. It takes time to rebuild a country from ashes."

"Rita Abramovna," Phil said, "what do *you* believe should be done to improve the economy and bring the country closer to Communism without using Capitalist methods?"

She smiled dreamily, gazing upward and sideways from under her half-closed lids, and sang her vision out in staccato as though she were teaching a nursery rhyme to children. As she spoke I decided that if I managed to get through the evening without either telling her off, or being yelled at by Phil, I would do everything I possibly could to avoid her for the rest of my stay. I completely forgot, needless to say, about the fifty dollars I owed her from her cousin Sarah in New York.

"If *I* were the leader," she was saying, "I would make children learn the values of Communism right in kindergarten. They should be taught to share and not to be selfish, to treat one another like brother and sister. 'From each according to his abilities, to each according to his needs.' We must work together, help each other as one big healthy family to reach Communism."

"That is exactly what they teach in schools now," Phil countered.

"And what do you know about our Soviet schools?" Rita asked derisively.

"I spent fifteen days last semester monitoring a Soviet school," Phil said. "It was part of my thesis."

Rita did not respond for a moment, and then said with finality, "Enough. It is not good to discuss such things. We must talk about *nice* things." She turned to me, "Tell us what clothes the ladies are wearing in New York this year."

Since my knowledge of the vogue was minimal and Phil's interest in it was nonexistent, the topic was rapidly exhausted. There was an uncomfortable silence, and then Rita said, *"Oy!* I almost forgot. Clintonotchka, I have something for you. Will you excuse us a moment?"

She grabbed me by the biceps and pulled me down the hall to her bedroom. On the bed was a fur hat. The hat was round and the fur was fine, short, and grayish-black.

"Here," Rita said, "we got a hat for you. You said you were going to buy a hat but we do not want you to spend your dollars on such things."

She handed it to me and I was greatly relieved to see that it was not a new hat. The fur around the edges had thinned and the white skin of the poor little beast was visible beneath it. Inside, the satin had been slightly stained by the sweat from someone's forehead.

"Was this your hat?" I asked.

"Of course not," she said. "I could never afford such a hat. A friend of Anna's owed us a favor."

"I really can't take it," I said, trying to push it back into her hands.

"It is insulting to refuse gifts in Russia. You must take it. Igor and Anna will be insulted."

"Well—how can I thank you?"

"We will talk about it another time." She turned toward the door. "So it is settled. That boy," she gestured with her head toward the living room, "I think he is not good for you. He is very opinionated and stubborn, is he not?"

"We have an expression in English," I said, attempting to seem good-humored although I was about to insult her, " 'The frying pan shouldn't call the kettle black.' " I did not know how to say "pot."

"I don't understand?" She looked up at me with her weird eyes and I became frightened.

"It is not important." My heart seemed to skip a beat.

Igor and Anna arrived at five. We drove to the restaurant in Igor's new Jhiguli car, which looked a bit like a Peugeot. I sat in the middle of the backseat between Phil and Rita. There were plastic slipcovers on all the seats, which squeaked unpleasantly when anyone moved. Rita was a little person but took up more space than Phil did. She pressed into my right flank as though she were trying to get my attention. I slid closer to Phil, who stared at me in disbelief. His look said, "How did I ever let you get me into this mess?"

Rita stuck her hand into the split in my coat and rubbed the material of my skirt between her thumb and index finger.

"You are wearing such funny pants! Ha ha ha!" Her laugh was forced and I did not understand what she could possibly have meant by it.

"It is a skirt."

She went into a euphoric speech on the wonders of the Opium perfume I had given her and Anna on my previous visit.

"It is so wonderful!" she said. "Everyone in the elevator asks Anna and me what we are wearing. Here it is impossible to get such perfume. I wear it every day!"

I did not smell the complicated scent on her, and wondered why she was lying to me and whether she thought I was completely stupid.

"How much does it cost, perfume like that?"

"I bought it on the airplane at a special price," I said vaguely.

"How much does it cost in the Beriozka, for example?"

"I don't know."

My heart was pounding and I did not know whether to laugh or scream. She did not seem to care what I thought of her; maybe she realized that I found her despicable, maybe not—all these considerations were probably irrelevant to her, as long as she got whatever it was she wanted of me. But what did she want? There was really so little she could get. And what did Anna and Igor feel? Were they in on the deal? They seemed to treat her with a certain deference. It was a total mystery.

"Enough, Rita," Igor said benevolently from the front seat. "Americans do not like to discuss the price of things the way we do."

"Never mind," Rita said happily. "We will go to the restaurant and eat delicious food and dance and we will have a marvelous time. And that's that."

Igor took off his sheepskin coat in the street outside the restaurant. There was a long, still, silent line of Russians already waiting in front of the door. On the lapel of Igor's jacket was a large, red and gold World War Two medal for bravery. Igor went to the front of the line and everyone glanced at his medal and kept silent. He exchanged mutters with the man guarding the door, turned and waved to us and we followed him in. "Do not speak English at all," Anna whispered in my ear.

The restaurant was pre-revolutionary. The high arching ceilings were decorated with frescoes that were framed in gilt. At the center of the enormous room was the dance floor, at the center of that was a fountain. The bandstand was crowded with music stands. There was an electric organ, a drum set, and four enormous speakers.

Igor sat at the head of the table with Anna to his right. Phil sat to his left (I gathered that he wanted to be as far from Rita as possible) and I sat next to Phil, across from Rita.

Within twenty minutes every table was taken and our *zakuski* had arrived. There was caviar, smoked sturgeon, potato salad, cucumber salad, sprats, slices of smoked pork, and little pastry shells filled with cheese and chicken liver paté. There was wine and vodka and sweet soda water to drink. "Eat eat eat!" Rita said.

Rita pouted if I left anything at all on my plate—even the fat which surrounded the slices of smoked pork. Igor asked Phil some questions about his studies. Phil asked Igor which fronts he had fought on during the war. Igor responded that he did not like to talk about the war. Anna asked me if I liked my hat. Rita and Igor and Phil ate, ate, ate, but only Phil and I drank.

The surly waiter cleared the small plates as the band was getting ready to play. Incredibly, the drummer began to beat wildly on his drums, the electric organist pounded on his keys, the guitarist made faces, arched his back and then bent in two, and the speakers blasted the music through the echoing dining room. The tune sounded familiar but I could not place it. The guitarist came forward and began to sing.

"Ah eeeup/Ah ca coo da/Da situasha go ra da rah . . ."

"What is he singing?" Rita yelled from across the table. "It is English, is it not?"

"I don't know," I said. This seemed to disappoint her.

"Abba abba cadaba/Ahmana reesha na gabya . . ."

He was singing "Abracadabra" by the Steve Miller Band. "Abra abra cadabra/I wanna reach out and grab ya." They had probably gotten ahold of a recording and had learned the words phonetically.

"*Dance!*" Rita yelled. "*You two go dance.*"

There were quite a few couples squirming and stomping on the dance floor; they were mostly well dressed and elderly, which struck me as bizarre, considering the music.

Phil pushed his chair back and took my arm.

He did a very strange New Wave version of the Charleston for a while and then took my hand and twirled me around, pressed me into his chest and pushed me back out again. He did his Charleston-style dance again, kicking his heels out sideways and backward, his arms flailing the air. People began to look at him.

"I despise that woman!" he yelled in my ear. *"I despise that woman and I think she's dangerous."*

After "Abracadabra" the band played a slow Russian song, and Phil waltzed me around the fountain.

"Listen to me," he said, "you're never going to understand anything about this place hanging around with people like that. That woman doesn't tell the truth about anything. Do you hear me? Unload her."

"I'm trying to," I said. The whites of his icy blue eyes were already pink. During the zakuski we had put a serious dent in the bottle of vodka.

"Tomorrow—no, some day soon, I'm going to take you to meet the other side."

"What other side? What are you talking about?"

"Dissenters," he said.

It was a blessing in disguise that Rita, Anna, and Igor were not people who talked much at the table. Phil and I danced quite a bit between courses (it took an hour between each) and Rita told me every time I poured a shot not to drink so much. Finally, at eleven, we said good night to them in the street outside the restaurant. Phil shook hands with Igor and thanked him for the dinner. Rita asked me when I would call her; I said "soon," and experienced an uncomfortable pang of guilt.

We were in the center not far from Red Square. A heavy mist hung in the air and the night was warm. Phil suggested a walk—the metro ran until one and he did not seem concerned about the curfew. My new hat kept me so warm that I had to open my coat.

We walked down the dark, cobbled streets toward Red Square. Every solitary light glowed as though seen through a diffusion filter. Red Square itself was an extraordinary sight. A silver light reflected off the stone slabs, off the red Kremlin wall and its pointed towers, which stood out magically against the royal blue sky. At the other end of the empty square stood the tallest watchtower, whose gigantic clock was striking twelve. Above it, at the very tip of its turret, glowed the red star. Just across the street from the tower was Saint Basil's Cathedral. Its crazy, multicolored onion domes defied the imagination; there were nine of them altogether, of all sizes and heights, and the closer one got, the more intricate and complicated their swirling, candycane-like patterns seemed. All the structures, including the boxlike mausoleum where Lenin lay at the foot of the wall, glowed harmoniously in the silvery mist. It was an awesome sight, which struck me as bigger than life.

I was seized by the sudden realization that I was fortunate to be in the one percentile of Americans to whom the enigmatic Enemy had opened its doors. Thank you, thank you, thank you, I thought. But then an indescribable feeling of emptiness and longing overtook me: in the larger sense, what had I learned? What did I understand? Everything was still a complete mystery. And I would not even be able to take my memories back with me, because after being home a while, the little things that brightened life here—soft toilet paper, hot coffee, or a cucumber—would lose their value and importance, and the memory of how it had been would die. Of course, there were students in the American group who had immediately discovered the embassy and embassy personnel. They used their washing machines and ate their fresh lettuce and avocados and tomatoes and spoke English all the time —what was the point? One of the reasons I admired Phil was that I felt he tried as much as possible to live like a Russian. He understood this way of life better than any other American I knew. What an asset he would be to the CIA! But he would never join; he wouldn't even go to the embassy doctor. I longed for Phil to want me unconditionally, and if, just then, he had said, "Come with me around the world" I would have said yes without any hesitation, leaving everything, even my expensive winter coat, behind. Although I longed to accomplish something wonderful and grand in my life I did not believe I ever would, and I would have settled for a life with him.

I took Phil's hand and squeezed it as hard as I could through my mitten.

"This is so romantic. How many girls will you be able to say you walked through Red Square with on a misty winter night, after a dinner which included dancing, Beluga caviar, and champagne?"

"I wonder what that woman wants from you," he said angrily.

"Can't you forget about her for a minute? Just look at the sky. Look how quiet and beautiful it is here."

"Did you know that Ivan the Terrible had the architect of Saint Basil's blinded so that he would never build another structure like it? During the thirties there was a movement to tear Saint Basil's down. Hundreds and hundreds of cathedrals in Moscow were torn down."

I let go of his hand. "During the day you treat me like we're business acquaintances and at night you lecture me on history. You're a pragmatic shit, you know that? Come on, let's go."

I started to walk toward the metro.

"You always get so upset over nothing," he said calmly. "What do you want from me? You want me to hide my thoughts just to please you? Yes, it's romantic here. There."

"Do you always treat women this way or are you paying every one of us back because some bitch broke your heart?"

"You don't understand. You feel like this now, but this is Moscow, U.S.S.R. When you get home you'll go back to your normal life and I won't even exist."

"Bullshit. You'd like to think that, because it takes care of everything."

"Nevertheless it's true," he said equably. "I've never lived in a big city. I hate New York. Every time I've gone into the City I couldn't wait to get out. We don't have anything in common except our interest in Russia, and that's not enough."

"I think you're scared."

"I'm not scared. I just know what kind of life you're used to and what you need and you'd get tired of me in two seconds back home. You really want to live in a tiny town in California? You like to surf? That's all I do besides study. We'll have tons to talk about. Surfing and Old Church Slavonic and Constructivism. How about Semiotics? That's fun. I don't have a fucking clue what I want to do and after this trip I won't have a cent to my name."

"You think *I* do? You think I care?"

"Yes," he said.

"Do you love me? Right now, I mean. Do you love me at all?"

"I don't know."

On the way home he read his Lermontov and memorized another poem. I stared at the people and knew how Ceppie felt the day she punched the hole through the bathroom door. We did not say a word to each other.

When we got back to the Institute we flashed our passes and climbed the stairs in silence. Walking down our hall, Phil said in a completely equable tone, "In the next couple of days I'll take you to meet these friends of mine," as though there had been no break in our conversation.

"Fine," I said.

I stopped in front of my door and turned the knob. It was bolted from the inside. Isabel had gotten used to sleeping alone. I banged loudly on the wood with my fist.

I was surprised at myself and Phil must have been too, because as he was sticking the key into his lock he froze and turned around. "Listen, you're blowing this way out of proportion. Come have a drink."

I heard Isabel's muffled footsteps coming down the little hall.

"I'm through," I said, and waited with a sunken heart for her to let me in.

"Who is it?" she cried.

"It's me!"

She stood in the doorway in her pink Lanz of Salzburg nightie, her pom-pomed slippers peeking out below the hem. She blinked as though she did not recognize me and I started to cry.

"I'm sorry to wake you," I managed to say.

"What's going on?" she whispered once we were both safely inside.

"I'm back," I said.

"For good?"

"I think so."

"Oh," she said, as though she either did not believe me, or could not have cared less.

18

VERA'S
TROUBLE

I awoke in such a state of gloom that climbing out of bed and dealing with the day seemed a totally useless and painful exercise. The morning was particularly cold and a heavy layer of frost had crystallized on the inside of our window. The early sunshine had turned the sky the color of champagne and I stayed in bed until almost nine, gazing at this lovely sight and wondering what Phil might be thinking of me if he was, in fact, thinking about me at all.

I spent the class day hiding from him, which was difficult emotionally but not in practice. I decided that the best solution was to avoid the Institute completely. I had plenty of people to visit who had nothing to do with him, after all. As soon as the last bell rang I ran back to my room for my coat.

The dezhurnaya was at her desk listening to a Walkman and reading a newspaper. One of the Americans in our group had lent her the Walkman and some tapes—she explained to everyone on the floor that she was getting an education in rock'n'roll. She had told someone that she was thirty-five, but she appeared much older. Her dark hair was specked with gray and the deep circles below her eyes gave her a wise, pained look. When she worked the night shift there was usually a party in the dezhurnaya's cubicle. She liked to watch the comings and goings and left the door ajar, and she and the Japanese student who serenaded her with a guitar could be seen drinking something out of tea cups which caused their singing to become progressively louder and more slurred.

I waved to her and continued down the hall.

"Dievushka!" she yelled, gesturing for me to approach the desk. "There's a letter for you." She held it up and waved it at me.

I recognized Dave's handwriting immediately. The script was so small you needed a microscope to decipher the return address.

"*Spasiba,*" I said.

"I like very much this man called Elvis Presley—we know of him, of course, but tell me, *dievushka,* he is not black?"

The word for Black in Russian was *niegr*—negro. If you said black —*chërny*—it was an insult. This was hard to get used to.

"*Nyet.* He's—white." (I said *biely,* the color, not knowing any other term for this.) "But he sounds black."

"That's what I thought," she said.

I left her to Elvis and went down to my room. One good thing about Dave was that he always seemed to arrive like the cavalry:

February 10, 1987
Dear Clint,

You probably should not have spent the night with me before you left. It threw me into a tailspin from which I am just now recovering (with the help of my friend Rémy Martin.) I never really believed you were going to go, but there you were and then poof! I am starting to understand how much it means to you and I'm sorry I gave you such a hard time about it. Now I am writing to you in Russia which reminds me of when I was little and wrote to Santa Claus and threw the letters into the fireplace.

Five months is a long time and there's no telling what will happen to you over there. I'll probably become an alcoholic if I am not one already. On top of which every time I flick on the TV there's another report about Russia. That's all they're talking about in every newspaper and magazine. It's a conspiracy.

They're trying to drive me nuts. All this to say that I feel for
you, I admire you for doing this, and I figure you're going to
need all the support you can get when you come home. You were
never too good at housekeeping, so when I think of you coming
home to that empty apartment I worry about your head. I'll still
be here and if you need a friend to talk to you can call me.

Guess what? I have a job on a soap for the next few months. I
play a doctor who has a huge ego and is angry at the world
because he's short. I might get killed off in two or three months,
but then if the public likes me I might not. It beats the hell out of
word-processing at that stupid law firm four nights a week.

Living with Joe isn't too bad. He drinks too much beer and
does too much coke and fucks ugly bimbos but the rent is cheap
and he usually leaves me alone.

I have never remained friends with an ex-lover, especially one
I was engaged to. But I guess there's a first time for everything.
Take care of yourself. I saw a show on AIDS in Africa on Sixty
Minutes that scared the shit out of me. Don't sleep with any
Africans. Love,

Dave

I put his letter with the others I'd received, in the suitcase under my
bed, and left the Institute with a much lighter heart than I had awakened with that morning.

Almost every day a new snowfall covered the city like a fresh coat
of paint, lending a brightness and an airiness to the landscape that was
almost surreal. On a sunny day the flakes glittered golden, at night, if
there was a moon it turned the snow silver. Under these conditions, the
drab, gray color of most of the buildings was not depressing.

Walking through the new snow, however, was serious work. By the
time I'd walked the half-mile to the booth at the corner, I had broken
into a sweat and was panting heavily. I called Vera to whom I had not
spoken in several days. The usual background noise of children roaring
like wild beasts was absent this time, and she sounded exhausted.

"Where did you disappear to?" she said.

I had learned recently that it was easier just to ignore these rhetorical questions.

"What are you doing today?" I asked instead.

"Nothing. Come visit if you like. Maybe I'll get Anna Yefimovna to sit with the children a bit. She doesn't mind and my *God* do I need to get out."

"Do you want anything?"

"Do you know—the strangest thing! I gave the baby that powdered juice with the vitamins and his . . . is gone."

"What is that?"

"On his skin. Red marks. *Gone!*"

"I'll get more."

"I don't like to ask you," she said. "But by God, it's for the children, not me."

"It's nothing," I said. "You feed me and keep *me* healthy."

The sun was pouring in through the kitchen windows, the baby Seryozha was asleep in his carriage on the porch. The two eldest were doing their homework in their bedroom, and the devils, Sasha and Petya, were—of all things!—playing quietly with a plastic truck in the hall. I gave Vera five jars of the powdered mix and a bottle of red wine. She put a steaming bowl of cabbage soup before me. There was bread and cheese and pieces of *selëdka,* salted herring, on the table. This was one Russian delicacy I simply could not eat. The fish was raw and of a reddish hue and smelled of dead things you might find in tide pools on the beach.

Vera looked emotionally bruised. Dark circles completely surrounded her eyes, and the silence between us was heavy.

"Has something happened?" I asked.

"*Nyet,* just another fight. You can't imagine, some days I feel a pain here"—she made a fist and placed it under her left breast—"that I think will kill me some day. Then the walls and ceiling begin to approach me and I feel the space I inhabit is as big as a *grob.*"

"What does that mean, *grob?*"

"The box in which you are put after you die. Shhhh."

The two little ones came in to see what I had brought. They licked their lips when they saw the jars of fruit mix but they were silent and shy and wide-eyed, like forest creatures. Vera mixed them each a cupful of the orange drink and they went back to their game.

Vera sat down at the large square table, her shoulders hunched. She picked up a piece of selëdka and crunched the fishbones with her back teeth.

"Have a piece," she said. "It is the best selëdka we've had this year."

"I can't, thank you."

"You can't? But it's a great delicacy."

"I can't eat it. I'm sorry."

"Anna Yefimovna is coming in a while. We can go for a walk."

"Where would you like to go?"

"It doesn't matter. Every place is the same. I am sick of living. Nothing new ever happens to me."

"Don't say things like that."

"But it is true. I am sick of everything. There is nowhere for me to go."

I was taken by an interesting, if dangerous, idea. Phil had said that the safest Beriozka store for Russians was the book Beriozka on Kropotkinskaya Street. For some reason Russians accompanied by foreigners were not usually harassed there. Phil had taken a friend of his to look at the books the previous semester, and his friend had been completely overwhelmed by the experience. Phil had spent sixty dollars on new, hardcover books that Russians could not get in their regular stores. I was feeling reckless, which often happened when I was angry or depressed, and I decided to take a chance.

"You want to go to the book Beriozka?"

She looked up at me in surprise. A spark seemed to have been ignited behind her eyes.

"You're joking, aren't you?"

"*Nyet.* My friend told me Russians go to the book Beriozka all the time. But I'll speak English to you, you pick out the books you want, and I'll buy them with dollars."

"And I'll pay you back with rubles."

"No. It will be a gift."

"What if they follow us?"

"What can they say? They are my books, I bought them to help my Russian, and you are helping me to choose the best literature of the Soviet Union."

"*Oy oy oy!*" she cried, sucking in her breath and shaking her hand limply. "What should I wear? What should I wear? You are not scared?"

"I am scared."

"I am not scared. I am a mat'-geroinya!" She pounded the table and the dishes jumped. We drank a few shots of wine and headed out. We were only a few subway stops from Kropotkinskaya.

When we came out of the metro it was snowing again. Just across the street was the enormous municipal outdoor pool. Thick clouds of steam rose from the round basin and people swam laps in the greenish water.

"They are crazy!" I said.

"Why? The water is heated," Vera said. "Come on, hurry before you change your mind." She pulled me down the street.

"Do you know that today is National Woman's Day? March 8. What a gift you are giving me! What a gift!"

When we got near the inconspicuous storefront with the BERIOZKA sign above it, we slowed to nearly a stop.

"*Oy,* my heart," she laughed.

"All right. Now, I will speak to you in English and you just say 'yes' and 'no' or shake your head. *Kharasho?*"

"*Yes,*" she said in English.

We approached the door. A man was standing just inside the glass, before the turnstile.

I started to speak loudly and ignored him as we went in.

"*So I've been meaning to check this place out for a while but we have so little time, you know.*"

"*No,*" she said.

"*Yes,*" I said. "*It's a fact.*"

The man barely glanced at us as we marched through the turnstile and up the little flight of stairs straight to the balcony. There lay the unobtrusive shelves of hardcover books without dust jackets. The downstairs section seemed to be comprised of art books and dictionaries and paperbacks by the leading Communist philosophers.

"And my friend told me this is the best bookstore in Moscow."

"Yes," said Vera. She stood statue-like before the books and gripped me by the biceps. *"Bozhe moy!"* she said. *"Kuda smotret'? Kuda smotret'!"*

I whispered that she could take anything she wanted but that she should not speak so loudly. A woman guard who sat at the other end of the balcony glanced up at us but did not say a word.

"Look at this!" Vera was unstoppable. She began to gasp and yell out in Russian every time a title appealed to her.

"They have the Collected Pasternak, Volumes One and Two!"

I lifted them off the shelf and cradled them in the crook of my arm.

"Shhh," I said. "Next."

"Look! Agatha Christie—*Collected Stories!* My husband will love this."

I picked that one up as well. The prices were marked in rubles, which then would be converted to dollars at the cash register. They were incredibly cheap. Three and a half to four rubles for the Russian books, and close to ten for translations of European and American books.

We picked up the *Collected Poems* of Anna Akhmatova ("Requiem" not included, of course) and the *Collected Essays* of Marina Tsvetaeva. For the children I picked up an illustrated Soviet edition of *Gulliver's Travels.* Vera was beside herself and was soon deep in conversation with the woman guard.

"They say soon there will be Pasternak's *Doctor Zhivago,* is that so?" Vera asked.

"So they say," said the guard.

"And Nabokov's stories as well," Vera said.

"So they say," said the guard.

Vera came toward me with her face turned to the shelves of books.

"There is so much *gavno* here," she said under her breath. "But there are also great things!"

There was Tolstoy and Dostoevsky and Bulgakov's *Collected Plays and Essays*—and his extraordinary satirical novel, *The Master and Margarita*, which had been prohibited for over twenty years, until some time in the late sixties.

"I should have *The Master and Margarita*," Vera said. "But I've already read it—I don't own it, of course. But I think I will have the *Collected Plays and Essays* instead because those I have not read. What do you think?"

"Have them both."

She stared at me a long while and her sad, dark eyes brimmed with tears. "It is too much. It will be too much money for you."

Under my breath and out of earshot of the guard, I eased her conscience. "They say that if we put it on our plastic cards—you know, when you pay later, sometimes the little bill never gets to America. I will pay on the plastic card, and who knows? Maybe it will be lost in the mail."

"Ha ha ha! The inefficiency of the system working for us! Ha ha ha! Incredible."

The women at the cash registers were much less friendly than the guard upstairs. They chatted between themselves about their boyfriends and their mothers. I couldn't imagine how they were keeping track of the prices on the books. They glanced at Vera scornfully, and made disgusted faces when I handed them my Capitalist Visa card.

"*Maybe you should stop jabbering long enough to get the count right,*" Vera said. "*Otherwise you might make a mistake in her favor and then you will be accused of inefficiency.*"

They did not say another word and handed me the Visa slip with the price scribbled on it in rubles. The exchange rate apparently varied from day to day and would not be converted until the bill reached the United States. It came to sixty-odd rubles, which meant probably close to ninety dollars.

They put the books in two plastic Beriozka bags.

"No bags," Vera said. "We'll carry them in our own bags."

She took all the books out and, handing me a third of them, shoved the rest into her enormous canvas satchel. We left the store like robbers escaping the scene, and trotted down Kropotkinskaya Street toward the metro. Vera looked over her shoulder every few minutes.

"Are they following us?"

"I don't think so," she said. "If they were going to arrest us they would have done it right outside the store. They might follow us just to know where I live. But for the books we are all right now."

We rode one stop going south on the red line and then changed to the brown line, which ran in a complete circle around the central section of the city. The brown line was always jammed at the stations closest to Red Square and the main business district. Vera grabbed my arm and pressed forward into the wall of people. An elbow fight ensued. Vera's opponent was a large woman in a red wool coat.

"*So much energy, Citizen! After such a long day of work? If it is not enough for you maybe you should work a double shift!*" Vera shouted. The woman mumbled something which I did not understand. Two stops later the woman began to nudge her way toward the doors, and Vera whacked her with the canvas bag. It seemed everyone got off with the woman in the red coat, and Vera appropriated two vacated seats.

"*Come here!*" she yelled to me. I never sat during rush hour because there was inevitably someone old, someone exhausted, someone pregnant or with a child, who deserved to sit more than I.

The car began to fill up with a whole new wave of people. Vera put her canvas bag down on the seat beside her and refused to budge. To avoid another scene I took the seat.

She put the bag on her lap and hugged it protectively. A devilish smile suddenly brightened her face.

"We fucked them didn't we?" she laughed under her breath. "*Bozhe moy,* does it give me pleasure to fuck them."

"Who?"

"*Them.* The ones who tell us how to live and what to eat and what to read. Them."

Her face went crimson with rage, or possibly satisfaction. She punched me in the arm. The car was packed once again, and pressing up against us was a wall of bodies carrying the pungent smell I'd come to identify as the collective odor of Russia: fried foods laden with garlic and onion, and the smoke of harsh brown tobacco that burned like dry autumn leaves. The soap here was coarse, like the traditional *savon de Marseille;* the detergents and shampoos were generic and did their duty without adding a perfumey scent; the odor of sweat was not camouflaged by antiperspirants. Not powerful enough to override all of this but noticeable nonetheless was a trace of industrial-strength disinfectant. All public places smelled like this, even the Institute, which was crowded with foreigners. It spoke of a difficult life but was not terrible once you got accustomed to it.

"Do you know what the trouble with my husband is?" Vera asked, pulling me out of my sleepy reverie.

"No, of course not."

"What is it with you foreigners that you are always exhausted? You are not as strong as we are, I think. *Nu, ladno.* Do you want to know what the trouble with my husband is?"

"It is not my business."

"You are my friend and therefore I make it your business."

She spoke in a mumble close to my ear.

"My husband is a *gomoseksualist,*" Vera said.

"Excuse me?" I leaned toward her mouth.

"Gomoseksualist. *Gomoseksualist,*" she insisted.

This, I thought, has to mean what I think. What else could it mean?

"He loves men?"

"You understand?"

"But you have five children!"

"Listen, the wind blows and I get pregnant."

"But still."

"I fucked your mother! We missed our whorish stop!" Vera said.

"We can get off at the next one and turn around."

"*Nyet.* Let's go around the city. In an hour we'll be back where we started and here at least we can talk. I don't speak about any of this in front of the children."

"Vera, what are you telling me? How long have you known this?"

"Since before I was pregnant with the second child. But he promised to stop. He swore, he cried, he begged me. I believed him. But that son of a bitch did it again. And again. I think he wants to hurt me, he hates me and wants to destroy me."

"But Vera, it is not something he has control over. It is not a choice."

"Yes, it is a choice. To sin or not to sin is a choice."

"We do not believe that in America. In the fifties psychiatrists tried to cure homosexuals by making them learn to love the other sex, but now they say that is wrong. It is against the nature of that person to love the other sex and it must be accepted as normal for that person to be that way."

"It is a sin. Here you go to jail for eight years. And what about SPID? What do you call it—AIDS? They say it is the gomoseksualisty and the Africans who brought it here. My friend was in the hospital last month and she said there were thirty or forty men with SPID in one room! This is a secret—no one knows if it is true or not but at the hospital that is what people were saying. Am I going to die?"

"When was the last time you slept with him?"

"When I became pregnant with the last one."

"So that is almost two years ago. Listen, here it is still a new illness. In America you would be in danger."

"But he eats the same food and uses the same bathroom as we do!"

"They say you cannot get it like that. You have to have contact through sex or through blood—"

"Sometimes he hits me, sometimes I hit him."

"Look—you must not hit each other in any case."

"Once he tried to kill me with a knife."

"My God."

"He said the only way he could live in peace was if I were dead."

"He will probably kill you with a knife before he gives you SPID. In any case you must not sleep with him. There is a test."

"*Ha!* And then he will go to jail for eight years for gomoseksualism. Do you know where he finds them? Others like him? In the public toilets, in the baths, in the street. There is something in the eyes, he told me. A look. They pass each other, they make a signal, they go to some dark place, or to a friend's apartment. Once he was beaten very badly. But you do not go to the militsia and say 'I invited a strange man to take a walk with me down a dark street' do you? Then he had one friend for a long while—that was between the third and fourth child —the man would phone and ask for my husband and I thought it was strange but I never said anything. I did not want to believe it. It is horrible. I am a *dura*. A complete idiot."

"But in the beginning—with *you*—in bed, you did not know?"

"How would I know? I never had another man. I thought something was wrong with *me*. When we got married we did not try it for three months. That was all right with me, I was scared. But then we drank too much vodka one night and tried. *Bozhe moy,* what a disaster. He could not do what he is supposed to do. I cried. He felt sorry for me so he went to the bathroom and did something for a while and came back and managed for a few seconds to do something to me, and then in a month I was pregnant with the first. And he was proud! We did not try again until I became pregnant with the second.

"Between the first and the second, whenever he drank at a party he became like a woman, with eyes full of desire for every man in the room. Then he was beaten so badly one night in the street he almost died—and I found out the truth."

"But really, Vera. What about for the children? It is not fair to them. Why did you continue after the first one?"

"I told you he swore never again, never again. After he was beaten he told me 'I am cured.' In any case, abortion is a sin."

"You are crazy. I do not agree with you."

We must have made a strange pair to an onlooker; we sat huddled together, our red and sweating faces inches apart, grimacing at each other and arguing in whispers.

"I am crazy. It is true. And now the boys are getting older. Volodya and Kolya bring home their little school comrades and I see that look in my husband's eyes. I fear more than anything that he will try something some day with one of them, and he will go to prison for certain and probably die there from a beating."

"You do not believe me when I tell you he cannot control it?"

"*No.* He does it to hurt me, I am certain. All his friends and work comrades think he is the lover of lovers, the man of men! *Piat' chelovek detiey!* Five children! Imagine. Ha ha ha! I laugh behind their backs. What protection I am for his other life. His life of sin and filth. He will not divorce. He has nowhere to go. And if I go to ZAGS—you know, the Bureau of Civil Affairs—and register for divorce, I need a good reason. Because they look very badly on divorces of *mat'-geroiny.* Mat'-geroiny simply do not get divorced."

"But you cannot live together, you are always in pain! Do not fight with him, Vera. He is afraid and alone and he cannot control it. You must convince him to get a divorce. You are young and you can find another man."

"*Ha!* What crazy man would want a mat'-geroinya with five children? No, speaking seriously—no. I went to Zagorsk last month and talked to the priest. He said if I choose to divorce I must never have another man, but his opinion is that I must be patient and wait. He said maybe my husband will change."

"That is crazy, Vera. A priest does not have to live your life. Listen to me: your husband is not going to change. It is not something he *can* change."

"How do you know?" she said, defensive suddenly.

"Tell me one thing—what is worse to the priest, homosexuality or divorce?"

"I do not know. I will go next week and ask him. Do not talk to me anymore about this, I do not like at all what you are saying."

We sat in gloomy silence for a while. I had never in my life heard such a story from someone's mouth.

I felt utterly helpless. There was nothing I could do and I did not have the right to offer her advice. I should not have said a word. Absolutely not. However, I wanted to continue the conversation because in my mind there was a distinct possibility she was not telling me everything. Russians often gave foreigners a personal interpretation of events while insisting that their story was the whole, impersonal truth. They became offended when questions were asked. So, it was up to us to weigh the facts and come up with a balanced view of Soviet life. The problem was this: how does one know if one has interpreted correctly? So many of us went home sounding like sanctimonious fools.

"I am sorry," I said. "I have no right to say anything to you. But I tell you what—through the embassy mail I will ask my friend to send articles in Russian about SPID."

"That would be helpful," she said. "Can I ask you something? Have you been in love? *Passionately* in love, I mean."

"Yes. Right now, in fact, I am in love and it is making me crazy."

"You are in love now? Not with a Russian I hope."

"No."

"With whom?"

"An American from my Institute. It is a very sexual thing—sorry, but it is true. And I believe you can love someone sexually and not like him otherwise, just as you can love someone for their mind and have no desire to sleep with them. Sometimes I think I confuse love and sex but this time I am not sure. I love his mind and I love sleeping with him. But he does not want me for good, only for now."

"You people seem so free with sex. Well, I envy you that you have known that kind of love. I have never felt it, although I love my husband and my children. I am waiting for it to happen but I believe it has passed me by. It will never be."

The next day at school was to be an excursion day (we were going to visit a school specializing in English which was located at the opposite end of town from the Institute) so I decided to spend the night at Vera's. This way I could sleep later, save the ten-ruble taxi fare home, and, since Vera lived close to the center, cut the morning's trip by half. That night her husband did not come home until after one. I was relieved because I did not think I could look him in the eye.

Vera put me in the room with the three little ones. I took off everything but my cotton turtleneck and underpants and slid into the double bed, next to Sasha the Terror with the leonine hair. He turned over. His round leonine eyes glared at me in the darkness. The blue

РЕСТОРАН sign across the street blinked on and off in the moist whites of his eyes.

"What is it?" I whispered, afraid he might wake the others.

He thought for a moment, as though he were trying to decide whether or not to trust me. "I am afraid."

"Of what are you afraid?"

"Of people."

"Are you afraid of me?"

"No. Of the ones who laugh at me."

"Who laughs at you?"

"The ones in my sleep."

He turned his back to me and began to cry into the pillow. I heard his muffled sobs against the even breathing of his two sleeping brothers.

"Do you want me to get your mama?" I whispered.

"Nyet."

"Do you want me to tell you a story?"

"Tell me a story about America. But speak slowly because otherwise I can't understand you."

"All right. One day Sasha comes to New York to visit his friend Clinton . . ." I ran the tips of my fingers through his curly hair and over his neck and shoulders. The slightness of his four-year-old bones moved me. He smelled vaguely of sweet things and milk, the way I imagined babies did.

The front door opened and closed suddenly. Sasha sat bolt upright in the bed.

"Papa is home," he said hopefully.

"Yes," I said, *"vcyo v poryadkie.* Everything is in order. Everything will be all right."

19

AN ENCOUNTER WITH SOVIET YOUTH

"Who was the first man in space?" the teacher asked. She wore a gray skirt and a navy blue button-down sweater over a white shirt, through which you could see the lumps in the padding of her bra. She probably looked the same as on any other school day except that she had recently been to the beauty parlor and her auburn hair curled stiffly and unnaturally around her head.

At her question all the little arms went up at once, pointing flat palms toward the front of the room. Above the blackboard was a touched-up and colored photograph of Lenin smiling down benevolently on the world. The walls were crowded with maps of the U.S.S.R. and children's drawings of space capsules, the red hammer and sickle insignia always right-side-up regardless of the angle of the craft.

"Yes, Kolya," said the teacher.

Kolya stood up, back straight and arms folded in front of him. Kolya's starched white uniform shirt was sticking out from the back of his pants. Tied around his neck, boy scout-style, was the red Young Pioneers scarf.

"Citizen of the Union of Soviet Socialist Republics, Yuri Alexeyevich Gagarin."

"Very good. And who was the first man to walk on the moon?"

Again the little hands went up and the teacher smiled at the five of us Americans crowded into the little desks at the back of her class. Our group of forty had been split up in this manner, and, at that moment, was spread out all over the Soviet secondary school that specialized in the study of English. We five had been assigned to a third grade Russian Grammar class.

"Yes, Masha? Who was the first man on the moon?"

Masha stood up and stepped into the aisle at the side of her wooden desk. "Citizen of the United States of America, Neil Armstrong."

"Very good. You may sit down now, Masha." Masha apparently liked to stand and waited a while before taking her seat.

"Now we will have verb conjugation." The teacher turned to the blackboard and wrote down three columns of verbs. As soon as her back was to the class the little faces pivoted stealthily in our direction. Their eyes were round with curiosity. They seemed to know instinctively when she was about to turn around and their noses shot back toward the front of the room before she faced them once again.

After conjugation came a dictation and afterward the children were called one by one to the board. When a mistake was made the teacher asked the student at the board to recite the applicable rule of grammar. The child then shouted out an incomprehensible series of words at a deafening pitch. Masha seemed to know the answer to every question and spent the hour with her arm in the air, moaning and squirming in her seat. Her counterpart was a round, fair-headed boy whose name we never learned since he was not asked to answer, doubtless because we were there. He sat by the window and stared out, leaning dreamily against his fist, the only student not wearing the Young Pioneers scarf. I wondered if this was a punishment or if he'd simply forgotten to put it on that morning. Like Ferdinand the Bull, he was completely disinterested in the competitive struggle going on around him and did not even seem to notice that there were visitors in his class.

When the bell rang Ceppie and I hurried off to find a bathroom. We had five minutes to get downstairs to the main auditorium for the grand assembly that had been organized in our honor by the entire school. In the hall Ceppie asked a serious-looking little girl for directions. The girl's brown jumper and white shirt were starched crisp, and at the top of her blond pigtails two gauze bows rested like large white butterflies. She wore the Young Pioneers scarf tied around her neck and a red pin in the shape of a star on her left breast, in the center of which was a photograph of young Lenin, aged probably ten.

Walking stiffly ahead of us with her chin in the air and her arm extended, she cut a path through the crowd of children. Ceppie and I were chest-high in a sea of bobbing heads and red scarves. White, powder-blue, and pink bows, some as big as pineapples, bounced past on the little girls' heads.

We went through a large, empty room with a shiny blue linoleum floor. At one end stood a four-foot plaster bust of Lenin surrounded by flowers, and above, on a red curtain, hung the same portrait as in the classroom. Red scarves and fancy bows flashed as the children, standing in neat ranks, swung their hips from side to side and bent down and touched their toes. They were singing in English, along with a teacher who stood at the front: "Clap your hands baby baby clap your hands/ On your hips baby baby on your hips/ Touch your toes baby baby touch your toes."

"Someone should tell her that's slang," Ceppie murmured.

At the end of the hall the little girl opened a door and the odor of urine and disinfectant wafted out. We went in. There were three open stalls lining the far wall, so that the crowd of girls waiting faced the girls peeing. Little and big girls squatted over the toilets, perched with their feet on the porcelain. There were no toilet seats and no paper and no one seemed to mind.

"Shit," Ceppie said. Our little girl was looking up at us worriedly. The other girls moved aside politely in the line.

"I can't pee when someone's watching me," Ceppie said.

"Well, pretend then."

This was a strange experience. I wondered if all Soviet schools' toilets were the same. It occurred to me that the U.S. Army employed a similar system, and I wondered if the reason for this was psychological, or simply economic.

There was a thin partition between the stalls, and with all the girls watching, Ceppie and I squatted over the bowls with our feet on the ground. I saw the top of Ceppie's curly black head sticking out from the other side of the flimsy wall. Her curls were shaking and I could hear her laughing. "Got some paper, *mujer?*"

The girls watched us impassively, feigning indifference just as their parents did on the buses and metro. I took a wad of toilet paper out of my bag and passed a handful to Ceppie. This seemed to interest them particularly and for a moment there was complete silence. I wiped quickly without looking up.

"*Spasiba,*" we said, thanking our little guide who had waited for us to finish. Ceppie gave her two sticks of Juicy Fruit gum. "It is chewing gum," she warned. "Not to swallow."

"Oh, I know," the girl said lightly. "We have *zhvachka* too but it is not as good as yours."

Then she became the center of an attentive circle and Ceppie and I made our way toward the main auditorium on the ground floor. We went down three flights of stairs while children of all sizes rushed past us screaming and shouting at the top of their lungs.

"This look yust like the school I went to," Ceppie said in her Puerto Rican accent. "Uniforms and everything, eccept we had mean old nuns and Jesus instead of Lenin."

The two front rows of the auditorium had been saved for the visitors, and once we were all seated children came and filled in the empty seats among us. Trading began immediately. Chewing gum and key chains and baseball cards and Star Wars stickers for Soviet *znachki,* the little pins everyone collected as souvenirs. A boy in front of me handed me a pin of the Tretyakov Gallery painted in gold on a white background. I gave him a key chain of a purple rubber palm tree and a roll of Life Savers.

A girl of around sixteen, probably a senior, got up on stage with an acoustic guitar. She stood alone, thin and pale and hunched at the shoulders, and began to strum. After a moment she cleared her throat and sang "Where Have All the Flowers Gone?" in a tremulous voice.

"Where have all the flowers gone?
Young girls picked them every one

When will they ever gone?
When will they ever gone?"

She sang the entire song and received thunderous applause from the
American guests despite the slight mistake. Then a group of little ones
got up and formed a chain with their arms linked in the air. They sang
while an instructor accompanied them on the piano.

We are peaceful loving people
We don't want war
We are peaceful angry people
We don't want war
We want to keep clear skies
We want to keep fresh water
We are peaceful angry people
We don't want war.

"We don't want war either, mang," Ceppie said in a loud voice. The
music instructor had probably put the song together herself, with her
limited knowledge of English. I wondered what "peaceful angry people" was supposed to mean and if it was meant to imply that the
children were angry at us for being the cause of their fear. They looked
so uncomfortable up there, standing stiffly with their mouths opened
wide and their frightened eyes staring at us.

After their song the children came into the audience and tugged at
our hands. The principal of the school stood up and demanded that we
go on stage and sing something. One of the American students took the
guitar from the thin Russian girl. He was a shy fellow of around
twenty, wore thick glasses and had long, stringy hair. He began strum-
ming "This Land Is Your Land" and we sat down on the edge of the
stage and started to sing. We were able to sing the first stanza, but no
one knew the rest of the words and our effort dwindled into an uncomfortable silence. This was a strange cultural difference between
America and Russia, and the children were obviously surprised; you
could gather any five Russians in a room and they would all know the

words to any number of traditional songs. Not in America, at least not our generation.

Our guitarist stood up and announced courageously that he would sing by himself. The tips of his ears turned pink and his lenses fogged.

"This is an American song about peace and about the world." He said *"O mirie i o mirie,"* because in Russian, *mir* means both *peace* and *world.*

"It is by John Lennon and is called 'Imagine.' "

His hoarse, high, pleading voice stung my heart; I did not think that most of the Russian students, especially the little ones who had sung "we are a peaceful angry people" would understand what he was singing.

> Imagine no possessions
> I wonder if you can
> No need for greed or hunger
> A brotherhood of man
> Imagine all the people
> Sharing all the world
> You may say I'm a dreamer
> But I'm not the only one
> I hope some day you'll join us
> And the world will be as one.

I looked over at the principal, who sat stiffly in the first row just a few feet away, and then at the instructor, who was still sitting at the piano but turned in our direction now. Their tough, round faces did not soften, but then the public Soviet face never did.

After the show we were allowed fifteen minutes in the main recess hall to chat with the upperclassmen. It was lunch break. A very tall and lanky blond teenager with large blue eyes began asking our courageous guitarist what music he listened to back home, and what were today's most popular groups. I was listening in when another student, a short, heavyset boy approached Ceppie and me. He wore a navy blue blazer with a white turtleneck underneath. His hair was dark and oily and his shoulders were specked with dandruff.

"Khow do you do? My name is Vadim. I am studying English next to ten years. I want to go to university after school and study to be a journalist or a lawyer. What will you do after university?"

Ceppie and I looked at each other as he waited with an enthusiastic smile for an answer.

"I am thinking about law school as well," Ceppie said.

I felt like a total failure.

"I do not know what I shall do after school," I said.

"You do not know? Wery interesting," said the boy. "It is true, then, that American students do not take a decision so early as Russians? I would like to wisit America and some day I will. I am learning English for the work purpose. Maybe I will be a big journalist. Maybe I will be a lawyer. I am so interesting to talk to Americans. You will be waiting and I get my coat, yes? I have no class this afternoon. I will go to the metro with you."

Ceppie looked around nervously. "Are you sure that's a good idea? You're not allowed to leave school, are you?"

"Certainly. They do not mind."

Vadim, Ceppie, and I walked away from the school in the bright sunlight. Vadim was explaining that he was the best student in his mathematics and English classes, and if he missed this afternoon he would get a 2 for the day (they were graded from 1, an F, to 5, an A) which would not affect his monthly grade since, he said, "I am a 5."

"But you told us you had no classes this afternoon," Ceppie pointed out.

"Yes," he said thoughtfully. What did he mean by that?

At che bus stop the tall lanky fellow was standing with our guitarist. They were still discussing rock'n'roll bands.

"You know Iron Maiden?" the tall fellow asked.

"I know *of* them," the American said. "Like I said, mostly I'm into country music, and you know, early rock'n'roll."

The tall fellow seemed disappointed and changed the subject. "You want to hear a not polite Soviet joke?"

Vadim wanted us to ignore the other student and told us in a loud voice that he admired America a great deal, but that overall he thought the Soviet Union was a better country. "In the newspaper they write that you do not want peace because you are a violent society. I believe this is true because here we have no poors," he told us, "we have no homeless, no crime. When you go home you will tell your friends this is true, yes?"

"Yes we will. But Americans do not want war either," Ceppie pointed out.

"Then why they hate us?" Vadim asked, surprised.

"They are very afraid of Communism," Ceppie said.

"Why?"

It did not seem appropriate to tell him that there were trade-offs involved. Yes, you could not walk in big city parks at night, and yes, there were neighborhoods to be avoided. But Americans would not trade their personal freedom for clean and safe streets. I did not think that filling him in on a few facts would help matters at all; he had his ideas, as everyone did. He would not believe us anyway.

"What does your father do for a living, Vadim?" I asked.

"He is an artist of placards for the government. He won last year the greatest award for artists in the Soviet Union."

Vadim asked us for our addresses back home. "If," he said, "I become a journalist in America some day, I will phone you and say 'Khello! Remember Vadim from Moscow?' and we will continue to be friends, yes?"

"Sure," Ceppie said, and took out a notebook.

"I am very interesting to collect moneys," Vadim said. "I have a money from 1867." He held it out for our inspection. "I am going to a special store to change this money for rubles."

"What kind of store is that?" I asked.

"A special store not in the street you know. You have any American moneys to give me?"

If a militsia passed by and saw us giving Vadim a dollar bill he would most certainly arrest us for speculating, and I wondered if Vadim knew this. I looked him hard in the eyes and received nothing but his regular, engratiating, wide-open gaze that did not offer any answers. I decided that he probably took us for fools.

"I have no American money," I said.

"I have no American money either," Ceppie said.

"Will you take me to your Institute and show me American moneys and records?" Vadim persisted.

"We are not allowed to bring guests into our Institute," I said.

"I will wait outside," he said.

"No," I said, "it is not permitted. And we must go to see friends now." This was not a lie; Ceppie had invited me to come along to a dinner at her friend Grisha's.

"To where are you going?" he asked. In Russia paranoia had become a way of life for us and I immediately imagined the worst: the school had sent Vadim, given him the afternoon off, to spy on us.

"We have to go now, Vadim." Ceppie slapped him on the shoulder and shook his hand. We hurried off, leaving him on the other side of the turnstile, and did not look back.

"Vsevo dobrovo!" he called after us, wishing us everything nice, everything good in life.

A SECOND
ENCOUNTER
WITH
SOVIET YOUTH

Before going to Grisha's Ceppie and I made a major detour. We could not arrive empty-handed and therefore went to the food Beriozka in the Mezhdunarodny Tsentr, which was the best hard-currency food store we knew of in Moscow.

This was your average three-hour production. From Shcherbakov-skaya station in the north, where the school we had visited was located, we took the metro south toward the center, changed onto the brown line at Prospekt Mira (Prospect Peace), rode west three stops then changed again onto the purple line at Barrikadnaya (Barricades) and rode two stops to Ulitsa 1905 Goda (the Street of the Year 1905). Then it was a fifteen-minute walk to the Mezh, our nickname for Armand Hammer's enormous steel and glass complex. The guard at the door would not let us in because we looked like poor students, not rich tourists. Ceppie shouted in English that it was an utter scandal that this hotel had been financed by an American and we, fellow citizens, were being denied entrance. The guard held fast, grumbling in Russian that we could not get in without a hotel pass. He must have been in a bad mood that day, because never before had anyone stopped me at the Mezh. We pretended we did not understand him and after acting out-raged for a few minutes, Ceppie flashed her American passport at him and pushed him out of the way. Force seemed the only method of persuasion, for he did not call the militsia or run after us.

We walked around the supermarket pushing a metal grocery cart. Soviet diplomats' wives in fur coats and a few Western correspondents were the only other customers in the store. There were no fresh vegetables that day except mushrooms and leeks that were ridiculously overpriced, so we settled for canned goods and alcohol. We bought a bottle of Stolichnaya, a jar of eggplant caviar, four tins of sprats, a tin of Camembert cheese from Denmark, a salami, and a six-pack of warm Heineken.

The good news was that from the metro station called the Street of the Year 1905 to Avenue of the Enthusiasts, where Grisha lived, we only had to make one change, and that was at the absolute other end of the city. We were on the metro an hour, and it was a fifteen-minute bus ride from the Enthusiasts stop to Grisha's. There was ice on the inside and outside of the bus's windows and by then the sky had turned completely black. Ceppie was nervous and irritable, and I was exhausted.

"I go over to Grisha's all the time. Hell, I don't have any other friends here except the guys Misha introduced me to when I first met him.

"The thing that kills me is how great it was when I was here last summer. Misha really loved me. Now he's always running away from me. He won't talk to me. He shows up at Grisha's once in a while, but not often, and less and less lately. He brings his dopey twat along and I'm too embarrassed to confront him in front of her. Every time I go over to Grisha's I expect Mish will show up without her and we'll be able to talk. He either shows up with her or he doesn't show up. Then I get drunk and depressed and I wonder what the hell I'm doing there to start with."

She complained that the party would turn into another drunken brawl because Alik, the friend who always cooked the food, never served dinner until after ten and by ten everyone was too drunk to eat. But Ceppie said she had to go because Grisha had begged her to. Grisha had been so kind to her, had taken her under his wing so to speak, and had remained her friend even after she and Misha had broken up (which was very unusual for Russians, with their acute sense of brotherly loyalty). I remembered that Ceppie had told me that Grisha was an America buff, and I became concerned.

"Does Grisha want something from you that he's not letting on about, like an American wife or something?"

"No, mang. He's my friend," she said, rolling her eyes. "He never wants anything. You know what he told me? He told me Misha is a coward. He wanted more than anything to go to the States. But he's afraid of starting over, in a new place and all that. And Grisha says Mish's afraid of me 'cause I'm stronger than he is. He's afraid of women. That's why Mish picked that blond twat who never says a word. You know what else Grisha said? He told me the only reason Mish is with that girl is because he knows I'm proud as hell and I'll leave him alone. Grisha says they don't sleep together."

I remembered Ceppie saying that Misha and the girl lived together. Something in the story was not right.

"Don't they live together?"

"Yeah. But I'm not sure if she lives like *in* his room or in the room next door. It's a communal apartment. I don't know anything, man. They don't tell you anything," she muttered.

I explained to her what Phil had explained to me: it was not unusual for Russians to get married simply to be able to stay in Moscow. You needed a permit to live in Moscow, if you were not a resident, but to get a permit, you had to have a residence; to get a residence, however, you had to have a permit—so you married a Muscovite with an apartment. Misha and the girl might have made this kind of arrangement, a business deal.

Ceppie was still enraged and not remotely convinced.

"Look, Ceppie, you're free to go anywhere you want. You're free to travel, you're free to leave. Misha's girl isn't. She's stuck here for the long haul."

I thought of Andrej, who had asked me to marry him, leaving out the small detail that he had a wife and child in Leningrad. It was no wonder the women felt threatened by us.

"If Misha doesn't tell you anything, I'd imagine he doesn't tell her anything either. Why don't you talk to *her?* She might just tell you the truth, whatever it is."

"She never would. That's why I want to chuck her across the room. She's got the little round face of a Suffering Innocent and she looks at me like I'm a behemoth coming to get her. I'm tired of this shit. Let's talk about something else."

"Like what?"

"Like how's Phil? I wanted to ask him to come to this party too," Ceppie said, thrusting her hands into the pockets of her olive-colored jacket and sinking her nose below the fur collar.

"Why?" I became apprehensive and felt slightly betrayed. I had not seen or talked to Phil since the night we'd argued on Red Square. Afterward I had gone to Ceppie's room and cried, hunched over at the side of her bed, the way she had the night she'd become enraged over Misha and punched the hole through the bathroom door.

"Because Phil saved my ass," Ceppie pointed out. "The man is good; he saved my ass and I consider him a friend of mine."

"You didn't ask him, did you? Because if he's coming I'm going home." Another hour-and-a-half ride back to the Institute was impossible; I felt silly, throwing around idle threats.

"Don't be silly, *mujer.* Of course I didn't do that. But can I say something? I think he's in love with you. Maybe he's scared too or something. You should see the way he looks at you when you come into the cafeteria and he's sitting at a table in the back. He watches you. He watches you until you look at him and then he pretends he hasn't been watching."

I became excited by the idea of his peppermint eyes looking me over the way they often did, as though they could see right through my clothes. I realized that despite myself I wished Ceppie had invited him. We were now going on Night Number Three of not sleeping together and it was beginning to hurt me physically as well as emotionally.

Ceppie sat glumly with her body slumped in the seat.

"I feel like I shouldn't be here, man. I'm wasting my time. I should've gone straight to fuckin' grad school or gotten a job in New York. Here I'm just wasting my time. I came back just to marry that fuck and now he doesn't even want me."

"Being in Russia can't be a waste of time," I said. "Although falling in love with an American in Russia seems crazy." I was in the mood to get blind drunk and was pleased to know that I would be able to do so without creating a scene because I'd just fade into the crowd of drunks at Grisha's; among these people I would not make a fool of myself.

The party had already begun. There were several bottles of vodka and Georgian wine on the kitchen table. There was a bottle of Cuban rum and a bottle of Armenian cognac on the counter next to the sink. I could not imagine where they had gotten this stuff; it was almost impossible to get alcohol in Moscow. There was, however, no food to be seen anywhere, although a large pot was boiling away on the stove. Its lid hissed and clattered from the pressure of the steam. Ceppie unloaded her knapsack on the kitchen table.

The cook, Alik, was wearing a frilly apron and drinking shots of rum by the stove. He came over to see what we'd brought, nodded appreciatively and said nothing.

"Please be introduced," Ceppie said in Russian. "My friend Alik."

Alik was approximately my height. He had the upper body of a person who trained with weights and legs that resembled chopsticks. His blond hair curled upward, away from his forehead, and came together in a duck's tail in the back. He had a narrow nose and jaw, sharp blue eyes and a perfect row of even white teeth. He kissed Ceppie on the lips with an open mouth and threw her back in a dip. She did not resist him, which astonished me. Then he gave me a big hug and stuck his tongue in my ear. He said something incomprehensible and I asked him to repeat. "Foo," he said. "Don't let life bother you. It's never worth it."

"What are you preparing, Alik?" Ceppie said, lifting the lid off the steaming pot.

"Do you like curry? I am making Indian curry." He brought his fingers to his lips and kissed them with a loud smack.

Alik was already quite drunk. He swayed a little and his eyes went in and out of focus as he spoke.

"We're not going to eat at ten again, are we?" Ceppie asked. "Because I don't feel like getting drunk tonight."

"Foo," he said, swinging the wooden spoon he held in his hand. *"Vcë vsegda nakryvayetsa pizdoy.* Everything always gets covered in cunt."

"That is an idiom, I presume," I said.

"It means something always goes wrong," Ceppie explained.

Grisha came stumbling in from the room at the end of the hall. Music was blasting from there and also from the little portable tape deck in the kitchen. It was on top of the refrigerator, surrounded by unsteady piles of cassettes that cascaded to the floor every time someone slammed the refrigerator door.

Grisha was exactly as Ceppie had described him: tall, thin, good-natured, with a pasty complexion and sensitive eyes. He had buck teeth and his mouth took up the lower half of his face and completely eclipsed his chin.

"I am delighted to finally meet you," he said, shaking my hand with a firm grip. *"Ochen pryatno.* What shall you have to drink?"

"I would love a glass of rum. It has been a long time since I have had rum and I have never tried Cuban rum."

"Cuban rum is the best rum in the world," he said, craning his neck proudly.

Ceppie said she would have a glass of water.

Grisha shook his head in disappointment. "Come now, Ceppie, it is a party. Come, for me, a little vodka. A little *vodochka* to make Grisha happy."

"All right," Ceppie said. Grisha gave her a shot of vodka in a little glass, toasted her, and drank his down to the bottom. Ceppie took one sip and while Grisha had his head tilted back, dumped her vodka into a glass on the table. Ceppie sat down in a chair near the stove. Alik's attention was on his curry most of the time, but once in a while he turned and kissed Ceppie on the neck and she returned his affections by whacking him in the behind.

Grisha stumbled in and out, in and out, never without his glass of vodka. A girl came in and sat down with us. She had a moon face and plain brown hair and wore heavy blue eye makeup.

"This is Sonya," Ceppie said.

"*Ochen pryatno,*" Sonya said.

"*Ochen pryatno,*" I said.

Alik put down his spoon and threw his arms around Ceppie's shoulders. His hands cupped her breasts for a moment, then Ceppie flew out of her chair and flipped Alik over her back. He laughed good-naturedly as he lay on the linoleum floor with his knees up and Ceppie's shin on his collarbone. "You have to teach me how to do that," Alik said. "I love it. Every time you do it, I love it."

"Behave yourself, Alik," she said.

Sonya sipped her drink impassively without the slightest change in her disinterested expression.

"You won't let me touch you so I have to grab you when I can," Alik said. "If you'd only let me, then I would not be ending up on my back all the time, you'd be ending up on your back all the time."

In came the tall, dark Misha. I knew this immediately because Ceppie's demeanor changed in a split second. She shot up from the floor and took her place back at the table, looked down into her empty glass, and grabbed the bottle of vodka.

Ceppie had told me Misha had Cossack blood, which gave him his piercing black eyes and shock of black, unmanageable hair, but he was more handsome than I had expected. His eyes, however, seemed shifty and his face seemed to be set in a permanent wince, as though simply being alive were too much for him.

"*Privyet,* Misha," Alik said, getting up. "I was just telling Ceppie that I'm in love with her."

Misha laughed uncomfortably and glanced quickly about the room. He nodded at me and looked away. I imagined that Ceppie had told him about me, as she had told me about him, which made us both feel exposed. I did not like him because he'd hurt Ceppie, and he probably knew that. But I could tell that he already had made up his mind not to like me, either.

Misha hurriedly filled his glass with vodka and left the kitchen. Ceppie filled her little tumbler to the brim and followed him out, vodka spilling over her hand. The doorbell kept ringing and the hall became crowded with people.

Alik poured rum into his glass and mine. There was a half a lemon by the sink and I cut it in two and dropped a piece into my rum.

"*Nyet, nyet, nyet!* That way you ruin the taste of the rum." Alik stuck three fingers into my glass. I pulled it away from him. He looked at me cheerlessly for a long time and then said, "Why do you look at me like that? I know you don't believe me but it is true that I have fallen in love with her."

He said *vlyubilsa*, "I have fallen in love," not *lyublyu*, in the present, which could mean either "I love," or "I like."

"Nobody believes me. They say American girls are easy to seduce. Do you see what happens to me when I try to seduce her? There is only one problem with her." He lifted an index finger to the bridge of his nose and held it there unsteadily. "She does not drink like a sailor. She looks at me like my own mother does when I am drunk. It makes me feel like a *podliets*, a scoundrel." He punched himself hard in the chest and a loud thump reverberated through the kitchen.

"And you *are* a podliets," said Sonya indifferently without looking up from the table. She had eaten almost an entire tin of sprats, laying one fish at a time on a slice of brown bread and popping the whole thing in her mouth, followed by a shot of vodka.

"You shut up," Alik said. "You don't know anything." Addressing me, he said, "I have a very good job. I am an exporter of vodka to Japan. I go to Japan on business several times a year and speak Japanese and so on. . . . I am not unhappy. And, do you know, with my eyes closed I could tell you the name of any vodka you pour into my glass. Shall we try?"

"Is there really a difference? For example, between Stolichnaya and Moskovskaya and Russkaya?"

"Are you joking? To me it is like the difference between rum and gin." He refilled our glasses with the Cuban rum, which tasted like a strong combination of cooking rum and Bacardi dark. He drank his down in a gulp, then placed a smaller pot on a back burner, poured in water and a heaping pile of rice from a generic paper bag that had РИС written on it in red lettering.

"You seem to be more of a drinker—she does not get angry at you?"

"No. But to her I am not a possible future lover."

"*Ha Ha Ha!* I like American girls because they talk like men. Do you know—Ceppie becomes angry when I try to open a door for her or pour her a drink? She wants to do it all herself. And she can throw me over her shoulder! What do you think of that, Sonya, if you are capable of thinking at all?"

"I think you are a heartless drunken swine who couldn't hold a door open even if you wanted to because you're always too drunk."

"If you want my advice, Sonya, you'd better learn at least to pretend to be soft and nice because no man is going to have you the way you carry yourself."

"Go to the devil. I wouldn't have *you* if you begged me on your knees."

"Foo. I want her, do you understand me?" He laid his outstretched arms on my shoulders and stared at me imploringly, as though I would somehow hand her to him on a platter. "*I want her.* It is supposed to be easy for us with American girls, what is it with her?"

"She is not American, she is Puerto Rican American. You know this. She is Catholic and to her it is important to love and respect someone before . . . before . . ."

"But she loves the *golubchik,* the little blue boy," he said, and laughed good-naturedly.

"What does that mean?" I asked, turning toward Sonya; Sonya, at the same time, screamed *"Alik!"* and threw her glass across the kitchen. It crashed against the wall behind the stove, shattered and flew into pieces.

"It's a good thing the . . . is on the curry or we would not be eating tonight," Alik said. "However, the rice must be started over again." He slammed the smaller pot into the sink. They started screaming at each other and I went out into the hall.

There were fewer people at the party than I had thought at first; five were standing in the hall, and ten or so sat on the couch-bed and on the floor in the living room at the end of the corridor. By Russian standards, Grisha had a large apartment for a single man, but twenty people made it seemed crammed.

The Soviet-made stereo lay on the floor surrounded by sleeveless and jacketless records. The most recent victims were stacked six-high on the spindle. Whenever someone stumbled by the needle bounced and skidded across the spinning vinyl.

Ceppie sat glumly in a corner while Grisha's lips mouthed words inches from her ear; his arm was around her and I imagined he was trying to talk her out of her funk. I felt lonely and went back out into the hall. I passed Misha leaning drunkenly against the wood paneling, the girlfriend (I presumed, since her hair was long and blond and she stood by like an admiring pet) watching him silently from a few feet away. In the kitchen doorway I came up against a bull of a man with a long scraggly black beard and round black eyes. He was holding a little girl on his hip. The child was fair and had blue eyes. They made an incongruous pair.

"Has anyone ever told you that you resemble Rasputin?" I asked the fellow. He seemed thoroughly pleased by this remark and his mouth bent into a self-satisfied little smile.

"Why yes!" he said. "So they say. Ceppie said so too. I did not know Americans knew anything at all about Russian history."

"It would be silly to study your language and learn nothing about your history. But Rasputin is one of the most famous Russian characters in America. Everyone knows him."

He had been ignoring the child, who began to wail.

"Shall I take her to her mother? Or shall I try to control her with my eyes?" He made a serious face and glared at the child; her howling became deafening. "I shall take her to my wife I think," he said, and smiled.

I went back to the kitchen. Sonya's eyes were puffy and bloodshot. Alik was stirring the curry with his back to the room. The rum was gone.

When I mentioned this to Alik he suggested the Armenian cognac. "It is the same color almost. That is a very important fact. You must always stay with the same color."

Sonya and I stayed in the kitchen most of the night. The silent, empty spaces in my mind became wider, more silent. At one point I asked Sonya what she did for a living; it seemed like an hour passed before she responded that she was an engineer. After a wide space I thought, how strange—everybody in Moscow is an engineer!

The curry was not ready until way after ten o'clock. When Alik finally placed a heaping dessert plate of the brown, unrecognisable food in front of me, I was so drunk I could not taste the curry, although other people were eating heartily and commenting on its excellence.

My head cleared slightly after the food, and I decided it was time to drink water despite my fear of the Giardia parasite that had given dysentery to half the students in the American group. At the Institute Isabel boiled our drinking water in her hotpot, but I wasn't about to ask Alik to boil me some water to drink. Russians did not like that at all; they considered it an insult. I convinced myself I'd be all right: there was enough alcohol in my system to annihilate Flagellum the Explorer.

I was on my fourth glass of water when Grisha came in and invited me to take a look at his collection of paperback covers. I had forgotten that he had another room. Ceppie had once told me about his strange hobby of cutting the jackets off English and American books and pasting them to the wall above his bed.

The door to the bedroom was camouflaged in the wood paneling of the hall. Grisha said he liked this, as very few of his friends were ever sober enough to find the door handle. He didn't like them to be in his room, he explained, "because drunken people have no respect." He pushed the door open and led me into the bedroom, which was just big enough to hold the double bed. Above the wooden headboard were the jackets of hundreds of space fantasies. The drawings were of lurid, half-clothed women and dangerous-looking extraterrestrials carrying bizarre weapons. There were a few spaceships and humanoid men in extravagant armor. At the very edge of the collection, above the bedside table, was *The Great Gatsby,* the book Ceppie had given Grisha the first time they had met.

"If you cut the covers off books they lose all their value," I said.

He shrugged indifferently.

"I don't care, they're only for me. Listen, come sit down a minute." He gestured toward the bed, flicked off the overhead light, and switched on the bedside lamp, which had a red bulb. In the red glow his large mouth appeared enormous and I tried to get up to leave.

"What is the matter?"

"Nichevo. I drank too much."

"Slushay—I want to ask you something." He patted the bed beside him. I sat down.

"But you must not be offended. Promise you will not be offended?"

"What?"

"Will you marry me?"

"Excuse me?"

"I want to leave. But you know, Ceppie is my friend and I would never ask *her.* I love her dearly and it would be an insult to our friendship to ask her. Look, I made a choice in my fate. I was going to be a very great film critic. I was the best student in Film Institute, and I was already writing about films for a newspaper. They asked me to join the Party and I refused. Now I am a secretary at the same newspaper. I type letters and answer the phone. I don't care. It is easier than to have the burden of being a member of a party for which I have no respect." He reflected a moment, sighed deeply, and went on.

"I love films, especially foreign films. I have seen so many films. I saw all the Hitchcocks. I even saw your *One Flew Over the Cuckoo's Nest* with Djek Nicholson. Did you see that film?"

"Yes."

"Did you consider that film anti-American?"

"No. It is against systems that attempt to control the minds of people. It is against bureaucracy, I think."

"Tochno. Exactly. It is about fighting for the freedom to think and act for yourself. That is why it is forbidden here. But I saw it at a friend's house who is the son of someone important." His eyes sparkled

mischievously. "Just as they have their own food stores and clothes stores, they have access to foreign books and films the people never get to see. But tell me—in America, the bureaucracy is American, therefore *One Flew Over the Cuckoo's Nest* could be considered anti-American, yes?"

"I don't think we think in those terms."

"Exactly! You see why I want to leave? It does not matter if a film or a book is anti-American in America. You can say and think whatever you want. Here we cannot. I consider you an intelligent girl, you are Ceppie's best friend here. We have had a nice discussion. So, will you marry me?"

I had no idea what to say to him.

"Thank you for the compliment," I said. "I am honored that you asked me."

"It is not a question of that," he said, frustrated now. "I am not asking you to love me."

"They say they will throw us out of the Institute if we get married. I do not want to be thrown out. I am researching the life of someone who lived here during the war and this is more important to me than anything else. I do not want to become an enemy of your government."

"They lie to you," he sighed. "It is not the truth. No one at the top cares at all about foreign students getting married here."

"But there is no . . . no . . . how do you say this? It is not certain that they will let you leave. Some people have been waiting eight years to get out who have married foreigners."

"Only if the person has been in trouble before, do they make trouble."

"No, listen. To speak honestly, I cannot make a decision like this now. I am sorry."

"*Ladno.* You are not offended at me? You will not say anything about this to Ceppie, yes?"

"Of course not." And feeling that I had to somehow make up in a small way for the letdown, I said, "Ceppie says you read English very well. I brought a few American novels. If you like, I shall give them to you."

He tried to kiss me then, coming toward me with his soft lips pursed in the shape of some kind of sea anemone. I stood quickly, pretending I didn't see this, and stumbled toward the door. Wanting to splash cold water onto my face before going back to the party, I crossed the hall and opened the bathroom door. A naked bulb hanging from a wire in the ceiling illuminated the room with a jaundiced light. On the edge of the bathtub sat Rasputin, his fly and legs spread wide. Misha's black hair was bobbing up and down, up and down between Rasputin's thighs. Misha's hands gripped the tub's edge on both sides of the other man's buttocks. His knuckles were as white as the porcelain. Both men's large and awkward Soviet shoes jittered wildly, close to each other on the floor. The men were so enraptured they did not hear the door open, or see me, before I managed to close it noiselessly and escape into the w.c. which was right next door. The vision was gone so fast it was as though I'd seen them in a camera's flash. And like a flash lingering behind my closed eyelids, the picture stayed with me for a long time.

I locked the door and sat down on the toilet to think. Muddled thoughts rushed through my head. Why hadn't they locked the door? I wondered if it was my business to tell Ceppie. I tried to imagine what would have happened if she had walked in on them instead of me. The sight was so bizarre and unnatural that as it played itself over and over in my mind it caused an uncomfortable tickle in my lower spine. It felt like a colony of ants had moved into my lumbar vertebrae. The sensation was somewhat erotic, and this disturbed me. They had wanted to be caught, certainly. They had wanted someone to feel exactly what I was feeling. I was overcome by shivers and decided that a drink was in order.

I made my way back to the kitchen, supporting myself against the paneling in the hall. I did not look back to see if the bathroom door was still closed; I was afraid they might have picked just that moment to come out. They would give me a wily look and smile contentedly and I would probably faint.

Sonya was gone, and there were many new faces crowded around the kitchen table. Alik was leaning against the sink. I went up to him and whispered in his ear,

"What does it mean, golubchik?"

He fixed me with an angry look that faded quickly into a smile.

"It is a joke," he said offhandedly.

"Don't talk shit to me," I said, translating this expression directly, which probably meant nothing in Russian. Alik seemed stupefied, so I stormed off to Grisha's room. He was still sitting at the edge of his bed, his arms on his thighs and his head drooping eerily in the strange light.

"Listen," I said. "I think you should ask Ceppie to marry you."

"She will be insulted," he said in a desperate voice.

"I don't think so. I just walked into the bathroom and saw Misha with that person who looks like Rasputin—"

"It means nothing; they do it for the strangeness of it."

"Ceppie does not know about it and I think it is not right at all. I think you people always hide the truth from us and it is not right. We are not at home here and it is so easy for you to fool us. Ceppie is pretty, it is true, but even the ugliest girls in our group have found Russian lovers. Everybody wants something from us but nobody will tell the truth. I could throw up it makes me so sick. I am going back to the Institute now. I shall catch a taxi in the street."

"I will catch you a taxi," he said, getting up. "I think you should take Ceppie with you and tell her everything. I'll tell you one thing, and you must believe me: I am not her friend because I am looking for a foreign wife. I love her [like her? he said *lyublyu*] and wish her nothing but good. And by the way, there was no need to be frightened, I was not trying to kiss you the way you think, I was trying to thank you for the books. You are always prepared for the worst, aren't you? You have a threatening look in your eyes that says 'Leave me alone!' And it is a look that has been there a long time. I can tell it is not a look you picked up in Russia."

"That is true, but it is also true that here in Russia we have an unnatural power that we do not have at home. It is no wonder American girls come back from Russia saying how wonderful it is. I do not believe it is reality, it is a fairytale. There is nothing worse for Ceppie than a man like Misha. I do not think he ever loved her, but thank God he was too honest or too much of a coward to fool her into taking him to America. I wish Ceppie would fall in love with someone like you. But even *you* do not tell her the truth."

"I will. I will tell her the truth. I will throw everyone out of my apartment but you must stay here tonight also, otherwise Ceppie will not stay. You can sleep in the living room, on the couch. *Ladno?*"

I thought about this for a moment, and it seemed to make sense. I was too tired and too drunk to think anymore.

"Ladno," I said.

21

AN AVOCADO
AND A TOMATO
IN MOSCOW

Ceppie and I left Grisha's at 7 A.M. The streets were deserted and the sky was still dark. A low ceiling of storm clouds threatened more snow. It was as though it were still night and the party had never ended. I had been uncomfortable on Grisha's couch, trying to sleep in my clothes, rolling around in crumbs and wet spots left behind by the partyers. It did not look like Ceppie had slept at all. Her eyes were swollen and miserable as we stumbled on toward the bus stop. She acted as if she were alone. I figured whatever Grisha had told her was none of my business, and if she wanted to tell me about it, she eventually would.

We climbed over a steep and slippery snowbank and onto the edge of the street where the bus shelter stood. Then, almost as if the divinities had felt we had had enough for one day, an empty taxi appeared on the horizon. I could see the little green light inside the windshield getting bigger as it approached us. I began to wave at it furiously, hoping beyond hope that it would stop. It stopped. Ceppie said in a whiny voice that she categorically refused to spend money on a cab. I said, "I'm paying; shut up and get in," which she did.

"Thank you so much," I said to the back of the driver's head after giving him our address, "you saved us."

"*Studienty?*" he asked. He had a thick pink neck and a leather cap tilted back on his head.

"*Da,*" I said.

"From where? GDR?"

"*Iz SeShaA,*" I said. Ceppie shot me a dirty look.

"*Amerikantsy, da?* You're coming from a party, eh? Your boys don't drink like ours, yes? Ha ha ha!"

He turned his head over his right shoulder and I saw that he was a man close to seventy.

"The way I see it," he said, "All young people are the same in their souls. I was in the Great Fatherland War, you know. I went right to Berlin with the Red Army. I met some Amerikantsy. They were nice boys." He shook his head now as if to say that since then the world had become a great disappointment to him. "I don't need to work. I have a pension and I had a good job—I was an engineer. But I am old now. Life is boring. This is my son's taxi. I drive it sometimes for amusement so he may stay home with his wife."

"We would like very much to have better relations between our countries," I said, "which is why we are here learning Russian."

"Good girls," he said.

The sky turned a pale gray before our eyes. The enormous deserted avenues rushed by. A weird sound droned inside my head. It was the sound I associated with exhaustion, when I'd gone beyond being able to sleep. I felt slightly mushy from the alcohol I'd consumed, but not drunk.

"Maybe we should stop and buy groceries," I said to Ceppie in English.

It would be a total breach of etiquette to pull up in front of the Institute in a taxi at seven-thirty in the morning, looking the way we did. To break the rules so blatantly would be an insult to the Institute. Yet the women who guarded the front door would pretend to ignore us if we arrived on foot with groceries. Even if the guards had not seen us go out, they would not say a word seeing us come in—that was the way it went. Everyone turned a blind eye on broken rules as long as excuses were available. And this excuse was perfect: the best groceries could only be found early in the morning.

We asked the driver to stop at the Dieta store. From there it was a ten-minute, downhill walk to the Institute. The meter read ten rubles, but he only wanted five.

"Good little girls," he said. "Go home and tell your President the Russians are good people."

The Dieta was a large square building with a high ceiling. It resembled an American grocery store in that you traveled through the aisles with a cart and picked the goods off the shelf and then brought them up to the row of cash registers in the front. The important difference was that the shelves were usually bare. Even when they were stacked it was with cans of generic pâté and fish stew—God knew what was in them—we'd tried a few once and they all tasted like dog food. You could always tell by a bustling crowd where the desired products were.

It was very early and there were few people in the store. In the back, on rolling metal shelves, the blue milk cartons were stacked without refrigeration (it didn't matter, they'd be gone in an hour.) There were also dark green glass jars of yogurt, and kefir in glass bottles that resembled small wine carafes; both were sealed with tin. Nearby, large chunks of Russian cheese, which looked and tasted like mild cheddar, filled an entire shelf. This type of cheese had completely disappeared from the stores three weeks ago, and no one could explain why. Suddenly it was back, but it, like the milk, would be gone in an hour. There were raspberry preserves and fresh apples and oranges—not bruised and greenish, but red and gold. The bread, also stacked on metal shelves, was still warm. Above, in the rafters of the roof, thousands of sparrows chirped happily and dive-bombed the bread and other things which interested them. They especially liked the floor, which was ne er swept and therefore littered with grains of rice and barley.

"Look at those goddamn birds!" Ceppie said. "This is worse than a New York City Puerto Rican bodega, for Christsake!"

I didn't give a damn about the birds; there was food available that morning, sanitary or not. We spent five rubles each on bread, milk, two large chunks of the Russian cheese, raspberry preserves, kefir, apples and oranges. They did not give you grocery bags in Russian stores, so we carried our groceries in our *avoski,* our "maybe's". This was the name given to the netted bags that you could roll into a ball and fit in your pocket or your handbag, in case you came across any goodies during your daily travels. The avoski bumped uncomfortably against our legs as we headed down the icy hill toward home.

The morning air was crisp and fresh and hard on the nasal passages and lungs. Along the Institute's front walk a wide alley with steps led down from the road. Often the steps were invisible beneath the snow, and on both sides of the alley all the way to the front doors, enormous snowbanks engulfed the two rows of streetlights halfway up the posts. The steps had been cleared and we went down them, acting normal and obvious, warmed by the protective walls of snow.

The linebacker babushkas at the door saw our grocery bags and waved us on through. I hadn't been home in forty-eight hours and it felt wonderful. A strange feeling of safety and comfort came over me as I smelled the slightly rancid odor the heat carried as it wafted up from the radiators along the corridors.

My room was toasty-warm in the pale light. Isabel was sitting on her bed in jeans and her pom-pomed slippers, writing something in her exercise book. Her pale blue towel was wrapped turban-style around her head, and she looked up at me with an unfamiliar longing in her eyes.

"What's up?" I said.

"Check it out." Isabel pointed her pencil to my bedside table, where two fire-colored roses and one white one stood in an old green kefir bottle. Next to the roses were an avocado of the Florida variety and a fresh, plump, red tomato. They were so incongruous and unexpected in our room that my mind didn't register them at first. It had been five weeks since I'd laid eyes on such a sumptuous sight. I lifted them up one at a time and squeezed their plump, giving textures with the tips of my fingers. Beneath them lay a note folded in two and sealed shut with Scotch tape:

March 8

Happy Woman's Day. It is customary in Russia to give a gift to the women one cares about. I do not want our silly fight to ruin our relationship and if you are willing to discuss a compromise maybe we can come to an agreement that is amenable to us both. I was thinking about you all day and knocked on your door tonight, although I half expected to get a frying pan in my face. Your roommate said you were not home so I left these with her. The red ones are for the wounds your heart and mine might have endured before we met and the white one is for a clean start for both of us.

Phil

I couldn't believe my eyes. Three nights ago I'd slammed my door on a pragmatic shit and here he was, turned romantic fool. I was completely flustered.

"Where did he find an avocado and a tomato?" I asked Isabel excitedly, as though they were my main concern.

"God knows. But you'd better believe the temptation to steal them from you was almost more than I could bear. They've been sitting there for two days. It's been absolute torture."

"Got any salt and pepper?"

"Sure do. Courtesy of Pan Am, in little packets."

Ceppie came through the bathroom to split up the groceries, and her eyes went wide at the sight.

"*Madre de Dios!* An avocado and a tomato! In Moscow, in winter? It can't be."

"But it is. Sit down, Cep. This is breakfast today."

We sliced the tomato into thin rounds and the avocado into thin strips, laid them delicately on a small plate, salted and peppered them, added a few drops of olive oil and dried basil (this was Ceppie's addition) and took our time savoring each tiny bite. The avocado was perfect: the two days had ripened it so that it melted against the roof of your mouth. The tomato did not taste like a winter hothouse tomato, which it probably was. Its texture was perfect and it was as juicy as an orange. We had some slices of black bread with the Russian cheese to prolong the culinary experience.

"Happy Woman's Day, *mujer!*" Ceppie said. "Now tell me: was I right or was I right? The mang es *nuts* abou' jou."

As soon as we were finished I crossed the hall and knocked on Phil's door. It was only a quarter to nine; we had forty-five minutes till first para.

"*Vkhoditie!*" he yelled.

I went in. Phil's roommate was sitting on the opposite bed. He was a thin, curly-headed fellow with freckles. I had met him a few times; he came by the room once in a while. But it was unusual for him to be there so early in the morning. I was confused by his presence and did not know what to say.

Phil was sitting on his bed, leaning against the wall with his head tilted back.

"Hi there, stranger," he said in a gruff voice. He did not move his head or look toward me.

"Hi," I said to them both.

"You didn't have another fight with Sofia from Sofia, did you?" I asked his roommate worriedly. Whenever Paul fought with his Bulgarian, it interfered with Phil's and my privacy. Luckily their fights never lasted into the night.

"No," Paul said distantly. He seemed slightly embarrassed. "Phil has some trouble at home."

There was a long moment of silence, and then Paul said, "Well, Phil. What can I say? Is there anything I can do?"

"No."

"Well, then. I guess I'll go down to breakfast. Let me know if there's anything I can do."

"Thanks," Phil said.

Paul gathered the notebooks lying next to him on the bed and stood up to leave.

As soon as he'd closed the door I sat down next to Phil, and waited for him to say something. He remained motionless, with his head tilted back and his eyes closed, and I took his hand. It was as cold as the air outside. I was afraid to ask him what was wrong.

"Thank you for the presents," I said in a quiet voice. "Where on earth did you manage to get a tomato, much less an avocado? They were delicious. I split them with Ceppie and Isabel. They were so happy. I can't believe you did that. Thank you. And for the flowers, too."

"They must be dead by now," he said from miles away.

"Phil, what's happened? What's going on?"

He leaned over, turned a tape over in his little disco box, and switched it on. "It was "Avalon" by Roxy Music. The sun began to streak through the ice on the windowpane. The pale light flooded over his bed in thin beams.

"My mother's back in the nuthouse again. She tried to do herself in. Again. I got a telegram yesterday from my father."

"Oh God, Phil." I caressed his cheek. "What are you going to do?" My first thought was entirely for myself: I thought he would leave and fly home on the next plane out. I hated his mother fiercely for doing this to us and I almost started to cry. Phil glanced at me quickly when he heard the tremor in my voice.

"Please don't cry," he said. "I can't handle it."

"Are you going to go home?"

"Are you kidding? I came here as a ten-monther to get away from this shit. I mean, California wasn't far enough. I can't stand it. I'm telling you, sometimes I think *I* should try it. Scare the living shit out of her and show her what it feels like." He shrugged angrily. "It probably wouldn't make a damn bit of difference. She's become completely solipsistic." He said this with such vehemence I was taken aback. Then, in a neutral tone and as though he were adding this as an epilogue, he said, "When I was little she seemed like the most beautiful, most perfect person in the world."

"She must be very beautiful if she looks like you."

He stretched out on the bed and crossed his arms behind his head. He looked at me openly and without flinching for the first time. His eyes seemed transparent and behind them was the black knot of rage and pain he was no longer concealing. For once I felt stronger than he and I did not like it.

"Yeah, right. She's vain to boot and the pills she's on make her lethargic and fat. So she stops taking them and everything's okay for a little while. 'Are you taking your pills, Millie?' my father says. 'Of course, dear,' she says. Then *bang!* Off the deep end.

"It's weird. She never really wants to die. I mean, taking twenty Valiums or so and drinking a bottle of gin might do you in, but she always does it and then calls my father at the office and tells him what she's done. He drops everything and comes flying home and gets her to the hospital in time. The problem is every time she does it, a little more of her brain gets fried.

"I talked to my dad yesterday afternoon. He said it wasn't even worth trying to call her because she's non compos mentis. That's what he said, 'non compos mentis,' that's the way he talks." He let out a bitter laugh that almost turned into a sob. I was frightened. If he began to cry I would not know what to do. I feared he would regret it later and close me out even more than I was closed out already.

"I called from the post office across the street from Patrice Lumumba Institute. You pay them your six rubles a minute for how-ever many minutes you plan to talk, then you wait for them to put the call through. There were all these Africans and Arabs from the Institute waiting for their calls. They were sitting there so quietly. The booths are made of wood and you can hear the Africans talking in English, very quietly, to their people back home. Happy birthday. How's the baby? Did you get the bicycle I sent you? Blah blah blah . . . After about twenty minutes the woman behind the big wooden desk yells out 'SeSHaA' and I went into my booth.

"My father is always so calm and together. Everything is mathematical, scientific. He starts giving me the medical terminology the doctors gave him. Something psychosis, acute paranoia. I started screaming at him. 'Don't give me this shit! Don't you give a damn? What's wrong with you?' 'Now just calm down, son,' he says. I paid for five minutes and after four-and-a-half the operator came on and said 'Your time is up, finish your conversation' and I started screaming at her in Russian.

'I fucked your mother, you better not cut us off!' I said. She cut us off. When I came out of my booth all the Patrice Lumumba people were staring at me. And the Russian lady who put the call through wouldn't even look at me when she gave me my receipt. You know how they feel about public displays. What an asshole I made of myself."

His eyes seemed to fog over then, and I stretched out next to him and put my hand on his chest. I wanted to say something soothing, something helpful, but having never been through such a thing, I felt utterly confused and helpless.

"Do you want me to rub your back? You're so tense."

"Sure." He took his T-shirt off and turned over. I straddled his lower back and began to knead the muscles in his shoulders and run my thumbs along the edges of his backbone. This excited me terribly and I felt rotten that at a time like this all I could think about was making love with him. I bent over and kissed the back of his neck where his blond hairs were as soft as down. He had a lovely wide back and his skin in the sunlight was the color of the white rose he'd left in my room.

"Ahh," he said.

"I'm sorry, Phil."

"For what?" he said.

"You know—for carrying on. That I wasn't here yesterday when you got your telegram. I didn't get your note till this morning. I've been gone since March 8. It wasn't on purpose, it just happened that way."

"Well you're here now."

After thinking silently for a long time, I said something I'd never said to him, something risky and terrifying.

"It's just that I love you."

His heart sped up, I could feel it begin to pump wildly beneath his rib cage. I pressed my ear to his back. After a minute his heart subsided. I did an experiment: I said it again.

"I love you." And his heart began to pump wildly again. Boom-BOOM boom-BOOM boom-BOOM.

I understood then that we were much more alike than I had ever thought.

Last night Grisha, who had never met me before, had told me I had a threatening look in my eye. A 'Leave me alone!' look. People who knew me well knew that it was only self-defense. The first time I met Phil I thought his eyes had a frozen look, a look as hard and impenetrable as a cement wall painted blue. Now suddenly everything started to make sense. He had recognized me as a safe bet; another hardened soul who could have a good time without falling in love. He'd been completely wrong. My threatening look had deceived him.

This, I thought, is what happens to people who have been abandoned or betrayed by their heroes. I wished for just one thing, and I wished for it more strongly than I had ever imagined I could; I wanted him to trust me enough to know that if he gave me a proper chance, I would never abandon or betray him.

"Where did you manage to get an avocado and a tomato in Moscow?" I asked him quietly, deciding that the worst thing I could do would be to push him.

"I have a buddy from college who's working at the embassy here. I think he's a spook. He got them for me at the commissary. I remembered you said once that the thing you missed the most here was avocados. You're so funny. Avocados, of all things!"

Then he laughed happily as though nothing else had been said and my heart flew up toward the ceiling, carried by the sound of his laugh.

PART THREE

22

DEAD
LENIN

I arrived at Red Square five minutes late and found my group gathered in front of the metal barricades the militsia put up on visiting days, to block off the street leading to the square. A young militsia man was talking to one of the American girls from his side of the barricade. Twenty feet behind him stood hundreds and hundreds of people. The line to visit dead Lenin began at the marble mausoleum that stood at the foot of the Kremlin wall facing Red Square, snaked to the right around the corner of the fortress, and through the Kremlin gardens, which flanked the southern wall.

It was snowing again though we were already in mid-April; the sun had been shining warmly for the past four days and most of the snow in Moscow had turned to mud. When I had gone off to visit Vera the day before it had been so warm I'd worn a thin leather jacket, my wool scarf, and sneakers. I had spent the night at Vera's (as I usually did on the eve of excursions) and now it was winter again on the day we were to see dead Lenin and had to stand in line. Most of the students were in their fur hats and winter coats. Only the miserable souls who had spent the night out had blue faces and purple lips.

"*Studienty?*" the young militsia man asked the American girl. The girl said yes.

"Where from?"

"Iz Ameriki."

"Your Russian is not bad," he said. "How do you like Moskva?"

"I like it," the girl said.

"Better than America?" the guard asked, and laughed.

"The weather is better in America in April," the girl said, and stamped her feet. I was not worried about her; she wore a pale blue Perry Ellis down coat.

Behind him the somber, self-conscious crowd stood two-by-two. The people wore patient, determined expressions, like the stargazers who stand for hours in subdued silence outside chic New York night-clubs. The waiting seemed much the same to me; often at Red Square as at the clubs in New York, big black limousines pulled up right to the door and the important people were granted entrance before the lumpenproletariat.

The breath of someone tall floated over my wool scarf, which I'd wrapped babushka-style around my head.

"Hi there."

I turned abruptly and found myself looking up at Phil.

"What are you doing here? You're not supposed to be here."

"Your group's counselor came down with Giardia and had to go to the embassy clinic. They needed a volunteer. I wanted to see Lenin again anyway, so I volunteered. As your acting counselor I'll have to report that you didn't come home last night," he said, and smiled.

"Yeah. I slept with my other boyfriend. I'm crazy about him. His name is Sasha and he's four years old."

Phil laughed. "I was hoping you'd make it, because I have plans to see those people tonight—the ones I was telling you about—and I wanted to ask you to come along."

A formal-looking woman in a brown fur coat and hat approached the militsia man who had been talking to the girl and said something. He suddenly became very serious and began shouting.

"All right, who is the elder of this group? We're late, who is responsible?"

"Excuse me. I have to deal with this," Phil said. He went up to the militsia man and the woman. He shook hands with her and said something obviously reassuring to the guard. A moment later he turned to the forty of us and addressed us in Russian in a loud, authoritative tone.

"Intourist has sent Biela Dmitrievna to be our guide this afternoon, and we are not going to have to wait in line. Knapsacks and handbags have to be inspected and checked into the coatroom if they are too large. No cameras are allowed." The militsia man slid the fence open and waved us through.

"Two by two," Phil yelled. *"Hold your bags ready for inspection."* Isabel approached him, probably asking about her camera, but it made me uncomfortable. In his new role Phil had to be shared.

He stood and chatted with the militsia man while we all passed through the gate. I saw Phil slip him a pack of Marlboros as he shook his hand and thanked him for his help.

Further up the street was another police fence, where we were stopped and our bags were searched. This militsia man was much less friendly than the last.

"This is not a bag, this is a suitcase," he said to me reproachfully. "Over there." He gestured angrily toward a door in the red brick building across the street.

As I left the group, I took my wallet and my address book out and stuck them in the pockets of my jacket.

Phil joined me in the line a few minutes later. "You didn't leave your address book in there did you?" I was pleased that he had come to stand in line with me, and even more pleased that my answer to his question was no.

"Of course not," I said.

"Good."

"My numbers are coded anyway."

"Better safe than sorry. Damn," he muttered, "I would have said something to everyone about that, but Miss Intourist speaks English."

Every few yards stood a militsia man with a club who shouted "Hurry up!" and "Keep your feet on your side of the white line!" which he pointed to with the tip of his club. There was nowhere to hurry to. You tried to hurry up and you bumped into the person in front. They treated us as though we were marching in a prison line, as though at any moment one of us would attempt to escape. The white line was four inches thick and ran along the large, even cobblestones all the way to the doors of the mausoleum. *What* was the purpose of keeping our feet on our side of the line? Red Square, entirely fenced in, was completely empty except for the militsia men. The air became heavy with our nervous apprehension. Everyone began to whisper and I could hear teeth chattering. The cold seeped up my legs through the soles of my sneakers. My ankles were already aching and numb.

"Move!" a guard yelled. "Hurry up!"

We finally reached the path that ran alongside the Kremlin wall. Headstones lined it on either side. Some were actually in the wall, and some were in the ground alongside it. We were not allowed to stop long enough to inspect the names carved on the plaques. I managed to read several, including Big Bill Haywood and John Reed.

"Who's Big Bill Haywood?" I asked Phil.

"A famous Communist."

"But what did he do?"

"He defected. I don't know. I'm not a History student, I'm a Russian Studies major."

We passed marble busts of Yosif Stalin, Dzerzhinsky, and Ordzhonikidze. A few seconds later we approached the doors of the mausoleum, where two guards with unblinking eyes stood facing each other like wax statues. "Hats off! Hands out of pockets! Hats off! Hands out of pockets!" someone barked, someone whose face was hard and cold and who stared each of us in the eyes momentarily, checking, presumably, for terrorists.

We went down a flight of stone steps into the bowels of the dark, marble tomb. Our breath hung over our heads. It seemed as cold inside as in the street. I unconsciously stuck my hand in my pocket to warm it and a guard jumped out and grabbed my wrist.

"What?" I whispered, opening my arms.

He remained silent and gestured for me to move along.

Lenin lay on a red cloth, on a bier surrounded by glass. He seemed very small and pink and waxlike, more so even than his guards, and the whole thing suddenly struck me as ghoulish and perverse. We were not permitted to stop moving and were rushed around the bier and up another flight of stairs and out into the bleak daylight. Altogether the visit with the father of Russian Communism had lasted less than a minute. Everyone seemed gloomy and disappointed.

The woman from Intourist herded us to the Lenin Museum, which was at the edge of the square, just down the street. We stood at the entrance while she and Phil went off to make arrangements and were assaulted by black marketeers. They looked as Western as we did, in down jackets and ski hats with names such as Adidas and Nike crocheted into the patterns.

"Tss, you—American?" one of them said to Ceppie.

"Can't you tell I'm Iranian?" she said. "I'm from the Patrice Lumumba Institute. I'm a freedom fighter and have had a good deal of practice in hand-to-hand combat."

This scared him off, so he began accosting a much less threatening-looking blond girl, who blushed and protested but could not rid herself of him until Ceppie intervened, adopting a karate stance.

We were shown around the Lenin museum by a tank-like woman who carried a pointed stick and spoke in a voice that did not break for breaths but certainly should have broken the glass displays. She showed us Lenin's baby boots, Lenin's report card from kindergarten. He was perfect even then. On and on she talked; we saw Lenin's grown-up boots, Lenin's overcoat and hat, as well as many manuscripts and newspapers from the Iskra days. In every single picture of the Old Bolsheviks, Trotsky had been blotted out.

"Where is Trotsky?" a bold person asked loudly, interrupting the woman. She did not skip a beat.

"Trotsky was an enemy of the Revolution and in any case, he was never close to our great leader Vladimir Ilyich Lenin. He was never trusted, therefore it is understandable that Lenin did not want him included in the photographs of the original Bolsheviks."

You would have thought from the way she talked that Lenin had been singlehandedly responsible for the Bolshevik Revolution, holding up the flag at the forefront of the peasants' uprisings. Her expression went from sanctimonious when she recited her version of history to beatific when she spoke of Lenin, and I decided after watching her for a long while that she was utterly convinced of what she was saying. With the long stick she tapped insistently on the glass displays, as if their mere existence proved her point. She was like a fanatical evangelist, and I felt outraged in her idolatrous church. I went and sat in the cloakroom in the basement to wait for Phil. The old woman who checked coats asked me suspiciously if I liked the museum. I said I loved the museum, but I wasn't feeling well. After that she wanted to feel my forehead and made me sit down with my nose between my knees.

After an hour the group dispersed and Phil stayed behind to thank the woman from Intourist. He gave her a little sampler vial of Pierre Cardin perfume and she smiled for the first time.

He then took me on such a complicated metro, bus, and trolley ride from Red Square that I could not have told where his friends' apartment was if I were tortured. They lived somewhere way out at the end of the purple line, but we got off the metro a stop before theirs and took a trolley car for a few stops, and then a bus. On the bus I told Phil that I was freezing. He took off his sheepskin coat, pulled his thick Irish knit sweater over his head and handed it to me. I took off my jacket and slipped it on. All the Russians stared at us as though we were apes escaped from the zoo.

"I was followed a few times on my way here," Phil explained as normally as he might if he were talking about being followed by a stray dog instead of the KGB. "I'd make arrangements over the phone to be here at a certain time and then I'd be followed by some sleazy guys who looked more like black marketeers than police. So now I make it harder for them. It's a game, really. They know me and they know when I'm visiting my friends because they tap my friends' phone. Pavel and Irina keep the phone in the closet, but the apartment is probably tapped too. Do you still want to come along?"

I shrugged indifferently, catching sight of his hands out of the corner of my eye. He had taken off his mittens and had crossed his fingers loosely over his spread legs. I was assailed by the absurd desire to kiss his hands—the palms and knuckles and the tips of each finger. How difficult it was not to fawn over him! I was constantly controlling my impulses, allowing him to act friendly and distant in the daytime and behaving accordingly. At night it was another story: in his bed I unabashedly set free all the impulses I'd kept pent up during the day. This he liked.

Distantly I said, "Tell me about your friends so I don't make a fool of myself."

"Pavel and his wife applied to emigrate about ten years ago but they were turned down. They're Jewish and their chances of getting out seemed pretty good then, lots of Jews were being let out. Since then he lost his job teaching Physics at the university and his wife lost her job as a gymnastics instructor. He figured he had nothing to lose, so he started writing letters of protest denouncing Soviet violations of human rights. They really speak their minds, which is what makes them interesting. The only problem is Pavel is unbelievably angry, and he just seems to get angrier and angrier. We argue all the time about politics. Don't mind if he starts to yell.

"They're still waiting to get their walking papers. Now there's a new wave of Jews being allowed to leave. They wait and wait. Pavel's an excellent photographer, and he gets paid off the books for his work and that's basically how they survive. I don't know much about it because that's the kind of thing people don't talk about over here. But Irina was on the Olympic gymnastics team when she was a kid. She's lost all her privileges since they applied to leave."

We walked from the wide avenue to a side street, and then down a path of mud that was banked by little piles of dirty snow. We trudged across a children's playground and through the courtyards of many housing blocks, to one gray building which looked exactly like all the others and had no number above the entrance. We took the elevator to the sixth floor.

The apartment door was opened by one of the most attractive women I had ever seen. She nodded curtly when we were introduced and moved aside.

This was Irina. She was in her early thirties and had the petite, wiry body of an athletic teenager. Her nose was so straight you could have put a ruler to it and her jet-black hair was pulled back into a tight bun at the base of her head, giving her face a severe look. But there was no severity in the sparkling, devilish eyes which slanted slightly upward above her cheekbones, or in the full dark lips which were almost frighteningly sensual.

"The lift is working?" she said abruptly.

"Yes," Phil said.

"Good. An unusual event."

They lived in two rooms. There was a living room with a double bed in it that also served as a couch. A long, rectangular table had been pulled up alongside it and set for dinner. Against the far wall was a cabinet crowded with books. The lower part of the cabinet had sliding wood doors which were kept closed. Nothing personal, nothing you would expect to find in a bedroom, was visible in the room.

A doorway led to a smaller room which in turn led to the kitchen. Apparently a child lived there; the room was in complete disarray. On the floor a naked Barbie doll lay face down, her legs twisted in opposite directions and her arms spread out at her sides. Her hair was a disheveled mess, and missing on one side of her head. The fancy little doll's clothes had been left lying about her and a pair of panties still dangled from one of her legs. She gave the sordid impression of a rape and murder victim. I picked her up on the way to the kitchen and began to straighten her out.

"I brought her for their daughter," Phil said. "Last time I was in Moscow she asked me for a doll with fancy clothes. Look what she's done to her."

I took my hairbrush out of my bag and tried to comb through her hair.

In the kitchen Pavel was frying meat with onions and potatoes in a skillet. He was enormous, red-headed and bearded, hunched over the stove like a bear standing on its hind legs. He turned and greeted us, spatula in hand, and laughed in a loud voice that sounded like it was coming through a megaphone. He hugged Phil warmly without putting down the spatula, which dripped grease onto the floor. Phil opened his backpack and took out a store of deficit items with Soviet

labels on them and placed them on the little round table. There were
two tins of caviar, red and black ("I have a friend who works in a
restaurant and he sells it to me at eight rubles a tin" Phil explained in
English when he saw my amazed expression), a jar of eggplant caviar, a
bottle of Stolichnaya, and several tins of sprats. Irina did not blink an
eye.

"We visited Lenin today," Phil said.

"And how is the old man?" Irina said, smiling derisively. Her eyes
turned brilliant when she looked at Phil and I became nervous.

"I asked him but he wouldn't say," Phil said.

"He's been closed for repairs on many occasions," she said, addressing me abruptly. "Just like everything else in this country, they didn't
. . . him properly. They say he began to rot and turn black so they
took him away and brought him back some time later with a nice, rosy
face. There's probably nothing left of him in there."

"Sit down, dear girl, sit down." Pavel produced a stool from under
the table and I sat.

"Let's have a drink!" Pavel rubbed his hands together vigorously.
Irina glanced at her husband, looking angry one moment and fatigued
the next. She sauntered over to the cabinet above the sink and brought
out four shot glasses, which she deposited on the table one after the
other with sharp, precise bangs.

A child ran in from somewhere. She was around eight and had a
black nest for hair, enormous black eyes, and a complexion so pale she
seemed slightly blue. She let out a horrendous scream and tore the
Barbie doll out of my hands.

"I'm sorry, I was trying to fix her hair," I said, quickly putting my
brush away.

"Forget about it," Irina said. "She'll just ruin it again. *Ona
nevozmozhna.* She is impossible."

The child came in a moment later wearing a militsia-style gray cap
complete with insignia—the shiny red star with the gold hammer and
sickle at the center of it—and brandishing a plastic sword. She made
siren noises and ran around the kitchen whacking at her father's legs
and whipping the sword through the air. The father said nothing so

everyone pretended she was not there and shouted above her noise, then all at once Irina snatched the sword out of her hand and whacked her lightly with it on the butt. The child went howling off to her room. The conversation, which I had not been following at all, continued, and Irina followed her daughter.

After a few minutes the child stopped crying and I could hear Irina's quiet voice cajoling her. Feeling that it might be a good time to befriend both mother and daughter, I got up from my stool and silently entered the child's room. She had thrown herself face down on the bed and was prostrate as her mother sat rubbing her back. "Ty nevozmozhna," Irina was saying. "You cannot be so wild. In the real world people will not put up with you."

Irina looked up. Her eyes were tired.

"I'm sorry," I whispered. "I should not have taken the doll. It was stupid."

Irina shrugged indifferently. "It has nothing to do with that."

After a moment she said, "Philip has not been around much lately. Less and less. We miss him. He is secretive, as most American men are. Are you his lover?"

I had to stop and think about this for a second. "Are *you?*" I wanted to say. But the child was there, her husband and Phil were in the next room.

"*Da.* But I do not know what that means. He keeps me away from his Russian friends." I laughed lightly as if I thought it was funny. The conversation droned on in the kitchen; they were not listening to us.

"We are not Russian," she said vaguely, "we are Jewish."

The look in her eyes changed; now she appraised me from head to foot and did not seem satisfied with what she saw. "What did you do to deserve your life?" her eyes seemed to say. We fixed each other coldly and neither would be the first to look away.

I wanted to shout, "It is not my fault that I am free to leave and you are not. It is not my fault that my life is easier than yours." But in a slightly defensive tone, I quietly said, "To us it is the same. You are both Russian and Jewish, as American Jews are both American and Jewish."

"And *there* is the great difference," she said. A strand of her rain-straight hair had fallen out of the bun; she tucked it in behind her ear. "I was certain that it was exactly such a thing that was keeping Philip occupied. But I, silly woman, thought it was a Russian girl, ha ha ha!" There was nothing joyous about her laugh. "He has to come all the way to Russia *three times* to find an American girl, ha ha ha!"

"Do you know," I said, "you are such a beautiful woman. I don't think I have seen a more beautiful woman than you."

"I used to be beautiful. I also used to be very stupid."

The doorbell sounded and Irina slipped out of the room. The child did not move. I couldn't think of anything kind or helpful to say and returned to the kitchen feeling defeated.

A terribly thin man, whose teeth were mostly missing except for a few in front, followed Irina into the kitchen.

"This is Dmitri," she said proudly. "He has been released from prison after fourteen years, comrades. Now he lives in exile one hundred kilometers outside Moskva. How did you get rid of your guards, Mitya?"

"Well, there are four cars parked outside my building at all times, I think I managed to get rid of three of them."

Everyone laughed and I stood against the wall not knowing what to say or what to do with my hands.

Phil shook hands with Dmitri and asked him how long he'd been out of jail.

"A month," Dmitri said. "And I just received my exit visa today. It is a celebration. Within three weeks I will be in Vienna, then Paris, and then with a little luck, New York."

"Yes. Dmitri is being used as a symbol. The General Secretary wants to show Mr-the-President-of-the-United-States that there is freedom in the Soviet Union," Pavel said in a sarcastic voice. "Dmitri is famous—but there are thousands more still in jail."

"What was your crime, may one ask?" Phil said. "You do not have to tell me, it is purely that I am curious."

"This time I was in jail for writing religious pamphlets—Russian Orthodox, you know. The first time was for signing a petition for the right to worship in peace, the second time was for marching with the Jews for the right to emigrate, and the third—well, you know how it is. Going to jail for me is an addiction. After the first time it is difficult to stop."

Everyone laughed and we toasted to Dmitri's future, then we went to the living room and sat down around the table. The zakuski had already been spread out on the plastic tablecloth. There was a bowl of cucumbers, the opened tins of sprats, the eggplant caviar, kolbasa and cheese cut into neat little squares on a plate, a slab of butter, and black-and-white bread sliced into rectangles. Irina went back and forth between the conversation and the kitchen.

"What do you think of your President?" Pavel asked me after his fourth shot of vodka. Phil and I were still on number two, sipping carefully and slowly because the evening was still young.

"I?" I asked. "I do not like to discuss such matters."

"We know what Philip thinks—Philip is a leftist liberal. But he doesn't know anything about the Soviet Union."

Irina leaned up against the door frame with her arms crossed over her chest. She laughed, and her upper body tilted forward. She reminded me very much, in fact, of some dark, exotic, sea plant.

"You're a good one to talk, Pavel. You're always talking about how wonderful America is, and you have spent *so much* time in America, haven't you? At least as much time as Philip has spent here."

Phil did not respond and, of course, neither did I. Pavel's eyes were already bloodshot and stared dully ahead, as though the point he were trying to reach lay straight before him on the table. It was unclear whether he'd even heard his wife.

"*We* like your President because he stands up against our government. Our government only understands force. It has never respected any of the treaties our countries have made together. SOI, in my opinion, is a good thing."

"What is SOI?" I asked.

"Strategic Defense Initiative. Star Wars," Phil said. "Here it's called SOI."

"What you are saying is crazy, Pavel," he added gently. "Absolute nonsense. SOI will never be effective. Ninety percent effective—*maybe,* they say. *Ninety percent!* And yet with one bomb you can destroy an entire city of millions. To compensate for SOI the Soviet Union will just continue to build more and more missiles. America will be trying to hold water in a sieve. The money our government spends is insane. If every dollar were a grain of sand you could already cover the whole surface of the earth with sand for the amount that has been spent on this thing. Instead of trying to stop Communism by building bombs they should think about preventing the spread of Communism by feeding the world. That is a completely ideological and impractical thought, I know, but nevertheless that is how I feel."

"You are just a silly humanist," Pavel said to Phil, "and there is no room for humanism in the Soviet Union."

"And there is no room for humanism in America. Everything is organized to prevent any radical changes in the economy. The corporations decide how the people spend their money and how the government spends its money. It's not a question of ideology or morality at all, it's a question of economics. You are crazy, Pavel, if you think the streets in America are paved with gold."

"You have freedom to vote and choose your leaders! Your people voted for your President, did they not?"

"There did not seem to be a big choice," I said, and immediately regretted having interfered.

"And if you are so critical about your own country, how do you feel about the Soviet Union?" he asked me in a joking, derisive tone.

"I think there are problems but I think your government is trying to change things for the better," I said, thinking about the bug in the phone and the bugs that probably infested all the walls of their little apartment.

"Nyet," he said.

"I like the people I have met and have good friends here now. I do not believe that we are so different as people and I would do anything possible to avoid fighting a war. That is one thing I believe we have in common, besides being terribly strong-willed and proud people. No one wants to go to war."

Pavel snorted. "At least fifteen million people were arrested and most of these were murdered during the purges between 1936 and 1938 —what kind of people does that make us? Barbarians, that's what.

"The system is dead. Imagine such paranoia that people would denounce their own neighbors, brothers, even parents, for crimes against the State! And such crimes!" Pavel shook his head and clasped both sides of his frizzy red head. "Like selling secret information to an enemy nation. *What* enemy nation? Like talking badly of the Great Leader, Comrade Stalin. And you were rewarded for denouncing! 'Your neighbor's apartment is bigger than yours? No problem, Comrade, denounce him and the apartment is yours.' The State has been dead since the beginning and the Party has poisoned the people with lies. These changes you are talking about are only prolonging the inevitable. The end will come and then there will be total chaos."

"But Russians love Russia," Phil put in. "This you cannot deny. Look at how they fought and *won* the Great Fatherland War."

"Half the deaths could have been prevented if Stalin hadn't been so concerned with maintaining his own power. The war wasn't fought by heroes, it was fought by people with guns at their backs. If a soldier tried to retreat the NKVD troops at the rear opened fire on him with machine guns. Oh, but since then the feats of the great Soviet system have been exaggerated out of all proportion. It is all a lie as well."

"I am sorry but I really cannot believe that," I said in a quiet voice. It was as though with that one sentence, the man had swept away the entire, tenuous Leggo castle of knowledge I had constructed concerning Russia at war. If Pavel were right, every sentence my father had written, and every belief that had been dear to him, was false. This could not be. I had figured a few things out from talking to people in the past two and a half months; for example, I believed now, as my father had, that the Soviets would always fight like wild animals, to the death, to protect their land. They were a xenophobic people. Not just the government, but the people themselves. And it was not just Russians, but everybody who had fought the Big War—Georgians and Azerbaijanis and Bielorussians and Ukrainians and Uzbeks and Mongols and on and on.

The Soviet Union would never capitulate during any kind of war, and annihilation was what a future without compromises between us and them, would bring.

"Look at what they did to Czechoslovakia in '68!" Pavel shouted. "Look at Hungary, look at Afghanistan! What do you call that? I call that old-fashioned imperialism, that's what I call that."

"And what about Chile? And what about Vietnam?" I said. "We put in fascists to stop Communism. I do not believe fascists are better than Communists. I do not."

"Vietnam—there's a perfect example. You should have won Vietnam. You should have made a complete war of it and wiped them off the face of the Earth, that is what you should have done with Vietnam. All that leftist liberal nonsense in America in the sixties was for ideological idiots—like you and Philip."

I began to feel sick at the thought that there were people in Russia who were even more reactionary than the men who had forced my father to leave the United States.

So much of what Pavel said was justified—the horrors were absolutely real—but given the chance, what would Pavel have done to change things? Lined up all the Communists in the Soviet Union and shot them? I did not speak up because there was no way I could express any of this in coherent Russian, and I was weary of arguing with a native who knew so many more facts than I. This was Pavel's next point precisely.

"You foreigners think you understand our country so well, but you really do not understand anything at all. You admire all the wrong things." Pavel pounded the table, filled the glasses, and apologized. Irina left her spot in the door and flitted away. The room suddenly seemed dark, as though a draft had blown out a candle.

"Pavel," Dmitri asked in a solemn, quiet voice, "why are you doing this to them? It serves no purpose."

"You are right. Let us talk without getting upset." Pavel wiped the sweat from his brow with the back of his hand.

"Philip, come here!" Irina called from the kitchen.

Phil left the table. I felt abandoned.

"I live in New York," I said to Dmitri, pulling myself together. I was grateful to him. "If it would be helpful to you I shall give you my telephone number. We will not be leaving Russia until July, but if it will help—"

"Certainly it will help," he said. "That is very kind. They say New York can be a terrible shock to Russians."

"It can be a terrible shock to Americans who have not lived there before." I wrote my name and number on a piece of paper and handed it to him. Again I thought of the bugs and my heart lost a beat. Would I get into trouble? Would my name be added to the list of undesirable Americans, so that I might never again be granted a visa to the Soviet Union?

"To New York." Pavel raised his glass.

"To New York."

One thing bothered me about all this; Pavel knew his phone was tapped, why was he putting us in such a spot? Maybe he did not care anymore. Russians seemed to believe that we Americans were exempted from their laws, which was absurd. There were countless horror stories concerning American students and journalists being arrested and thrown either in jail or out of the country after being bodysearched and interrogated for committing crimes against the State.

"Excuse me," I said, getting up. "I will see if I can help in the kitchen."

"Sit down," Pavel ordered. "They can manage just fine, and in any case, you are a guest."

"*Ladno,* I will not help, but I must go to the toilet."

I went through the child's room. She seemed to be asleep. Out of some need to be near Phil, I went to the kitchen, trying to be neither silent nor loud.

"Can I—" I had begun to speak just as I reached the door, but then froze completely. They were standing by the sink with their backs to me. Irina was pressed into Phil's side with an arm draped lightly around his waist and her head tucked under his chin. I had to maintain face until I could at least leave the room, so I finished my sentence, "—help with something?"

I tried to tell myself that I was inventing trouble, but my mind could not argue with their body language. There was something so intimate and gentle in the way she leaned against him and in the way he allowed her to, that the upper half of my body felt suddenly drained of blood.

Irina moved away from Phil, lifted the plate of meat and potatoes that was steaming on the counter, and slid lithely by me as I stood paralyzed in the doorway. "No, no," she said sweetly, "everything is ready. Come eat."

I felt as though my bowels were about to give way and all at once I lost both my sense of gravity and all feeling in my legs.

Phil turned toward me and squeezed my neck as he passed but he did not look at me. I followed him, unable to feel the floor beneath me. I went to the w.c., then to the bathroom to splash water on my face, and joined them at the table. During dinner I did not say a word or eat a thing. The whole situation had suddenly become agonizingly clear to me, and I hated them all.

I drank quite a lot of vodka and then excused myself, explaining that I wanted to see the view from the porch. The porch was crowded with rusty scraps of metal, a broken baby carriage, and some planting tools. Down below, the playground and the pathway were dark. The patches of snow looked like cirrus clouds seen from an airplane at nightfall.

I pressed my forehead against the railing and the cold sliced through my skull to the back of my neck. "Daddy, Daddy, Daddy," I mumbled, beginning to cry because I felt helpless against Irina's anger and envy, and I imagined my father watching me, unable to help in any way. The look of pain in his eyes when he tried to explain something bad about the world when I was a child had been more painful to me than any words he might have said.

I needed to be wise and gentle, as he had been, and understand what I was dealing with. Logically, I knew I had no right to hate Phil for not telling me about Irina (after all, we were in no way committed to each other) but I *did* hate him, and I hated Irina even more, and her husband the most, because he was the biggest fool of us all.

A long time must have passed because someone came and knocked gently on the windowpane. I had not taken my coat, and, although my breath rose like cigarette smoke from my nose and mouth and tears had frozen on my face, I did not feel the cold. My arms were crossed over the metal railing, supporting my head, which was turned to the side.

"Yo, Clinton, are you all right?" It was Phil. Earlier I would have given anything to have him follow me out there, but the thought of his seeing me in this condition almost made me retch.

"What?" I managed to mutter.

"Can I come out?" he asked calmly.

"Go away."

He came out anyway. There was barely room for both of us among the scraps of metal. He pressed warmly into my side, a little behind me. "Are you all right?" he said, just as calmly as before.

"I'm just great, Phil," I said.

"Jesus Christ," he said, letting out a terrible sigh. "It is *cold* out here."

"You're fucking her. Why didn't you tell me at least? You could have warned me."

I heard him swallow hard behind me.

"I'm not fucking her," he said hoarsely. "I fucked her once two years ago. Pavel was my friend even then and it was just one of those things. Look, she wanted to pursue it but I told her to pretend it never happened. I was a bit infatuated with her; you understand that, don't you?"

Understand that? The vision of him touching her, kissing her, and loving it, almost made me pass out.

"But if I'd known then what I know now I never would have done it, I swear. Do you hear me? I'm telling you the truth."

I could barely talk. "You should've told me before."

"Look—nobody else knows about this, why should I have told you? Anyway, that was two years ago and how was I supposed to know she was going to make a big deal about it tonight? Pavel has *no* idea."

"Men are so stupid."

We stood on the balcony for a while, looking down at the dark courtyard. Phil pressed against me and crossed both arms over my chest. We rocked like that, slowly, and I was afraid he would go away.

"I don't like them," I said.

"Pavel's changed so much. You wouldn't believe it. He still has his good moments, but they're getting less and less frequent. He used to be so funny and gregarious."

We were silent a while, then I spoke.

"My mother says I always pick men that are no good for me. I get into relationships I know can't last. She read some book by a lady analyst and figured out it's because I have a subconscious fear of being abandoned. You know, since my father died. It's like I'm afraid to replace him. Maybe she's crazy. But she definitely picked up on a pattern. You really hurt me, Phil. All the time."

He lit a cigarette and smoked it fast, inhaling deeply and flicking the ashes over the railing. When he put it out on the railing the red cinders fell in a shower toward the ground. Like fireworks, they went out long before they hit.

"Well I guess you could say I'm the same way. It's been a long time since I've felt this way about anyone. I don't like to feel like this. I don't like to have to worry about someone else. I don't like to think life won't be the same when that person's gone. I didn't want to fall in love with you and I guess when I started to feel it I got scared, and then I got pissed off."

"Are you telling me you're in love with me?"

"I was thinking, if you want to . . . I mean . . . it's a lot to ask, but if you can hang tight till I get back from my trip, maybe we can work it out back home. I have to take this trip. You've got to understand. I saved up all my pennies and organized and planned for months. That was way before I met you."

"Can't I go with you?"

"You want to go with me? You don't have a visa and you can't get a visa to travel in the Soviet Union once you're in the Soviet Union."

"I can try." I could see the letter now: *Dear Mommy, Please lend me five hundred dollars because I have to go to Bali with Phil, the American I told you about. . . .* My mother would die of worry. She would think I'd finally, truly flipped my lid.

"All right. Try." Phil said.

I knew I never would.

But because of our conversation, I did not hate Irina anymore and was not worried about facing her or her husband. I felt magnanimous because I had won. All the terrible questions and doubts which had tormented me an hour ago had gone comfortably to bed in my mind.

23

YELENA DAVIDOVNA'S ASPIRIN

"Of course! Of course," I had promised Yelena Davidovna the first time we'd met, "I will get you thousands of American aspirins." But I had not brought any aspirin to Russia; I was allergic to it and in packing for my six-month trip I had only been thinking of myself.

I had two bottles of Tylenol and two of Advil and brought a bottle of each to her the next day.

"Is it aspirin? I will only take aspirin," she insisted.

"Tylenol is a sort of aspirin," I said.

She inspected the bottle, bringing it up to her nose. She saw the word aspirin and was satisfied.

"What is the other one?"

"It is Advil. It is a pain reliever that is not aspirin."

"I will not take it then." She pushed the bottle back into my hands. *"Narkotiki* are addictive. I do not want to become a drug addict."

"But Advil is not addictive. I promise you. I take it all the time for headaches and menstrual cramps."

"You are probably addicted."

I believed that Advil, being a muscle relaxant, would help her as much as Tylenol and I argued and explained and cajoled until I was exhausted, but to no avail. Yelena Davidovna was at times a very stubborn woman.

I asked around the group during the next few days and tried to barter my Advil for aspirin, but no one would trade more than a couple of tablets. Everyone had become stingy about medicine. We had learned the hard way in our first month that it was almost impossible to get pills from Doctor Belinka at the American Embassy clinic.

Doctor Belinka was inconsistent and nasty with students. He refused to examine girls with gynecological problems when his nurse was not on duty—and his nurse was mostly not on duty; in fact, while we were in Moscow she went back to America on a three-month pregnancy leave. Sometimes when students showed up at the clinic with Giardiasis he gave them a few days' worth of Flagyl, and sometimes he sent them home with nothing. Students did not get rid of Giardia once they caught it, because Flagyl (I found this out later) has to be taken in large doses and for at least two weeks to be remotely effective.

We had been in Moscow three weeks when a student's lung collapsed. It was a Sunday and our counselor Rebecca from the University of Chicago phoned Doctor Belinka at home in a panic. She told the doctor the student knew what it was because it had happened to him before, back home, and he needed X rays immediately. Belinka said, "You shouldn't accept students with health problems on your program. I'm not on call today," and hung up.

In a rage she called Doctor Sebastien of the French Embassy, who agreed to see the student immediately although he was not on call that Sunday either. From then on we nicknamed the American physician Doctor Treblinka and went to the Frenchman for serious emergencies.

To Doctor Treblinka, as to the rest of the American Embassy staff, students lay in the dung heap below the first rung on the priorities ladder. I figured it had to do with the fact that we were in Russia because we'd chosen to be, while most of the staff members would have given anything to be assigned to another post. It seemed our government purposely hired people of average intelligence who did not speak Russian and had no interest whatsoever in Russia. They were a patriotic, isolationist bunch. They acted as if the embassy were the Alamo, and we looked much more like Mexicans to them than fellow patriots.

A strange irony: the embassy staff, although it despised the Soviet Union and everything it stood for, had adopted a Soviet attitude toward conducting business. Upon walking into the embassy, students were treated with the same hostile indifference they found in the Soviet grocery stores. The attitude was, "We have nothing to give you here so stop bothering us."

We were given the excuse that recently all the embassy's blue-collar employees (Soviet) had been fired in retaliation for some incomprehensible political move the Soviets had made in Washington. The shortage of coolies meant that persons in high positions were assigned menial jobs, and they were infuriated beyond belief. (This probably did not improve Doctor Treblinka's attitude, as he doubtless had to mop his own clinic floor.) But I had it from Phil, who'd been in Moscow three times—twice before the firing of the coolies—that the embassy had been just as inefficient five years ago.

New restrictions concerning the mail were passed down the ladder to us. "No packages arriving from home will be accepted for students who are here for less than ten months," we were told. This was unconditional and final. Then suddenly packages for our group began to arrive.

Phil, because he was a ten-month student, had special embassy privileges and in principle could receive rather large packages of "research materials." However, his materials (banned Soviet books which his father swore he'd sent months before) never arrived. Meanwhile students in our five-month group received photographs and college yearbooks and cassette tapes. One girl received a hermetically sealed bag of peanut butter. Whether or not a package arrived for a student seemed to depend on the mood of the official in charge that day.

Phil went to the embassy to complain. The official in charge that day told him in a nasty tone of voice that the staff was overworked and many packages had been sent back. Phil mentioned that people in the five-month program were receiving peanut butter, and the official said, "You must be joking." No explanation beyond that was given. A week later, Phil's research materials miraculously turned up.

I decided that I had to attempt to get my mother to send some aspirin to Phil. My mother, however, was not known for her ability to deal with technicalities. She was incapable of putting a video cassette in her own VCR and could not figure out how to listen to the messages on her answering machine. I would have written to my Tante Claire, who was much more technically minded, but this would have caused a controversy between them. "Why does my daughter ask *you* instead of *me* for help?"

It also seemed a perfect way to introduce the existence of Yelena Davidovna to my mother without making an enormous to-do about it. I diplomatically offered my mother the choice of handing the business over to Tante Claire if it was too much trouble for her.

This was my letter:

March 2
Dearest Mommy,

A few days ago I met an old woman who knew Daddy during the War. She is a painter, a very good one, and has the most terrible arthritis I have ever seen. It is in her hands and it hurts me to see her trying to paint. She will not take Advil and Tylenol does not seem to help much. I know this is a lot to ask, but could you please send a couple of bottles, BIG BOTTLES, of BUFF-ERED aspirin to me? She is very old and Soviet aspirin makes her sick to her stomach, on top of which it is really lousy.

The thing is, I am not allowed to receive packages, so you must send them to the AMERICAN EMBASSY *NOT* THROUGH SOVIET MAIL, to my friend PHIL CHASE and write RESEARCH MATERIALS on the package in big letters.

There is no guarantee at all that they will get through, but it is worth a try. I can't stand to see her suffer like this. She has the courage of a lion and the kindest heart in the world. She has had a hard life. Her only son died of cancer fifteen years ago. She has not told me much about Daddy yet but I'm hoping once she feels better, she will.

If you do not feel like doing this, you can ask Tante Claire, who I am sure won't mind. Please remember NOT to send the package to me, but to *Philip Chase* (the surfer I told you about who is going around the World after the end of the Program,) and write RESEARCH MATERIALS in large letters on the front and back of the package. One more thing. Do you remember the poem by Robert Louis Stevenson that Daddy used to read to me, about a little kid who doesn't want to go to bed? "In winter I get up at night . . ." The reason I want the poem is that Yelena Davidovna, the old lady, remembers it from years ago but neither of us can get beyond the first stanza. If by any chance you still have that book and could send me a copy of the poem, I will never forget it for the rest of my life. Thank you so much, Mommy, for helping out. Love,

Clinton

I did not believe for a second that the package would arrive. Between the embassy's inefficiency and my mother's airheadedness (she often wrote me at the embassy's Helsinki address but included the number of my dorm room at the Institute on the envelope) the obstacles seemed insurmountable.

I tried to make dates to visit Yelena Davidovna once or twice a week, but she did not like to plan ahead. She said I was too young to make dates with a boring, crippled old lady. "Your time in Moscow is too short," she said. "I do not want you to feel obligated to keep appointments with me. You never know—something much more interesting might come up."

Few things, however, were more interesting than spending time with Yelena Davidovna.

There were days when she was in a reminiscing mood and talked longingly of her youth. She had been born a few years before the Revolution and had never learned to spell correctly because she had been in grade school when the old Cyrillic orthography was changed to the new, simpler style, and the teachers had been as perplexed as the students. She had a college degree in Art History and had read practically every book published in the Soviet Union. She also read English quite well, though she did not like to speak it. She told me she owed her brains and her education to her father, a Jewish intellectual and a Bolshevik, who had managed to stay out of trouble with the government until 1941.

"I am sorry," she told me one day, "I lied to you when we first met. I did not know you then. My father was in jail in Moskva at the beginning of the war, not in the hospital. I did not evacuate because I wished to be near him."

I accepted this new information the way I had learned to accept everything Russians told me: without anger and without the slightest surprise.

She also told me that two of her cousins had died in the Kolyma prison camps. They were taken away one night in 1938 by the NKVD. There was no information available on their deaths—they had simply disappeared somewhere in Kolyma. Another friend of hers had come back from the Arctic camps in the summer of 1955, after Khrushchëv had begun to liberate Stalin's victims. This man had returned with several toes and fingers missing from frostbite and self-inflicted wounds, "to get off work detail in the gold mines, you see," Yelena Davidovna explained. "But his mind was sound until the day he died."

Yelena Davidovna was rarely gloomy but there were days when she was not in the mood to talk. She would take down art books from her crowded shelves and show me paintings. Her favorite were Chinese. She owned an enormous volume of paintings of lotuses, and many volumes of Russian and Soviet art.

One day she showed me a collection of minute, fragile figures cut out of single pieces of rice paper. She kept them in a hand-painted cardboard binder that I had to untie because she could not. "It is the work of patient little Chinese peasants," she said. "Imagine the precision, the concentration."

She told me excitedly that she had bought them for the gigantic sum of two rubles in 1950.

I had never seen anything as beautiful as these little oragami-like figures that came in thin white paper envelopes that you held up to the light. With the light behind them the figures appeared black and white.

There were exquisite snowflake patterns, fish with many tiny scales and long, flowing tails, and blooming flowers.

In the binder beneath these, glued onto eight-inch by four-inch rectangles of brown felt paper, was a series of little Chinese rice paper figures dressed up in bright warrior costumes.

"You see, first they cut them out of the little piece of rice paper, and then, after glueing, they color. To color they use the thinnest brush imaginable; a brush made of sable hairs so fine it can paint a line as thin as a needle," she explained.

My favorite warrior had an evil gray face and a dragon wrapped around his shoulders. The dragon's face was blue, his eyes yellow, and his whiskers pink; his pointed claws, which dug into the warrior's suit of mail, were painted many shades of red. The most delicate work was in the purple suit of mail: it was a pattern of tiny connecting diamonds, and through each diamond you could see the brown felt underneath. In one hand the warrior brandished a long white sword.

"You may pick one," she said.

"I wouldn't think of it."

"I started out with many, many more! Over the years I have given them away to special friends. Take one," she insisted. The little warrior became mine and I began to worry about protecting him from all the harm he might encounter between Yelena Davidovna's apartment in Moscow and mine in New York.

Although I learned about Russian and Chinese art and about Russian history, I heard little about Yelena Davidovna's dead son, or her relationship with my father. She talked about them sometimes but never in concrete terms, only as abstractions, as though they both held only spiritual positions in her consciousness.

I made certain to keep at least one day free a week and phoned her from the street, as though I had run out of interesting things to do.

I always brought a little something to Yelena Davidovna's. I knew instinctively that she would be offended by trivial gifts, such as a bar of American soap or a tube of toothpaste, and even more so by large, expensive gifts, so I brought Soviet pastries, or wine or brandy from the Beriozka. She liked it when I brought something Russian, like the fancy mocha layer cakes you could find in the bakeries (if you happened along at the right moment). This was because she did not want me to spend my dollars on *chepukha*, foolishness, and thought it was a good experience for me to stand in Soviet lines. The only thing she had ever asked me for was aspirin, and it was the one thing I could not give her.

Once, almost a month after our first encounter, her arthritis was so bad she could not get out of bed.

"Dochka, I fear you will have a night by yourself. I am so ill I cannot even paint. Today it hurts in my back and my legs as well as my hands."

"Did you take the aspirin called Tylenol I gave you?"

"*Da*, dochka, but that kind of aspirin is not the kind of aspirin that helps much."

I was so angry that such a woman should have to endure great pain that I spent the entire evening helplessly crying in my room.

In the third week of April, just as the snow drifts and the ice turned to mud and the falling snow to sleet, Yelena Davidovna's aspirin miraculously arrived. Phil's counselor dropped the package off at his door, and he immediately brought it to me.

"I guess carrying on at the embassy helped," he said, pleased with himself.

I threw myself around his neck and kissed him as though he were a knight in armor who'd come and saved my life.

RESEARCH MATERIALS!!! was printed five times on the package in bright red ink by an angry hand that seemed to warn that this package damn well better get through or else. The plastic bottles were at least seven inches tall. I had never seen such big aspirin bottles. "Special Discount. 1000 Tablets of Buffered Aspirin for $2.99!" the label said. Buffered no less! My mother had included the poem by Robert Louis Stevenson, written out carefully in her long script on a separate sheet from her letter. It was a strange letter, filled with questions and warnings and worry.

March 25

What are you telling me, Clinton? You are not telling me anything is what you're telling me. Who is this woman who knew your father? How do you know she knew your father if she won't tell you anything about him? I wouldn't trust her, Clinton. You never know. Those people will try to take advantage of you. No matter what she tells you you better just remember that you are his only daughter and I am his only wife.

And what about this surfer from Long Island? Why is he going around the world instead of finishing his PhD? Is he rich or something? He sounds confused. You always seem to get involved with these boys who can't give you what you need and who can't protect you emotionally or financially. I am getting old and at this rate I'll never get to be a grandmother.

The last one was a disaster and thank God you got out of it before it was too late. Right from the beginning you said that sexually between you and Dave it was not what you had hoped it would be and let me just tell you that those things don't get better with time, they only get worse. I hope this Phil is a great lover at least because if you come home a wreck at least you will have had a good time. Sometimes I worry that you will hurt yourself and I don't want you to get hurt because you are my only baby and when you hurt, I hurt. Sometimes I have dreams that you are crying and in pain and I try to think of ways to call you but I know that would only make you worry.

Well, anyway all your tantes and I are glad you didn't marry Dave and you should be glad you didn't marry Dave as well. Tell the surfer he can come visit us next summer in Wainscott and he can surf all he wants. That is what those boys dressed up in black suits and sitting out there in the water like ducks are doing, isn't it?

How old is the old lady anyway? I miss you and love you and can't wait for you to get home. Do you think the CIA reads my letters?

Love, your Mama.

After class, I took the aspirin with me and went out to call Yelena Davidovna.

"Allo?"

"Eto Clinton. I have a surprise for you."

"Dochka, I am not well today."

"Precisely, Yelena Davidovna, your aspirin has arrived."

"But I look awful. I do not want you to see me like this. I frighten myself, even, when I look in the mirror."

"I will only drop off the aspirin at your door, Yelena Davidovna. I think it will help you."

"Nyet. You cannot come all the way and turn around at once. *Eto neprilichno.* It is not proper. I will make a pot of tea."

"It is not necessary. Please, Yelena Davidovna. I shall just bring you the aspirin."

"Very well," she said. "Then you shall make me a pot of tea. I am warning you, I am not even dressed."

She opened the door in a fuzzy blue dressing gown. Her face was a paler shade of blue. She looked quite beautiful; her silver hair was slicked back behind her ears and her gray eyes shone feverishly, full of life. Their kind, welcoming expression told me that she was pleased to see me despite her illness.

"Dochka," she said, putting her thin arms around me, "how can I thank you?"

"You do not have to thank me at all, Yelena Davidovna. You have made my life here so pleasant. You have treated me as your own."

"And so you are," she said vaguely. "You are my own." She headed back toward her two rooms at the end of the hall.

"I put the kettle on but I did not have the strength to prepare anything else."

"It is not necessary," I said. "I will make the tea. Please, Yelena Davidovna, take two or three aspirins right away."

"I will."

In the kitchen I took four large pinches of the Georgian tea leaves out of their metal, hand-painted container and dropped them into the little teapot. I filled it with boiling water and then ran her a cold glass from the sink.

She was lying on her bed, propped up on pillows and wrapped in an old knitted blanket. I unscrewed the childproof cap of the aspirin bottle for her and handed her three pills and the glass.

"I will have to teach you to open this," I said. "It is made so that children cannot and is quite complicated."

"Ha ha ha! Americans think of everything."

She took the pills in her crippled, twisted hand and put them in her mouth. After throwing her head back, making a face and swallowing, she said, "I would not mind this disease if it killed you fast." She breathed deeply and then said, "My son's cancer did not kill him fast either. It took a year. At the end I bribed the nurse and stayed at the hospital all the time. He could not eat anything at all but I tried to feed him grains of caviar, one by one, from a tiny spoon. His wife was there with me, but once he died she would not see me anymore. She said it was too painful to her because he looked and acted so much like me. Would you like to take a closer look at his picture?" She pointed a crooked finger toward the glass cabinet across the room from the bed, where three pictures of a young man had been stuck between the two sliding panels of glass.

"Take them out," she said. I went and took them out. The corners of the black-and-white photographs curled in toward each other in my hand. He did look very much like her, a handsome, dark-haired fellow with an angular, oddly noble, intelligent face. He had kind, sweet, happy eyes in the pictures.

"He does look very much like you." I sat in the sofa-chair next to the bed.

"Not now," she said, laughing lightly. "But there." She pointed to one of the long, thin artists' drawers that filled the large space below the cabinet. "Open the third one. There. Bring that top folder to me."

She took out a pastel drawing of a serene and noble-looking young woman with dark red hair and thick black eyebrows that almost came together over her nose. The aquiline nose and the gray eyes were Yelena Davidovna's; they had not changed at all, but the overall impression of the woman in the drawing was of an Italian lady. I kept wondering why Italian, and all at once it dawned on me: the portrait looked disturbingly like my own mother some fifteen years ago. I wondered why I had not noticed their similarities immediately, and decided it was because the reality was too frightening.

"I looked a little bit like you, didn't I?" she said, smiling thoughtfully as she studied the drawing. "My husband drew this."

"You look so much like my mother it is frightening," I said. Yelena Davidovna glanced at me, put the drawing back in the folder and shut it.

"Is that really so?" she mused.

"Yes," I said.

I had forgotten about the tea and went back to the kitchen to fetch the cups and teapot. I brought everything in on a tray and set it on the bed. We drank for a while in silence. Then I took the poem out of my bag. "Look what my mother sent me, Yelena Davidovna. It is the poem we could not remember."

She perked up, straightened herself on her pillows, and blinked. "Really?" she said. "Read it to me, please. Slowly."

" 'Bed in Summer,' " I read.

"In winter I get up at night
And dress by yellow candle-light.
In summer, quite the other way,
I have to go to bed by day.

"I have to go to bed and see
The birds still hopping on the tree,
Or hear the grown-up people's feet
Still going past me in the street.

"And does it not seem hard to you,
When all the sky is clear and blue,
And I should like so much to play,
To have to go to bed by day?"

I looked up from the page on which my mother's pretty handwriting stretched from top to bottom, and saw that tears were running along Yelena Davidovna's cheeks from under her closed eyelids.

"That is the way I feel now, dochka. There are so many things I would like to do. I would like to travel with a group of artists to Tallinn this spring; I would like to go to the Caucasus again as well. My time is running out and here I am, unable to move. Like a child forced off to bed."

"The warm weather will be here soon," I said, trying to sound hopeful, but my voice would not carry it. It cracked in mid-sentence and my eyes brimmed with tears. "Already the snow and ice has melted," I managed to whisper.

"Now it is a muddy mess. It snows off and on through the first week of May most years, dochka. But the summer! The summer is something to see. We will take walks together when it is warmer."

"We certainly will."

"Shall I tell you about your father?"

"Yes. Only what you want to tell me."

"*Ladno.* I told your father in December of 1942 that he would die from his heart. He had an attack right in my apartment. He came back from his visit to Stalingrad with that man Gavrilov—dochka, Gavrilov was NKVD. But do not get upset." She reached for my hand and held it.

"Not all wolves will eat you. Gavrilov was a decent man, an orphan who got picked up by that horrendous organization when he was still just a boy. He was very intelligent, very artistic. A poet. But he was also violent, and wild, as your father was. Your father knew Gavrilov was NKVD and he didn't care. Gavrilov was probably assigned to watch him, but a real friendship developed between them. If Gavrilov had not been so powerful, your father would never have seen Stalingrad before the Germans fell.

"Your father came back from Stalingrad sick. I knew as soon as I saw him—I was living near Red Square in my husband's family's flat at that time. My husband's family was well connected and I had little to fear in being friendly with your father, or Gavrilov. Your father climbed the four flights of stairs (the elevators were not working, of course, and we were so cold because there was no oil to heat the buildings) and when I opened the door his lips were blue and he was out of breath. He did not faint or anything like that. But he said he had a slight pain in his arm and that his heart was not working right. I told him he had to go to a doctor immediately but he said no. He was afraid they would send him home.

"We sat in the darkness of the apartment—we had no electricity—and drank strong tea with sugar he had brought me.

" 'Lena,' he said, 'I saw German prisoners who said they would not survive in Soviet hands. They wanted me to take some pictures and notes back to their people. I could not do it; Gavrilov was watching from a distance. They will die, won't they?' He had the most horrible look of despair in his eyes.

" 'Maybe not, Sasha,' I said. 'The Red Army is a good Army.' At the time I hated the Germans as much as any Russian did and I didn't care if we killed all of them. But now I am old and I don't hate anybody."

She lifted her teacup and brought it with difficulty to her pursed lips. Her hand was shaking as she put it down on the saucer, which did not match.

"Did you know that they threw 350,000 German soldiers into the battle of Stalingrad? Out of those, about 210,000 were left when the Soviet Army captured the city. And out of these 210,000 prisoners, 900 went home at the end of the war.

" 'Lena, it was too much for me,' your papa said. 'The prisoners were already freezing to death and half-starved. The Soviet soldiers are dressed properly and are well fed. They are as strong as bears and seem to have no fear except the fear of losing the war. Every day they too die by the thousands. Everyone is suffering so much, and for what? Soon our countries will be enemies again. After this war ends there will just be another. I am going to do everything I can for the rest of my life to stop that from happening. We cannot have another war like this one.'

"Your father did not talk like that in the beginning. He liked the violent stories of Soviet infantry fighting against Nazi tanks. He loved the Red Army for holding out in Stalingrad. It was all exciting and extraordinary until he saw death with his own eyes.

" 'You are becoming a pacifist. Your heart is too fragile,' I told him. 'You will die from your weak heart.'

"He laughed at me, can you imagine?

"Then he said that if my husband did not survive—my husband was in the East, in the navy stationed in Vladivostok; it was a comfortable place to be and I felt guilty for all those poor men dying whose parents were not powerful enough to secure them a safe position—your father said that if my husband did not survive the war, he would take me and my son back to America. My husband survived the war. He is still alive, in fact. We were divorced long ago, long before my son died." She paused for a moment. "I am sorry, dochka, I do not want to hurt you in any way."

"My father could not have picked a better woman. If I had to pick a mother in the world beside my own, I could not pick one better than you."

She laughed heartily at this.

"So you see, you are my *rodnaya*."

Rodnoy is a strange Russian word that does not exist as one word in English. It implies "own," "indigenous," "related," all these things in one. Its opposite is *chuzhoy*: "foreign," "alien," "unknown."

"Did you know, dochka, that after your father recovered from his fall off the tram, he went right on working although his knee gave him a great deal of pain.

"This is something I am sure you know about: your father was one of the first foreign correspondents to see a *contzlagir*, the Nazi camps where they gassed children as well as adults. That was in August of '44, when the Red Army reached Lublin, in Poland."

"I read a chapter in one of his books. It was hard to read. I don't remember very well because it hurt too much. It was hard to imagine him having to see that."

"He wrote article after article about the Maidanek camp because he could not get it out of his mind, but the American newspaper thought he had been influenced by Soviet propaganda. They did not believe he could be telling the truth! They believed he was exaggerating. Exaggerating about Nazi atrocities, imagine! After that I was certain his heart would not hold out because he again had those dizzy spells and the pain in his arm.

"I worried about his heart in 1956, when Khrushchëv admitted that Stalin had been a criminal. I had not seen or heard from your father in over ten years. That was how we had left it. There was nothing else to do. Your father knew that many Party leaders had been shot during the thirties, but he had no idea of the violence and the wanton terror under which we had lived. You cannot imagine, dochka, how powerful the Secret Police were in those days. None of us knew how many had died. We still lie about the numbers. And the purges started again after the war. Even Gavrilov, as powerful as he was, was sent to Siberia. Many, many, many who had become too powerful or had dealt with Westerners during the war were sent off to camps. If my husband had died and I had married your father, I would have had to wait years for an exit visa, and *I* would have been sent to Siberia as well.

"I could not imagine how your father would have taken this information. He had believed and hoped for peace between our two countries. I was so afraid he would become convinced that the Soviet leaders were as evil as Hitler. He would perhaps look back on all the time he devoted to trying to understand this country and find that he had in fact understood nothing at all, been betrayed by us. You are lucky, my dear, that your father's heart held out as long as it did. I would give anything to know he did not look back on his experience here with feelings of regret."

"I wish I could tell you, Yelena Davidovna. I don't know. And he was so open with me about everything. Everything except that."

We sat in silence for a while. The grandfather clock ticked loudly in the other room.

"I feel better, dochka. Will you see what we have to eat? I know there is some kolbasa and some cheese left. And there is a can of some kind of meat. Would you like a little drink of vodka? I saved a bottle. It is in the usual place, in the other room. You see, all my son's friends want to come take care of me when I am ill, but I will see no one. You are the first."

"I love you very much, Yelena Davidovna."

"And I love you very much as well."

24

THE DOG
FROM HELL
REVISITED

B eatrice's letter did not arrive until the end of April. By then I had dismissed Natalia Ivanovna and her junkie daughter from my mind. I had decided that I had done all I could back in early February by writing to Beatrice and asking her to investigate. I had not believe for a second that Beatrice would find the daughter, although I knew she would look for her.

March 15

Dear Clinton,

You wouldn't believe it but the East Village has become yuppie chic. You should see them with their briefcases and suits going off down Avenue A at daybreak and coming back at nightfall. Our President, that light of lights, tells us in his State of the Union Address that things have never been better. Well I beg to differ. He should clarify: "things have never been better for white people with money." He should take a walk down here some time. You'll forgive me for sounding like a socialist but I am convinced that there is a direct correlation between the gentrification of my neighborhood and the rise in the number of homeless I see in the streets.

Third Street between C and D (where your friend's daughter

lives) looks a bit like Coventry after the bombing. Some buildings are gutted and some are not; most are lived in regardless.

I went down there Friday afternoon. It was early enough, about three pm. Things are fine around there until dark. Your letter intrigued me. I was curious to see what one of those buildings looked like from the inside. So I left the article I was working on to check it out (it wasn't going well anyway).

Vika and her man (?) Pedro live in one of the better buildings on Third, closer to D than C. I started to laugh thinking about the look of terror on your face the first time you came to visit me down here. You were trying to be so courageous but you were scared shitless. That was nothing, that was A and 10th. You wouldn't have liked this scene at all. I've learned to fade into the scenery: black coat, black scarf, black shoes. Remember what I told you once when we took the subway home from Columbia at four in the morning after that party? Pretend you're invisible and they'll think you're invisible. I don't look like I have anything to give.

I've walked down there by myself quite a bit in the daytime. Even in winter people seem to live in the street, on the stoops, inside wrecked cars. There are drooling babies with skin rashes crawling on the stoops and wood fires burning in small metal pails on the sidewalk. The folks hanging out around the pails aren't old but they don't have teeth. Most of them are Latino and this is how I envision Central American countries in the middle of revolutions. Except the white junkies kind of throw the picture off. They're ghosts. The cold doesn't seem to bother them and they don't look for the warmth of the burning pails. I guess New York is also going through some kind of Revolution. It doesn't upset me any more, which worries me.

I found the building. Some black guys were hanging out on the stoop. One of them was showing off a butcher knife he had stuck in his belt. He lifted up his sweatshirt and the sun glinted coldly on this twelve-inch blade. My heart started pounding. I was thinking, Is this fuck nuts enough to slit my throat for no reason? I've felt danger before around here and the thing is not to panic, to look invisible. I gave them my best invisible look and climbed the stoop. They wanted to know what kind of drug I was looking for and I thanked them and said I had it under control.

I couldn't read the names on the buzzers because of the graffiti and if I could have I would've been seriously surprised. As always the lock on the door was busted so I went in and climbed the stairs. The stairwell was so dark and clammy it was Medieval—heaven for rats and roaches. There was a Puerto Rican woman rocking a sick child in the hall of the second floor. What she was doing out in the hall I couldn't imagine. The child was really sick. It could barely breathe and had the most helpless look of pain on its little dark face.

"Your baby needs a doctor," I said as gently as I could. People don't like to be told how to take care of their kids, I can tell you that from my own experience with my son.

She stared at me with terrified eyes and I thought, shit, I can't get my ass involved in this. I told her about a clinic my friend runs not too far from here. I don't know if she understood. She understood when I asked if she knew Pedro Gonzales or a Russian girl called Vika. As she was pointing down the hall she leaned toward me and the child sneezed a glob all over my chest. The next day I came down with the worst flu I've ever had in my life. I'm just recovering now.

I knocked on the door and a Latino opened it. He had on a sort of cowboy hat. His face was in the shadow of it and I couldn't tell what kind of eyes he had but I could see that his nose was pointed and his chin was square and hard-looking. When he saw me he tried to close the door on me but I stopped it with my foot and started talking. I stuck your letter through the crack in the door and said, "I'm here from Vika's mother in Moscow."

"Viky don want nothin to do wid dat shit."

Terrific, I thought. I hate these hardass macho spic bastards. I controlled myself. No point blowing it now.

"Well maybe you'll let her tell me herself," I said. "Look, I live around here and my friend who's in Moscow just wants to know if she's all right. I have some money for her." As soon as he heard money he let me in.

There was crap everywhere. Just crap, I mean take-out paper bags and cups and shoes and blankets and dirtballs and blood-specked rags used for God knows what. Apparently there are two other small rooms connecting to this one. Pedro goes over and kicks the shit out of one of the doors with the toe of his boot.

"Viky get you ass out here now."

Then he goes and sits behind a card table as though it were a desk and starts answering the phone that hasn't stopped ringing since I came in.

Three girls come out at the same time. One is Latino, dark-skinned, one is black and one is white. I figure Vika has to be the white one. She didn't seem ready to deal with anything.

He tells the other two to get lost. He treats all three like dogmeat so I figure he's banging them all and they get their junk from him and probably fuck anybody else he tells them to. My favorite kind of scumbag. The two others slink out and Vika lies down on this couch-bed that has definitely seen better days. Everybody is flying high except Pedro. No men came in while I was there.

"Who de fuck are *you?*" she says. This girl must be around your age, twenty-five or so. Her teeth are green and her eyes are like two cigarette holes burned through a blanket. At one time she must have been good-looking. She has delicate features, delicate shoulders and hands. She's blonde I guess but her hair is so oily and stringy you can barely tell. The face is scary. A horrible ashy color speckled with little white and red bumps. Who'd fuck that? I had to ask myself. Someone definitely looking to die.

She's lying there gazing at Pedro like a hungry dog waiting to be fed. He throws something at her that lands next to her on the couch-bed. It's a vial of some kind. She opens it, sticks the spoon attachment in and then brings it to her nose. After she's taken a few big whiffs Pedro comes over and takes it away. It's just enough to brighten her up.

"My name's Beatrice," I say, "I live around here. My good friend is studying in Moscow and met your mother. You want to read my friend's letter?"

"No."

"Your mother says she hasn't heard from you in over a year. My friend says your mother's blood pressure is terrible and she's overweight. She cries all the time."

"She always was a fat pig and she always cried all the time.

The whole time I'm in high school if I'm not home by nine she cries."

I never heard a Russian-Puerto Rican accent before. Interesting combination.

"Your daughter is doing fine," I offer. I figure if I maintain my noncommittal look I'm not going to scare anybody and nobody's going to scare me. "Your husband speaks to her in Russian so that she won't lose her roots."

"My husband's Russian sucks. Where is the motherfucker anyway? He still at Yale?"

"I don't know. I don't have his address."

"No kidding. He don't want me to know. That motherfucker knew I was an opium lover back when we use to do it together in Moscow. So he can't tell no one he didn't know what he was getting into. He won't let me see the kid."

"Well." Well, I'm thinking, what do I do now? What do I say?

"My friend wants me to write her through the American Embassy in Helsinki and tell her if I saw you and how you're doing. Do you have anything you want to say to your mother?"

"Tell her I'm fine. Tell her I'm a waitress or some shit. Tell her I'm working hard and don't got time to write right now. When I got time I will. Tell her I don't got a phone. Tell her to give your friend money to bring back for me."

Nice girl, this Vika. She's gone far in America. If I were her husband I'd have done the same thing—hightailed it away from her as fast as I could. I knew that playing the good samaritan and offering help was going to be about as effective as trying to turn Manson toward God, but what the fuck.

"Look, I have friends running places that can help you. We can try to push you through without the waiting list. You want to check it out? If you get it together they'll give you back your daughter."

Pedro moved in then.

"Aint your business," he says. "Get the fuck out of here."

"All right." I'm thinking, I'm not going to argue with this fuck. They're probably all dying from the new plague and I'd better not touch anything or get touched by them. A big gray mouse or a small gray rat skittered like a ball of dirt allong the edge of the wall and hid under the couch-bed. I don't mind them; it's just to give you an idea.

"Your mother wants to know if you're still playing the violin," I said. This seemed pretty funny to me but I was afraid if I laughed she'd get seriously offended.

"Still playing the violin! Ha ha ha! Pedro you hear that?"

"She got to go mang," he said.

"And did you get any of her letters? Apparently some came back to her 'Addressee Unknown' or something."

"Yeah, a few I got. Look, Pedro getting pissed off."

All I had on me was a 20-dollar bill. I took it out of my pocket to give to her but Pedro grabbed it out of my hand.

"I appreciate your patience," I said. "Sorry to take up so much of your time." Looking at the shadow below the brim of his hat I wondered if he detected the irony in my voice.

"Es cool," he says. The bill disappeared so fast I don't even know where he put it.

So that's all. For the $20 you can buy me a few drinks or take me out to dinner when you get back.

I think I'm going to try to write about this somehow. It was an extraordinary experience. Usually I'll go into bad situations with a cold heart and I'll just suck people dry for information without getting involved. Something threw me here. I raised my son alone, like that fat emotional woman in Moscow raised Vika. I watched him go off to school in this neighborhood for years and years and really had to concentrate to stop myself from being terrified. The idea of a scumbag like Pedro getting ahold of my kid made me so sick with rage that I imagined pointing a shotgun at that man and watching for a while while he begged for his miserable life and then shooting him without mercy. This is definitely not healthy.

On a lighter note, new things are happening to me. After years of being a single mother I have fallen in love. I was writing an article about stunt men for this magazine and I interviewed this little powerhouse of a Guinea who works in Hollywood. Having been raised and fucked over by Italians all my life I knew that this was not the man to have an affair with and I brushed off his advances. But he charmed me by offering to throw himself down the stairs of my building. I said sure, go ahead. I was curious. Before he hit the landing of the third floor I was seduced.

Take care of yourself. I hope Vika's tale of woe is the exception and not the rule. If you want to go see her when you get back I'll take you.

Lots of love,
Beatrice

Beatrice's letter caused me severe anxiety: the sun had begun to warm the tired city, the trees were beginning to bud, and people were taking out their spring clothes, reminding me daily that my time in Moscow was running out.

I began to have dreams in which I went to Vera's or Yelena Davidovna's apartments and they were gone. The new tenants wouldn't tell me anything and pretended they could not understand me. It was as though I were unconsciously preparing myself for the day some years hence when I would come back and everything would be changed. I had begun to hoard my hours. People who upset me or bored me or tried to take advantage of me I resented almost violently; I did not want them to steal my time away from those I had begun to love and worry over.

The day I received Beatrice's letter Isabel and I read it together after class. Isabel walked around our little room in a daze, considering our alternatives. She had new friends as well; a widow and her little child had become dear to her, and she too felt her time running out.

We remembered all too well the strange evening we had spent at Natalia Ivanovna's back in early February. We had listened in horror to her apartment-mate's anti-Semitic rantings; Natalia Ivanovna herself had raved stubbornly on, convinced that her angelic daughter was the innocent victim of some Capitalist conspiracy, while Sharik, the dog from hell, had taken every opportunity to dig his teeth into us.

How could we tell those women the truth about Vika?

It did not seem possible. On the other hand, we simply could not ignore them.

"It's your fault," Isabel said as she paced back and forth in front of her bed with Beatrice's letter dangling from her hand. "You had to write your friend."

"I told the mother I would. I felt sorry for her."

"Well." Isabel had a snippety, schoolteacher way of saying that word which infuriated me and left me speechless.

"Maybe we should give Natalia Ivanovna a watered-down version of the truth," she went on. "Something along the lines that her daughter is having a certain amount of trouble with drugs. That her health is suffering—I mean, if the girl dies at least it won't be a total shock. We can tell her that Vika's living with a man who takes care of her. Nothing about prostitution or the 'new plague.' Look, at least the girl's alive, right? At least we can tell the old bitch that her daughter's alive."

"You call that alive? No matter what we say we're going to be in it up to our ears."

"We can't just pretend we never got the letter!" Isabel shouted. *"Can we?"*

I grabbed the letter out of her hands, pulled my leather jacket off the coatrack and headed for the door.

"Where are you going?"

"I'm going to ask a friend of mine whether or not we should tell them the truth."

"Absolutely not," said Yelena Davidovna.

We were walking down Malaya Bronnaya Street. The buildings cast long shadows on the sidewalk and there was a sudden chill in the air. We came to a park in the middle of a square that was still bathed in sunlight. A tent had been set up by the pond and vendors were selling glasses of apple juice and little chocolates and butter cookies. Three white swans and a black one glided idly toward the children who were leaning over the pond's edge, throwing them bread.

"Shall we take a seat and have a glass of juice?" Yelena Davidovna took her change purse out of the pocket of her brown wool coat.

"Look at how well my fingers are working today!" she said excitedly, wagging them at me inside her brown crocheted gloves. She wore a matching brown crocheted hat with a little red crocheted rose on the side, above the brim.

"I take one aspirin every morning when I wake up. When I feel badly, I take more, of course. There are three hundred and sixty-five days in the year, a thousand aspirins in each bottle—so, I will not run out before I die." She smiled happily and squinted up at the blue sky. My heart pounded furiously in my chest and then seemed to drop toward my stomach.

"Please do not talk like that, Yelena Davidovna. It upsets me."

"Forgive me, then, dochka. I am a selfish old woman. But I am a happy selfish old woman. Even if I do not get to Tallinn this spring I shall be painting in the Caucasus this summer."

"Then I am a selfish girl because I want you to stay in Moscow until I leave."

"Ha ha ha! Please, allow me to buy the juice." She gave a few kopeks to the fat woman who poured the juice from the warm glass bottles into the paper cups.

We took the paper cups over to a park bench that faced the pond.

"May I see the letter your friend wrote?" she asked. I took the crumpled aerogram out of my jacket pocket.

Yelena Davidovna put on her reading glasses and bent over the letter.

I watched the children feed the swans while she read. The sun was warm on my back and I unraveled my wool scarf.

"No, no, dochka. If I were you I would not tell this Natalia Ivanovna this horrible story. She does not sound like a very bright woman. But from what you have told me she sounds terribly opinionated. Invariably such women will place guilt anywhere but on themselves. One can ruin one's children by loving them too much, overprotecting them from cruel realities. Her daughter obviously had a problem with drugs even before she left Russia, but the mother refuses to admit that. She refuses to see anything but what she wishes to see. She will say it is a lie because her daughter is an angel in her mind. Allow her that concession. Let her live with her dreams because she will never see her daughter again in any case. Hopefully—and please forgive my saying this—she will die before her daughter. I hope so for her sake."

Yelena Davidovna looked out over the pond with a hard expression, her jaw jutting forward. "It is such a fine line," she mused. "How does a parent know what to say to a child? How does one protect a child? Is one to pretend cruelty and violence do not exist? That is a lie. Your Natalia Ivanovna seems not to know the difference between a reality and a lie."

She turned her head toward me and gazed at me affectionately with her lovely gray eyes.

"Your father was not easy on you," she said. "I can see from the way you deliberate and drive yourself crazy over the things that perplex you. You are a great deal like him.

"Listen to me, dochka, but don't take my advice unless it suits you. You must try not to stand on the deck of someone else's sinking ship. The type of people who allow you to become involved in their private miseries are people who would not hesitate to drown you along with themselves. If you ever decide it is time for you to sink, do it on your own. Do you understand me? I believe the best thing you can do is call the woman and tell her you have heard from your friend. Tell her the daughter is alive and living at the same address. That is all you are obliged to say. Nothing else. You do not have to go spend an evening with her if you have better things to do."

"Yelena Davidovna, I have another terrible problem."

The way I said this must have frightened her because she turned completely white.

"Bozhe moy, you are not—*beremënnaya."*

"No, no. I am not pregnant. I am in love. He is an American from my Institute. I think he is in love with me as well but he is leaving me. He is going around the world and I am so angry at him I feel sick inside."

"Men are men, you know, dochka. When they are young they think they are independent and strong and do not need anyone. And then there is the role of fate. You cannot change what fate has intended for you. If it will be, it will be. With your father, for example. I never loved a man that much before or after, but I knew from the moment I met him that he was not my fate. Let me meet your boy. Bring him to me next week and I will tell you what I think. I cannot say anything without knowing him. Every man is different, even if they are all quite similar."

"I am burdening you with my silly stories."

"Not at all. Tell me more. I find it utterly charming that things are still exactly the same as when I was your age."

So I told her all about Phil. I even told her about his dissidents and his affair with his friend Pavel's wife.

"I don't like that," she said, shaking her head.

"I don't either. But he says he made a mistake."

"They always say that afterwards."

We had a good giggle over that. The building's shadows grew longer and longer until they finally reached our park bench, and Yelena Davidovna shivered.

"We must go," I said.

"All right. It is teatime. Home we go." She stood and linked her thin arm through mine. "The first chapter of *The Master and Margarita* takes place in this very park, did you know? Ivan Bezdomny and the Director of MASSOLIT were sitting on one of these benches when the Devil Woland walked up to them, dressed as a foreigner."

"I remember!"

"Woland told the Director of MASSOLIT that he would slip on the spilt oil and lose his head beneath the tram's wheels. And then Anna spills the oil, there." She pointed just ahead, to the street crossing beyond the park's gate. "And the Director of MASSOLIT slips and loses his head. The tram no longer runs there. But I will show you the exact spot where the Director of MASSOLIT lost his head."

After classes on Saturday, Isabel and I phoned Natalia Ivanovna from the booth at the corner of our street. We held the receiver between us, the sides of our heads touching, as Natalia Ivanovna yelled excitedly into the phone. "Girlies, the most wonderful thing in the world has happened. I have received a telegram from Vika for my birthday. It was only a day late! 'SDNËM ROZHDENYA. VSË KHARASHO. Happy Birthday. Everything is well,' it says!"

It was possible that Beatrice had somehow reawakened Vika's dormant sense of conscience. I was happy for Natalia Ivanovna.

The terrible dog Sharik was barking and growling furiously in the background, almost as though he knew it was we on the phone and he was warning us to stay away.

"Oh God, that stupid dog," Isabel muttered, covering the mouthpiece.

"That is wonderful, Natalia Ivanovna," Isabel said. "How happy you must be. My friend received a letter from New York. Your daughter is fine. Vika lives at the address you gave us."

There was some incomprehensible shouting at the end of the line and Isabel handed me the receiver.

"Did your friend see my Vika?" she shouted.

"Yes. My friend saw her for a few minutes. Vika is very busy. She is a waitress and works very long hours. She is very tired. She says she is sorry for not writing to you in such a long time, but that she is too busy."

"Why have my letters returned to me then?"

"I don't know. Maybe your government did not want them to get through."

"Or maybe your government."

"Maybe."

"Has she heard anything from her husband? Has she seen the child?"

"No. She does not know where they are."

"Can you imagine such a man?" Her voice hardened. "She should come home to Russia. She would be much better off here. She would not have to work so hard and she could live with me. What else did Vika say?"

"She asked that you send her money," I said.

Natalia Ivanovna sighed deeply, hissing into the phone.

"Money! Always this story about money! What is wrong with your country that a girl has to work like a beast and she still has no money or time to live a normal life?"

She began yelling about how rotten our country was and would not stop. I held the phone a foot away and Isabel and I waited. The dog continued to bark. After a minute or so Natalia Ivanovna must have realized that she was yelling at no one. She quieted down and, coughing slightly, asked, "Are you there?"

I brought the phone back to my ear.

"Yes, we're here," I said.

She explained that she and Olga Vladimirovna were on a severe diet and could not have guests to dinner this week.

"It is a healer's diet, you see," she said in a dainty voice. "We are to drink a glass of our own urine a day and eat only potatoes."

"What'd she say?" Isabel asked impatiently.

"I'll tell you later."

"You will come visit us before you leave," she said, a sentence somewhere between a demand and a question.

"Of course," I said.

"Because I will give you a few things to take back to my Vika."

"We have a weight limit. We are only allowed ten kilos per suitcase."

"Oh, very small things," she said lightly.

"Give our regards to Olga Vladimirovna," I said.

"Thank you, girlies."

When I hung up I told Isabel about the urine diet. She did not believe me.

"Maybe you misunderstood."

"If *mocha* doesn't mean pee, what does it mean? I'm not going back to visit them," I said. "You can if you want."

"Let's blow it off," Isabel said flatly.

It seemed terribly cruel to me. But as we stepped away from the phone booth I felt exuberant, released. We were no longer in the middle of their bloody kick-boxing ring, we'd taken back-row seats. If Natalia Ivanovna wanted to believe her dreams it was her business. If she wanted to drink urine it was also her business. If Vika wanted to kill herself it was not my problem, not mine and not Isabel's.

25

THE FIVE-YEAR PLAN

On the plane, everyone except Isabel was in a rotten mood. No one wanted to go to Odessa. For our four-day mid-May vacation our group had planned to visit Tbilisi in Soviet Georgia. At the last minute Intourist announced that they could not accommodate forty students in Tbilisi because of the film festival and we were being carted off to Odessa instead. Nothing was happening in Odessa and there was plenty of room.

Phil's group (they were only ten) had gone to Tbilisi without us and I was devastated. It was like being back in first grade. There had been days when the monitors were in a bad mood and made us sit alphabetically at lunch time. I was certain the monitors' and Intourist's actions were equally sadistic: Intourist hated Americans as much as our monitors had hated children.

Elsa, Ceppie's roommate, had been looking forward to Tbilisi for months. She was still involved with her tall and skinny black marketeer whom she'd met on our very first day in Moscow. She had not spent a night in the Institute since. Elsa had recently told Ceppie that although her boyfriend was madly in love with her (he wined and dined and made love to her with great zeal), intellectually, the fellow was a vacuum. Tbilisi was going to be the "intellectual portion of my Soviet experience." Elsa had arrived in Moscow without contacts, but a Geor-

gian professor at her university had given her the phone numbers of
some very important Tbilisians. She never ceased to remind us of this.

Elsa was sitting across the aisle from Ceppie, staring straight ahead
in a dumbfounded rage.

"That's what old Born Free gets for hanging out with black marketeers," Isabel whispered to me. She was sitting by the window; I was
between her and Ceppie. "Poor Elsa, she's so foolish—she really believes that fellow's in love with her. *I* had no contacts in Moscow, but
you didn't see *me* taking off with black marketeers. Who *wouldn't* want
to meet a *nice* Russian man? Where are they, I ask you? The ones that
approach us in the street are all slimebags. *Ha!* 'The intellectual portion
of my Soviet experience.' She doesn't have enough intellect to feed a
small aquarium of tropical fish. Tbilisi, Odessa—what's the difference?
It's a learning experience, a change of scenery. We all need a change of
scenery. And imagine, we'll get to see the Potëmkin Steps!"

"Shut up, Isabel," Ceppie said in an exhausted tone that didn't
conceal her rage. The only explanation she'd offer us was that it made
no difference to her if they sent us to Odessa or Novosibirsk, she
simply did not want to leave Moscow.

"We es all goin' to die on dis plane," Ceppie said. She kept glancing
up at the baggage compartment above her head; there was no latch to
close it and jackets and bags and metal baggage carriers had been hap-
hazardly shoved into the open space by the Soviets sitting behind and
in front of us. We had tried to put everything heavy under the seats
like good, practiced American flyers. There was no compartment for
oxygen masks above our heads.

"You think Aeroflot has anything like an FAA?" Isabel asked in a
shaky voice.

Every once in a while the plane's engines seemed to stop dead—and
Isabel screamed. It must have been a normal idling of the engines
because the Soviets flying with us did not blink an eye. They were
curious about us and laughed every time Isabel screamed.

The Soviets on the plane were loaded down with Moscow goods.
They pulled smelly sausages and bread and cheese out of canvas bags

and ate. The plane was like a busful of peasants heading back to the country.

"It's only going to be four days, Cep," I said, trying to bring her out of her gloom. "Then we'll be back in Moscow."

"Four days is a lot, *mujer,*" she said in a low voice. "I'm getting married on June 11. That's in less than three weeks, and I'm trying to get to know my future husband."

"What?" I shouted. "They're going to throw you out of the program!"

"Shhhhh!" she hissed. "No one knows."

"What's going on?" Isabel said impatiently.

"None of your business," Ceppie said, and Isabel turned back to the window in a huff.

For an American student to get married in the Soviet Union, the student had to get special signed permission from the Director of the Institute before he or she could apply to ZAGS, the Bureau of Civil Affairs. Once the Institute knew about the marriage they informed our American counselors, who sent the student home on the next plane. Catch-22. It was one of the rules they drilled into our heads before we left Philadelphia.

"Ceppie," I mumbled, "how the hell did you manage to apply for a license without permission from the Institute?"

"Grisha has connections. We bribed someone."

"They're going to find out, Ceppie. They're going to send you home. What the hell are you doing, Ceppie? You're not in love with him. He could be stuck here for years trying to get out and you'll be married and alone in New York!"

"When I get home I'm going to apply for a relative's visa. It's for three months. When I come back and live with him for three months, they'll believe it's real and they'll let him out."

"Oh my God. You're nuts. Why are you telling me this *now?"*

"Because I want you to be my best lady at the wedding. Leave me alone, *mujer.* I have to think."

Why was I telling her that four days was nothing? Four days was excruciating. I imagined Phil with the other ten-monthers, climbing

the mountains around Tbilisi with dark-eyed Georgian girls—falling
in love, maybe. Georgian people were famous for their hospitality and
their amorous nature, and they adored blonds. My God, if I didn't trust
him not to fall in love in four days, how would it be when we'd be
apart for seven or eight months?

I started thinking about the day I had taken Phil to meet Yelena
Davidovna. It was May 9—Victory in Europe Day—and we'd gone
with her to see the veterans gather in Gorky Park in the cold rain.

We met her in front of her building and she and Phil shook hands.
She did not look at him peculiarly or for long and did not ask him any
questions. On the metro going to Park Kultury they talked about
Soviet literature of the war period. We crossed the wide bridge over
the Moskva River in a crowd of thousands. Yelena Davidovna looked
around her at the old and young faces carrying flowers and said that
this holiday affected her worse than any other except for New Year's
Eve, which was when Soviets put up their Christmas trees and exchanged gifts.

The veterans wore their splendid war medals on their best sports
jackets. The people offered them flowers in the street. It had been cold
enough for my down coat that day, especially in Gorky Park, which
stretched along the bank of the Moskva River. But the veterans were
in their jackets and so were we. Yelena Davidovna wore her wool coat
and crocheted hat. She was shivering and I was concerned about her
arthritis. A drunken veteran with a haggard, ravaged face stumbled by.
There were so many colorful medals on the lapels of his tattered jacket
that it seemed to pull the shoulders down toward his chest.

Phil approached the old man before he passed us. "I congratulate
you on your day of victory," he said, and handed the veteran a red
tulip. The old man added it to the wilting flowers he already held in
his hand.

"Thank you, young man," the veteran said. He looked up at Phil
with bloodshot eyes. "Thank you . . . Germans?" he asked after a
moment of reflection.

"*Nyet. Amerikantsy.*"

"Ha ha ha!" The old veteran slapped Phil on the shoulder and took a bottle of samogon out of his jacket pocket. "To you!" He glanced over his shoulder, drank, and passed Phil the bottle. The liquid was yellow and sirrupy-looking. Phil took a long stealthy pull and handed it back, making a face.

"You were our allies then," the man said dreamily, and wiped the cold from his eyes with the heel of his callused hand. The wind was howling on the banks of the river. Carnival music wafted over us and disappeared in a gust of wind. Up ahead a Ferris wheel went slowly round, the gondolas swinging dangerously in the purple sky.

"It's a pity you didn't start fighting the fascists sooner. A lot of brothers would have lived to celebrate this day," the veteran said sadly.

"I agree with you," Phil said.

He walked with us a little way, toward the big fountain around which many food stands had been set up for the occasion.

"May 1 was such a warm day," Phil said. "Pity today is so cold and rainy."

"Nyet. This is perfect weather for such a day," the old man said. He saw someone he recognized in the crowd and waved. "Well, *vsevo dobrovo,"* he said and stumbled off. Twenty feet ahead a little girl with huge pink bows in her hair handed the old veteran another flower. He was accumulating quite a bouquet.

"Philip," Yelena Davidovna said, taking his arm, "why do you like it here so much?"

"I don't know, Yelena Davidovna. I fell in love with Moskva five years ago, when I came here the first time. The people, I think. The culture. It fascinates me. Also, the difficulties one encounters in everyday life here make the difficulties of my life at home seem so much less serious. And I like to be away from my people."

"You are brave and honest to say so. Then your family is not Russian?"

"No. Not at all."

"I know I am an old and stubborn woman and that it is not my position to say anything to you, but I feel very close to this girl for many complicated reasons. I do not like to see her distressed. I wonder if you are not afraid of close ties, Philip. I must tell you that a girl like this one will come your way only once or twice in your lifetime. If you are afraid of her you will lose her to someone who is not afraid."

"I know. I have been thinking about asking her to marry me so that we could come live here together for a year."

I threw Phil an outraged look, expecting to find a silly smile on his face because he could only be joking. I saw nothing but a concerned, straightforward expression and I almost collapsed on the pebbles. I was walking on the other side of Yelena Davidovna, and when my knees began to buckle I grabbed hold of her tiny arm. Her strength shocked me; it was as though I'd wrapped my fingers around a metal pole.

"How does that sound to you?" Phil inquired, leaning forward. "We would come back in a year from September."

I could not speak and stared at him, shrugging stupidly and nodding.

He said to Yelena Davidovna, "I want to go to Moscow State University as a special graduate student."

"But now you are going on a long trip." She behaved as though they were discussing whom to invite to a tea party.

"That is something I cannot change," Phil said in a hard voice.

"Clintonochka, are you going to wait for this prodigal son to come home?"

"If he writes to me, I will."

"Then young man I suggest you write her often from your islands, and very long letters. What a pity that I will not be with you for your wedding."

"We will have a celebration with you when we return to Moskva," Phil said.

"I will try, then, to live that long."

"I might be getting married too," I whispered to Ceppie below the drone of the plane's engines.

"No kidding? That's great. Before you leave Moscow?"

"No. When he comes back from his trip."

She breathed out a long and terrible sigh. "Life back home has nothing to do with this here. How do you know it'll work? How do you know you'll still want it when he gets back?"

"I'll want it. I think maybe he won't want me. Shit, Ceppie."

"What are you scared of, *mujer?* It is what it is. You can't change it."

An Intourist bus took us from the airport to our modern, clean, Intourist hotel in the old section of the city. Isabel and I shared a room on the tenth floor that faced an Orthodox church. Its silver steeple and fat onion domes glinted in the sunlight. Below the church were stone courtyards and tin roofs. All the buildings had a yellow tint. Isabel had bought a map in the lobby and had spread it out on her bed. I stood out on the balcony with the cooing pigeons and looked down at the busy street. I resolved to make the best of the situation and concentrated on purging myself of my depression.

"Well, we've got two hours before dinner. Let's take a walk. What do you say?" Isabel said.

Ceppie had wanted to sleep, so Isabel and I headed out alone down the long, straight avenue, which had many stores and cafés on it. None of the buildings was as tall as the hotel. The blander buildings reminded me of old sections of Paris, while the pink and red and yellow ones that had intricate carvings in the stone above the windows and on the balconies were reminiscent of Leningrad.

We stopped in front of a grocery store that was selling vegetables and fruit. The stores generally seemed better stocked than the ones in Moscow. We had black Turkish coffee and vanilla ice cream in an outdoor café. There were no lines and the little metal tables were attractive with their bright parasols. Loud, canned Soviet rock 'n' roll blared from speakers that had been set up outside the café.

Looking at her map, Isabel said, "The Potëmkin Steps are right at the end of this street, somewhere. And the opera house is down here. Let's go look at the Potëmkin Steps."

Two drunken men at the next table were staring at us. One started whistling and making faces at Isabel. She threw him an outraged look and got up.

The avenue widened into a downhill promenade in front of the opera house, which was a wildly beautiful, eccentric, colorful building with pillars and fancy windows. There was a little park with complicated flower arrangements in the center of the grassy expanses. Children were running on the dusty paths. The afternoon was warm and dry and the Odessans looked relaxed and content.

Out of the corner of my eye I saw two tall figures walking just a little to the left, behind us. Isabel was still looking for the Potëmkin Steps on her map.

"Do you remember that scene in *The Battleship Potëmkin?* Saw it in film class. Never got over that baby carriage flying down the steps. Water at the bottom and everything," Isabel said with her face in the map.

"What do you think," one figure said to the other in a soft boyish voice, "East Germans?"

"Swedes or Danes," the other one said. His voice was deeper and calmer, more self-assured. "Look how they're dressed. East Germans don't dress like that. Nice legs on the blond one. Skinny, but nice. Nice hair on the other one."

"Hey, Vanya, try your English on them. Swedes speak English." The boyish voice became hopeful and enthusiastic.

"Nah."

"Come on."

They circled us widely and were suddenly just in front, glancing over their shoulders. Isabel was too concerned with her Potëmkin Steps to notice them.

"Check it out, Isabel," I nudged her, giggling. They were in their early twenties, well groomed, shapely, and sweet-looking. They wore European clothes: jeans and colorful cotton jerseys. The taller, stronger one walked with a certain nobility; he carried his head high even though he was blushing furiously.

Isabel appraised them from head to foot in a fraction of a second. *"Yes!"* she said excitedly, close to my ear. "Why *not* have a chat with them? Maybe they'll show us the Potëmkin Steps."

"Excuse me," I said in Russian, "do you know where are the Potëmkin Steps?"

They stopped short and spun around.

"You speak Russian?" the thinner one with the boyish voice asked. He had a lovely shock of dirty-blond hair, which hung over his forehead and was very short and even in the back. His face and neck were deeply tanned. He had enormous, curious, aquamarine eyes in a tender, almost feminine face.

"We are students in Moscow," I said. Isabel and the bigger one were pretending not to check each other out. He was dark and had an exceptionally strong and handsome Russian face; the straight nose, square jaw, high, square cheekbones, and pale eyes. Isabel was studying her map; he approached her, looked over her shoulder, and pointed out the steps to her with his index finger.

"Where are you from?" he asked her in an aloof tone.

"From the United States of America," Isabel said.

The Odessans glanced at each other for a second. It was as though in that tiny moment they had discussed and decided everything concerning us. I decided that they were great friends and had known each other a long time.

"We'll take you to the Steps," the thinner one said. "This way. You are not really from the United States of America." He threw me a wily smile.

"Yes we are," I said.

"Americans don't speak Russian and don't walk around the streets of Odessa by themselves," he insisted, laughing now.

"Some try," I said.

"That's really something," he said, shaking his head. "We are students at the Merchant Marine Institute. We get to travel a good deal. I've been to Italy, Turkey, and Finland. The ships sometimes go to America. Boston or New Orleans, but I have not had that opportunity yet. In principle we are not permitted to talk to you. We signed a statement in school that we would not befriend foreigners. It's for the safety of our country, you see. Down by the Steps our gang hangs out. When we pass them do not speak in English, *ladno?* We will say you are Estonians if they ask. Plus, if they find out you are Americans they will be jealous and will want to start trading with you."

Isabel and the big one were still wordlessly pretending not to be checking each other out.

"Vanya speaks English," the thin one said. "He's the best student in the class."

"Shut up, Kolya."

"What are your names?" Kolya asked.

"They call me Clinton, and they call her Isabel."

"Is-a-bel," Vanya said as though tasting something utterly new and delicious.

"Say something to me in English," Isabel said.

"Nah." He was so red his face seemed almost violet.

"Come on."

"*Ladno.* Khow do you do? I em fine. I em kheppy to meeting you."

"That's good!" Isabel said. She smiled; color rose in her pale cheeks and her eyes became watery.

Vanya smiled.

"Vanya is shy. He always turns red like a tomato in front of girls," Kolya said, punching his friend in the arm.

"*Bozhe moy,* would you shut up?" Vanya sighed.

"After we show you the Steps we'll have a walk. Then we'll take you to have something to drink; all right, Vanya?"

"All right."

"But we have dinner at the hotel at six," Isabel said with a certain amount or apprehension. By nature, Isabel was defensive; it was obvious she liked Vanya, but was becoming suspicious that they might want something (like dollars) from us.

"The Intourist food is terrible," Kolya said. "Eat with us. We'll pay, right, Vanya?"

Isabel also was not one for breaking patterns or rules, even when they did not exist. No one had told us we had to be back for dinner.

"We don't have to be back for dinner, Isabel," I said in English in a slightly angry tone. "I'm much more interested in talking to them than sitting with our group in an Intourist hotel."

"What did she say?" Kolya asked Vanya.

"I don't know. She has a strange accent and she speaks too fast."

"*Ladno,*" Isabel said. "We'll come with you."

"I am pleased," Vanya said.

"We have never met Americans before. You are supposed to be the enemy and you look like angels from heaven. Strange thing, isn't it? Are all the American girls as pretty as you?" Kolya asked. "Because if they are I will not be able to stand Boston or New Orleans. I *love* pretty girls, and you know how it is after you've been on a boat without seeing a woman for months and months—"

"Shut up, Kolya, for God's sake," Vanya said in a low voice.

We stood at the top of the Potyomkin Steps, gazing down at an enormous dock where big merchant ships were moored. There was an observation tower of some kind surrounded by steel cranes. There was no longer water at the bottom of the Potëmkin Steps.

"What happened to my Potëmkin Steps?" Isabel said in dismay. "Where's the water?"

"They built this recently," Vanya explained. "Odessa is one of the greatest ports in the Soviet Union. See that ship? My father is the captain of such a ship."

"That's right," Kolya put in, "Vanya's father is a very important captain. We're going to be captains too some day, in about five years if we don't mess things up."

"Your father is a captain?" Isabel asked, apparently greatly relieved by Vanya's credentials.

"Yes," he said proudly, his chin jutting out.

"What do you mean mess things up?" I asked Kolya.

"Oh, you know. Normal things. Drinking. On that paper we signed there was also a rule about not frequenting any places where alcohol is sold. Everybody drinks, though. It's just a matter of not getting caught."

Going down the steps we passed a group of young men and women sitting on the cement bastions at the edge of the steps. They said hello to our two companions and looked Isabel and me over as though we had green hair.

"Estonians!" Kolya yelled to them. "We're showing them around!" He stood protectively between us and his old friends.

"It will look better from the bottom looking up," Vanya assured Isabel. "Did you see that movie, *The Battleship Potëmkin?*"

"*Yes!*" Isabel said. They moved on ahead, talking about the movie. At first they were a foot apart, then six inches; by the time they reached the bottom step their shoulders were touching. When we got to the bottom of the steps I looked up and realized how far we'd descended. They were beautiful, majestic steps. Vanya was explaining to Isabel that they were in fact slightly uneven, which gave them their geometrically even look. I had no idea what he was talking about but Isabel seemed to understand. She was nodding pensively, staring up at him.

Afterward we walked down the main alley that stretched above the quay. Rows of gigantic chestnut trees in full white bloom lined the walk. Hundreds of people were promenading in their colorful spring clothes and sitting on the benches beneath the rustling trees.

"What a pity it isn't late June. The cherry blossoms bloom and everything in Odessa is pink. Like pink snow. You see, this is where young people come to meet," Kolya said. "Vanya and I were out looking for girls. We never meet anyone new. How extraordinary that you happened along at the exact same time as we. Maybe it's a good thing that it isn't June because we might not have passed you in the street," he reflected.

They took us down side streets in the old section of town. Kolya showed us the apartment building in which he lived with his mother. All the buildings were four or five stories tall, made of limestone and painted bright pastel colors.

"The stone comes from the ground underneath the city," Kolya said. "The quarrying created catacombs where our resistance hid during the Great Fatherland War."

"Are you Ukrainian or Russian?" I asked. "You speak Russian as though you were Russian."

"Can't you hear the accent? We say 'kh' instead of 'g' all the time.

Khovorit' instead of *govorit'*. I am Ukrainian but all our schooling is in Russian. I speak Russian better than Ukrainian. Vanya is Russian. But he was born in Odessa."

They took us down a sloping street lined with shops. We passed a clothes shop, a bookstore, and a poster store. The poster store had extraordinary anti-alcohol posters in the window. On a black backdrop a blood-red hand held a white water glass over a little, drunken man. The scalloped edges of the glass were like prison bars across the beaten man's face and body. AGAINST DRUNKENNESS WE WAGE WAR! said the red caption. Another one showed a black-and-white photograph of a terrified woman and child looking up at the black silhouette of a man drinking from a bottle. STOP NOW BEFORE IT IS TOO LATE! that one said.

There was an anti-nuclear poster which showed the world being chopped in two by an evil-looking Uncle Sam holding a bloody axe.

"Don't look at that one," Kolya said. He took up a position in front of the shop window, arms and legs outstretched.

"We don't mind," I said. "We are used to it. In any case, I agree, in principle, with the idea."

"You agree?"

"Yes. I do not want the world split in half by nuclear bombs."

"And you are American? They told us in school that America is the center of Capitalism and that all Capitalists want to take over the world."

"It is not so simple."

The café they wanted to go to was jammed, the line stretched out to the sidewalk. Vanya was embarrassed and perplexed and stood stiffly on the sidewalk appologizing to Isabel.

"It is always like this," he said. "I don't want you to have to wait. Guests should not wait."

"Forget it, Vanya." Kolya took him by the arm. "Let's go to your place with a bottle of champagne."

"Are you crazy?" Vanya mumbled. "My father is in town. He's sleeping. Can you imagine bringing Americans over? My God."

"Vanya's father is a big Party member," Kolya explained to us, then turned back to his friend. "Look, they speak Russian. If we wake him up we'll say they're Estonians."

"We don't want to get you into any trouble," Isabel said. "Maybe we should go back to the hotel."

This convinced Vanya immediately.

"*Nyet*," he said. "You wait down here at the corner while we go buy some champagne."

"Where are you going to buy champagne?" I asked.

"It's a secret. But it's better if they don't see you with us," Kolya said.

Isabel and I stood at the corner and waited, feeling like prostitutes. Isabel pretended to be reading her map.

"I think Vanya likes me. Do you think he likes me? I think they're sweet. They seem honest. They travel, so what would they want from us, in terms of Western stuff? Right? I mean, the father's home. They don't want any trouble, they're just being friendly."

"How old do you think Vanya is?"

"Probably twenty-three."

"Hmmm."

They came back ten minutes later with two bottles of champagne in a plastic bag.

"We thought you would have gone," Kolya said. "I am really pleased you did not go."

"I em also," Vanya said in English.

"I am not worried about my father," Vanya whispered as we entered the courtyard of a very old and beautiful building. "He sleeps like the dead. It is my mother who I am worried about because she is curious and has ears like an elephant."

We crept up the creaky old stairs to the second floor and Vanya opened the door with a key. "*Shhh*," they said.

We were led into a long hallway with fourteen-foot ceilings and enormous doors leading off of it. Vanya pointed to the far end of the hallway and we all crept on tiptoe past his parents' bedroom.

We went through a bathroom to get to his room. His room also had fourteen-foot ceilings. It had a couch, a round antique wooden table, four antique chairs, a fancy tape deck and large, dark paintings on the red walls.

"I'll go make tea and find something to eat," Vanya said.

Kolya stuck a cassette in the tape deck and turned up the volume. It was "Beat It" by Michael Jackson. "You like Mickael Djekson? We got this tape in Italy." He locked the door behind Vanya and opened it for him when he knocked stealthily a few minutes later.

We sat there and ate cheese sandwiches and drank tea and lukewarm semi-dry champagne and listened to Michael Jackson.

"This was all they had," Vanya said, filling the little glasses again, starting, as always, with Isabel's. "We wanted sweet."

"We like the dry better so for us it is lucky," Isabel assured him. Soviet champagne came in five categories: sweet, semi-sweet, semi-dry, dry, and brut. They all cost about seven rubles, but dry and brut were the hardest to find and were often as good as Moët et Chandon.

"To friendship."

"To peace."

"To accidental meetings."

At one point his mother knocked on the door and Vanya told her he was entertaining and to go away. They never once asked us for anything and only wanted to know about Boston and New Orleans.

"I have a friend in New Orleans I went to college with," I said. "I will give you his number and if you are there he will show you around."

"That is nice. But it is impossible. We always get off the boat in threes. There is one senior always. He watches us. He lets us buy things and look around. But we are not to talk to anyone."

"What are you doing tomorrow night?" Vanya asked as we stood to go. By then it was past midnight. They insisted on walking us back to the hotel.

"We must go see *Swan Lake* at the opera house with our group," Isabel said.

"Will you meet us after?"

"Why not?" Isabel said. I was completely taken aback by how fast she'd agreed.

"Will you come with us to my parents' *dacha?* It is just outside the city."

"We are not allowed to leave the city limits," Isabel said flatly.

"But it is still inside the city limits."

Isabel took out her map and asked Vanya to show her where the dacha was. He pointed to a little tiny dot which exactly straddled the border of the city limits.

"That is not *inside* the city," Isabel said.

"We consider it inside the city," Vanya said. "You don't trust us?"

"It's not that. If we get caught outside the city, especially with you, we will get thrown out of the country."

"It won't happen. We will get a car and go and bring you back first thing the next morning. It is on the beach, there is no one around because it is too early in the season. We will invite our other friend from the Institute and his girlfriend as well. We will swim.

"Swim! It's much too cold to swim," Isabel said.

"Then we will not swim, we will eat *shashliki* which we shall marinate all day in onions and vinegar. We will cook them on an open fire and drink vodka. It will be wonderful. Here we cannot drink and make noise because of my parents. I swear to you on my word as a Soviet seaman that I would never do anything to offend you."

"I swear too," Kolya said, putting his hand over his heart.

"What do you think?" Isabel turned to me.

I was terrified; not of them, but of the consequences of getting caught. Not just for us, but for them. Their careers would be completely ruined, and probably Vanya's father's career as well.

"Please say yes," Kolya said. "We want you to have a good time in Odessa. Please."

"All right," I said. "I am scared, but all right."

On the way home Isabel and Vanya lingered twenty paces behind us, walking arm in arm and talking in hurried whispers. Kolya and I waited for them ten feet before the spot where the bright light of the hotel's windows began to illuminate the sidewalk. Isabel and I finally walked into the light and waved goodbye to the two long silhouettes that remained in the shadows.

The next morning the group piled onto an Intourist bus and drove around the city. A woman with a terrible screeching voice spoke to us through a microphone as she pointed out the sights. We saw the opera house and the Potëmkin Steps again. We saw the Black Sea and the spa where people came to rest. It was only about sixty degrees and the sky was cloudy but the Soviets were in bathing suits, sitting and lying on wooden chaise longues. Out on the dock there were men in raincoats fishing with poles.

On one avenue near the beach were rows of extraordinary mansions. "These are rest homes for the people," the woman shouted. "Before the Revolution they were privately owned, now they are owned by the people."

We saw the war memorial, a black obelisk at the edge of the sea. It was guarded by young Komsomols in uniform.

All day long Isabel talked about Vanya. She said his nature and attitude toward the world were so much like her own she could not believe that he was Russian. "He believes in their system," she told me. "The way I believe in our system. He's rigid, you see. The way I am rigid. He comes from a line of very successful Communists. The family is ancient. They have a bloodline all the way back to Peter the Great. Apparently they have a relative who was one of the original masons of Leningrad. He bought his freedom from serfdom by building for Peter the Great. My family came to America on the Mayflower. So you see, we have so much in common."

"Don't get carried away, Isabel. We're only here for four days."

"Everything can happen in four days," she said. "Do you know what he said to me last night while we were walking back? He said, 'You will think I am foolish, but you are the girl I have been dreaming of since I was twelve. You are an apparition. You are beautiful *and* perfect because your head is not filled with silly, girlish ideas. You are a *serious* girl.' That's what *I've* always thought about myself—that I am *serious*. And did you see the way he was always filling my glass? Whatever happened to gallantry in America?"

Swan Lake was ridiculous. The music was taped and you could hear scratches in the recording. The chorus did not keep exact time, which gave the impression their arms and legs were flailing about. Isabel and I sneaked out after the second intermission. Kolya and Vanya were waiting for us in a dark garden behind the opera house.

They did something so outrageous that as the elder of the bunch I was horrified. They stood in the street and flagged down privately owned cars. Someone finally stopped and for a large sum of money agreed to drive us to the dacha. Going off to a dacha in the middle of the night, miles from the center of the city and in an area completely unknown to us, in a private taxi, no less, was crazy. Absolutely crazy. I was so frightened that my whole body began to shake. In the Soviet Union militsia men stand on the side of the highway and randomly pull cars over. They do not need an excuse to ask for your papers and search the car. This was all I could think about as we drove through the night. After we'd been in the car half an hour and had not passed a single house I decided that their dacha was certainly not within the city limits.

"This is so exciting!" Isabel said in English, in the back of the private car we had hailed in the street. I thought I was going to faint. Kolya, who was squeezed in next to me in the backseat, put his arm around my shoulders and whispered to me to stop shaking like that. "Nothing will happen," he assured me.

The car dropped us off on the paved road near some railroad tracks. The dacha was at the end of a long dirt path. On both sides were thick shrubs and thistles and dogs howling. The plots of land seemed close together, like houses in American suburbia.

The electricity at the dacha had not been hooked up for the season yet, and Vanya climbed up on the roof to attach a cable to some kind of antenna. It was so dark we could only see his black silhouette on the roof. There was lightning in the sky and once in a while he was lit up by a flash of it that seemed to tear the sky in two.

"He's going to die," Isabel said. "He's going to die and we're going to have to go for help. What are we going to do then? Get down from there, Vanya!" she yelled.

"We need lights or we can't stay here," he said calmly from the roof.

It took him a long time but he finally hooked the cables up. Kolya meanwhile stood on the ground between Isabel and me, trying to comfort us.

The kitchen was a room separate from the rest of the house. It had its own door and was a small, comfortable room with summery drapes hanging over the windows. The table and chairs were wicker, the stove seemed pre-revolutionary. The water from the faucet was brown. There was an outhouse at the end of the path, by the dirt road. They apologized for this, embarrassed. We assured them that we did not mind. When we had to pee they escorted us down the overgrown path with a flashlight, holding back leaves, and stood outside the door and waited.

In the middle of the vegetable garden no one had started that spring, they made a circle of stones and lit a big fire. The flames shot high in the air. The pork shashliki which they had marinated in a large glass jar all day were speared onto long metal skewers, and these were placed over the fire, straddling the large stones.

"You are not going to burn the house down, are you?" I said to Kolya.

"We are sailors, my dear. We know how to make a fire."

The other couple arrived in a separate car. The fellow was round and pale and had big round eyes and full, sensuous lips. The girlfriend was blond and wore enormous plastic heart-shaped earrings and a good deal of eye makeup and lipstick. She and I prepared a salad of scallions, radishes, tomatoes, and cucumbers with sour cream. We boiled water for tea. There were five bottles of vodka, of which I drank an enormous amount, just to settle my nerves. A dog in a nearby yard was howling. I was much calmer once we settled down in the kitchen. The world outside seemed far away, and I knew we would be safe until the ride back in the morning.

The shashliki were delicious. Everyone got drunk and sang Russian songs which Isabel and I had learned in singing class at the Institute. They were impressed.

"Do you know the words to 'Yesterday' by the Beatles?" Vanya asked.

"I do," Isabel said. Her pale face was flushed and her eyes were watering. She and Vanya sat against the wall in the corner, pressing so close to one another they were beginning to overlap.

Isabel began to sing the song in a tiny, high-pitched voice.

Vanya hummed along with her and soon he was crying.

"You have the most beautiful voice I've ever heard."

"Shit," I thought.

"My God," he said, and punched himself in the chest with a loud thump. "I am falling in love."

Everyone laughed except me.

They taught us swear words I'd never heard and told Brezhnev jokes. Here was one: Brezhnev is so old he is senile and his speeches have to be written for him. For the Olympics he stands on the podium and unfolds a piece of paper. "O-O-O-O-O," he reads. I almost died laughing.

There was an uncomfortable silence as bedtime approached. There were three rooms, one had a single bed and the others had doubles.

Isabel retired first. She was not a big drinker and the vodka had gone to her head.

"Where should I sleep?" she asked, getting up from the table and looking around with a dazed expression.

"In the best room," Vanya said. "My parents' room. I'll show you."

He came back a few minutes later and sat down again, perplexed.

"Well, Isabel said I should join her but then that means Kolya and you will have to share the other double bed."

I thought about this for a moment and looked at Kolya, who was quite drunk and smiling happily.

"We have to climb through the window because we can't find the key to the door," he said.

"I don't mind." I wondered if it was going to be one of those tug-of-war nights where you watch the sun come up after having spent the entire night trying to explain to the fellow why you won't have sex with him. I was not afraid of Kolya, in fact I liked him quite a bit. I did not want to hurt his feelings, and I also did not want to ruin Isabel's night. It amused me thoroughly to see her so relaxed.

"All right. Lead the way," I said to Kolya. We went out into the yard. He was carrying the flashlight and a blanket draped over his shoulders. He put a chair in front of the window and gave me his hand to help me up. The room was so dark I couldn't see what was in it except for the bed. I lay down in my clothes and stared at Kolya through the darkness.

"You do not have to worry about me," he said. "I gave you my word as a Soviet seaman and my word is good."

He stretched out next to me and ran his hand over my face and hair. "But if you want to do it I am not against it," he said.

"It is not that I don't want to sleep with you. It is that I am in love with someone else."

"Who?"

"An American. I do not want him to sleep with someone else so I feel I must treat him the way I expect him to treat me."

"*Molodiets!* Bravo! Finally I meet someone who thinks like I do. Here you finally are and you are American. The world is a strange place. You know we go off on ships for months and months at a time. We leave our girls back here in Odessa and in a week they have someone new. You can't imagine what it is to be on a ship and worrying constantly about your girl."

"You chose a hard life."

"It's better than staying in Odessa. We get to see the world. We get to have nice clothes and things like that. I have a question to ask you. This has been bothering me for a long time and maybe you can help. They tell us in school that Capitalism is the oppressor of the working class. How can Capitalism be the oppressor of the working class if the working class is getting paid well for its work? I was in Italy and in Finland. I saw how they live. They live much better than we do. Here we get paid badly, terribly. So badly that people have to take recourse. Black marketeering, illegal methods, just to make ends meet."

"What you are saying is true in a way, but it is not that simple.

Some people in the West don't work at all and suffer terribly. Some live in the streets."

"Why don't they work? They don't want to work? Or they can't find work?"

"I don't really know the answer to that. Both probably."

"And I don't understand why the General Secretary's wife wears enormous diamonds."

"But she has to look good in the eyes of the rest of the world."

"That is not Communist."

The walls of the dacha were thin and the sounds of love crept through. The blond girl and her friend were howling like dogs. The bedsprings in Vanya and Isabel's room were creaking but their voices could not be heard.

"Have you slept with many girls?"

"No. I fell in love once, when I was seventeen. My heart hurt so much that I couldn't sleep at night." He slapped his chest with his open palm. I liked that about him, the way he showed his emotions with his face, his hands. He was not afraid of telling me things. Maybe, I thought, he is not afraid because he knows that I will be gone in three days and he will probably never see me again.

"We are not supposed to drink, you know. If they catch us wandering around the streets drunk we are thrown out of the Institute. My father drank too much and left my mother a long time ago. I never met him. Then last year he sent me a letter telling me not to drink. So I don't drink too much."

What is too much? I wondered. We'd put away five bottles of vodka between six people, and Isabel had only had two or three shots.

"I have to be careful," he said.

"I have to be careful too."

"You know about that passenger ship that sank about a month ago? There was an explosion. I was on a training cruise in the Black Sea and we had to go pick up the survivors. Three thousand people were on the ship, five hundred died. Those kids who crewed that sinking ship were the bad boys from our Institute. They are the drinkers, the ones who aren't allowed to leave the country. They have to stay in the Black Sea.

I saw those boys save the lives of children and women. Lots of them died while the officers and older ones did nothing. Just because a kid drinks doesn't mean he doesn't love his country, that he doesn't have pride. If I had to go to war, I would fight just like the best of them."

"I hope there never is a war between us. Never."

"So do I. After meeting you and Isabel it would be much harder to fight. Now I would never be able to kill an American without thinking that I am killing someone like you."

A while later the bed next-door stopped creaking and Vanya yelled out, "You two are jabbering like old ladies over there!"

"Can I kiss you?" Kolya whispered in his boyish voice.

"Yes."

"Can I kiss you everywhere or just on the mouth?"

"You do that too?"

"Of course."

"What is it called?"

"*Miniet.*"

"That's a strange word. It does not sound Russian."

"I am certain that it is a practice brought to us from the West. Russians would not think of it."

I started to laugh. It seemed such a pity in a way that I would be going home without having slept with a Russian. A merchant marine, no less.

"Well?" he asked.

The bed next-door began creaking again.

"It is a complicated matter. If we start, it will be hard to stop."

"I gave you my word."

He kissed wonderfully, passionately and openly. I let him run his smooth hands over my chest, I hugged him close to me and kissed his neck. When his kisses began to move downward I stopped him and pulled him back up.

"Don't," I said.

"All right. We'll stay like this, then." He nestled in against me like a child. I thought of Phil in Tbilisi and tried to imagine him nestling in against someone else. The notion seemed no less threatening than a passionate sexual encounter. Could he blame *me* for this? No, I decided, because he knew better than anyone that in the Soviet Union our whole world was turned upside down and nothing made normal sense.

The next morning, sitting around the same kichen table that we had not cleaned off before bed, Isabel announced to me that Vanya would be coming to Moscow in June and that she would return to Odessa for Christmas vacation. "I have a great aunt who died and left me a good bit of money which I only use for traveling. Why not come back?" she said. The vodka fumes were still fogging up my head and the sight and smell of the table made me feel utterly empty and sick. The table was crowded with half-filled glasses of vodka, wet cigarette butts ground into tea cups, and dinner plates where the sour cream had melted and the pieces of fat from the shashliki had hardened. A few mangy cats begged at the open door. I dumped all the leftovers onto one plate and set it on the stoop.

"If it works out," Isabel went on excitedly, oblivious to the surroundings, "Vanya and I are going to continue the relationship."

They both looked exhausted but relaxed and had nice rosy complexions.

"After all," she said, "in five years he will be a captain. They might even send him to work in America because he has English. I could stand living here for a few years, as long as I could leave whenever I wanted. If we plan carefully and remain determined, lots of good things can happen in five years."

At that point Kolya gave me a cup of strong tea and poured several large shots of vodka into the used glasses.

"Take this," he said. "Medicine. *Nado opakhmelitsa.*"

I took a glass from him and raised it to Vanya and Isabel, who sat hugging each other across the table.

I was afraid for them but did not see any point in contradicting them with logic.

"Who knows," I said, "you might even be able to improve our international relations." I brought the glass of vodka to my lips and turned it upside down.

26

AN
UNEXPECTED
ENCOUNTER

Isabel cried the whole way home from Odessa Sunday night and was still crying on the way down to breakfast Monday morning. The Institute did not give us any kind of break. We were told we had to attend classes Monday, since we were behind on the planned curriculum they had assigned us upon our arrival in February. We were completely exhausted.

After classes I went out to make phone calls—I wanted to let Vera and Yelena Davidovna know that I had returned safely and make plans to see them as soon as possible, since our time was now really running out. Then I intended to sleep until midnight, which was when Phil was supposed to arrive from Tbilisi.

I walked out into a warm, windy, dusty day. The heaters and the hot water had been turned off inside the Institute and it felt ten degrees colder inside than out. The young trees which had been planted on the sloping Institute lawn only a few years before were tottering frantically in the wind. The air carried the taste of summer and made me thirsty for change; now, I did not want to be reminded that the arrival of summer would bring the end of our stay. Then we would be gone (a new batch of Americans would arrive for the eight-week Summer Program) and life would continue here without us. It would be as though we had never existed at all. As a collective group we were replaceable; the black marketeers would find new girls in need of affection and end up with their fancy tape decks and fancy jeans. And the Soviets looking for U.S. passports to marry would have endless opportunities to try again. But it was apparent from the frantic way people in our group were behaving that not one of us believed, or hoped, that other Americans could be substituted for us.

I thought about all this as I ascended the dusty sidewalk to the main road. Just a month and a half ago we were fighting slippery ice and deep snow on this very sidewalk—now it was dust and debris from the unfinished neighborhood construction which whirled about in tiny tornadoes.

Across the street, by the bus stop, a muddy white car was parked in a small dead-end street between two buildings. The horn was blowing insistently and I paid no attention. Strangers often honked at us like that, to lure us into a trade or some such illegal thing. But someone was waving furiously from the driver's seat. I stopped and looked hard at the car. It was a Lada. A hand beckoned me. I approached slowly, keeping a certain distance.

Andrej stuck his curly black head out of the driver's seat window and smiled. Even from the other side of the street I could see his wandering eye looking nervously toward the Institute behind me. Through the cloud of confusion that descended on me a bolt of nostalgia broke through; he had given me the only taste of Soviet "Khaigh laife" I had known. It was his contacts, after all, who had led me to Vera and Yelena Davidovna. I had learned so much since that February night when he'd taken me off to his mother's apartment!

After that night, I had tried for a month and a half to get hold of him by phoning his sister Klara at her office. Andrej had vanished and I was furious; he'd opened a door that was now locked to me, had given me a view of Moscow's artistic, privileged world and then slammed that same door shut in my face.

The first time I phoned Klara she informed me, in a sweet and apologetic tone, that Andrej's play had hit some difficulties in Leningrad and was going to take longer to open than expected. She said to call back in a week. I called back in a week and was told that in another week or so Andrej would be back in Moscow. After two more weeks she became nervous: Andrej had been called to Minsk to bury an aunt. Five days later her voice seemed desperate as she explained that Andrej had returned from the funeral of the aunt and had spent three days in Moscow waiting by the phone for me to call. Klara and he had expected that I would try her at work during that period, but I was angry and did not. The next time I called Klara (several weeks later) the message from Andrej was that he'd been called back to Leningrad because there was a new problem with his play, but that I should be patient and wait for him. I was to call Klara at work in another week, which I did. She told me, excitedly this time, that Andrej was at their mother's apartment waiting by the phone and that I should call him immediately. She sounded so thoroughly relieved to be rid of me that I decided that no matter what I would not call her again.

The nasty old mother answered the phone. Recognizing my voice, she told me without hesitation that Andrej had been sent to Baku for a rest cure. Now that I knew (thanks to Vera's gossip network) that Andrej had a wife and child in Leningrad, I understood why the mother did not want him to associate with me. So I tried to calmly explain to the mother that I was aware of the new wife and baby in Leningrad and that this did not concern me at all. She must have misinterpreted, which only weakened my cause.

"I only want to speak to him about some important business," I had tried. "I want to thank him for helping me locate certain people—"

"I don't understand you," she interrupted, and hung up on me once again. I gave up.

Now I walked up to the muddy white Lada and leaned over the open window. The wind blew the dust and my hair into my mouth and eyes.

"Greetings, Andrej."

"You look like a thunderstorm," he said nervously, looking at me with one eye and looking off toward the Institute with the other. "I have been back in Moscow three weeks waiting for you to call. You never call me, naughty girl."

"Don't fuck my brains, Andrej," I laughed. *"Nie yebi mnie mozgi;"*

he, in fact, had taught me this expression. "The last time I called your mother told me you were taking a rest cure in Baku."

"I don't believe it."

"But it is true."

"I can't believe it. I will speak with her." He seemed sincerely perturbed. "I have been trying to think up methods of locating you," he went on. "Finally I decided to sit here and wait. I knew your classes ended at three and I thought, 'If she does not walk out within the hour, I shall leave a message with the gate-watchers.'"

"That is dangerous and silly."

"I don't care. I wanted to see you again."

"You know, I tried to call you about a million times."

"Your Russian has improved. Where are you off to?"

"To make some calls. We just got back from Odessa last night."

"Odessa? Whatever for? Nothing happens in Odessa."

"*Lots* happens in Odessa," I said. "My roommate fell in love with a sailor."

"A *sailor?*"

"A merchant marine."

"Ha ha ha! That is too much."

"We even had dinner with his mother the night before we left. They have the fanciest apartment I ever saw here, except for your friend Boris Mikhailovich's."

"He has asked about you, and his wife as well. They wondered why you never called them."

"Because they never gave me their number."

He sat behind the wheel, tapping it with his fingernails, a perplexed expression wrinkling his good-natured face.

"I am going to Boris Mikhailovich's now, in fact. Would you like to come with me? A seventeen-year-old rocker is coming there to audition for a documentary film my friend intends to make. He wants me to write it because of the success of my last play—you know, the one you saw about young struggling musicians."

"What is a rocker?"

"Punks. They aspire to become Western-style heavy metal musicians and play violent songs about emotional deprivation. It should be interesting, in any case."

What is he doing here? I wondered. What does he want from me? All I wanted was a chance to tell him that I knew the truth, and that I did not care. In the past several months I had come to understand that between Russian men and women, it was most often everything or nothing; 'coeducational' friendships were a rare occurrence. I wondered if I could talk Andrej into being my friend.

"I'll come with you."

I walked around the front of the car, slid into the passenger seat and slammed the door. I felt an ache in my throat; a fraction of a second later my mind acknowledged that I was afraid of not getting home, of not seeing Phil that night.

"I have to be home by midnight," I said to Andrej.

"Ladno." Andrej raced off down the dusty street. The construction pits with the garbage-strewn lots seemed to beg for attention; they were as sad and carcass-like as abandoned Hollywood sets. Paper wrappers and empty bottles skidded and rolled along the street's gutters. These were the ugly realities you never saw in winter. Moscow in spring no longer resembled the silvery drawings of fairytale books.

"You will not believe what happened with my play in Leningrad. I had to stay there for weeks more than I had intended. And then my aunt died and I had to go to Minsk. And then Leningrad again because something else went wrong—with the censors this time—and now that I am back and have been waiting with a palpitating heart for you to call, you do not."

"How are your wife and your baby?" I said in an equable tone.

"What?" He almost drove onto the sidewalk.

"I said, how are your wife and your baby?"

"Who told you that? Mama? It was Klara. I am furious."

"It was not Klara and it was not your mama. It was someone who knows someone who knows you. Someone who said Moskva is just a small village full of peasants who know everything about everybody."

"I must explain to you. It is not what you think."

"In Russia it never is." I was laughing now and the whole thing did not seem terribly serious, though it did to him.

"Listen. She is not my wife. I never intended to marry her but she wanted the child nevertheless. I support the child and the child carries my patronymic and my family name."

"What is the first name?"

"Yelena."

"That's a nice name."

"This woman—she designed the costumes for my last play. You know how it is working on plays. It was just a little something. Then that happened. What was I to do?"

"What you did, I suppose."

"I intended to tell you. I swear it. I am outraged that someone else told you first. Who told you?"

"I am not going to say."

"It really is a town full of nasty peasants. I am a moral man and I support the child in every way but I do not have anything . . . anything . . . well, you know—to do with the woman any longer."

"You have a law here that you are obliged to support the child. There is nothing special about that. If you did not support the child they would throw you in jail."

Andrej did not respond to this.

"No wonder your mama and your sister did not want you to see me. You could have told me everything right in the beginning, Andrej. Then I would not have felt like such an idiot in front of your mother. It doesn't matter in any case; I only want to be friends with you." This time, after months of practice in Grammatika class, I said it right: *"Priyately."*

"Let's talk about something else now, *ladno?* What have you been doing for the past three months? Did you discover anything interesting about your father?"

"Yes. And it is all because of you. You were very kind to me, Andrej. The connections you gave me have changed my life here. Without your help it would have been miserable. My God, so much has happened."

"Have you fallen in love with any Russian men? Any merchant marines, ha ha ha!"

He slapped my knee as he had done on that February evening so long ago, when the royal blue night had hung over Moscow like a curtain veiling endless mysteries. How things had changed since then! In turn, I slapped his hand.

"Don't make me angry, Andrej," I said in a complacent tone. "I don't care about the woman and the child. It is not my affair. I am not interested in fairytales, do you understand? I want to come back and live here for a year. Not like a tourist. I've only begun to understand things. So do not talk to me about marriage and fate and silly things. All right? Just tell me the truth."

"You want the truth? There are so many different truths, which truth do you want? Today, in any case, with this kid musician you will get a little piece of truth, whatever it's worth."

The large bay windows were open and the breeze carried the white lace curtains fluttering into the room. Boris Mikhailovich was sitting at the round table in the dining room, in the exact spot he had occupied the first time I had met him. His young wife Sonya was in the kitchen preparing some food and came out and hugged me warmly.

"Ah," Boris Mikhailovich said, rubbing his hands briskly, "here is our young playwright and his young American."

Auntie was still knitting across the table from Boris Mikhailovich. "Summer is on its way," Auntie explained, "so I am taking the opportunity to prepare for the winter."

It seemed nothing at all had changed since my last visit. There was cognac and gin on the table and small glasses and ice, and a plate of sugar cookies.

The two seventeen-year-olds sat quietly at the table drinking straight warm gin and smoking harsh-smelling Soviet cigarettes one after the other. One was fair and one dark. There was another man at the table, a large, bearded fellow who jumped up when Andrej and I came in. They kissed warmly on both cheeks. The man took us out into the hallway and explained to Andrej in a hurried, raspy voice that he had discovered Pëtr by complete accident. He had been in Saratov filming a newsreel on the local mining operations when some reporter mentioned this kid musician who played in basements and garages to crowds of many hundreds. The kid had not wanted to come to Moscow at first because he'd been in trouble with the authorities already and did not want more trouble.

The large man lowered his voice and, taking Andrej by the arm, said, "You see, the kid's own mother is a censor for the local Communist paper and she had him locked up in a mental institution at the urging of the local Party cell."

"Good God," Andrej said. We went back to the dining room.

Everyone was introduced. The blond boy, who had a frighteningly pale face and terrible broken teeth, was Pëtr. When I thought of "punks" I thought of the whips-and-chains and black-leather types who hung out in the bad streets of New York. This Pëtr's brown leather jacket was too small for him and torn at the elbows. His hair was chicly cut to stand away from his forehead, and formed a duck's tail in the back. There was nothing threatening or unpleasant about him. His eyes were sad and intelligent and had a curious twinkle in them. The other fellow, the dark one, seemed to shrink in discomfort whenever he spoke. He was introduced as Zhenya, Pëtr's manager. Pëtr did not say a word, the manager spoke for both of them.

Boris Mikhailovich ignored them for the most part and filled their glasses with gin every now and then. He asked me about my stay in Moscow. I told him that I wanted to come back and spend a year doing research on my father. When Pëtr heard my accent he looked up from his gin and a vague smile flitted across his thin mouth.

"We might be able to organize a special grant for you through the Ministry of Culture. When would you like to return?"

"In a year from September," I said, thinking about Phil being at Moscow University and how nice it would be to have a job here and not have to depend solely on him.

"Because of all the new happenings around here we might even be able to get you access to special files. Did you see, for example, that they are publishing letters of Tarkovsky's in *Ogonyok?* It is wonderful. It is extraordinary."

Sonya brought in a tray of sandwiches.

"Young men," said Boris Mikhailovich, "have something to eat and then we shall listen to Pëtr play."

"God, do I love heavy metal music," Sonya said with the smile of a child gourmand.

"I do not even know what it is," Auntie said, chuckling to herself.

"I am afraid you might be offended, Auntie," Boris Mikhailovich said. "Maybe you should not listen."

"Why pass up the opportunity to experience something new?"

"Where's the young man's guitar?" Boris Mikhailovich asked.

"He doesn't own one," the manager said quietly. "He smashed up the last one he had." He rearranged his tattered blue jean jacket and shifted in his chair.

"Tell us about your music," Andrej said gently, addressing Pëtr directly for the first time.

"Well. I can't read music. I learned from listening to records and tapes. Mostly black market stuff. We don't get much in Saratov. I was playing in this garage, see, with friends. But we became too big and they closed us down. We almost started a riot one night. That's when I broke the guitar."

"Sonya," Boris Mikhailovich said, "bring your guitar for this young man."

Sonya promptly came back with an acoustic, Soviet-made guitar.

"Thanks," the kid said. He slid the waist of the guitar up to his groin and pulled back the beaten-up sleeves of his leather jacket. There were deep red vertical slashes on both his wrists.

He made chords for a while. His long fingers stroked the neck of the guitar while he tickled the strings with his other hand. He tightened the keys and brought his ear close to the strings.

"I usually play electric when I can get my hands on one," he smiled apologetically. "This won't sound great. Can we close the curtains and turn off the lights? It's hard for me with all this light."

Sonya shut the heavy curtains and turned off the amber light that hung over the table.

"You're American?" he said, addressing me with his chin. It took a moment for the slits in the curtains to light up his ashen face. He used the familiar *ty* which no one in Russia had ever done upon first meeting me before.

"Yes."

"You know this song?"

With only the slightest accent and without a single false note either in his high, scratchy voice or in the guitar, he began to sing.

" 'Blackbird singing in the dead of night/ Take these broken wings and learn to fly/ All your life/ You have only waited for this moment to arise . . . You have only waited for this moment to be free.' " He hit a strange cacophonous chord and looked up at me. "That is me. *Ya* want to be free."

"Where did you learn English?" I asked him in Russian.

"In school. Till I got thrown out. I look up words in the dictionary. Sometimes I hear a word in a song and I look it up and it doesn't exist. I guess I'm not hearing it right. I don't speak English really."

"Play your own songs," Andrej said. "I am interested in what you write yourself."

"This one is called 'Yellow House' " Pëtr said in his mild voice, and then screamed as though he'd been stabbed. He beat a complicated time, drumming on the guitar's body and stamping his foot. His song engulfed the room, the darkness. The self-effacing boy was suddenly a libidinal rock 'n' roll terror. He made such ecstatic, horrific faces that Auntie dropped her knitting needles and clutched at her throat as though she were about to faint.

> Yellow house.
> House of fools.
> Yellow house.
> Idiot house.
> Cut your wrists.
> Hang yourself.

Screw it up
That's where they'll put you.
In the yellow house
They tell you life is great.
That's the biggest lie.
Say, "Life is great!"
Like they do,
They'll let you out.
Don't, and you'll die
Alone, unloved,
A liar,
In the yellow house.

Boris Mikhailovich coughed loudly and leaned back in his chair.

"How about something a little more quiet for Auntie?" he said amicably.

"What strange music," Auntie said. "It reminds me of when my father used to slaughter the pigs on the summer farm and all the other animals would become crazy and flutter and stampede and shriek."

"I think it is extraordinary," Sonya put in. "Simply extraordinary. And he's only seventeen!"

"Play the one about the kid and his father," his manager said quietly. "That's a nice quiet one."

"*Ladno.* This one is called *'Degenerat.'* "

My father comes home drunk and yells,
"Degenerate! Junkie swine!
When are you going to go
Work in the mine,
Like everybody else around here?"
"What for?" I say, "So they can steal
My mind, just like they've done to you?"
Then he beats me. I don't care.
It's not his fault.
The beating he takes is always worse,
Working in the mine.

"Papa," I want to say,
"Can't you teach me to fly,
Teach me to be myself,
And not to listen to their lies?"

Auntie seemed quite perplexed. She picked up her knitting needles and went on working.

"My goodness, where does he come up with such words?" she said in a tremulous voice.

"The one about the yellow house he wrote in his head when they locked him up. The other one is about a friend of ours. Pëtr himself doesn't have a father," his manager said.

"Play some more," I said to Pëtr. I was becoming irritated at the way they all talked as though he were a monkey performing tricks for them.

"For you I will," he said quietly, gazing across the table at me with a sweet twinkle in his eye.

The kid musician had an enormous repertoire. He'd written reggae-style songs and heavy metal songs, blues songs, and even songs that were reminiscent of old Russian folk classics. While Pëtr played the manager sat back in the semi-darkness and smoked, a beatific and serious smile lighting up his thin white face.

"How much is an electric guitar?" I asked Pëtr a while later. His pale face was flushed and wet.

His manager responded, "God. A thousand rubles at least. Pëtr shovels dirt for a living. He makes one hundred and fifty rubles a month. There's no way on earth we can afford a guitar."

"Listen, Pëtr," I said. "If I had a guitar I'd give it to you. But I brought a whole lot of cassette tapes from America. If you meet me somewhere tomorrow I will give them to you. What is your favorite music?"

"Heavy metal. Iron Maiden. Def Leppard. Do you have any of that?"

"No."

Pëtr seemed disappointed, almost crushed. His manager sat forward in his seat.

"But listen," I went on, "I have the greatest blues musicians in the world. From way back before anybody thought of heavy metal. They are the original, you understand? You can learn from their playing. And I have some newer rock 'n' roll. Eric Clapton, for example. He is one of the greatest guitarists in the world. And there's a man called Mark Knopfler. And a man called Michael Bloomfield."

"I know Eric Clapton," Pëtr said. "And Beatles?"

"I have one mixed tape of the Beatles. My friend made it for me. I will give it to you." My ex-fiancé would have been furious if he'd known that I was about to give away almost all the tapes he'd ever made for me. It seemed to me a worthwhile cause, however. The kid guitarist would never get a chance like this again. Back in New York, I could make new tapes.

"Unbelievable," Pëtr said. "You people are just like I thought. Those tapes are worth a fortune on the black market. You could sell them and you're just going to give them to us?"

"We'll organize a place to meet tomorrow," I said. "Not in the street because they'll think we're trading."

"I'll come by with the kids," Andrej offered. "I'll bring them to the Institute after your classes tomorrow."

"That's great, Andrej. Thank you," I said.

"I must say," said Boris Mikhailovich, "Americans do have the most extraordinary attitude."

"What do you want from me and Zhenya? What can we give you in exchange?" Pëtr asked.

"Keep playing," I said. "Just keep playing no matter what. And you mustn't try that again," I added, pointing to his wrists.

27

RITA'S
LAST
DEMAND

Even if Soviets tried to get into our Institute they were usually stopped at the door. There were some brazen types—the black marketeers, the casanovas in search of U.S. passports—who succeeded in bribing the gate-watchers and roamed the Institute in search of prey. We were convinced that these people were in one way or another involved with the KGB, because our true Soviet friends avoided our home as if it were a plague-infested hospital. At times, when certain Soviet acquaintances became too cloying, we used this to our advantage. We stopped calling them and nine times out of ten, we were rid of them. Regular people did not pursue us into our Institute because everyone believed the Soviet authorities watched it carefully and took notes.

I had stopped calling Rita and her relatives a few weeks before our Odessa trip. The few times I'd called before that, Rita had harangued and badgered me and the more she did, the more stubborn I became. I invented endless excuses for not having time to visit them.

Upon our return from Odessa, Rita began to call the Institute looking for me. Almost every day the floor dezhurnaya handed me little notes after classes with Rita's name and phone number scribbled on them. There was always some pushy statement included, such as "It is *imperative* that you phone . . ." or *"Immediately* phone . . ."* I threw the notes in the toilet and went about my life feeling guilty because I still had not dealt with the fifty dollars her cousin Sarah had given me to buy Rita "something" in the Beriozka store. I knew I would have to see Rita one last time, and postponed this encounter as long as possible.

One afternoon, about two weeks after our return from Odessa, I went out for groceries after classes and came home to find Rita sitting on my bed.

Rita and Lidya Dmitrievna, the floor dezhurnaya who wore her blond hair tied in a large knot on top of her head, were having a friendly discussion about the weather.

"Very warm for early June, Lidya Dmitrievna. We are lucky this year," Rita was saying with the utmost conviction.

"But as they say, Rita Abramovna, the warmer the spring, the colder the winter." Lidya Dmitrievna was leaning up against the desk with her arms crossed comfortably over her large chest.

"Couldn't be any worse than last winter," Rita said.

Isabel sat on her bed surrounded by notebooks, looking completely perplexed. This was an extravagant breach of Institute etiquette and did not fit into Isabel's understanding of things. I saw her glancing furtively at the strange contraption we'd nicknamed Igor the Bug, which hung in the middle of our ceiling. Rita looked completely at home and there was a comfortable, self-satisfied expression on her tight little face. She had managed through some impetuous act to bore her way into my safest haven.

I wanted to run, to spin around and run down the hall, but it was too late. I stood frozen in the doorway. Rita looked up from her conversation. Her head turned slowly toward me, puppetlike in its stiffness. Her sleepy eyes gleamed rapaciously for a moment and she jumped up as though something had pinched her behind. She moved with the swiftness of a cockroach to the doorway and grabbed me tightly by the arm.

"*Clintonotchka!*" she shrieked. "*I have been waiting for you for hours.*"

My heart was a knot in my throat. "How did you get in here?" I said in the gloomiest of tones. I could not disguise my discomfort, but

Rita couldn't have cared less. Her goal—whatever it was—was the only thing on her mind.

"Oh, it is no problem at all. They are quite charming at your Institute. I went to see the Director and asked him to find your room for me. Come come come! Our friends are waiting for us in the car outside. Come! We're taking you off today."

"I can't go today. I must meet some friends."

"Where?" The shrill edge in her voice attacked me like a woodpecker drilling into a tree.

"First we'll take a little drive and then we'll drop you at your friends'." She pulled me toward the outside door.

What could I do? "I have to unpack these groceries," I tried.

"No time for that," she said, taking the avoska bag out of my hand and dropping it next to Lidya Dmitrievna on the desk.

"Well, goodbye, Lidya Dmitrievna, it was a pleasure talking with you." Rita pushed me out the door.

"I must stop by Phil's room first," I said. "We are to go to our friends' together."

When I knocked on Phil's door my heart was pounding in my head. If for some reason he was not in, I would have no choice but to go with her alone.

"Vkhoditie!" Phil yelled. Rita was right behind me, not even a foot away, in the hall. She pushed through the doorway before I could say anything. Since Rita was in front of me Phil saw her first, and his eyes displayed no emotion whatsoever. He simply looked at her with his cement-wall expression and said nothing. Using my eyes, I gesticulated wildly at him from behind Rita. *"Help me! Please Phil, don't let me down."* Rita turned back to me to see what I was doing. Then Phil started gesticulating at me by shrugging and widening and narrowing his eyes.

Phil and I had made no plans together for that evening but I started to talk and would not stop so that Rita could not get a word in.

"Phil, Rita wants me to go for a drive but I told her we were to meet some friends later and since I don't know how to get to their apartment it might be better if you came along for the drive, no?"

He lifted his arm and looked slowly at his watch.

"We don't have much time, in fact," he said. "We should be leaving here pretty soon to be there on time. Couldn't you go for a drive another day?"

"*Absolutely not!* My cousins are already insulted beyond repair that Clinton has not called us in weeks! What kind of behavior is that after we went through so much trouble to get you tickets to the ballet and theater and even gave you such a beautiful winter hat?"

I never asked you for anything, I wanted to say, but not a word would come out.

"*Ladno,*" Phil said, getting up from his desk and stretching his back. He took his blue jean jacket and his backpack, which were lying on his bed, and was ready to leave.

"You don't have to come along, Philip," Rita said sweetly, "if you don't want. We are interrupting your studies."

"Not at all," Phil said coldly. "Clinton and I were going out anyway." It seemed she did not hear anything, or believe anything, we said.

"Where do the friends you are going to visit live?" Rita asked him in the same sweet voice as we headed down the hall.

"I already told you, Rita Abramovna, that I make it a policy never to discuss Soviet friends with strangers. Especially in the Institute."

This statement was followed by a dead silence.

"Where are we going?" Phil asked once we were settled in the backseat of the car with the plastic seat covers that heated up your arms and legs and stuck to you like wet Saran wrap. Rita was in the middle, pressing into my thigh.

Phil had gone straight to the point, which I never would have done. They wanted something, obviously, but were pretending we were out for a friendly pleasure cruise.

Igor, who was driving, said in a matter-of-fact tone, "Since Clinton is leaving in less than three weeks we decided it was time to settle the matter of the fifty dollars which belong to Rita."

I watched the back of his wife's head. Anna sat complacently in the passenger seat as though none of this was going on at all. She was all dressed up for her outing. She wore a dark blue cotton suit with a frilly white blouse underneath. Her short hair had just been done and curled stiffly in big loops at the top of her head.

"I told you I'd give you the fifty dollars and you can do with it what you want," I said.

"And I told you that is illegal. If we go to the Mezhdunarodny Tsentr and you buy me something with the fifty dollars, that is not illegal."

"Yes it is," Phil said. "They can send us home for that if they want."

"They will not send you home," Igor said condescendingly, and laughed. "They never send people home for that. Your silly program tries to scare you but there is in truth nothing at all to worry about."

Could this be considered abduction? I wondered. It was certainly coercion. I did not have the slightest experience on which to base my reactions. My fury sat heavily in my chest like steam building up and I had to do my slow and concentrated yoga breathing to remain calm. Just get through it as fast as possible, I thought, and end it once and for all.

Igor parked across the street from the enormous steel and glass complex and we walked up the drive to the back entrance. I noticed that Igor was wearing his war medal on the lapel of his jacket, as he had done when we'd gone to the restaurant. They kept Phil and me back while they said something to the guard and then the glass doors opened and we all marched in to the plush mall-like interior of the hotel. We were on the mezzanine level, where the fancy shops and restaurants and bars were located. Muzak was being piped in through invisible speakers. Rita began to shout excitedly as she looked in the store windows. The bookstore (I could have bought many books for fifty dollars) did not interest them in the least. It was the clothing store they wanted to see. We went in and Anna and Rita immediately began to rifle through the coats.

"Look at this fur, Anna! Three thousand rubles. What does that make in dollars?"

I thought I was going to faint. Igor would not go in the store but wandered around outside on the wide balcony.

The shop attendants glared at us with open disdain. Phil squeezed my hand. Fear took such a hold of me that every small thing seemed to portend disaster: the looks on the attendants' faces, the stocky men in gray suits who walked by the store window several times; once, one of the attendants picked up the phone and whispered hurriedly into the receiver.

Phil wrapped a hand around my neck and brought his lips close to my ear.

"Don't sweat it," he whispered. "If Rita thought this could be dangerous she wouldn't be here. I guarantee."

Rita and Anna had moved to the sweaters and polyester attire. The prices were outrageous. Sixty to seventy rubles for Polish and Hungarian polyester blouses and dresses, and fifty for the sweaters, which were some kind of angora and polyester blend. Rita and Anna seemed to gravitate toward the garments that had sparkling sequins in the shapes of flowers and moons and stars sewn into the fabric. Most of the patterns were horrendous.

"Try it on," Rita said to Anna, taking a blue and black dress off the rack. The design resembled lightning bolts going in all directions and there was an enormous black sequined rose adorning the left shoulder.

"It's too expensive," Anna said.

It cost sixty rubles, which would come to approximately one hundred dollars. At that point I did not care and would have bought the dress just to get out of the store.

A tall, dark woman in a leather pantsuit came in followed by a short, well-dressed man and a Western woman who was wearing a cream-colored suit and a white shirt with a high collar and a big bow at the neck. Her hair was teased high off her forehead and curled neatly outward at the shoulders. She looked like a Wall Street executive.

"Oy," the woman in leather said, flipping her long dark hair over her shoulder, "there is deodorant! Look Fedya, deodorant! They never have deodorant. We must have some."

The woman in leather asked for six cans of deodorant, which one of the attendants brought out of the glass display case and put down on the counter with several loud bangs. The Western woman seemed as ill at ease as Phil and I and stood back while her Russians went like a whirlwind around the store. The goods piled up on the counter next to the cash register. A little while later the Western woman took out an American Express Gold Card and paid while the Russians stood by and said nothing.

"Try it on!" Rita insisted.

Anna took the dress into a booth. A moment later she stuck her head out of the curtain and said, "It fits perfectly." Her kind, round face was wrought with longing and despair, like that of an orphan looking into the window of an expensive toy shop.

Rita was going through the sweaters again. I watched her face as she gazed up at the rack. Her expression was once again rapacious. I suddenly felt sorry for them, for their desperate greed. There was a black sweater with gray stripes that Rita seemed particularly fond of. This one cost forty rubles, approximately sixty-six dollars once converted.

"Rita," I said, approaching her, "I cannot afford to buy you both the sweater and the dress for Anna. I simply cannot."

She gazed at me from beneath her drooping eyelids and a derisive, coquettish smile formed on her lips.

"I am certain that you have enough dollars to buy everything in the store," she said. "After all, your father was a successful man."

"How dare you say such a thing to her," Phil said quietly, stepping in. "Who the hell do you think you are?" He pulled the sweater off the hanger and swiftly took it up to the cash register. He threw it down in front of the hard-faced attendant and said, "Ring this up quickly before I change my mind."

He handed her a Visa card and she gazed at him stupidly for a while. She yawned and languidly turned her attention to the cash register.

A few minutes later, Anna came out of the dressing room carrying the black and blue dress folded over her arm. She already wore a resigned expression. I slid the dress off her arm and took it to the cash register. The girls obviously liked to take their time. One was just putting Phil's sweater in a Beriozka bag while the other handed him the slip to sign.

"This too," I said. "On another card." The girl threw me another disdainful look and took my Visa card in two fingers as though it were a square of soiled toilet paper.

We took our Beriozka bags and walked out of the store into the mezzanine. Igor had disappeared.

"Carry the bag out into the street," Phil said to me. "Don't give it to them until we're back at the car. That's when they nab you, if Russians are carrying the Beriozka bags on the way out."

Phil flew through the glass doors and headed toward the car.

"*Why, Philip.*" Phil was walking so fast that Rita had to run along beside him to keep up. "*You do not have to act so offended! Please do not be offended, Philip! We will give you rubles for your dollars, one for one, better than at the bank. Do not be concerned.*"

He spun around and looked down at the little woman with disgust.

"To hell with the money. I wouldn't take your rubles if I were completely destitute. You think we are fools."

"*What are you talking about, Philip? Why are you offended, I don't understand?*" Rita's voice kept rising so that by now it had reached an impossible, hysterical pitch.

He grabbed the Beriozka bag out of my hand and thrust both bags into Rita's arms. Rita took them, completely bewildered. She was flushed and shaking and her mouth twitched as though she were about to cry.

"*What is wrong with him, Clintonochka?*" She grabbed my arm and squeezed my wrist, pulling me down toward her so forcefully that I winced. She stood on tiptoe and her face was inches from mine. The bags were pressed up between us, close to her chest.

Igor and Anna were trailing us by a hundred yards. She had waited for him inside the hotel. As they approached I saw a childishly open look of pleasure and contentment on her face and I felt sad.

"Shhhh," Rita said to us. "Now stop this nonsense. We mustn't offend Igor."

As Igor came upon the scene the look of contentment similar to his wife's left his face. A dark shadow replaced it and his eyes turned cold.

"What is going on?" he demanded.

"Igor, give this young man his rubles. I have somehow offended him and he is furious at me." Rita's mouth puckered up into a pained grimace and I was certain in another second big tears would come rolling out of her eyes.

Igor quickly unlocked the car, got in behind the wheel, took his wallet out of his breast pocket and began to take out bills.

"I already told you that I would not take your rubles," Phil said.

Igor looked up, squinting. There was a dangerous gleam in his eye. "What is this all about?"

"Rita, you are hurting my arm," I said, trying to pull away.

"Let go of her arm," Phil said to Rita in a calm voice. "Let go of her immediately."

Rita removed her hand from my arm.

"We're going to walk to the metro now," Phil said slowly, like a policeman talking through a megaphone and trying to reason with hostage-holding criminals.

"*Clintonochka, let him go!*" Rita shrieked, going around in crazy circles, arms flailing the air. "*Let him go and come with us. We'll take you to dinner at our friends' house. He's gone mad. He's gone completely mad!*"

"You are the one who is behaving like a madwoman," Phil continued in the same tone, "look at you."

There were so many things I wanted to say, but I stood paralyzed with my mouth agape. The fiasco had been stretched to its limits. The whole thing was so twisted, so bizarre it could have been a scene in an Ionesco play. I focused on one thought: all this is an act; she has worked herself into a state of hysteria because she cannot stand the thought of her one and only Beriozka source slipping out of her hands.

"Forget about all this," Igor said dismissively. "Get in and we'll drop you wherever you're going."

"No," I managed. "We will walk to the metro."

Igor sat perplexed and fuming in the driver's seat. Anna seemed about to cry. Her large brown eyes filled with tears and she blinked blindly as though someone had just slapped her for no reason.

"I don't understand," she muttered. "I don't understand. . . ."

Feeling embarrassed, and guilty somehow, I followed Phil away from the car, up the steep hill toward the metro stop.

Rita shouted after us in her hysterical voice to stop behaving like crazies and come back immediately.

"You amaze me, Phil." My voice broke and I took his hand.

"Oh hell," he sighed. "It didn't do any good anyway."

When we reached the top of the hill we turned back to see if they had gone. The car had disappeared.

"I feel so sorry for this country," Phil said. "I keep hoping things will get better and then I meet people like Rita who have the balls to call themselves Communists—it makes me want to throw up."

I imagined the three of them sitting in the car. Anna would be sniffling into a handkerchief and Rita and Igor would be yelling at each other. No major conclusions would be reached as to who was to blame for the fiasco. Crazy Americans, they would eventually say. They get so offended over nothing.

I hoped, but was not convinced, that Rita would stop phoning the Institute. By the next day she would certainly have reconstructed the whole scene in her mind; she would have erased the parts which did not comply with her final, definitive version, in which she was cast as the martyr.

Never again would I be able to climb the Institute stairs without agonizing over the possibility that Rita might be sitting, victoriously and comfortably, waiting for me on my bed.

28

CEPPIE'S
WEDDING

After classes one Saturday afternoon, Ceppie stormed through the bathroom which connected our two rooms and said nonchalantly in her Puerto Rican accent, *"Mujer,* I got to talk to jou abou des shit."

I had been trying to get her to talk to me about her wedding for weeks, but Ceppie had a gargantuan streak of Latino obstinacy. Ever since our Odessa trip she had been moping around silently, irascibly, often disappearing right after classes and not returning until late at night.

There was no telling how she felt about her future husband or the impetuous decision she had made. I worried that she had agreed to marry Grisha at least partly to slight Misha, the one she had originally returned to Moscow to wed. I worried that she had no conception of the seriousness of her decision and was avoiding the ugly realities. Ceppie was a mule; the more actively I nudged and cajoled her, the more steadfast and stubborn she became.

So on that Saturday afternoon, a week before her wedding day, we went for a walk in the birch forest behind the Institute. I was angry that she had waited so long to talk to me and we walked through the thick greenery in silence. Old people and young lovers and mothers with baby carriages sat on tree trunks made into benches or strolled along the peaceful footpaths. I could hear the rumbling of quiet voices all around us. The forest seemed a haven for secrets.

Ceppie walked with her head down and her hands in her pockets, kicking stones and roots with the toes of her Herman Survivor boots.

"You know," she started in an irritated tone, "ever since we got back from Odessa I've been acting the part of the perfect future bride and I'm tired of it. Grisha's mother and grandmother really think we're in love and they tell honeymoon jokes and cry all the time cause their own husbands are dead. I hate to lie, you know?"

She had discussed the wedding feast with them, discussed Grisha's future with them; his mother, who was quite frantic about the whole thing, made Ceppie swear that she would not abandon or divorce him, even if it took years for him to reach America.

Ceppie swore to appease the mother; but she'd made a different deal with Grisha. Grisha had asked her to wait for him one year. After that, if they did not let him out, she was free to divorce him from America.

"But listen to this, *mujer,*" Ceppie said with a big sigh, "his mother gave me her goddamn engagement ring! It's been in their family since before the Revolution, a ruby as big as this." She made a small circle of her thumb and index finger. "I don't want the fucking ring and anyway there's no way to get it out through customs. I tried to tell her this but she wouldn't listen. What am I supposed to do?"

"Give it to Grisha before you leave and let him deal with it."

Ceppie threw me a long sideways glance and her mouth curved downward at the corners. "Yeah," she said. "That's what I was thinking too."

"Why are you doing this, Ceppie?" I asked, remembering with a pang of guilt the night of Grisha's party, when I had drunkenly suggested to him that he ask Ceppie to marry him instead of me. At the time it had seemed a fairly good idea; I had hoped it would give Ceppie a new understanding of her friends' complicated and difficult lives. At the same time I had wanted to lift the burden of Grisha's request off my shoulders. But I had not thought for a second that Ceppie was going to agree to marry him.

"Why am I doing this?" She thought for a moment, looking around at the silver birch trees. "Wouldn't you do it for a good friend?"

"I don't trust anybody that much," I said.

"God, are you cynical." She exhaled and kicked a tree trunk. "I knew you were going to have only *bad* things to say and since I already have enough bad things to say to *myself,* I figured I'd give myself a break and avoid you for a while. But I guess I'm just a masochistic jerk because here I am asking you your opinion. Fuck it, *mujer.* Let's go home. I'm going to do it anyway no matter what you think or say."

She spun on her heels and started heading back the way we'd come. I ran after her and tugged gingerly at the patched-up elbow of her blue jean jacket. Ceppie did not like to be touched and she might just have been angry enough to chuck me right into the shrubbery.

"I'm sorry, Cep. I'm just worried about you that's all. You just have to know *why* you're doing it, you know? You have to be doing it for the right reasons." This sounded sanctimonious, even to my own ears.

"And what's the right reasons?" Ceppie said, stopping short. After a silence she slid her arm through mine. "Come on, let's walk. I'll tell you what happened. I know you think I'm doing it to piss Misha off and maybe I am, a little. But Grisha, he's got guts, man. Do you understand that? He's got guts. Do you know a lot of guys our age with guts? *I* don't. I don't know any."

Ceppie began to explain what had happened between her and Grisha the night of his party.

She had been in a state of drunken gloom after Misha arrived. He had fallen into his usual pattern of eluding her by hiding behind his girlfriend, who gazed at Ceppie with the eyes of a beaten mongrel.

Grisha had spent the entire evening keeping Ceppie away from Misha, talking her out of a confrontation. He insisted that Misha would walk right out the door if Ceppie confronted him. Ceppie did not want Misha to leave because then not only would she not be able to talk to him, she would not be able to look at him. Grisha filled and refilled her glass with vodka as she watched Misha from a distance. It simply killed her that his eyes flitted past her as though she were just another face in the crowded room. How could she remember every detail of their fairytale and he nothing at all? What had happened to all the vows, the secrets they had shared last summer?

By the time Grisha threw out his guests and told us to stay, Ceppie was so annihilated that there was simply no physical way she could have left. While I collapsed fully clothed on the crumb-covered couch, Grisha took Ceppie back to his room and sat her down on the edge of his bed.

In a swift and gentle voice Grisha said, "Misha has certain problems concerning his sexuality."

At first she did not understand what he meant. "What are you talking about? What does that mean?"

Grisha paused momentarily, gathering strength. "Misha likes boys as well as girls. He likes boys better than girls." His tone had become so morose he could have been announcing the death of a lover to a close friend, and that was exactly the kind of shock Ceppie felt. A terrible stillness descended upon her and she sat cross-legged and immobile on Grisha's double bed for a long time. She stared up at his odd collection of paperback covers while tears tumbled from her eyes. How could she have let herself be fooled? Why hadn't anyone had the honesty or the manners to tell her? She opened her mouth to voice these thoughts but the words would not make themselves heard.

"Listen to me, Ceppie," Grisha said gently, "I admire you more than any woman I know. I am only sorry that I waited such a long time before telling you. I hoped you would see it for yourself, but as they say in Russia, love is blind. Misha thought he wanted to leave and start a new life in America. The truth is he is not strong enough to give up everything he has here, everything he knows, to start all over again. Here, you do not have to work hard to stay alive. No one expects you to work hard. In America, it is necessary. He is terrified of that."

Ceppie continued to stare at the paperback covers, although every word Grisha said sunk into her head with the permanency of coffins being lowered into the ground.

"I do not think he has ever had a——how should I say this?——a real affair with a woman. Maybe he's slept with a few girls he did not know well but I don't think he enjoyed it. I think sleeping with you terrifies him as much as leaving Russia. I know all this is awfully hard to listen to, and maybe you do not believe me."

His voice was so even and sad that Ceppie could not help but believe him. In the red glow of his bedside lamp she turned to his steady eyes and saw that they were filled with compassion. She wondered, despising herself for her idiocy, why on earth she could not have fallen in love with him instead of his best friend. At that moment, she was not alarmed by his large, soft-looking, sensuous mouth.

"I wanted to give him something no one else could. I would have helped him in America," Ceppie managed to say, believing for the first time that she was speaking of the past, that Misha no longer existed in the present or in the future.

"He doesn't want such an opportunity." Grisha made a disgusted face. "He doesn't know what to do with such an opportunity. I am ready for such a thing, but he is not."

"*You* are ready to leave forever?"

"I am. And I am not afraid."

"*You* want to leave everything and everybody behind?" Ceppie was dazed. He had never mentioned anything like this to her before.

"Yes. I know I would miss everyone and even certain places. But I am not afraid. I can say that since I know I will never leave this country," he laughed quietly, self-effacingly.

Ceppie decided suddenly that Grisha had a right to a little hope in his life. Her heart felt terribly light as the brilliance of her idea struck her.

"I'll marry you, if it will get you out."

Grisha's expression did not change. It was almost as though he could not believe what she had said.

"You and I are good friends," Grisha said after a moment, "I could never ask you to do such a thing because we are such good friends. If I ever thought you might believe I would take advantage of you, I would kill myself."

How Russian, Ceppie thought. How gallant and how silly!

"Maybe they will not let you out. What if I go home and you're here for years and I meet someone else I want to marry?" Ceppie asked.

"We will get divorced. You can divorce me from over there. Just give me one year. Our marriage will not count for you in any case because it is not before God. It is only before the civil authorities of the Soviet Union."

"All right," Ceppie said. It seemed to make good sense to her.

"If they let me out, all I will need is a place to sleep and a map of New York City. I would never bother you or ask you for anything else. And then as soon as I have a job I will move to my own place and get out of your way."

"Don't talk like that Grisha, we *are* good friends. Don't talk as though you're going to be a burden. I've been a burden to you here. You've kept me fed, kept me from throwing myself at Misha, kept me from going crazy. I owe you a lot."

It was absolutely true that the marriage would not count before God, or before her parents, or before the nuns who had educated her. The thought of Misha hurt a great deal and only made her more determined. Let him rot in hell, she thought. He'll be sorry some day.

"Ceppie," I said as we walked on through the woods. The leaves were so thick above us we could not see the sky or any of the tall buildings that we used as markers. "Ceppie, I don't know much about our immigration laws, but aren't you held financially responsible for your spouse? I mean, if he does come to America you're really going to have to take care of him."

"What's he going to do, sue me? For what? The clothes on my back? Look, you don't know him the way I do. This is an honorable guy. Plus, I can come back and live here for months without being a student. That'll be a good experience."

We got lost. It seemed to me we'd gone around in wide circles, and none of the paths we'd taken had led us out of the forest. Twenty paces ahead, two Vietnamese men were sitting on a log, chatting amicably. We asked them in Russian if they knew how to get back to the Institute.

They looked at each other a moment, whispered a few words, and then one of them said, "Do you speak Engrish?"

"Yes," Ceppie said. "We're American."

"How foltunate. We allived from Ho Chi Minh City yesteday and speak not a wold of Lussian. Institute that way." He pointed down the path in the direction from which we'd come. Beyond his bony brown finger was a wall of thick green leaves and silver trunks.

"Thank you. Good luck," Ceppie said. We walked on in silence, listening to the forest sounds, the rustling of the fresh leaves above us and the soft squish of the old dead ones underfoot.

"What about a dress, Ceppie?" We had come to the edge of the forest. The land dropped radically where the trees stopped and at the bottom of the hill was a lake surrounded by a slanting cement embankment. There were children leaning over the embankment, pushing at wooden ships with long sticks and yelling at each other excitedly.

"What do you mean?"

"What are you going to wear to your wedding?"

Frowning, she thought about this for a moment, then shrugged. "I'm not going to worry about that now," she said. "I don't want any fancy bullshit. I just wish I didn't have to pretend in front of Grisha's mother. It's awful. But he insisted, because he's worried about upsetting her."

We watched the children play at the edge of the water for a while and I felt calm about the whole thing although I had a pain low in my throat. Ceppie seemed emotionally organized and since the Soviet authorities had not bothered her up until now, it seemed they were not going to give her any trouble. I was not afraid for her, but I felt oddly melancholic. Ceppie was a hardheaded person with a strong moral sense, but she had a touch of the Catholic martyr in her as well. She would most probably not divorce Grisha if he were not out within a year. I believed that she would wait, just on principle, as many years at it might take. She would then be chained to a nonexistent lover, while all the other men who might have made her truly happy would lose patience, and pass her by.

Early on the Sunday morning in mid-June that was the wedding day, I crossed the hall from Phil's room to mine. Isabel, who had been invited to the wedding and sworn to secrecy, had decided that as a little surprise we should wake Ceppie together and help her dress, as girls do on such occasions. Isabel, who a month ago would have fainted at the prospect of Ceppie's breaking the rules in such a radical way, was completely "gung ho on the idea." Her encounter with the Odessan merchant marine had transformed her. She had become a fastidious and expert rule-breaker. The merchant marine had come to Moscow to see Isabel, and had been smuggled into the Institute on Phil's identity pass. Vanya had spent several nights in our room (Isabel had diverted the dezhurnaya while I whisked Vanya down the hall into our room), and I was grateful to him because love had a wonderful, softening effect on Isabel. Now he had gone back to Odessa and Isabel was more determined than ever to join him there for her Christmas vacation. "My mother would simply die if she saw Vanya's mother's apartment. That art work! Some of those paintings are from the eighteenth century, my dear. And that hand-carved oak furniture! My mother is an art historian. I think our mothers would get on famously, don't you?"

They had all gone crazy. My roommates were doing pirouettes on a tightrope and I was watching, electrified, from a front-row seat.

Just as we were about to cross through the bathroom to wake up the bride-to-be, Ceppie came through from her room wearing blue jeans, flat blue espadrilles, and a white, short-sleeved, button-down shirt.

Isabel shrieked.

"You simply can*not,* Ceppie. It— Well, it isn't done, and that's that!"

"I don't have any dresses," Ceppie said, looking down at herself. "I have one corduroy skirt and it's brown and anyway it's too hot for it now."

"But you know how the others will be dressed! You simply can't. You'll insult him."

Isabel was wrapped in her powder-blue towel. She had spread a pretty mauve dress out on her bed and her pink pumps lay on the floor underneath.

"It's not for real, woman," Ceppie said, her eyes darkening.

"But you don't want *them* to know that, do you?" Isabel pointed out. "Let's see." She opened our closet and went through the hanging garments. "Clinton's got that one sort of flowery, light blue dress which she will doubtless be wearing because it's all she's got. She's got a gray cotton skirt—that won't do—I have that pink sundress. Wait, this is what it will be!" She brought out a pleated white cotton skirt and a gauzy white shirt with little pink and blue embroidered roses around the collar, buttons, and cuffs.

"With a pink belt, Ceppie. It will be beautiful."

"You're a foot taller than me," Ceppie said gloomily. I'll look ridiculous. Plus I don't have shoes."

"What size shoe do you wear?"

"Six."

"Well I'm a seven and my foot is very thin. Clinton has those warmth insoles for her sneakers—we'll cut them, fit them into my white pumps, and we're all set."

"Damn," Ceppie said. "How did you manage to pack all the stuff you brought into those two suitcases?"

"There's a method to packing, I'll have you know. You learn these things when they send you off to camp and boarding school."

We practically had to pull Ceppie's clothes off but eventually got her into the skirt and blouse.

"I never wore high heels in my life," she grumbled. "Grisha is going to shit."

"Well let him shit," Isabel said. She pulled and tucked and re-arranged the clothes on Ceppie, who stood limply in front of the closet mirror.

"We can see your bra through the shirt," Isabel said, stepping back. "Camisole, definitely. You must try on my pretty pink camisole underneath."

"What are you, nuts?" Ceppie said.

"Try it on," I said with authority. "We're running out of time."

Ceppie took off the shirt and slid the camisole on over her bra. The skirt was a bit long on her, but that was fine for the occasion. She looked beautiful and did not give the impression she was wearing someone else's clothes. Her ankles turned in the high white pumps, however. She practiced walking back and forth in the room. I had never noticed that her calves and ankles were so delicate and feminine.

"We need a white or pink bow for your hair," Isabel declared.

"No fucking way, woman," said Ceppie.

Isabel pointed up to Igor the Bug and said, "I am not going to fight about this with you right now. But this is a solemn and momentous occasion and you want to 'fit in' as much as possible. Don't you agree, Clinton?"

"I agree. We don't want to stick out like sore thumbs."

"All right. A bow. But no makeup."

"I hear you," Isabel said. "Okay, so we took care of the something old and the something borrowed, there's something blue in the blouse —now we have to think about the new."

"This isn't for real, Isabel," Ceppie muttered.

"It's pretty damn real, Ceppie," Isabel said.

"I've got a pair of turquoise earrings that will look nice with your outfit," I suggested.

"Fine," Ceppie said. "And since I'm a virgin I'll be the something new."

Isabel tied a wide, white cloth belt around Ceppie's head and made a fancy bow on one side, above her ear. She pulled Ceppie's black curls out in front, twirling them, and fluffed the longer strands out in back.

Ceppie stood in front of the mirror and turned first to one side, then the other, adjusting her head to get a better look. Her tight face relaxed and she smiled for the first time that morning.

"That's me? I look like someone else."

Then it was our turn to get ready. Isabel yelled at me because I had not shined my flat red Capezio shoes, the only ones I'd brought for the warm months, which I wore almost every day. They were badly scuffed and muddied. Isabel got down on her knees in her powder blue towel and scrubbed at them with a rag.

Phil knocked on the door at nine-thirty. He was in a pale blue shirt, a paisley tie and his tweed jacket. It was a little warm for the jacket but we all had to make do.

"My God, I think I'm dreaming," he said. "Is that you, Ceppie?"

"That's what I said," said Ceppie.

Phil looked at his watch. "We'd better move," he said solemnly. He was carrying an enormous bouquet of white roses wrapped in wax paper. He did not hand them to Ceppie until we were outside the Institute. It was a warm and windy day and dust was swirling around on the lawn. As Ceppie's hand encircled the bouquet I saw the antique ruby ring sparkling on her wedding ring finger. The sun glinted in it for a moment, and then the perfectly clear blue sky was invaded by a galloping herd of black clouds. The rain began to fall in a tinny clatter. We all reached into our bags for our collapsible umbrellas (they had become a daily necessity in the Moscow spring) and hurried up the drive to the main road. It was impossible to see fifteen feet ahead. The Russians squeezed and pushed into doorways and under the bus shelter and stared at us disapprovingly for remaining in the street. Phil stood in the gutter and was splashed by passing trucks and cars until he managed to stop a cab.

Phil was muddied from head to foot. Ceppie laughed happily, pushing the wet curls away from her forehead, while Isabel shouted obscenities at the sky.

Twenty minutes later the taxi stopped in front of a large, two-story yellow building which seemed ancient compared to the cement-block buildings surrounding it.

"Who's getting married?" the driver asked, turning his head.

"Our friend here is getting married," Phil gestured toward Ceppie.

"Pretty bride," the driver said. "Well, you'll have good luck. See, the sun is coming out just for you."

Phil paid and gave him a large tip.

Just as we stepped out of the taxi the rain stopped and the black clouds galloped off into the distance. In a matter of seconds the sky was clear again. Here and there floated a white puff of cloud and a bright golden sun shone down on the wet street. The old yellow mansion, the trees, the pavement, and the gray cement buildings were suddenly splashed with a dazzling coat of gold.

Grisha, his mother, and his friend Alik (the cook from the night of Grisha's bacchanalian debauch) were standing under a tree with umbrellas. Only the mother was not smoking and pacing. She stood primly, head up, clutching a little white purse in one hand and her umbrella in the other. Grisha and Alik were in dark blue suits. Grisha wore a thin black leather tie and Alik wore a big, fat, shiny striped thing. There was a Soviet flag flapping above the doors and a large, engraved silver plaque that said DVORETS BRAKOSOCHETANIY, Palace of Weddings.

Grisha spotted us and ran up, smiling his wide, lippy smile. Grisha and Alik's eyes were bleary and red, which probably meant they'd spent the whole night drinking.

"By God, I was getting nervous. You look absolutely beautiful," Grisha said to Ceppie as he kissed her on the cheek. She blushed uncomfortably and changed the subject; she asked him if Misha was going to come.

"I don't know," Grisha said, shrugging apologetically.

Grisha introduced his mother to us and shook hands with Phil. Alik took my head in his hands and planted a big, wet, alcohol-soaked kiss on my mouth.

Phil glanced down at this short, squat fellow who lifted weights and then glanced at me. "I gather you've met before," he said in Russian.

"Certainly," Alik said. "We got very drunk together."

"Something new and different," Phil said.

Other wedding parties were gathering around outside, and some were heading into the building.

A few more of Grisha's close friends arrived. I recognized several faces from his party, including Rasputin and his wife, and Sonya who had chucked the glass across the kitchen, missing Alik's head by inches. Misha did not come. We went up the steps into the grandiose old building.

We walked into a large hall filled with flowers. There were enormous bouquets of all sorts and some plastic green plants with gigantic leaves. A chandelier hung from the ceiling and below us was an ancient, colorful Asian rug. A woman clerk in a tight gray suit stood before a hallway and directed us to follow her. Twenty feet down the hall she motioned for the women to enter a room to the right. The men were ushered off to the left.

"You will be called when it is your turn," she said without emotion, and closed the door behind us. Ceppie, Grisha's mother, Rasputin's wife, Sonya, Isabel, and I found ourselves in a waiting room crowded with wooden benches, coat hooks, and mirrors. There were paintings of early Communist weddings and portraits of Lenin and Marx hanging on the walls.

Four other brides were already waiting in the room with their parties. All were dressed in floor-length gowns and wore short gauze veils. There was something a little off in each outfit; the brown shoes of one had been painted white with what seemed to be wall paint; the pattern on another's veil resembled a table doily; the neckline on a third's dress had been sewn unevenly with egg-colored thread. Everyone held large bouquets of colorful spring flowers. The Russians chattered nervously among themselves and fixed their hair in the mirrors. They often glanced at Ceppie with curious smiles. Ceppie and Grisha's mother sat demurely on one of the benches. The older woman wore a light blue dress with a corsage on the bosom. She was a heavy blond woman with a kind, square face and the same large, soft mouth as her son. She was crying into a little handkerchief and holding Ceppie's hand.

"Please don't cry. I promise you it is a good thing," Ceppie mumbled to her future mother-in-law.

"A good thing . . . a good thing . . . God only knows. It will be a good thing if it all turns out all right. I am so afraid he will get into trouble. He is so stubborn. He wants to live his life his own way, not anyone else's. Thank God for him and for me that his father was a successful man with quite a few friends in high places. And"—she lowered her voice even more—"who knows—if he goes to America, maybe they will allow me to visit?" Her face brightened at the prospect and she stopped crying. She lifted Ceppie's hand and gazed lovingly at the ruby ring.

"They certainly will, the way things are going now," Ceppie assured her. Isabel approached and began to fiddle with Ceppie's bow.

"Get away from me, woman," Ceppie said.

"Now now, behave yourself." Isabel slapped Ceppie lightly on the shoulder.

The lady clerk came through another door at the opposite end of the waiting room and called out a name. One of the brides threw her hands up, gasped, laughed, and went out, followed by her entourage of close to fifteen. Through the closed door we heard four bars of Mendelssohn's Wedding March being played, and then the music was abruptly cut off.

Seven minutes later the lady clerk opened the door again and called out, "*Concepcion*, Maria-Manuella," and Ceppie and I went out, followed by Grisha's mother and the rest of the women.

The men were being let in through a door across from us; they came tumbling out, awkward and enthusiastic, like little schoolboys after the recreation bell has sounded. We all gathered together behind Ceppie and Grisha. The same four bars of Mendelssohn's march were played again as we walked up toward the small wooden desk at the other end of the long room. Below us was another expensive Asian rug. There were flowers everywhere. A small woman in a well-cut, conservative dark blue suit sat behind the desk with a pile of papers in front of her.

The ceremony took all of five minutes. The official read their names from the sheet before her and then gave the bride and groom a speech about friendship and love and duty. The duty of any married couple is to have children, she stated. She talked about the importance of being faithful and helping one another to strive for perfection in the home, the place of work, and in society. They said their vows and when the woman asked for the wedding bands Grisha stepped forward and said that he did not have them yet. The woman was nonplussed and made some comment under her breath to the effect that this was not done.

Grisha apologized and promised to get them as soon as he could. The papers were signed. Alik and I signed as witnesses.

"This is an important marriage because it is an international marriage," the official said in closing, in a high-pitched, booming voice. "We wish you the best of luck and hope that the differences between our two nations will not impede your success. We are a friendly nation and wish nothing better than to have peace among all the nations of the world." She stood up, rearranged her skirt, and shook their hands. Another clerk ushered us out through yet another door which was off to the side, behind the desk. Just as the door closed behind us the Mendelssohn march began again.

Neither Grisha nor Ceppie had any desire to be photographed leaving flowers on the Tomb of the Unknown Soldier at the foot of Kremlin wall, or to visit dead Lenin without having to wait in the long line. But they did so to please Grisha's mother; in her eyes it was a sign of her son's good will toward the government she was so afraid would punish him for his infidelity. Grisha, Ceppie, Alik, the mother, and I piled into Alik's car and drove to the Kremlin. White gauze had been tied to the door handles and the antenna. It was one of those traditional moments the mother wanted to hold in her memory.

The others went back to Grisha's apartment to arrange for the festivities.

The mother took photos of the four of us in front of the very warlike Tomb of the Unknown Soldier. Like a good Soviet bride, Ceppie left a few of her roses on the tomb and then we walked to the front of the line of waiting people to visit dead Lenin one last time.

A veritable feast awaited us at Grisha's. There was champagne, vodka, cognac, caviar, and all sorts of other Soviet delicacies which Grisha's friends had somehow managed to procure. We drank toast after toast and danced and sang. Grisha paid special, gentlemanly attention to Ceppie, who sat next to him at the head of the long table for most of the evening. He filled her glass and asked her constantly if she wanted anything more to eat. Ceppie did not like to dance and Grisha, as a good host, made the rounds and danced with everyone else, including his mother.

Late in the evening, Misha showed up alone and gave Ceppie a bouquet of yellow tulips. He had not shaved in several days and the bristles on his face made him look unkempt and dirty. His eyes were tired and sunken and he seemed even paler than usual. He did not greet Rasputin with any special attention, which surprised me and brought back that uncomfortable tickle in my lower spine. There was something perverse about the fact that they were lovers and that almost everyone except Ceppie knew this. Misha sat at the opposite end of the table, near Alik and Sonya, and had a glass of vodka. Ceppie excused herself and stumbled off in the high white pumps to the bathroom. I followed her. I did not knock on the door but went in, as I had on the night of Grisha's party. Ceppie was sitting on the tub, exactly where Rasputin had been. Her hands gripped the porcelain edge while she sobbed. Her small shoulders shook in the pretty white blouse.

"Ceppie," I said, sitting next to her and laying an arm across her shoulders. "The guy is a coward. The guy is gay. The guy is nothing."

"The guy is nothing but the fucker is burning a hole through my insides with a blowtorch."

At midnight Phil drunkenly gathered us together and stated that we had to leave to make our curfew. We had classes at nine the next morning. Grisha hugged each of us and kissed us with tears in his eyes.

"You'll never know . . ." he mumbled. "You'll simply never know what you have done for me."

Ceppie looked subdued and brokenhearted. Grisha held his bride tightly against his chest for a moment, rocking her from side to side. He did not want us to leave but Phil insisted we had to leave if we were to make our curfew.

"It will be all right," Grisha told Ceppie. "I promise you everything will be all right."

Everything was not all right, however. Moscow, as my friend Vera had once told me, was truly a small village where everyone minded everyone else's business. A friend of Grisha's had somehow met a girl from our program and had told her about the wedding. By Tuesday, the entire group had been informed that Ceppie had gotten married.

She was called to the Director of the Institute's office and was forced to face the Director of the American Program, who was in a hysterical rage. Our Director was a strange woman. One of our younger counselors had told me in confidence that the program found it difficult to convince good professors of Russian to come live in an institute in Moscow for a year, and therefore had to make do with whomever they could lure over. This particular Director was "in between jobs" and had not visited the Soviet Union in fifteen years. She had no conception of how to make friends with our hosts at the Institute. She treated the Soviet Director and all his staff condescendingly, as though she had nothing to learn from them, and treated the American students as though they were badly behaved ten-year-olds. On some mornings she stood at the front doors and tried to catch people who had spent the night out, while she could have spent that time trying to organize trips for us, or seeing an official who needed buttering up.

Once, she had taken our month's stipend—close to eight thousand dollars in cash—to be changed at a Soviet bank, and had forgotten the money in her briefcase on the backseat of the taxi. Fortunately, the counselor who had accompanied her had remembered the cab's identification number and had immediately reported it to the authorities. Luckily for the driver, he had not considered stealing the money and had handed the briefcase over to the police.

We called her Babayega, the Russian wicked witch, because she seemed to do everything possible to make our lives in Moscow unbearable. If a student got into trouble, she always took the side of the Soviet authorities and yelled even louder than they did. There was no one the Soviet authorities respected less than a person who did not defend his or her own people, right or wrong.

Ceppie told me later that as soon as she walked into the Director of the Institute's office, our American Director began to scream like a hysteric. The Director of the Institute and a fellow we had nicknamed Mr. Head KGB Man sat quietly while Babayega raged on.

For some reason, neither Mr. Head KGB Man nor the Director of the Institute wanted Ceppie to be sent home on the next plane out. It was never clear whether they feared repercussions from The Top, were concerned about maintaining their quota of students, or simply did not see anything wrong with Russo-American marriages. Ceppie herself was convinced that the Director and Mr. Head KGB Man were just softhearted guys.

"The rules are the rules," shouted Babayega in a voice which attempted to sound stern and authoritarian but managed only to be annoying. "We informed all our students back at orientation that if they married a Soviet citizen, we would send them home on the next planc out."

"But she has not broken any of *our* rules," the Director of the Institute said evenly. He was an enormous man with a weathered face. He had won many medals for bravery in the Second World War. "She is a good student, she has attended all her classes, and she has not spent nights away from the Institute." (This was not true.)

"May I say something?" Ceppie asked. "I love it here and I intend to apply for a relative's visa and return as soon as possible to live with my husband. I intend to find a job, and it seems absurd to send me home now when I am only two weeks away from finishing the program and receiving my diploma. I have not done anything wrong."

"You have harmed the reputation of our program," insisted the American. She turned to the large man behind the big wooden desk. "We must use her as an example. We do *not* want our students getting married. If we do not follow our own rules we will not be taken seriously by the other students. She has been deceitful. To get married, Americans must have permission from the Institute. How did she manage to arrange this so that you were not informed?" She pointed an accusing finger at Mr. Head KGB Man.

"We run a tight organization here," said Mr. Head KGB Man, taking offense. "We have twelve hundred students from all over the world residing in our Institute. Certain people are bound at some point to fall through the cracks. We cannot be blamed for that. If you send her home you will be calling attention to us all. It is better to let the matter drop." At this point, Mr. Head KGB Man turned his head the slightest bit and winked at Ceppie.

The only thing that kept Ceppie from breaking down was her fascination with Mr. Head KGB Man's incongruously handsome face and blond hair. He was a fellow of around forty, whose button nose was adorable, but whose icy blue eyes divulged nothing, not even a cruel streak. They were the eyes of an interrogator. He had half a finger missing on his right hand. But which finger? Ceppie kept staring, trying to pinpoint the mutilated one. It was his job to watch us and to watch out for us.

While the two Soviets and the American argued over Ceppie's fate, she remembered the story that had gone around the program about him. Several years before, when the American government had had the absurd idea of bombing Libya, five Libyan students at the Institute had gotten drunk and come after two American males with hatchets. Mr. Head KGB Man intervened just in time. He overpowered the Libyans with the help of a few assistants, and sent them home the next day without blinking an eye. The Institute had refused Libyans as students ever since.

"In fact," the Director of the Institute now said, "I would be willing to give her a special pass so that she may spend the nights at her husband's, and return in the morning for her classes. After all, she will only be in Moscow another two weeks. Let the couple spend as much time as possible together."

Ceppie felt herself blanch. She had had no intention of spending every night until our departure at Grisha's, but now she would have to make an effort to stay there at least four times a week and be blatant about it.

"It seems cruel to me to be so unbending. Why should marriages of love be subjected to petty rules invented by you Capitalists, rules which involve politics and have nothing to do with our students?" concluded the Director.

"I must agree with our Director," Mr. Head KGB Man put in. "We will be highly displeased if you send her home. We might even be so displeased as to cut the number of Americans by half next year."

The American Director stormed out, a trail of papers falling from her briefcase, and left Ceppie with the two Soviet officials.

"We sure fixed that Capitalist nitwit, didn't we?" Mr. Head KGB Man said to Ceppie, winking again and squeezing her arm as he graciously escorted her to the door.

29

MOSCOW FAREWELL

1

We had four days' worth of last nights. Classes had ended, exams had been passed, and we were finally free of school. But we had only exchanged one form of imprisonment for another. Our Russian friends suddenly became so possessive and childish that visiting them became a burden. There was too much to eat and too much to drink, and if you did not drink and eat enough to kill yourself, they were unhappy and pouted or threw tantrums. They also did not want to share us with anyone else, so we were forced to invent intricate lies to avoid hurting feelings. "Why must you leave? Why can't we see you tomorrow? Have another drink."

Each banquet was richer and more elaborate than the last; it was as though our Russian friends had found out from spies what we had eaten the day before and were purposely trying to outdo each other. Needless to say, we were completely inebriated from the beginning of the festivities to the end.

There was a party at Boris Mikhailovich's four days before we left for Leningrad, which we were visiting on the way home. Boris Mikhailovich and his wife Sonya were not insulted that this was our last meeting because they were busy people with many important friends, but Andrej harangued me the entire evening because I could not see him the following day. I finally promised to *try* to meet him for lunch the day we were leaving for Leningrad. This was not the first of a series of lies I had been forced to tell just to get my Russians off my back.

Driving me back to the Institute later that night, he cried out and slapped his thigh as though he'd been suddenly struck by genius. "I will come to Leningrad and spend the last four days with you!"

"No! Please don't do that. We have all these group tours organized already."

"But I know Leningrad very well. I can be your private guide."

"*Nyet,*" I said with finality. "*No.* I do not want you to do that."

As he pulled up into the shadow of the tall building and came to a stop, he began once again to talk about Fate and God and our roads crossing at such an appropriate time in our lives. I told him he was a great friend, kissed him on the cheek, and escaped into the light of the glass doors.

There was another bacchanalian debauch at Grisha's the next evening. Grisha was insulted that Phil, Isabel, and I had made other plans for the next two evenings, and spent the night making bad jokes on this subject.

There was a party at Yelena Davidovna's the day before our departure, and two parties, one at Vera's and one at Phil's dissidents, on the final night.

Only Yelena Davidovna insisted that I should not waste my last night in Moscow with her and refused to see me that evening.

She said, "How absurd that a girl your age should spend her last night in Moscow visiting an old lady when there are so many fun things to do!"

Yelena Davidovna had invited several of her son's friends to our farewell dinner and they had managed to procure enough alcohol and delicacies for a major feast. The Russians always seemed able to pull rare deficit goods out of nowhere, like magicians, when it was necessary. There was roasted duck with apples, a salad with purple basil leaves, fresh coriander and tomatoes in sour cream, fried whitefish, fried potatoes, brandy, vodka, and wine. For dessert there were three kinds of torts, the fancy layer cakes smeared with thick chocolate cream.

Among Yelena Davidovna's friends were an Azerbaijani bassist who was a party official and the mayor of a sector of Moscow, a Jewish painter from Kiev, and the woman Ph.D. who was an expert on ancient coins and had read almost every American novel published in the Soviet Union. She was particularly fond of "Djoseph Geller," "Ernest Gemingvey" and "Villiam Falkner."

The discussion over dinner was whether or not rigorous censorship improved writing.

Yelena Davidovna said absolutely not because censorship spreads fear and the Azerbaijani, whose name was Khudat, said absolutely yes because by trying to restrain artists you gave them a higher will to break the restraints and create more fervently.

"All right," Khudat said, "I will phone my friend who is a famous writer and ask his opinion."

The friend was a writer so famous that Phil began to laugh as though it were a joke. Khudat picked up the phone and dialed a number. After Khudat posed his question, he listened intently and then said, "Please hold on, sir. There is a foreigner who would like to send you his greetings." He handed Phil the phone.

It turned out that the famous Azerbaijani writer agreed with Yelena Davidovna. Censorship, in his opinion, did not improve one's writing in the least.

Yelena Davidovna winked at me and gestured for me to follow her into the other room, her bedroom, which held the many canvases stuffed into the large, flat, artist's drawers.

The guests were laughing and shouting in the other room. Glasses clicked. Yelena Davidovna went to the cupboard and opened a tiny wooden door which protected a deep pigeonhole. She brought out a four-inch square, hand-painted cardboard box and carried it gingerly back to her desk. She sat before it and carefully began to pull the lid off. "Come here," she said.

I stood beside her chair, leaning over her shoulder. With her swollen fingers she finally pried open the lid and poked around inside the blue box.

"Oh well," she said, and dumped the contents out on the square of green felt before her. There were gold and silver chains and tiny diamond pendants, rings and earrings and broaches. I saw a lizard and a cat with diamond eyes. She picked a small scarab out of the pile and dropped it into the palm of her left hand. Its body was made up of three sapphires separated by gold thread; a heart-shaped one for the thorax and abdomen, and two smaller ovals below it for the wings. The tiny head, legs, and antennae were of heavy, probably fourteen-karat, gold.

"This is for good luck." She brought her palm up toward me. I backed away.

"I can't take this, Yelena Davidovna. It is worth a fortune. I couldn't take it out of the country in any case."

"I noticed you wear a tiny gold chain around your neck. Just attach the zhuk and wear it as if it had always been there. No one will say a word. Dochka. I have no grandchildren, I have no nephews or nieces. Please take it and remember me by it. It will bring you good luck." She took my hand, opened my fingers and dropped the scarab gently into the center of my palm. I removed the gold chain from my neck, unfastened it, and slipped the scarab over the tiny ring. Once it was on my neck I felt it had always been there and decided that like my father's ankh ring and silver bracelet, I would never take it off again.

"The value of material things is relative, dochka. Money really means very little. I don't have any money but my son's friends take care of me. The government pays me for my paintings and I have a small pension. The zhuk is valuable because it is a good luck charm and I gave it to you because I am fond of you. Let me tell you a little story. On New Year's Eve of 1943 there was no electricity, no heat, barely any food, and it was dark. I managed to get a tiny pine tree and I had some paints left, you see, so I dipped cotton and old newspapers in paint and made them into the shapes of vegetables: tomatoes, cucumbers, carrots. There were lots of carrots and tomatoes because I had lots of orange and red paint." She laughed easily and wiped at her eyes.

"My little boy came home to me from his camp and was completely overwhelmed to see a pine tree covered in vegetables. Your father spent that New Year's Eve with us, God bless him, for he brought most of the food. He wept when he saw my crazy decorations. They were worth nothing, they did not fill our empty stomachs, but they made us think about the future in a happy way. Every year after that my son wanted those same decorations on the tree. And I still have them although they are now almost dust.

"Now bring Philip in here and I shall take out my paintings. You must each have one to take home to America. And one I will give you for your mother."

"I brought you a little something as well," I said. I gave her a rust-colored box of Chinese design which contained Opium perfume. It was the last of the Opium I had bought on the plane and I thought it was a gift delicate enough not to offend her. Plus, the Chinese design, I thought, would please her.

"*Oy! Religia.*" She held up the box and turned it around in her fingers. "Such a pretty box."

"I don't understand. 'Religion'?"

"*Da.* That is the street name for this perfume in Moscow. Because religion is the opium of the people. But, dochka, you must have a younger Soviet friend who would need this more than I."

"Absolutely not. It is for you."

"In that case." She took the little box and placed it on her shelf behind the sliding glass panels where she kept the pictures of her son. "I will wear it the next time a man asks me out dancing."

All the guests gathered in the bedroom and Yelena Davidovna dragged her low casel out of a corner and set it in the middle of the floor.

"You may pick from these," she said, setting a pile of paintings on the desk and placing them, one at a time, on the easel.

I had seen all of them before, the serene landscapes and the wild, violent skies. Her skies, I had come to realize that spring, were common in Russia. They were turbulent and frantic and often had nothing to do with what was going on below. Phil had not seen her work and would not allow her to change each painting for many minutes. He went up close and knelt on the floor and took off his glasses, backed away, approached from different angles. There were landscapes of Georgia, Latvia and Estonia. One aquarelle was of a wide, fast-flowing river. An old wooden dock stretched away from the sloping green bank on which stood an old church and a wooden *izba*. Little rowboats of many colors lined the dock.

I paused on this one.

"That is the Volga, *dochka*," Yelena Davidovna said. "Not far from Volgograd—which used to be Stalingrad, as you know."

"I want that one," I said.

"Done," she said.

Phil, after what seemed hours of deliberation, settled on an aquarelle of the Caucasus Mountains. The painting focused on a house and an enormous tree. The mountainside and the house were tinted many shades of rust and red. Only the tree, dark and deep in color, was green.

"I was in Tbilisi just over a month ago," he explained. "And this looks so much like the mountains I saw."

"You have made good choices," Yelena Davidovna said. "Now I will give you each a few prints of Leningrad, and an aquarelle for Clinton's mother."

The one she picked for my mother was not of the bunch we had been allowed to choose from. It was a pink mimosa tree in full bloom, seen from below, as though you were standing leaning up against the trunk, looking up. The long, thick, and graceful branches drooped down toward you and behind them was the wild, galloping, pink and purple sky. The aquarelle was a masterpiece, by far one of her best.

"My mother has a mimosa outside the window of her little summerhouse," I said. "She will faint."

"You tell your mama that this painting is from an old Russian lady who greatly admired her husband. And that is all." She slit the air in front of her with a flat, horizontal movement. "Do you understand me, *dochka*?"

"I understand you."

"Now. You must not let the customs people find these, you understand? Philip, you will be traveling for many months, therefore I recommend you allow Clintonochka to take your painting back for you."

"I have a better idea. I will send them tomorrow through the American Embassy," Phil said. "I have special privileges, you see. I will say they are research materials and send them along with some books to Clinton's address in New York."

"Very well. That pleases me a great deal because now I will be certain that you two will have to see each other again, after Philip's voyage."

She gave him a long, sharp, appraising look, and stood up.

"Now let's continue to eat and drink and laugh and generally have a good time."

Phil and I smiled at each other wearily. We had not gotten home from Grisha's until eight that morning. At about three in the afternoon, Phil had crawled across the floor on his hands and knees and plugged his Soviet-made hotpot into the wall socket. He poured two large spoonfuls of freeze-dried Beriozka coffee and two generous shots of fifteen-year-old Georgian cognac (which he'd brought back from Tbilisi) into our cups and that was how we had started the day.

We had managed to maintain some kind of equilibrium, but like cocaine addicts, we needed a shot of alcohol every half hour or so to avoid complete internal collapse.

I was drinking a good deal at Yelena Davidovna's, but did not seem to get drunk. Finally, at a quarter to one, we prepared to leave. It only hit me then that Yelena Davidovna had maintained her jovial humor, her smile, her benevolent tenderness, and the sparkle in her eye, to protect me. She was exactly like my father, and I suddenly was struck by a terrifying thought: we were finally saying goodbye, and the future—whether or not I would ever see her again—was completely out of my hands. Her face changed as she pressed me tightly against her fragile frame. She backed away, holding me at arm's length, and there was sorrow and longing in her tired gray eyes.

"Do not worry, dochka, I will live until you return."

I tried to speak but the walls began to cave in around me. I was suddenly blinded by tears.

"Go now, quickly," she said in a gentle voice. "Philip, you take good care of her, do you hear? Take her by the hand—there." She removed my arms from hers and handed them to Phil as though they were two branches. The rest of our goodbyes were quickly said. Phone numbers had already been exchanged. Phil held me against his hip. His chest was level with my ear and I felt both near and far away from his heart. I saw nothing, and heard nothing but the silence inside my head until Phil and I were out in the tree-lined street. He took a deep breath and looked up at the green, rustling branches and the stars far beyond them. A blind was drawn, a window opened above us and amber light spread out from it in a fan shape. Khudat and Yelena Davidovna came out and stood on the balcony among the flower pots and waved. Khudat's arm was wrapped protectively around her frail shoulders.

"Goodbye! Goodbye! *Moyi rodniye!*" she called out in a faint voice, bringing her index finger to her lips. "Do not worry, I will still be here in a year's time."

2

I went to Vera's alone, early on the afternoon of our last day, carrying two enormous plastic bags filled with all the sundry toiletries and articles of clothing I was leaving behind. Because of the weight limit of ten kilos per suitcase on international European flights, we were severely limited as to how much we could take out. Vera had offered to take anything I left behind.

I gave Vera—and with a great deal of satisfaction—many of the articles of clothing Rita Abramovna had brazenly asked me for; there were several long wool sweaters and thick pairs of socks, my snow boots, long underwear, and panty hose which had not even been taken from their packages. "But I don't wear these!" Vera said. "Well then sell them or give them away, I don't care," I responded. I gave her two cotton men's shirts for her oldest sons, a Star Trek phaser complete with batteries, and Star Wars decals for the younger ones.

The sundries included soap, laundry detergent, shampoo, Tampax, toothpaste, razors, shoelaces, Advil, and baby oil which Vera needed desperately for Seryozha's diaper rash; all these products were useful to her and she was not offended. I had brought most of this to Russia to give away, but had not been able to. Even Rita had turned her nose up at these small gifts, stating flatly, *"Zdies, y nas vsyo yest'."* "Here," she had said, "we have everything." So I told Vera that it was all left over from my own stash.

"My God, you people arrive as though you were being sent to Siberia for ten years!" she said. "You don't know someone who might want to sell or donate a winter jacket, do you? I have a friend, a priest, who has just been released from jail and he is in dire need of everything. If you do, I can come to the train station tomorrow to fetch it."

"No. Sorry."

She uncorked a bottle of red Georgian wine I had brought (I had exhausted the Beriozka's supply of Chianti Classico).

"You see," Vera said, pouring the wine, "with all this talk of loosening things up, people still sit in jail for opening their mouths."

Vera was kneading dough for blini. A large pot of potatoes was boiling away on the stove. She put the dough in another pot and sat it in the sink in cold water. She carried the potatoes down the hall and dumped the boiling water into the toilet. The sound of the water hitting the porcelain was like that of a person getting sick. She returned, sweating, slammed the pot onto the kitchen table and began to mash the potatoes with a metal utensil, adding big square chunks of butter and many cups of milk.

"But you have to admit that things are getting better, more relaxed," I said. "Look at the articles printed in the news now. Two years ago they would never have printed a letter by Tarkovsky about the evils of censorship and why he was forced to leave the Soviet Union."

"This is all I have to say to you," Vera said, taking a sip of wine and then slamming her glass down on the table. The wine splashed over her hand. She licked it away as she spoke and continued to attack the potatoes. "There are three things all Russians know instinctively regarding their relationship with The Powers That Be: *'Nie vieri, nie boysia, i nie prosi.* Do not believe, do not fear, and do not ask any questions.' That will not change for a long, long, long time. Yes, maybe things look better. It is out of favor now to be conservative. Now we are allowed to speak out, even to criticise the latest thaw, but there are limits. The problem is, no one knows how far to go because the limits have not been clearly defined. So, you think it is different? It is not so different. You've been in Moscow five months and you think you know everything that's going on, but this is a gigantic country and you can't assume that what is happening here is happening everywhere. It always amazes me how little you Westerners understand us."

"Why do you people always say that?"

Vera was in an unusually irascible mood and had already put away half the bottle of Georgian wine.

"And where is Philip?" she demanded, as though he'd slighted me by making me arrive alone.

"Philip had to go to his friends' who are also having a party for him, but he will come here later on." An unpleasant, defensive, and guilty feeling was building up in my chest, and I was afraid that was exactly what Vera wanted. I had come to learn that she did not like to take her ups and downs by herself.

Over the past few months I had kept my visits down to once every week and a half. Her mood swings were radical and unpredictable, and her anger, which was really directed at her husband, was flung at the oldest two boys and at me. The smaller three were like floating wood in the waves of her emotions; the angrier or sadder she was, the more they screamed, the more they fought. Sasha and Petya beat up on the baby Seryozha as soon as no one was watching. I would leave her place feeling completely beaten myself, and sapped of strength.

"Why did you not go with him to his friends?" she asked, sighing deeply. This was Vera the martyr; I could imagine her thoughts. *You do*

not want to spend time with me since things have been working out well with
your lover.

Responding was useless so I remained silent. Sasha and Petya ran
into the kitchen from the hall and scrambled under the large, rectangular table. They were bashing each other on the head and me on the
kneecaps and toes, fighting for possession of the phaser. It made a weee-
oooo-weee-oooo sound and lit up green and red whenever they pressed
the trigger. This was a present Phil had brought for his dissidents' little
daughter. But seeing that she was developing into quite the monster
child, and considering the noise factor, he'd given it to me to give to
Vera's boys, since he spent less time at Vera's than at his dissidents'.

Sasha, the terror with the mane of amber hair, had a sticker of Han
Solo's spaceship on his forehead and one of Darth Vader on the back of
his left hand. He bashed Petya on the forehead with the phaser under
the table. Petya began to howl. Sasha, brandishing the toy, ran from
the room.

Vera sat Petya down at the table, gave him a chocolate, slammed the
door, and came back to her potatoes. The chocolate seemed to ree-
nergize the child immediately. "Aaarrrgh," he cried, his mouth a
brown circle, and ran out after his brother.

"The priest at Zagorsk said I should get divorced. He said my
husband is not performing his conjugal duty and therefore we are not
living in holy matrimony and should divorce. But I can never remarry.
So I went to ZAGS to apply for divorce this week and they were
horrible to me. 'A mat'-geroinya with five children, applying for divorce? Comrade, where is your head?' The woman was like a Soviet
tank. Exactly like a tank. I told her he chases me with a kitchen knife
and frightens the children."

"What does Oleg say about it?"

"To hell with him. He would let it go on like this forever. He says
it was a fictitious marriage all along in any case, that he married me just
so that he could get an apartment in Moscow. He says his mother told
him I was too low-class for him right in the beginning. That wretched
cow! At one time Oleg's mother and father—that poor man, he was
like a beaten dog—and my mother and *her* mother and Oleg and I and

the two oldest boys all lived right here, in this apartment together. Our mothers fought all the time. I thought I was going to lose my mind. Once, they came to blows. My mother was stronger, of course, being that Oleg's mother is so 'high-class' she never did a stitch of work in her life. My mother said to Oleg's mother, 'You raised a runt, a mama's boy; *my* Vera wears the pants in this marriage.' *Whack!* Oleg's mother slaps my mother across the face. *Whack!* My mother slaps her back, knocking her on the floor."

Vera acted out the scene, pantomiming the slaps and the evil facial expressions of Oleg's mother. She pointed to the exact spot on the floor where Oleg's mother had fallen. "She banged her head and a week later they moved out. They rented an apartment illegally until their legal permission to move was approved."

"Vera, did *you* know he felt like that in the beginning, about the marriage? *Was* it a fictitious marriage, Vera?"

I stared her in the eyes a moment, her lids dropped, and she returned to her potatoes.

Several weeks earlier, Vera had invited me over for a "party" to celebrate the fact that she had gotten a job. I was the first to arrive; she led me to the kitchen and pointed enthusiastically to a shoe box lying on the table.

"That is my new job! I am a matchmaker for unhappy people who cannot find someone to love. Look!"

She randomly pulled an envelope out of the box. Inside was a cover letter. A photograph of a rather normal-looking, dark-haired young man was stapled to the left-hand corner. His only stipulation in terms of a match was that he wanted the woman to be blond. *Blond* was underlined several times. On a separate sheet of paper he had written out in careful detail his family history for the past hundred years.

"He wants a blond," Vera mused. "How do I know if he means a real blond or will he settle for a fake blond? These are important questions. Never mind. I'll think about it tonight."

Soon, Vera's two friends arrived. It was the first time I had met them and could not understand why she had suddenly decided to introduce me.

Galya was a tall, pale Jewish woman who had applied for immigration and had been refused. She had absolutely nothing but bad things to say about Russia and wonderful things to say about America. During dinner, while the children screamed and the TV blared, Galya told me in a loud voice that her immigration application was for Israel, but that she would not remain in Israel for thirty seconds. She wanted to go to America because in America there was wealth and opportunity. "God, you are so Jewish!" Vera said to her.

The other was Katya, a quiet, pretty, black-haired woman with a ravaged face that seemed to have been wind-beaten and scrubbed too often with a hard brush. Her husband, Vera had told me, was in jail for some political crime against the State.

After dinner, Vera and Galya went off to put the children to bed (Oleg, as usual, had not come home from work). Katya and I sat, breathing deeply in the refreshingly silent kitchen. A fight was in progress down the hall. Someone would not go to bed.

"It is such a pity that things have turned out so badly between Vera and Oleg," I said. I was trying to subtly learn something more, since Vera's version of the story seemed so one-sided.

Katya stirred her tea thoughtfully for a moment, and ate a chocolate without saying a word. Then, looking up, she spoke to me in a quiet, gentle voice.

"I was friends with Oleg before I was friends with Vera. We came from the same small town and I have known him since I was ten. Everyone knew, even when we were fourteen, that he was the way he was. He even told me that he knew ever since he was a small child. Vera pretends it is not so, but it is. She has changed the whole story in her mind to suit her vision of her tragedy. And now she yells it on the rooftops, she tells everyone, and that is very dangerous for him."

The silence had suddenly become oppressive in the kitchen. Now the baby Seryozha was crying and Vera was singing a lullaby in her attractive, throaty voice.

"You must never say a word about this to her," Katya said, touching my forearm. "I do not care for me because we are such old friends it will not matter. In any case, I have told her what I think, and our relationship has suffered. But for you—if you disagree with her she will be very angry at you. If she knew you talked to me about this, she would probably never speak to you again."

"I already told her that her story does not make sense. I told her not to be angry at him because it is not something he can help. In America doctors say this is a fact and I tried to tell her."

"That was a mistake. She cannot bear to hear anything but the facts that she has made up in her mind."

"She is so religious, where is her forgiveness?"

"She did not used to be so religious. That is a recent development."

Vera came back into the kitchen with her other friend.

The silence continued to be uncomfortable. Vera, as though struck by a brilliant idea, jumped up and went to a cabinet. She produced a bottle of Rémy Martin cognac I had given her a few weeks earlier for her birthday. The ladies were ecstatic, their faces became flushed, and good humor was restored.

"To American women," Vera said, raising her little, stemmed glass. "Because they have learned to be independent of men." There was a bitter edge in her tone but it was cloaked in her wide, pretty smile, and everyone laughed.

Vera bashed the potatoes with the masher, slamming it from side to side in the pot as though she were imagining that the potatoes were her husband's entrails.

"Vera, tell me. Was it a fictitious marriage in the beginning, or not?"

"I knew how it was," she said angrily. "But I also knew that if there was a woman he could love it was I, because I am more like a man than a woman."

I felt such a pang of despair for the children who were trapped in the middle of this insanity that for a moment I wanted to hit her, to scream at her, *You have no right!*

"Anyway, soon it will be over. He will go live with his precious mother and I will finally be in peace." She slid her pot of potatoes further toward the center of the table and brought over the pot of dough from the sink. "Here." She handed me an empty water glass. "Make little rounds with the glass in the dough, and then we will put potatoes in the middle, and then we will fold the dough in two, pinch it closed at the edges, and then we will fry it." She smiled neatly as she demonstrated on one little round of dough.

"You think it will work back home with your Philip, but I don't think it will," she said as though she were talking about the possibility of rain the next day.

"Why do you say that?"

"Because here he is in control," she said almost coquettishly, with a twinkle in her eye. "He knows more than you about Russia and he is the boss here and that excites you. Back in America it will not be like that. In your mother's cultured environment, he will be like a fish without water."

"You don't know anything about my mother," I said in a hard voice. My cheeks became flushed.

She had inadvertently hit two sore spots. One, my mother *was* a bit of a snob. She wanted me to marry a millionaire; an intelligent, kind, cultured millionaire with a sense of humor. Good luck. Two, my mother, who was famous for speaking her mind regardless of the consequences, had a philosophy concerning me and men. *You're always getting involved with these types who try to control you. You like someone to make a box of your environment and tell you exactly how to live in it. That's called reverting to your childhood. Just because a guy controls you doesn't mean he's strong; it's exactly the opposite. And you get bored and unhappy. Adam never tried to control you, and look what you did to him. Maybe you like to be unhappy. Maybe by being unhappy you think you're holding on to your father. You need a man who's going to let you be yourself, who'll let you run your own life. Do me a favor, next time, pick on someone your own size.*

Was Vera saying that Phil was not big enough for me?

"You don't understand. I don't want a boss, I want to be equal with him."

"We'll see," she said cryptically. I wanted to tell her to go to hell; I wanted to leave, walk right out of her apartment. But first I wanted to tell her a few things. *For all you know about men you should shut up. For all your complaining against the System, your father was the System in spades.* Her father, after all, had been NKVD. I was about to speak when the doorbell rang.

It was Katya, bearing goodbye gifts for Phil and me. She'd brought a little set of six hand-painted, lacquered shot glasses on a matching, tiny tray for me, and a matryioshka doll of birch wood for Phil.

Phil arrived two hours later. He was quite drunk and his hair was tousled, sticking out at strange angles around his head. The thought did cross my mind: he slept with Irina again. Then: no, no, don't be absurd; after all Pavel was there. Vera, Katya, and I had drunk two more bottles of Georgian wine.

When Phil walked into the kitchen, Sasha and Petya were flinging their dinners at each other and at their older brothers. The baby Seryozha, feeling left out, howled in his high chair. Volodya, the eldest, finally threw his plate into the sink and went out, slamming the door. A few minutes later he returned, complaining in a whiny voice that he could not find the pajamas he wanted. Kolya, the second oldest, had spilled orange drink all over his mathematics homework and was asking his mother to recopy it for him since she wrote much faster than he did. Sasha, my bedfellow, approached me with a determined expression and stabbed me in the hand with a fountain pen. He gazed into my eyes with a look of cold curiosity that sent a shiver down my back.

"I thought we were friends," I said. Tears had formed from the sting and the shock. Blood and blue ink mixed in the small hole and dripped down my hand.

"No, we are not friends," he said. "Piss. Shit."

"I can't help you with your mathematics when I am completely drunk and entertaining guests, can I?" Vera shouted at Kolya. "Get out of here, all of you!" They laughed when she yelled at them.

Phil had not moved from the stove. He was completely stupefied. He was somewhat used to Vera's children, having spent quite a few evenings sitting around the kitchen table drinking wine. Usually his presence calmed them down. Now it was beyond control. Their unruly behavior had crescendoed all evening until it had reached this frenzied pitch.

Vera finally told Phil to sit down, and she put the kettle on for tea.

"You see?" she said. "These days Oleg leaves before anyone gets up and comes home after everyone is asleep. He no longer helps me and the situation is out of control."

I wondered foggily if Oleg really never did come home, or only did not when she entertained guests. How would I know since I was a guest? If he thought that all her guests knew about him, it was no surprise he did not want to come home.

Vera started an argument with Phil. She always argued with Phil about politics and women's rights and they both seemed to enjoy it a great deal.

"American men are almost as chauvinist as Russian men. It is just that your women have taught you a lesson. Here we are at least twenty years behind you in the Women's Liberation Movement. We are still second-class citizens." She slammed her fist onto the table and shouted that all men were cowards because they refused to take responsibility for birth control. I could not imagine where this was coming from since she was so adamantly against birth control herself.

"*Pazhaluysta,*" Phil said calmly. "If there were a pill that men could take, I would be happy to take it."

I left to go soap my wound. I was not in the mood to listen to them argue.

I ran into Volodya in the bathroom. He had finally found his pajamas and was now washing his face and combing back his wet, reddish hair. He resembled his father so much it was almost as though he'd come out of a miniature mold of the older man. He was tall and thin, physically immature for a boy of thirteen, and his face had not yet taken on the deep and anguished lines of his father's.

"Sasha attacked me with a pen," I said, showing him the wound. He inspected it, saying, "Hmmm."

The eldest was the least talkative of Vera's children.

"You know there's trouble in the air," I said.

He nodded almost imperceptibly. I stuck my hand under the cold water and soaped the little wound. I was suddenly grateful to have it, for this business of cleaning it made talking to Volodya less difficult.

"I am drunk and my Russian is pretty terrible anyway."

He smiled, just the smallest twitch of the mouth.

"But, will you listen to me for a moment?"

He nodded again. He was leaning against the sink, his head and shoulders sagging under some invisible weight.

"There is trouble in the air between your parents. I do not know when I will be back. You have to help your mother as much as you can. With the little ones and so on. Do you understand? Sasha is angry and completely confused."

"So am I," he said gloomily.

"Kolya is much more calm and levelheaded and things don't seem to upset him so much. Maybe that is not so, I do not know you all very well. But you must try to help and tell Kolya because he is second oldest to help and not be angry at your parents. When they fight they say things they do not mean. Kolya will listen to you because you are the oldest. Please. Will you try?"

"Yes. Why are you leaving?"

"I have to."

"Can't you live with us, as a relative?"

"I have a mother back home too. I have to go see her."

His eyes seemed to become heavier suddenly, as though he might fall asleep on his feet.

"Give me a hug, will you?"

"All right," he said. His hug was stiff, awkward, given at arm's length. I went back to the bedroom he shared with Kolya to kiss him goodbye as well.

This was my farewell from Vera: "Let me come see you off at the station tomorrow."

We were standing in the dark hallway, next to the coatrack.

"No."

"It is customary to see one's friends off."

"No. I can't take it. Please understand."

"But everyone else will have friends there."

"I don't care. Let us just say goodbye as if I were coming over tomorrow."

"You never came over two days in a row. You were always too busy."

"Come on, Vera. Stop it, now."

"All right. Until tomorrow, then."

"Until tomorrow." We hugged each other tightly, she hugged Phil, punched him in the arm, and we went out into the dark street. It was a quarter to one and Katya had left with us to try to make the last metro.

"You probably should not be seen with me," she said as we hurried down the wide, empty street. "I am often followed."

Once in a while a lonely car sped by, raising dust.

"At this point," Phil said, "what difference does it make? They know what they want to know about us. They know we are not dangerous."

"You people seem to love Russia so much," Katya said with a sigh. "How strange. I love and hate it *so* much. I fear I have wasted my whole life trying to decide which is the stronger emotion. It is an endless cycle. I do not think I could ever leave, however. Just as with Vera and her husband. It seems we cannot learn to live without guilt and pain and without oppressing one another."

30

LENINGRAD

1

With four days left before Phil and I would separate for at least seven months, our combined groups were herded off to the station to board the night train to Leningrad. It was called the Red Arrow and was an old-fashioned sleeper with four bunks per coupé in second class. Our combined groups would take up two full cars. Everyone wanted to share a coupé with their best friends so that they could stay up late listening to music and eating and drinking tea and vodka, and this was what we were all discussing on the bus ride to the station. At that moment, it seemed the most important thing in the world to me: to be able to spend the night in the same coupé as Phil.

Phil did not have to say much to drive me to tears. Now, just a comment said the wrong way or indifference in his tone sent a meat hook through my chest. I felt as though I were dangling from one in a freezer somewhere. The last four days had fallen all at once, like the last four sticks in a game of Hokkaido.

At the train station everyone was tense, everyone was upset. Many Russians had come to see us off, and they had no reservations about expressing deep-felt emotions in public. We Americans were by nature much more restrained but, at the Leningrad train station, almost all of us had tears in our eyes.

Grisha was there to see Ceppie off. The newlyweds stood whispering at the edge of the platform near the doors that led into the well-lighted hall, adding last-minute details to their plans for the future. A tear rolled from Grisha's eye every so often and Ceppie wiped it away with the backs of her fingers. The first announcement for the Red Arrow came over the loudspeaker and Grisha suddenly looked up from Ceppie's face. Then, he took her curly head in both his hands, stooped and pressed his mouth to hers. Her arms flew up around his neck and they were suddenly kissing like Humphrey Bogart and Ingrid Bergman in *Casablanca*.

Edmund Byrnes, the tall blond fellow whom I had sat next to in class (the one whose Soviet-made condom had broken while he and his Russian girlfriend had been making love in the dark stairwell of her apartment building), had come to the station accompanied by his girl. He was being kissed passionately again and again by the small, slight girl as he leaned unsteadily against a steel lamp post. The girl's thin white arms dangled from his neck while she pressed up against him and her long dark hair swung from the fancy vertical barrette that held it back. Edmund Byrnes had recently told me (we'd run into each other on the way into the Institute at one in the morning and he was quite drunk) that he and his girl had never, in five months, had the opportunity to make love in a bed, but that he was getting very good at doing it in the stairwell. The reason for this was that her father was a captain in the Soviet army and if he'd ever found out that his daughter was sleeping with an American, he doubtless would have sent her to Siberia to finish her studies. Fortunately, she had not become pregnant that first time; the condoms, however, had kept on breaking, month after month. Edmund Byrnes had told me that night as we climbed the Institute stairs that he was beginning to wonder if he was not sterile.

Now Edmund seemed to be having trouble keeping his balance, even with the help of the lamp post. The girl was sober in comparison and quite determined to get in as many kisses as possible before the final whistle blew. Edmund was trying to be a good sport but his greenish complexion betrayed his emotional and physical discomfort. It was likely he would be sick as soon as he boarded the train.

I was glad I had begged Yelena Davidovna and Vera not to come. There were two things in life I could not bear: hospitals and goodbyes. Had they come, I would certainly have been in worse shape than Edmund Byrnes. I stood alone, off to the side, and watched, feeling like a coward, while my friends were obliged to withstand the tears and cries of their friends.

Phil's dissidents were there without their monstrous child. Irina's arms were around Phil's waist and tears streamed down her beautiful, devastated face. Her husband Pavel's big, bearded hugs intermittently engulfed Phil so that he became completely invisible. Phil was behaving incredibly well considering he was one of those people who could not handle scenes of any kind. He patted his friends on the back and remained tightlipped, shaking his head as they cried.

We had been drunk for the past forty-eight hours and I was in one of those clear-headed, emotional stupors which can only be maintained by more drink. Hanging from my shoulder was a Spanish wine sack filled with hunter's vodka, which I lifted to my mouth every once in a while. It was the fuel which kept me running and the anesthetic which kept me from collapsing. Phil and I were both stretched so thin we were like rubber bands about to snap.

Pavel and Irina hugged and kissed him over and over again, and held him back, even as the others crowded around the closed doors of the train's cars.

I left them alone and weaseled my way up to the doors so that I could help in securing a coupé for Phil, his roommate Paul, Isabel, and myself. Already the idea of sleeping in a separate bunk was awful. Everything hurt so much I began to confuse old hurts with new ones.

In one sense, the thought that in four more days the ordeal would be over was reassuring. On the other hand, I was tormented by the thought that things could have turned out differently: I could have made an effort to change my plans, change my visa so that I could have traveled with Phil. He could have changed his plans—but that thought would have never occurred to him.

There was an enormous difference in our perspectives; Phil was thinking about his wonderful trip and I was thinking about going home to my empty apartment and my empty life. The prospect of reconstructing from zero was exhausting and terrifying.

When I looked at Phil's face I could not imagine that in four days I would not be seeing it any longer, that maybe I would never be seeing it again. His complacent expression had disappeared in the past few days and had been replaced by the stony, wall-like one that was completely impenetrable. This had to be a defense mechanism, I was certain of it, but this intellectual knowledge did not help me at all in dealing with my emotional devastation. Sometimes I wondered if he felt anything beneath his stony countenance; I wondered if he thought about me at all. I could not stop thinking about my father. In the throes of my paranoid stupor, the two of them were inextricably connected. With me were vile memories of past pain, past betrayals, people who had left me. Phil's self-control infuriated me.

Isabel and I managed to secure a coupé. Phil and I took the upper bunks and Phil's roommate Paul and Isabel took the bottom ones. The conductress had a little cabin at the end of the car and for kopeks served tea from an enormous samovar, in glasses supported by silver holders. We drank large quantities of tea with sugar, and shots of hunter's vodka from a bottle Phil had brought. Isabel began to take slugs of vodka to forget her merchant marine, Paul drank to forget his Bulgarian—Sofia from Sofia—and Phil and I kept drinking out of habit and some strange need to continue to avoid facing the truth, which was that in four days this particular time in our lives would be over forever.

There was a table between the bottom berths and we sat around it like traveling Russian peasants, slicing bread and cheese and pieces of kolbasa with an army knife and popping them into our mouths, followed by a shot.

"S'gonna be all right. Sofia'll find another American ina couple weeks," Paul said after his fifth shot. He straightened his glasses on the bridge of his nose and drank another shot. His face was purple, and the way he sat hunched over the little table with his head sagging gave the impression that he was completely uncomfortable. I am so happy, I thought, that Phil and I still have four more days.

"The problem with Vanya," Isabel was explaining to Paul, "is that they go off on these cruises for *months* at a time—four months, three months. How is he going to write to me from on board ship? And they're watched so carefully in port." Isabel wore a glum, concentrated expression, as though if she thought hard enough, an answer would come to her.

"You're dreaming," Paul said, shaking his head.

"How would *you* know, you've probably never been in love. Poor Sofia from Sofia."

"What do you know about Sofia? She's hard as nails. Pardon me for being frank, but even in bed I never felt it was *me* she was making love to but my passport."

Ceppie came in then and sat down next to Isabel.

"Can I have a shot?"

Paul poured vodka into his empty tea glass and handed it to her.

"Guess what, people," she said, "I think I am falling in love with my husband."

"Why Ceppie!" Isabel brought her hands together in a gigantic clap.

"Now when I come back on my relative's visa maybe I'll get pregnant and everything will be fine."

We ran out of vodka at around 3 A.M. Ceppie had left, Phil had gone up to his bunk, and Isabel and Paul had already passed out in their clothes. I crawled up onto my bunk and sat with my feet dangling over the edge and watched Phil undress. Soon he was down to his Soviet-made, purple-paisley boxer shorts and a guinea T-shirt. He looked at me watching him, hesitated, and then flicked off the light. I felt abandoned.

Unfortunately, mine was a lucid drunk and sleep did not come easily.

In the darkness the space between our beds seemed like a bottomless pit. When the train passed a light along the tracks I could see the whites of his eyes. Darkness and then light, darkness and then light—

that was the way it was between us. There was nothing to grab onto and then a spark of some kind would ignite in him and the world became a perfect place. Now he was staring at me, even in the blackness, without being able to see me. Now he was leaving me probably forever and I thought my soul was going to rip into two again.

We lay on our sides facing each other, staring over the rift for a long time. He reached out and took my hand, caressing it as though it were my entire body.

When my first love affair had come to an end, I ran to my father in the middle of the night. He was sitting at the kitchen table in his old terry cloth bathrobe, watching a ghost movie on TV. I could tell from the tenseness in his back and the way his ears seemed to prick up that he had been expecting me. I sat very close to him and wept like a young widow with my face against the cold, waxed, oak table. *At your age love seems so black and white, doesn't it?* He had a soothing, old man's voice.

This seemed profound and enigmatic, and I stared up at him, frowning through my tears. He spoke slowly, with patience and not condescendingly, about what he thought love meant. He thought love meant so many different things that there should be a hundred words for it, like the Eskimos have for snow. *It's only going to get worse as you get older. I'm so sorry, Honey. There's nothing I can do to help you.*

Two months later, my father died. In following years only one person ever treated my feelings with the deference my father had shown my fifteen-year-old heart.

You expect people to treat you the way he did? Adam, that other person, had said. This must have been four years later, in college. *He was your father. I can't be your father, now can I? What do you expect from me?*

I wanted everything. My soul was like a cold room with long, sharp icicles hanging from the ceiling. I had expected Adam to move into it and build some kind of gigantic fire to melt everything down. But no matter how hard he tried, the room remained ice-ridden and windswept. He took the beatings I inflicted without a sound.

He was a short person, no taller than I when I wore one-inch heels, and he carried around the burden of me, my grief, my schoolwork, my memories, and all of his own as well. He was on the wrestling team at 122 pounds and starved himself to lose the weight that was only water to start with. For two days before matches, he sucked ice cubes and his face turned gray.

Why do you do this to yourself? Why?

Shut up about this. You can do anything you want, say anything you want, but about the wrestling, shut up.

I thought he was a masochist and liked impossible challenges. I was wrong; he was not that much of a masochist.

Do not worry, dochka, I will live until you return.

Don't worry, Baby, I'll see you tomorrow. Those were my father's last words to me from his hospital bed. He even winked at me. But tomorrow never came.

The train rolled on through the night. The rickety-rock, rickety-rock jiggled the bunks from side to side. Our hands were still touching. In the middle of this I had begun to sob in silence. Finally I leaned into the black rift that separated us and kissed his hand.

"Phil," I choked. "Help."

He flew over to my bunk in a flash and lay facing me in the darkness that was sliced only for seconds, and at large intervals, by the pale lights from outside.

"What? What? Drank too much?"

"Help."

"Want some water?"

I shook my head, coughing, choking on the fluids that seemed to be pouring out of every orifice in my face.

The neck of his T-shirt was soaked in seconds.

"Want some air?" he whispered. "Let's go out in the hall and get some air."

"You don't understand. . . . You don't und—"

He jumped down and went out into the hall. Seconds later he was back, bare-chested, holding the now-drenched T-shirt in a ball in his hand. He climbed back onto my bunk and pressed its icy wetness lightly against my face.

Hours seemed to pass before I calmed down enough to speak. All of my defenses had finally collapsed and I did not care if I shocked him so much that he bolted like a hare. It made no difference whatsoever because, as Ceppie would say, it is what it is. If he's going to run, I thought, he might as well run now.

"They're gone," I whispered. "I can't believe they're all gone."

"Who's gone?"

"Them." I felt so much pain I wished I were dead. "They left me. My father and Adam. They were there and then suddenly they were gone. And Yelena Davidovna—maybe she's gone too. Maybe she'll die. And you—maybe after Leningrad I'll never see you again."

"I told you I'm coming back."

"And Adam told me he loved me more than anything in the world. But he said I was too crazy and he couldn't stand it anymore and then he left and slept with my best girlfriend who is now dead too as far as I'm concerned. He did that so that he could never come back to me. He made it death by guillotine instead of slow torture. And my father told me 'I'll see you tomorrow' when he knew he was going to die that night."

"He said that to protect you," Phil whispered while he slid the wet hair away from my face.

"And Adam, he slept with my ex-best girlfriend to protect me, too?"

"Probably," Phil said.

"Bullshit. And you're going to go away forever to protect me, too."

"It's too late. I already told you that. It's too late now."

"I don't know if I believe you and I can't stand it."

2

The Pribaltiskaya Hotel, a modern complex built by the Swedes, stood on the edge of the Gulf of Finland. It resembled a Hilton, all chrome and steel and equipped with the most modern Western furniture and appliances, and so big you could easily get lost in it. The hotel, unlike the Red Arrow, was not "coed" by room and it was only out of the graciousness of Isabel's and Paul's hearts (they assured us that they did not mind being roommates) that Phil and I were able to sleep together in Leningrad.

The fifty of us were checked in by nine in the morning. We looked like a caravan of desert nomads; our luggage covered the lobby floor all the way to the front doors. We were told that after dropping our baggage in our rooms, we would be served breakfast in the main dining room. Immediately after that we were to board the Intourist buses to go out to Pushkin to visit a palace of Catherine the Great's which had been leveled by the Nazis and reconstructed from scratch by the Communists after the war.

From the window of our room on the fifteenth floor Phil and I had a view of the large, stone pavilion that led from the hotel to the rocky beach and the flat, dark, misty Gulf. The morning fog swept across the pavilion in clouds and rose to the second floor of the hotel.

"Fuck it." Phil flung his backpack onto the twin bed closest to the window. The beds were separated by a formica table that had a radio built into the vertical panel at the front. The radio was on rather loud and I left the window to shut it off. I found that, as with the Institute radios, it could be turned all the way down but not off. I decided that it was probably a listening device.

"I don't want to go to Pushkin," Phil said flatly as he gazed out at our view. "I'll go out to Petrodvorets tomorrow. I don't need to see seventeen reconstructed palaces. I already saw Pushkin anyway. Everything in Leningrad was destroyed during the war so everything is reconstructed. I need to sleep is what I need."

I should've shut up, I thought, aghast. I shouldn't have told him anything last night.

I sat down on the bed he had not appropriated with his backpack. Phil came back from the window with a single-minded, concentrated expression in his eyes that frightened me. I thought he was going to say something awful to me, like "You'd better room with Isabel after all."

"I'll go down to breakfast," I mumbled, getting up. He pushed me back down onto the bed.

"You don't need to see Pushkin either."

As he completely overpowered me I imagined the poor KGB man leaning over his console, tapping his earphones, somewhere in the bowels of the hotel. An incubus had come to lie in Room 1509 of the Pribaltiskaya Hotel.

Sitting on the rocky beach later that afternoon under a feeble sun, I drank a warm Heineken from the hotel's Beriozka and had the awful sensation I was losing my grip on the situation. He had not said a word to me since "You don't need to see Pushkin either," except for "I'm going down to the beach," and I had followed him like a mute, accepting child. It was barely warm enough to sunbathe and now and then a chilly breeze from the water swept over the rocks.

Without a word he stood and waded out up to his waist in the oily, murky water. I watched his blue nylon lifeguard trunks disappear slowly. He paused for a moment, his V-shaped back to the beach, and ran his hands flatly over the surface of the water. He gazed out over the Gulf and I was jealous and angry because I was not privy to what he was thinking and feeling. I knew him well enough to know that if I asked him to tell me he would only become less willing to talk. While I watched his handsome back I wondered if there really was a problem or if my alcohol-induced paranoid stupor was in fact controlling my thoughts.

Ceppie, whose room was just a few doors down from ours, had

opened her door just as Phil and I had been heading down to the beach. Her eyelids were enormous and her face was puffed out as though she'd had an allergic attack of some kind. "I was just going to see if you were around," she said in a hoarse voice. She said she had fallen asleep and missed the excursion. While I talked to Ceppie, Phil kept walking and disappeared around the corner of the hall.

Now she came up from behind and sat down next to me, spreading a white Pribaltiskaya towel out on a flat rock. She was wearing a black tank top and purple-paisley boxer shorts. About a month before there had been an onslaught of purple-paisley boxer shorts in the Moscow stores. Within a day everyone owned a pair.

"Your face looks like my mother's used to when my father got sexy with her," she said. "Your cheeks and neck are all red." Her chin jutted out toward the water. "Something wrong with him?" I shrugged. "I understand," she said. "There's lots to be sad about and he's a guy who doesn't like to be sad. Don't waste your last few days, *mujer*. Like I think I should have slept with Grisha, you know?"

Phil dove into the water and began a butterfly stroke, making whale-like splashes until he was way out in the flat water. It was too cold to swim. I'd followed him down to the beach but I was not about to follow him into the water.

"I have to pee. I'll be right back." I squeezed her taut shoulder and got up. There was a clump of bushes and trees just beyond the beach and I headed in that direction.

I scrambled down into a small ravine surrounded by trees. A circle of large stones had been constructed at the bottom, like the one the merchant marines had made to cook the shashliki in Odessa. The ground at the center of it was charred. When I reached the bottom I squatted near the stones and pulled my shorts over to the side. After a moment I felt a strange chill and looked up. A young man was staring down at me from the top of the ravine with a twisted smile on his face, both guilty and derisive. He wore a red shirt and orange shorts and had curly brown hair. I shrieked but could not stop my bladder, and had to wait while he continued to stare at me.

Had he been watching from the beach, waiting for someone to go looking for a place to pee? Or was it me particularly he had been watching? He smells sex on me, I thought. He knows. I bowed my head and squeezed my eyes shut and tried to pretend he was not there. When I was finally finished, I forced myself to look up. He had fled. The place he had filled between the two large bushes was empty, but his ghastly presence remained in the rustle of the leaves and the blank space that continued to stare at me, like his cold eyes. I ran up the incline and toward the beach without looking back.

Phil was still out in the dark blue water, swimming a crawl now.

"Ceppie! Ceppie!" I tried to shout but my voice failed me, as in a nightmare. All I could muster was a hoarse whisper. "There was a man staring at me. There was a man—"

I started to hyperventilate and Ceppie took off at a run to look for the man. Phil came out of the water and sat down, glistening beside me on a large rock.

"What's going on?"

"Some guy just watched me pee." I was trembling and my voice was still unsteady. The foot of space between us seemed enormous, as big as the black rift had been between our two bunks on the train.

"Sick bastard," Phil said, and shook his head.

"Ceppie went to look for him."

"What for?" He seemed perturbed.

"He scared the hell out of me. You don't care, do you?"

"What do you want me to do about it?"

"Sometimes you're such a prick, Phil." I picked up my towel and headed back toward the hotel.

The man was sitting on a step just below the pavilion. I recognized his red shirt, orange shorts, and curly brown hair. He was staring at me; his body faced the water but his head was turned fixedly in my direction. I felt a chill pass over me again and I started to run for the hotel. Why me? I am alone and needy and miserable, that's why me, I thought as I stumbled on over the rocks.

Back in the room I watched the pavilion and the beach from behind the billowing white gauze curtains. Ceppie and Phil were still sitting on the rocks with their backs to the hotel. They seemed to be deep in conversation and I became jealous of Ceppie. The man was gone. In my T-shirt and shorts I crawled under the blankets of the bed we had made love in, and put the pillow over my head.

I'd been in a car accident in college. My friend had driven a VW Rabbit under a gas truck and I had been in the passenger seat. All I remembered from it was the agonizing sound of metal twisting and glass shattering like bones as the back fender of the truck came through the windshield, stopping only a foot from my chest. I had gone into shock and it had manifested itself in exactly this manner: I had gone to bed and slept dreamlessly for fifteen hours, until my worried friend had come and knocked on my door.

I did not hear Phil come in. He crawled in next to me and pressed against me from behind so that my face was up against the wall.

"You're totally covered in sweat," Phil said.

"Go away."

"Come on, get up, I'll give you a bath."

I felt a bit as I imagined torture victims must feel once they've reached the psychological breaking point where resistance is impossible and compliance seems much simpler. I let him pull me from the bed and undress me.

He got into the long, high tub with me and washed me as though I were five years old. He scrubbed my back and my neck; behind the ears, under the arms. He scrubbed my heels and between my toes, shampooed my head and rinsed it afterward, using a glass from the sink. At the Institute we had taken only showers. I had not been in a tub in five months and the feeling was warm and good and safe.

We made love in the bathtub and the sounds emanating from Phil were completely new to me. It was almost as though he were speaking in tongues. I decided that I was not going to drink anymore.

At dinner that evening in the large, high-ceilinged dining room which had enormous glass windows facing the Gulf, the other students seemed to stare at us. Phil was not perturbed one way or the other by the silence so I shrank into myself, concentrating on the food. I drank apple juice because Phil had checked my hand as I'd reached for the carafe of water.

"Don't drink the water," he said. "Giardia is bad in Leningrad."

A whisper seemed to pass like a wave across the room. "Don't drink the water. . . . Don't drink the water. . . ."

3

It was after our visit to St. Isaak's Cathedral, now a museum, that Phil disappeared. The inside of the cathedral was so overdone, so grotesquely rococo it was hard to believe. I was in a bad mood when we walked out into the harsh sunlight and by the time my eyes adapted, Phil had disappeared down a side street. I spent the hour of free time we'd been allotted by Intourist looking for him in the crowds of tourists in the shops and hotel bars. I could not concentrate on anything else and was more furious with myself than with him. A whole hour! When he finally showed up at the buses at the appointed time and took his seat next to mine, I stared out the window and would not speak to him. He did not seem to notice and we ended up not speaking to each other for the rest of the day.

That afternoon we went on the Intourist buses to Aleksandrovskaya Lavra, the cemetery where the dead of the Leningrad blockade had been buried in mass graves. It was unbearable. Loud, gruesome dirge music was being piped in from speakers which stood on metal poles every twenty yards or so. "Why do they have to *do* that?" Isabel whispered. No one was speaking and only the music filled the air.

Isabel and I had to link arms to make it through from one end to the other of the cement walk which split the cemetery in two. Red flowers lined the walk, and flowers of all kinds had been left by visitors on and in front of the cement slabs which marked each grass-covered mound. The mounds were lined up like graves in a regular cemetery, but they were enormous, and stretched out in even rows in all directions, as far as the eye could see.

There were no names on the slabs; each mound was marked by only the year. 1941 . . . 1941 . . . 1942 . . . 1942 . . . and on, and on. During the 900 days of the Leningrad blockade, 750,000 people, a modest estimate, had died. The bodies had been carted out to this place on sleds, by family members who were starving to death themselves, to avoid infesting the city when the spring thaws came.

Phil had disappeared again. Back at the buses I gazed out the window and waited for him. Just as the buses were about to leave he appeared. He had put his dark shades on over his glasses. He sat down beside me and stared straight into the back of the seat ahead of him. His nose and cheeks were red and, once, he sniffled.

"Don't you want to talk to me?" I squeezed his large, damp hand as it lay limply between the seats.

"No," he said flatly. "I want to fuck your lights out."

Something the size of a grapefruit dropped from the back of my throat to my stomach. In front of all this death he was talking about fucking and there was only one thing I knew for certain: I wanted him so badly that the deaths became vague to me suddenly. We were as perverted and barbaric as the peeping Tom and this behavior was foreshadowing the end for us. I knew from my experience with Adam that the last thing to go was the sex. Something so enormous and horrible welled up in my chest that an exchange of words seemed impossible but I knew I *had* to talk to him.

"You don't have the right to treat me this way," I said hoarsely. "Who do you think you are?"

I put my sunglasses on also and sat in the comforting green darkness and pretended I was surrounded by a soundproof glass wall.

"Goddamnit," he muttered. "Listen. I'm not used to being with someone all the time, you know? I'm not used to having to talk about how I feel. All that fucking futile death. All those poor children and women and old people. And then you get scientists and politicans who tell us we can *win* a nuclear war? No problem, everybody: we'll lose fifty million but *they*'ll lose a hundred million. I feel sick, Clinton. I feel sick."

"Why do you fight *me,* though? I'm not the enemy; I'm not out to hurt you, for God's sake!"

"You're not out to hurt me but all you have to do is tell me to go fuck myself and I'm ready for the nuthouse."

The incubus visited our room again that afternoon before dinner, and after dinner as well, and every day and night until the end. We missed excursions to important museums. We did not phone any of the contacts we were supposed to phone in Leningrad. If someone back home were to ask me later, "What did you see in Leningrad?" I would be forced to answer, "The ceiling and the floor of my room in the Pribaltiskaya Hotel."

We were given three hours to see the entire Ermitazh on the afternoon of our last day. I stood transfixed before an antique Italian table whose round, stone surface was an intricate cityscape done in the most minuscule mosaic I had ever seen. I stood transfixed also for at least an hour before a Rembrandt of Jesus being taken from the Cross. The only light in the somber painting is from a candle which a man shields with his cap. He stands near the top of the Cross, like the point of a pyramid, and the light sheds from that spot downward and outward toward the black edges of the canvas. I could not leave this painting, although Isabel kept appearing at my side, insisting that time was running out and we hadn't even gotten to the Impressionists and Post-Impressionists.

On the third floor, there was an entire room of Picassos from his red period, and another from his blue period. There were Monets I'd never seen, and four very early Van Goghs I didn't know existed. Matisses filled one very large room. There wasn't time to look at anything carefully.

I asked our Intourist guide in English (she was not allowed to speak Russian to us inside the museum, for some reason), "Where did all these paintings come from?"

"They belonged to rich, Capitalist collectors before the Revolution. Now they belong to the people," she said.

The long, winding queue the Soviets waited in outside the Ermitazh seemed never ending, while we tourists crowded around a back door and were let in in droves. The Soviets waited entire days, as they did in Moscow to see dead Lenin, but at the Ermitazh they were rarely admitted. I wanted to say something to the guide but thought better of it. After all, it was not the guide's fault, and regardless of what she thought personally, what could she do but throw me the Party line?

At ten to five the guards began to herd us toward the exits. Isabel ran up to me, pale and horrified, and said that I simply had to go downstairs with her to see the Van Dycks before the museum closed. With Isabel consulting a map of the Ermitazh, we ran down hallways like crazed rats in a maze. We finally came to the large double doors behind which hung the Van Dycks, but the woman guard in her dark blue military-looking suit had already closed the doors.

"*Nyet,*" she said, standing steadfast and shaking her big square head.

"But please, we are leaving tomorrow and will never be back," I said.

"*Nyet.*"

Isabel covered her face with her hands.

"No!" she cried out, and her whole body seemed to crumple in on itself.

"All right. All right," the guard said. She opened the door just enough to let us through. "But hurry up. You have five minutes."

Isabel's eyes were so filled with tears she could barely see the dozens of enormous, dark canvases that lined the walls. There was no artificial lighting and the shadows were deep in the large, high-ceilinged hall. I saw great brown faces and hands, and anguished eyes the size of chicken eggs staring down at me.

Afterward we sat on the base of the Aleksandrinskaya Column. It stood at the center of the Winter Palace court, and at the top of the column was a winged angel holding a Cross. Isabel and I stared at the pale blue walls of the Winter Palace for a while, weeping in silence.

"This," Isabel sniffed, making a large circle of her outstretched arm, "is the very place the workers and priests marched into to address the Czar on Bloody Sunday. And the Czar's guards opened fire. If the blasted guards hadn't opened fire and the stupid Czar had had a *clue* maybe everything would have turned out differently and we could see the Ermitazh any day. Here is history. We are sitting in the middle of history. I can't believe it. They kicked us out of the Hermitage."

On the last night, ten of us bribed one of the Intourist bus drivers with a carton of Marlboros and thirty rubles, to take us across the Nieva River and wait for us while we watched one of the drawbridges open to allow the ships in and out of port. We sat on the lower quay, close to the water's edge. It was June 30 and the sky never turned black that night. At two-thirty in the morning dusk fell over Leningrad and remained. My wine sack was filled with orange soda and there were many bottles of vodka being passed around. We sang the songs we had learned in the Institute singing class: "Katyusha," "Vykhozhu odin ya na dorogu," "Kalinka." We had learned war songs and love songs and children's songs and we sang them all with tears in our drunken, blinded eyes. Edmund Byrnes was passed out cold against the stone rampart with his legs spread out in front of him and his head lolling on his chest.

We made so much noise that a patrol boat came up to the bank and flashed a big round searchlight into our group, though it was light enough to see without it.

Phil stood and went to talk to the young Soviet patrolmen.

"We are American students. We have been here for a long time and are leaving tomorrow. We are sad to be leaving and are spending our last night awake in your beautiful city."

"You like our country?" the young men laughed jovially.

"We *love* it!" everyone shouted drunkenly.

"Well, then. Good luck to you!" They sped away.

I was leaning against the stone rampart, next to Edmund Byrnes, looking out at the river, which reminded me of Venice's Grand Canal. In the back streets of Leningrad were smaller canals which reminded me of pictures I'd seen of Amsterdam, except the architecture in Leningrad was completely its own. Suddenly a bright red or pink or green house with fancy ornamentation and statues above the windows would appear, and you knew you were nowhere else in the world. It was such a tourist's city, really. But there were no tourist shops, no colorful awnings, no Yves Saint Laurents and Cardins to catch your eye and tempt you in. This is what I was thinking when Phil appeared before me with his hand outstretched.

"Come for a little walk with me," he said.

I took his hand and pulled myself up. We went around the corner of the cobbled lower quay.

"The quay reminds me of Paris," I said.

"Does it?" he said. "I'll end up in Paris probably in February, on my way home. I'm flying out of London. Figure I may as well go to Paris too."

"Go to hell."

"Here." He handed me a very small, square box wrapped in Beriozka paper. I tore the paper off and shoved it into the front pocket of my pants. It was a pink cardboard box and inside was more paper, white tissue paper.

"Careful now, don't drop the goddamn thing or we'll never find it."

"I'm not drunk."

I sat down cross-legged on the cobbles and continued to tear at the tissue paper with indelicate fingers. I had never been good at this sort of thing. I uncovered a gold ring. Its setting was an unevenly shaped amber stone secured by six golden claws. In the center of the honey-colored stone was a petrified mosquito. Because the light was vague and dusky, it took me a while to realize that it was indeed a mosquito and not a spot of some kind. Amber encasing petrified insects was the rarest and most expensive kind.

"You're so proud you never even asked me where I went that day I disappeared. I went to the jewelry Beriozka. I put it on my father's Visa card," Phil said. "I couldn't afford to pay cash for it, not right before this trip. My father's going to shit but what the hell. Look, I've got to give you the receipt so they won't give you trouble at customs on the way out. That's really rude, isn't it? You shouldn't ever know how much gifts cost. Don't worry, I'll pay him back."

"I love to know how much things cost," I said. Trembling, I slipped the ring onto the fourth finger of my left hand. It fit perfectly.

"How did you know what size?"

"Remember I tried your ankh ring on my little finger once?"

"What if you change your mind? What if you meet some Burmese or Thai chick or some Australian champion surfer girl in Bali? Do I have to give it back?"

"Of course," he said, and pushed me so that I rolled onto the cobbles on my back. I stared up at the dusky sky and watched purple clouds pass over me. None of it made any sense at all and I was afraid that in the long months to come, I would only remember the bad days which made no sense, and nothing else.

"I love you much more than you think," Phil said. "You're so damned insecure and proud you don't even see it."

"You're so damned insecure and proud and self-involved you can't even see when you're hurting me."

"Listen," he said. "When you get back, will you call my father? Just tell him who you are. I already wrote him about you. And maybe you could call my mother, too, at the hospital."

"All right," I said. "It's going to be weird, talking to them with you so far away. I wish I were pregnant. Then this wouldn't seem so final."

"I'm glad you're not. I couldn't go away if you were pregnant."

4

Everyone traded phone numbers and addresses in the Helsinki airport. Ceppie, Isabel, and I sat in one of the open waiting areas and tried to be jovial but tears streamed silently, uncontrollably, from our eyes. "Goddamn language. Can't tell the ladies' from the men's room," Ceppie muttered, looking through her backpack for more toilet paper. "Look at that sign—klbgrndsmialsstr—what the fuck?"

Isabel and I laughed, causing more tears to fall. The airport's sounds, all silence and echoes, were oppressive that day. They did not portend excitement and a mysterious voyage; they represented the dead end, the morning after.

An elderly woman was sitting beside us in one of the metallic chairs. She reached into her pocketbook and handed a little traveling pack of Kleenex to Ceppie, who was closest to her.

"Don't worry, dearies," she said in a tremulous voice, "I'm sure you'll have the time of your lives, being away from home." She spoke in the slow, twangy singsong of the Midwest.

"No, no," Ceppie said, shaking her head while she took the Kleenex from the elderly lady, "you don't understand. We *are* going home."

"Is that so?" She seemed completely perplexed. "Well, where have you been, then, that you are so sad to leave?"

"We've just spent five months in the Soviet Union," Isabel said, pulling a Kleenex out of the plastic wrap and pinching it daintily against her nose.

The woman blanched and red spots appeared on her face. "The S-Sov—" She sat stiffly with her hands in her lap, shaking her head.

"Yes, we have lots of friends we've left behind," Isabel tried to explain, but the woman was frozen in her seat. After a moment she picked up her little square carry-on case and scuttled off toward another waiting area.

"That's what it's going to be like back home," Ceppie said in a heavy voice. "From now on, that's what it's going to be like."

"We're on a goddamn plane of fools," Ceppie said. As on the flight to Odessa, we managed to appropriate three adjoining seats. Isabel was by the window, I was in the middle, and Ceppie was on the aisle. Ceppie and I were drinking Virgin Mary's, the first Ceppie or I had ever had. Being totally sober was an interesting experience. For some reason my moods were not fluctuating radically any longer, and I was feeling the full impact of my grief with a conscious, controlled mind.

Isabel was sipping, of all things, a mint julep. She had explained to the American stewardess that we had been in the Soviet Union for five months and that if she did not have a mint julep with real mint immediately, she was going to die. God only knows where the stewardess had found the mint.

"Here we all trade phone numbers and none of us are ever going to see each other again," Ceppie said. "Es hard to swallow, mang."

"You're both welcome to come visit me at Yale," Isabel said, piqued that her loyalty and her good intentions were being questioned. I could not imagine going to visit Isabel at Yale. I had not gone to visit anyone at a college since I had been in college myself.

"No, you come down to New York and stay with me, Isabel," I said. "You'll probably be looking for a job in the City soon anyway."

"It's a deal," Isabel said.

"Yeah, my family's moved up in the world, or should I say down? We're in Queens now. We started out in Spanish Harlem. You guys can come over and my mom'll cook you a wicked meal. Chorizo with black beans and rice." There was a bitter edge in Ceppie's voice which I did not like and which was about to bring me to tears again. The idea of being separated from them was horrible. Who was going to understand me now? It seemed unfair that the program had given us three days of orientation on the way over, but now was dropping us like old sacks at Kennedy Airport, forcing us to work through our reverse culture shock by ourselves.

I had sublet my apartment to a French lawyer I barely knew and she was supposed to have been gone by yesterday. What was I going to find? What was I going to do? I would call my ex-fiancé, probably, for moral support; call my mother in the country and take the train out to see her the next day. There was too much to explain to her and to everyone else and no way to explain anything. *That's the way it's going to be from now on.* Ceppie's voice rang in my ears.

"I don't want to go home to my parents'," Ceppie said in a flat, matter-of-fact tone. "I can't deal with it right now. Probleign be— ain't no place else to go, mang."

"Come to my place," I said before I'd even thought about it. "You can move in. I have a one-bedroom that I can't afford and the bedroom is all the way at the other end of the hall from the living room. I'll sleep in the living room and you can have the bedroom. I don't know what the hell I'm doing, Ceppie, and neither do you. And I don't want to be by myself right now."

"How much is your rent?" she asked, her eyes narrowing as though she suspected I might try to rob her.

"Seven-fifty. That means three seventy-five each a month."

"I can swing it for a couple of months. By then, I'll know what I'm doing. All right," Ceppie said. "Can I call my people from your place?"

"Unless the French lawyer who's been living there didn't pay the phone bill and it's disconnected," I said.

This did not worry me so much as how I would handle my first tour of the local Korean grocery store around the corner. It would be chockful of fresh and delectable fruits and vegetables—avocados galore, and fresh basil! There would be mozzarella cheese and all the ingredients necessary for Bolognese sauce. There would be a whole shelf stacked with colorful boxes of different types of pasta—no more pasty, mushy generic noodles that crumbled and stuck together as soon as you put them in the water. The days of waiting in line for tomatoes and cucumbers were over. There would be as much Boston lettuce and vinaigrette as I wanted. And there was a Burger King down the street. Heaven! A Whopper with cheese!

There was another side to it: there would be the bums living in the street, the mad people, the junkies, the whores, the youth of America on MTV, and the street billboards advertising everything from panty hose to cars in bright colors that caught your eye and made you long to be rich so you could buy things you really didn't need. How long would it take before we forgot what life was like without them? Our papers would doubtless tell a different story about the Soviet Union than the one we believed. "The West looks down at us from the ceiling," the Russians say. There was a certain amount of truth in that.

I had taken a ten-milligram Valium to help me through the last few hours with Phil. He did not know. We walked on the rocky beach in the white night and he warned me about the culture shock. *One time we had to spend the night in Helsinki and I went out in the street to make a phone call from a booth. I forgot I could call from the hotel. It takes a while to get used to the idea that you're not being listened to and watched.*

New York is going to look like a combat zone to you, like some underdeveloped Black African city. There are beautiful buildings and beautiful people but in the streets you'll notice the poverty and sickness in a way you never have and you won't believe your eyes.

Before he left for the train station he took my head in his hands and stared at me as though he were afraid he would forget what I looked like. I had snapped so many pictures of him in the past few days I would never forget what he looked like.

I thought of Phil and tried to imagine him at that very moment. I saw him sitting on his bunk on the Trans-Siberian train. He was discussing history and the price of beets with a peasant from Irkutsk. And a sailor on the way to Vladivostok was interrupting, offering Phil his opinion on the nuclear arms race.

Can you hear me? I yelled out to him in my head. Can you hear me?

The plane's engines droned on all around.

Why does he do that, Mommy?

Your Daddy has nightmares. Ever since I've known him he's fallen out of bed in the middle of the night. He screams out in Russian and sometimes in German and then he falls out of bed with a bang. It scared me to death at first but now I'm used to it.

I remembered—sometimes I was sick or couldn't sleep and crawled in with them. I remembered the moans and the mumbles and the screams, but at that time Russian was completely foreign to me. I had wanted to help him, to reach out and touch him. I knew that waking him was dangerous. He lashed out.

Don't ever be afraid to fight for what you believe, even if they kick the shit out of you.

Yes, Daddy.

But what did I believe?

I realized with a certain amount of apprehension that all of us who had gone with the willingness to open our minds would be alone together for the rest of our lives.

The following books were instrumental to the author's understanding of the Soviet Union and to the writing of this novel:

Seweryn Bialer, *Stalin and His Generals* (1969), and *Stalin's Successors* (1980); Charles Bohlen, *Witness to History, 1929–1969* (1973); James Edward Brown, *Russia Fights* (1943); Mikhail Bulgakov, *The Master and Margarita* (1967); William H. Chamberlin, *The Russian Revolution*, Volumes I & II (1935); Marshall Vasily I. Chuikov, *The Beginning of the Road* (1963); *An Army of Heroes: True Stories of Soviet Fighting Men*, translated by Elizabeth Donnelly (1944); David Eisenhower, *Eisenhower at War* (1986); John Erickson, *The Road to Stalingrad* (1980); Sheila Fitzpatrick, *The Russian Revolution, 1917–1932* (1982); Walter Graebner, *Round Trip to Russia* (1943); Andrea Lee, *Russian Journal* (1979); Larry Lesueur, *Twelve Months That Shook the World* (1943); Roy A. Medvedev, *Let History Judge* (1971); Charles Messenger, *The Pictorial History of World War II* (1987); *History of the U.S.S.R., The Era of Socialism* by Progress Publishers (1974); Harrison E. Salisbury, *The 900 Days: The Siege of Leningrad* (1969); Ellen W. Schrecker, *No Ivory Tower: McCarthyism and the Universities* (1986); John Scott, *Behind the Urals* (1942); Varlam Shalamov, *The Kolyma Tales* (1981); Hedrick Smith, *The Russians* (1976); Colin Thubron, *Where Nights Are Longest* (1983); Donald W. Treadgold, *Twentieth Century Russia* (1981); Robert C. Tucker, editor, *The Lenin Anthology* (1975); Adam B. Ulam, *The Bolsheviks* (1965); and Alexander Werth, *Russia at War* (1964).

Special thanks to Beverly D'Onofrio for allowing me to borrow from her letter in Chapter 24.

KJ